Book One of the
Third War of the Realms

**Martin J Lake**

This paperback edition 2022



ISBN: 978-1-7396926-1-2



Cover design: Jemima Catlin

*To my wife, Catherine.*

# Prologue

Eyes as black as the heart that beat in her chest looked out from a face that had once been flawless, at one time as exquisite as it was fearsome.

But that had been many centuries ago. Now her face was withered, skin wrinkled and ancient beyond even the incredible longevity usual for her kind. Her body was kept alive by the malice that ruled her every thought.

The throne on which she sat motionlessly was raised above the assemblage, affording her an uninterrupted view of the Great Hall. A murmur of conversation arose from those gathered, small isolated groups scattered across the floor, their muted conversations punctuated by an occasional covert glance.

She didn't need to hear them though. She knew they all were plotting and scheming, even those of her own extended family. Some conspired against each other, but most were against her. All were trying to gain an advantage over the others, looking to increase their own status and power.

And she knew, chief amongst all their petty schemes or elaborate plans was their one overriding problem.

*Why wouldn't she die?*

A rare smile, almost hidden amongst the creases of her lined face, startled one who had momentarily glanced her way.

Let them fear her. Her rule required absolute control. Let them plot to kill her; they would fail, as had many others over the centuries.

For she would not die while her vengeance remained unsatisfied.

She would see them all dead first.

# Chapter 1

SUNDAY, 8TH NOVEMBER

"I don't bloody well know why," Camron shouted. He grasped the edge of the oak table and took a steadying breath, slowly exhaling as he tried to compose himself.

"I just don't know why," he repeated in a softer voice, looking over to his wife. Midnight-blue eyes blazing with anger met his gaze.

"I'm sorry," he said lamely.

"You're sorry! Well, that's alright then. Never mind that yet another weekend is ruined because you're in a foul mood. Just so long as you're sorry! Why should it matter that you can't explain it, and just because someone wants to move some sodding stones," Rachel retorted, her voice laced with sarcasm.

"Stonehenge isn't just some *sodding stones*. They're important."

"But they'll put them back. They're only being moved for a couple of weeks," said Rachel.

"I know," Camron replied. But the truth was he didn't. He did not know at all why he felt this way. He couldn't explain the anxiety and dread he felt every time he heard a report about the archaeological project to temporarily move the giant stones at Stonehenge.

Camron sat down at the kitchen table as Rachel turned her back on him and filled the kettle.

"I'm scared," he said in a small voice.

"What?" Rachel asked over the sound of the running tap.

"I'm scared," he repeated.

"What do you mean? What are you scared of?" she asked, turning to him.

"That's the point. I don't know. I just don't know. But something about the stones being moved scares the hell out of me."

"What, are you scared our heritage will be damaged?"

"No, it's nothing like that. I get this deep-rooted fear in the pit of my stomach whenever I think about it. I know it's irrational," he said, seeing the sceptical look on her face. "But I can't shake the feeling that something bad will happen if the stones are moved."

"Really?" Rachel's tone dripped with mockery, "Are you sure you're not just having a mid-life crisis?"

"You tell me," Camron retorted, his anger resurfacing as he rose from the table to face Rachel, "you're the nurse." Shame burned his cheeks and he regretted his words immediately.

Anger flashed across her eyes as she turned from him, saying, "Just clear off and take Flint for a walk will you and give me some space."

Camron stood there, looking at her willowy figure as she busied herself making a cup of coffee, her stance stiff and unyielding. Part of him wanted nothing more than to put his arms around her slender waist and hold her tight, wishing everything was alright. He glanced at his wife's solitary coffee mug on the worktop. Almost of its own volition, his hand reached for the dog lead hanging on the hook by the back door.

Sighing, he tore his eyes from her and said, "Flint, come on boy. Let's go for a walk." The dog looked up from his basket and bounded across the kitchen floor, following Camron outside. The gravel pathway crunched underfoot as they headed for the garden gate.

It was a beautiful crisp autumn afternoon. A spectacular array of fiery reds and oranges crowned the trees, their leaves gently falling, swirling to the ground. The sun had made a rare appearance after the persistent rain of the past few weeks and sunlight sparkled off the many puddles in the lane. The beauty of his surroundings would normally have touched Camron, but today he barely noticed, his long legs striding at a pace that caused Flint to trot to stay alongside him.

Thick hedgerows bordered the narrow lane, obscuring the fields from view. The pair left the road, following a public footpath signpost that pointed the way through an empty field. Flint approached the familiar wooden stile at a run and leapt over it. Camron followed suit, vaulting effortlessly. At forty-two, he was still in pretty good shape and hadn't entirely lost his physique from his sporting youth. He landed with a squelch in the puddle on the other side. His boots took the brunt of the spray, but the rest of him received a spattering of muddy water. He wiped the back of his hand across his narrow angular face to remove the mud.

"Great," he announced to the world in general. He trudged along the path as it wound around the edge of the field, head down and hands thrust deep into his pockets.

Ducking his six-foot frame to avoid an overhanging branch, he spoke to Flint absently, "She's right. They're only stones. Why should I care?"

Camron looked down at Flint, who was looking up at him expectantly, tail wagging in anticipation. Flint clearly was not the sympathetic ear he might wish for.

"Off you go then," he said and watched as the white German Shepherd bounded across the field to investigate the nearest hedgerow, looking for rabbits in need of chasing.

Camron traipsed through the field dejectedly, eyes looking unseeing at the ground before him. As he walked, his mind drifted back to earlier that day. It had started out with the promise of being a perfect Sunday – until Rachel had switched the radio on.

Stonehenge was at the heart of the news again. The prehistoric circular monument of standing stones in the middle of Salisbury Plain captured the media interest, as it had all week. Radio Four had a heated debate concerning the controversial plan to move some of the great stones, albeit temporarily. Archaeologists and Stonehenge experts believed they might find the key to understanding the mystery of the henge by examining the recently detected objects buried beneath them.

There had been widespread objections. Druids had been permanently encamped near Stonehenge since the proposal was first mooted some months ago, protesting vocally but peacefully. Since then, the camp had grown several-fold as more people joined them. Public opinion and pressure were increasing. The campaign already had an unofficial slogan, *'No Rolling the Stones.'* The discussion on the radio was lively and dominated by the protestors' plans to disrupt the work.

Rachel had not really been listening, engrossed in scrubbing the roasting tin from their Sunday lunch. But Camron had and he stood, wet plate and tea towel held motionless as unease and fear had gripped him once again. By the time Rachel had realised and switched off the radio, it was too late.

Camron knew he was acting unreasonably, but he couldn't let it go. Their pleasant Sunday lunch had ended with a pointless and futile row and now he found himself plodding across the hills feeling thoroughly miserable.

He stifled a yawn. Tiredness definitely wasn't helping his mood. For the past few weeks, fleeting images of unimaginable horrors had plagued his sleep until the sheer terror would wake him with a jolt. He would lie awake in the dark, details of his nightmare slipping through his grasping memory like tendrils of fog. His thoughts whirled in confusion and he struggled to understand what was happening to him as he lay, shivering and surrounded by bedsheets that were damp and clammy from his sweat. And Rachel would be there for him, holding him tenderly in her arms, reassuring him with gently whispered words. Looking at him with concern in her eyes.

Her eyes!

He felt he could spend an eternity gazing at them, and a hint of a smile creased the corners of his mouth.

"Flint. Flint, come here, boy." The dog stopped his investigation of the hedgerow and looked towards the voice. Seeing Camron beckon, he gave up his hunt and trotted obediently towards him.

"Time to go home and face the music, I guess." Turning around to retrace their steps, they headed back. The hilly landscape surrounding the small Dorset village of Winterbourne Cerne was peaceful. A world away from the frantic pace of life in London where Camron lived and worked during the week.

Camron resumed his monologue with the dog as they drew nearer the cottage.

"I hate it when we argue." He lapsed into silence and then a thought struck him. "I could nip to Covent Garden this week and buy a bottle of the perfume she likes so much. Do you think she'd like that?" Flint wagged his tail enthusiastically, a sign Camron took for approval.

He opened the front gate and Flint bounded around the side of the cottage looking for Rachel. Camron followed, making his way to the kitchen door. As he turned the corner, he saw her kneeling in the garden, attacking some weeds in the flowerbed with greater force than was strictly necessary. Flint already lay on the grass beside her, watching every movement with the absolute attention only dogs seemed to master.

She was dressed in the old clothes she kept for gardening. Her luxuriant hair, the colour of burnished mahogany, scraped hurriedly into a ponytail. A smudge of dirt was on her cheek where she had wiped the back of her hand across it.

He knew she was aware of his presence but was determinedly ignoring him, her focus solely on the weeds. It didn't matter anymore. Seeing her there reminded Camron of just how much he loved her. Gathering his resolve, he walked towards her.

# Chapter 2

MONDAY, 16TH NOVEMBER

Today was the day, after months of committees and meetings and defeating the protestors' arguments. Not since the 1960s had the stones been moved. And for the first time ever, the remaining Great Trilithon was to be lifted. New discoveries and research over recent years had led to fresh theories, and it was hoped that this project might finally solve the ages-old mystery of Stonehenge.

Professor David Underwood stood amid the great stones and looked around, his breath visible in the clear, crisp morning. No matter how many times he visited, he found himself captivated by its splendour and marvelling that the site was 5,000 years old.

David leant against one of the massive bluestones, sipping from a mug of strong coffee. His eyes that drifted to a recently erected perimeter security barrier were as brown as his coffee. Protestors were lining the far side of the fence, vocal in their opposition. On this side of the fence, his team was beginning their preparations alongside an array of machinery and heavy lifting equipment.

David was leading the project to excavate beneath the stones. As a professor of history at Cambridge University, his knowledge was prodigious, but this went beyond pure academia. Stonehenge was his passion and he had spent almost thirty years studying the stones. Even after all this time, David still sought answers to some fundamental questions; why it was made? What was its purpose?

Recent advances in ground-penetrating radar, analysis using magnetometers and 3D laser scanners have generated the most detailed three-dimensional subterranean maps ever. This had led to the discovery of several new, as yet unidentified, objects buried some metres under the site. Gaining access to these objects was the primary purpose of this project.

"How are you feeling?"

The voice startled him.

"Damn," he exclaimed, shaking off spilt coffee from his hand.

"Sorry," said Clare, "didn't mean to make you jump."

"That's ok. I was miles away."

"You ok?" Clare enquired.

David knew she wasn't asking about his hand. Despite being a commensurate academic, he had been unable to avoid being embroiled in the dig's controversy. Many groups were opposed to moving the stones, and the diversity of opposition was incredible.

"Yeah, I'm ok," he replied, removing his protective yellow hard hat and running fingers through his hair that was now more grey than brown.

Clare was not entirely convinced. "Come on David, I've told you a thousand times, you're the best person to lead this project. Nobody else has your knowledge or your devotion to *the henge*."

"You're very kind to say so."

"They aren't just platitudes," answered Clare, "it's true. Look, we'd all rather we could do this work without disturbing the stones, but we've explored every alternative, and we just can't. And if it wasn't you in charge, then it would be someone else, and they might not be as protective as you."

David sipped his drink, grimacing at his now tepid coffee.

"Thank you," he said smiling at Clare, "I'm glad you're on this project with me. I'm not sure we would have got this far without you."

David emptied the dregs of his coffee on the ground.

"It's going to be a busy few days," said Clare

"Let's hope our spectators' plan to disrupt us doesn't work," David said, looking towards the protestors. The local police were out in force, and no one had managed to get onto the site to chain themselves to one of the stones or some such nonsense.

"Well," said Clare, "we're done with all the planning. Shall we make a start?"

David nodded and they headed towards the rest of the team.

The heavy lifting equipment was ready, just waiting for the go-ahead to start moving the trilithon stones that formed the central horseshoe. Satellite imagery, laser technology and advanced GPS would ensure the replacement of the stones to within millimetre accuracy.

Carefully, almost reverently, the whole team began preparations to move the first of the stones that had stood on Salisbury Plain like sentinels standing guard over the landscape for countless centuries.

The soil around the first stone was removed, and the special lifting cradle was placed around it. Both the team and the protestors held their collective breath as the crane slowly began to lift. At first, the ground seemed to cling to the stone as if reluctant to relinquish its' millennia-old grasp. Still, the power of modern mechanics won, and the stone swung free.

David let out a sigh of relief as he watched the stone being carefully manoeuvred into one of the custom-built crates that would protect it. He unclenched his fists and was surprised to see red marks left by his fingernails digging into his palms.

The shouts of the protestors very nearly drowned out the noise of the cranes, diggers and lorries as the meticulous process was started over for the next stone. Still, they remained peaceful, and the police and private security successfully thwarted any attempts to disrupt the process.

On the fourth day, only one more stone remained to be moved.

This was the only surviving stone of the Great Trilithon. David knew this would be the most difficult. It would take enormous care, precision, and considerable engineering power to ensure this part of the operation went smoothly. The crane lowered the heavy slings, and meticulous preparations were made to lift the largest stone at the henge. Everyone waited as slowly, very slowly, the crane took the weight of the stone and began to raise it, inch by delicate inch. All eyes fixed on the trilithon. Another few centimetres and it would be free of the ground.

*Crack!*

The noise was explosive, sounding like the shattering of granite under immense pressure. It resounded and reverberated through the very bones of the onlookers, who gasped as the massive stone swung slightly, suspended in a cradle of nylon straps.

David shouted into his radio for the crane operator to stop. Nobody dared move. Every eye strained to catch a glimpse of even the slightest crack in the stone's surface.

David took a few tentative steps forwards. His movement broke the inertness of his colleagues, and several others likewise headed towards the stone.

An hour of meticulous checking followed, including the use of X-ray tomography. They found no new faults or cracks, either on the surface or inside the stone. Nobody could account for what had caused the noise, despite everyone in the immediate vicinity clearly hearing it.

However, the strangest part of the incident happened several hours later, during a detailed review of the video footage. The team could not find any recording of the noise; despite determining the precise moment of its occurrence from the reactions of those on the tape. A conundrum David put to the back of his mind for later reflection.

"Maybe one of the straps had slipped?" Clare ventured.

"I'm not sure," answered David sceptically.

"Well, at least the stone is ok," she said, nodding in the directory of where the massive trilithon now lay alongside the other stones.

David nodded in agreement.

"And tomorrow the real work begins," she continued.

"It does," said David, still unable to shake off a feeling of unease.

"You coming to the party?" Clare asked.

"Party?" David queried.

"Well, just burgers and a couple of beers, but we thought it would be nice before we start excavating."

"Yeah, maybe in a bit," said David. "Save me a burger," he called as Clare turned to leave.

David wanted to review the video footage of the noise one more time. He managed to waylay Toby, the video engineer, on his way to the party. Despite some grumbling but assuaged by a couple of beers, he agreed.

However, even after reviewing the video several more times, they could still not find any recording of the noise. David was astounded as they repeatedly replayed the moment. Both the visual and audio parts of the video were working correctly, confirmed by the crane's engine noise and the onlookers' murmurings. But the ominous crack everyone had heard was missing.

As Toby headed towards the party, complaining the beer would be warm now, David headed in the opposite direction.

He wandered amongst the remaining stones, still feeling a sense of unease. He knew this project should be just another piece of work, but to David, learning about the past was as important as advances in science and technological progress. Somehow, though, this project felt different. He couldn't shake off a feeling of foreboding.

He sat on the edge of the pit where the base of the Great Trilithon stone had so recently stood and gazed up at the stars, lost in thought. He sat for a long time, trying to make sense of his inner turmoil.

Eventually, the cold and damp seeping through his jeans got the better of him, bringing him back to his present surroundings. He glanced at his watch and realised it was late. He had another busy day ahead of him tomorrow. The noise from the camp had lessened as the party wound down, and David decided it was time for bed.

As he stood up from his perch on the pit's edge, he noticed a silvery glow. Startled, he stopped and stared, astonishment etched in his expression.

"Bloody hell," he exclaimed. *I must be more tired than I realised,* he thought.

Shaking his head to clear his thoughts, he deliberately removed his glasses. He carefully cleaned them with the corner of his handkerchief, keeping his eyes averted. Replacing them, he took a deep breath of the crisp autumn air.

David lifted his gaze, and there, right in front of him, a faint, shimmering light outlined where the Great Trilithon stone had so recently stood. He gaped in renewed disbelief. Was this a trick by one of the protestors? The shape appeared to be floating in mid-air, insubstantial and ethereal as if it were the ghost of the stone.

David took a tentative step forward, reaching towards the glowing outline with trembling fingers.

Suddenly he stumbled, losing his footing at the edge of the pit. He cried out once as he tumbled into the darkness.

# Chapter 3

WEDNESDAY, 18TH NOVEMBER

Try as she might, Rachel couldn't ignore the signs anymore. Not only was she nearly two weeks late, but she had also been sick most mornings and felt tired much of the time. Worst of all, she no longer enjoyed chocolate!

She plucked up some courage and bought a pregnancy test kit on her way to work. Actually, she got three. It was too monumental an event to leave to a single reading. When she arrived home that evening, she delayed for as long as possible. She tidied the already clean cottage, made herself dinner and even took a long bath. Immersed in the warm water, her mind lurched through thoughts of possible motherhood.

Rachel considered herself fortunate. She knew some women without children desperately craved motherhood. However, her job as a community nurse brought her into daily contact with babies and children, so she had never really had a chance to miss them. It wasn't that she was too old to be pregnant at thirty-eight. It just wasn't what she had planned. Rachel had wanted children when she was younger, but she accepted the fact and got on with life when it hadn't happened. She was very content with Camron and the subject of their becoming parents hadn't surfaced for a long while.

The evening dwindled on and Rachel eventually got out of the bath. Steeling herself, she took the pregnancy test. Half an hour and three tests later, Rachel could no longer deny that she was pregnant. *I'll be sixty when she graduates from university. And I will definitely have to use Photoshop for any wedding photos that I'm in.*

Rachel decided she would break the good news to Camron when he returned from London at the weekend. It was good news; she was sure of it. She had spent much of the day deliberating and decided that it was definitely good news. Camron would have to relinquish the second bedroom he used as a study. Still, if she was going to put up with stretch marks and a rapidly changing body shape, he also had to make sacrifices.

She decided they would go out Saturday evening, and she would tell him then. Despite their bickering of the previous weekend, Rachel resolved that this would be a happy occasion. They had hardly been out since the summer and what better excuse could there be for a celebratory meal. One of the things she liked about living in Winterbourne Cerne was the fantastic pubs in some of the nearby villages, many of which took great pride in serving good beer and excellent home-cooked food. Rachel booked a table for Saturday evening at one of their favourites, *The Waiting Dragon.*

Friday came and Rachel stood in the twenty-minute waiting section of the car park at Dorchester train station. She leant against the bonnet with Flint by her side, his ears upright and alert, knowing from the numerous times before that he would see Camron soon. On time for once, the Waterloo train arrived, discharging the regular crowd of travel-weary passengers. Rachel waited as the passengers made their way out of the station.

Flint began straining at his lead. He barked once, facing the station exit. Camron walked out of the train station with his bag slung over his shoulder. Rachel always parked in the same place, and when he saw them, a huge smile broke on his face. He looked tired as he walked towards Rachel, but Camron always did when he returned from another week working away. She knew his work was stressful, but he enjoyed the challenge. His London salary, combined with her income, meant they had a good lifestyle, not extravagant but comfortable.

"Hello you," she said as he approached, smiling.

"Hi, gorgeous. I've missed you," Camron said before pulling her into an embrace and kissing her lovingly. She savoured his presence, their argument from the previous weekend wholly forgotten as he held her in his arms. She could have stayed like that for ages, except he didn't properly smell of Camron. He never did after London. There was always the subtle, or sometimes not so subtle, hint of city life. People crowded too close together, the

London Underground and the unavoidable presence of city living.

As they were driving home, Rachel said to him, "I've got a surprise for you. I've booked a table at The Dragon for tomorrow night. I thought it would be good to go out. We haven't for ages, not since the summer."

Camron smiled and felt some of his weariness lift.

"That's a brilliant idea." The Dragon was probably his favourite pub.

Camron hoped that as Rachel was arranging this little treat, she would offer to drive, and he could partake of a pint or two. These thoughts kept him pleasantly occupied for the short ride home.

The following morning Camron woke early, feeling the soft warmth of Rachel's silky skin as she snuggled close to him, her breathing soft and a look of peace upon her face. He lay there, savouring the memories of the previous night. Their lovemaking was always passionate after his return from London, but last night the urgency of their reunion had been surprising. Eventually, they had fallen into an exhausted sleep, wrapped close in each other's arms.

Unfortunately, Camron's improved temperament didn't last long and shortly after breakfast, he had descended into another black mood. Even Flint was getting in his way and he snapped at him uncharacteristically. Rachel didn't know what was wrong but was determined to make everything about today as perfect as possible. The news she would tell him that evening demanded nothing less.

"Why don't you take Flint for a walk? He misses you during the week."

"Maybe," he grunted noncommittally.

"Well, the choice is yours. You can stay here and help tidy the house or take Flint up to Cerne Abbas."

Camron gave in. He couldn't be bothered to argue and definitely couldn't be bothered to help around the house. He donned his wax jacket, pulled on his wellies, grabbed Flint's lead and headed out. He would hardly need to use the dog lead. Much of the route to Cerne Abbas was across fields and on footpaths, perfect for a dog who loved to roam free.

The weather, though a little chilly, was still glorious. The sun shone brightly, heedless of Camron's gloomy mood. Flint meandered back and forth across the fields, enjoying himself immensely. It didn't take long to cover the couple of miles to Cerne Abbas. Instead of entering the village, they skirteds around the edge. The hill with the Cerne Abbas Giant carving rose to their right. The huge hill figure, dating back to Saxon times, was cut into the chalky white hillside and depicted a naked man about sixty metres tall and famous for an impressive phallus.

They climbed the steep slope and Camron sat alongside the fenced off figure. It was peaceful and gave him space to think. He often sat there, sharing a quiet companionship with the giant. It wasn't always this tranquil as it was a popular tourist attraction. During the summer, the village was often bustling. Today, however, he had the giant to himself.

Camron thought about why he was in such a bad mood. He couldn't understand it. He wondered if it was the Stonehenge thing but dismissed the idea. They had moved the stones now, so there was no reason for it to affect him anymore. He sat on the grass, disconsolately contemplating his mood. Sad that his normal happy relationship with Rachel had become strained for the second weekend in a row. Thinking of her brought to mind the image of her waiting at the train station, the depth of her smile and the warmth in her eyes.

Those same midnight blue eyes had captivated Camron twelve years ago when he had met her on the day of her twenty-sixth birthday. There was a near-collision in Starbucks, a nervous laugh between strangers, and a look as their eyes met. She had smiled at him and her eyes had danced vivaciously. Alluring, yet with a mischievous glint. That chance meeting with this beautiful and intelligent woman had changed the life of a thirty-year-old confirmed bachelor forever.

Since then, his life had been good. Nothing extraordinary or exceptional, but good nonetheless. And it was being with Rachel that made his life good, he reminded himself.

*Nobody else would put up with me,* he thought with a smile.

Camron knew he was being unfair to Rachel. His general grumpiness and black moods were entirely his fault. Still, he hadn't been able to shake the growing apprehension he had felt ever since he first heard that the stones at Stonehenge were to be moved. He couldn't understand why this affected him so much, but nothing he did could shake the dread he felt every time he thought about this, which was with increasing regularity.

However, brooding on a hillside would not make things any better. Camron stood and looked around for Flint. He was standing on the other side of the wooden fence, right in the middle of the giant's chest.

"Here, boy," called Camron, but Flint uncharacteristically ignored him, staring fixedly at the giant's head.

"Flint, come here," called Camron, forcefully this time, but was again ignored. "Stupid dog," he muttered. A hint of his recent ill-humour resurfaced as he clambered over the fence.

Flint didn't move. He continued staring at the giant's head, hackles raised.

"What's the matter, boy?" Camron said, pulling the dog lead from his coat pocket as he reached Flint. He glanced towards the giant's head and stopped, dumbfounded.

A faint blue glow outlined the head of the giant. As Camron gaped, he felt his own head tingle. The light grew brighter, expanding to encompass the entire giant. The tingling around Camron's body intensified and he felt a strange pulling sensation within him, a feeling that was almost impossible to describe. He felt as if his body was collapsing in on itself, pulling him inside himself.

Bathed in blue light, he fell to his knees beside Flint. The sensation grew more forceful. He tried to resist, but the glowing outline of the giant was now contracting around him. His head throbbed. His body felt like it was on fire. He tried to get up but couldn't move. Pain coursed through him as if a thousand tiny shards of glass had punctured his skin. Flint whimpered and Camron made a desperate lunge towards him. As blackness claimed him, his hand closed around Flint's fur.

* * *

Rachel glanced at the kitchen clock. It was gone one o'clock. Camron should have been back well over an hour ago. Maybe he was getting whatever was going on inside his head out of his system. Nevertheless, she rang his mobile and heard the distinctive ringtone coming from his study. Typical, she thought.

She decided to give it another hour.

Two o'clock came, and Rachel was beginning to worry. She left a note for him on the kitchen table and jumped in the car, heading for Cerne. She parked in the car park by the viewpoint opposite the giant, and as she couldn't see him on the hill, she put on her walking boots and set off.

She ended up walking all the way back to the cottage, but there was still no sign of him. Her note on the kitchen table remained untouched. She walked back to Cerne Abbas, taking a different, slightly longer way, just in case Camron had detoured from his regular route.

Once back in Cerne, she checked both the pub and the village shop, but no one remembered seeing anyone of Camrons description with a large white dog. Rachel retrieved her car and drove home.

The next few hours passed like a nightmare.

She called a few of their friends to see if anyone had heard from him. Trying not to sound too concerned, she reassured them nothing was wrong but that he had left his mobile phone at home and she was merely attempting to get in touch with him.

Finally, she decided she had no choice but to call the police. They took some brief details over the phone, but as Camron had only been missing for a few hours, they said there was no cause for alarm. He would most likely return home soon. However, if she was genuinely concerned, she could come down to the station and make a formal statement. She left another note on the kitchen table and drove into Dorchester.

Rachel had to wait for nearly an hour before seeing the desk officer on duty. The officer was very understanding, recorded her statement, and took a recent photo of Camron from Rachel. The policewoman tried to alleviate Rachel's obvious worry.

"He will probably turn up of his own accord," the officer said, "He might even be at home waiting for you right now."

Rachel muttered that she was probably right and thanked her for her time.

Rachel returned to her car and drove home, but the cottage remained empty. She curled up on the sofa, waiting for the phone to ring. Her mind worked overtime with worry.

The phone rang at 8:30 pm. Rachel jumped and scrambled to answer it.

"Camron?"

"No, sorry, it isn't. Is that Rachel?" said a voice on the phone.

"Yes. Sorry, I thought it was my husband calling."

"It's Tom from *The Waiting Dragon.* You had a table booked for eight o'clock. We were wondering if you were still coming."

She dropped the phone, clutched her knees to her chest and burst into tears, sobbing uncontrollably.

# Chapter 4

SUNDAY, 22ND NOVEMBER

Rachel lay awake as daylight crept into the bedroom. Her thoughts were in a tumult even as her ears strained for the sound of a key in the front door. Surely if anything had happened to him, he or Flint would have been found by now. But if nothing terrible had happened to him, then that meant he had gone on purpose.

She tried to recollect the past couple of weeks. Had his routine altered, had there been any changes in his character, had she noticed anything different, no matter how small or insignificant? In her mind, the link between him disappearing, his bad moods and the stones at Stonehenge were all she could come up with. It was all pretty tenuous, but desperation made her grasp at any possibility, no matter how unlikely.

Could he be at Stonehenge?

The stones had been moved now, but the excavation continued, and the protestors remained.

Had he decided to head off and join the protestors? It would be entirely out of character for him to do something so spontaneous and inconsiderate. Surely, he would have let her know, although he had left his mobile phone at home when he took Flint for a walk. And how would he have gotten there? They only had one car, and it was parked outside their cottage.

Try as she might, Rachel could not come up with any other explanation. Refusing to believe anything dreadful had befallen him, she convinced herself that he must have gone to Stonehenge. Even though Rachel wasn't hungry, she quickly ate a bowl of cornflakes, unsure if her nausea was due to the pregnancy or her anxiety. She printed off a handful of pictures of him, hoping someone might remember seeing him, then scribbled a note explaining where she had gone and left it on the kitchen table.

As Rachel turned off the A303, heading towards the protestors' camp almost a mile from Stonehenge, she saw a police checkpoint ahead, with one or two cars turning around. Presumably, the police had refused permission for them to proceed. As she neared the checkpoint, a police officer in a hi-vis jacket put out his arm, signalling her to stop. Thinking quickly, Rachel showed him her NHS identity card. She informed him that one of the protestors was pregnant and she needed to check on her following a call from their doctor. Much to her relief, the policeman didn't question her but waved her through the barrier with a smile.

Rachel hated having to lie, but voicing the truth was not only unbearable but also implausible. *'My husband has gone missing; I think he might be having a mid-life crisis and has joined the protestors at Stonehenge.'* No, a simple white lie was better.

She pulled into the makeshift car park and did her best to park on one of the remaining pieces of grass rather than in the mud. The thought of finding someone to tow her out later didn't appeal. She walked carefully round to the boot and retrieved her wellies, grateful she had thought to bring them. Clutching her bundle of photographs, she made her way into the camp. It had been there for several weeks, and she was surprised by its air of permanency.

There was quite an extraordinary cross-section of society present, everyone from the curious to the steadfast. Some protestors were seasoned campaigners and knew how to make their stay as comfortable as possible. Alongside these were the druids, mainly dressed in white, although now mud seemed to be a predominant adornment to their robes. Also, there were defiant young couples, a handful of pensioners, middle-class professionals and, of course, a constant police presence.

She spent the next couple of hours moving through the camp and speaking to anyone who would listen to her, asking if they had seen Camron. The answer was always the same: no. A few thought they had seen someone who looked like Camron, but they couldn't be sure. One colourful character said he had definitely seen him. Rachel's hopes lifted until the guy said he had shared several bottles of local cider with him last Wednesday.

Rachel wandered away, eyes fixed on the ground, lost in her own misery. She was startled when someone tapped her on the shoulder.

"Excuse me, miss, are you alright?"

Her stomach sank as she turned towards a young police constable. Guilt flashed across her features as she thought her ruse to get into the camp had been rumbled.

"Are you okay?" he repeated. "I saw you were talking to lots of people, and you seem quite upset."

"I'm fine," she said unconvincingly, looking up at him. He seemed genuinely concerned for her.

Her gaze faltered, and she stifled a sob.

"It's my husband, you see. He went missing yesterday, and I know it sounds ridiculous, but I thought he might have come here."

"Oh, I see," said the officer. "Let me see if I can help. Have you spoken to your local police station?"

"Yes, but they told me it was early days, and he'd probably turn up of his own accord."

"Well, they're probably right," he said, but seeing her crestfallen look, added, "but if you think he might have come here, then why don't you leave it with me? It sounds like we're going to be here a while. I could ask around for you. Would you mind if I had a few of those?" He nodded towards the bundle of photograph copies in her hand.

"Thank you," said Rachel. "That would be most kind." She smiled gratefully and handed some of the copies to him.

"Would you mind if I took a few details, please, miss? So I know who we're looking for," he said, reaching for his notebook.

Rachel gave him the information he asked for, which he noted down and thanked him, reassuring him she would be okay and would be going home soon.

She spent another half hour speaking to a few more people and then decided to stop for the day. It was a miserable drive home, the cloudy weather finally giving way to rain, and the conditions outside the car perfectly matched Rachel's mood.

When Monday morning came, Rachel couldn't face going to work. Her job was demanding at the best of times, and right now, she couldn't possibly deal with the myriad of problems the families on her caseload presented. She telephoned her manager and explained what had happened, asking if she could have a couple of days off. Her manager agreed and made her promise if there was anything she needed that, she would call. Rachel thanked her and rang off. She sat on the bottom step of the staircase and wondered, for the thousandth time, what had happened to Camron and Flint.

Rachel was thinking about going to the police station again when the doorbell rang. She jumped, startled, before getting up to answer it.

A man and a woman stood waiting on the doorstep. In his late thirties and wearing an ill-fitting brown suit, the man held out a police warrant card.

"Hello, my name is Detective Sergeant Burridge from Dorset Police. This is Detective Constable Shaw. It is Rachel, isn't it? May I call you Rachel? Could I come in, please? It's about your husband, Camron." DS Burridge tumbled the words out without pausing for breath.

Rachel blanched, her mind reeling in shock as she imagined the worst.

DC Shaw must have seen the look on her face. "No, no, don't be alarmed; it's nothing bad. We just need to ask you a few more routine questions, get some background, that sort of thing."

"Oh," said Rachel, the panic slowly ebbing from her,

"Sorry," said DS Burridge, "It's my mistake. I should have made it clear why we were here. It was thoughtless of me to spout it out like that. Anyway, may we come in?"

Rachel showed him into the kitchen.

"Can I get you some tea or coffee?" she asked.

"No thanks, we're fine. I just had one at the station, but thank you anyway."

The three of them sat down at the kitchen table. DC Shaw pulled out her notepad and flicked through a couple of pages. She went through a couple of questions, confirming when she had last seen Camron and if she had had any contact with him since.

"Um, you were at the protestors' camp at Stonehenge yesterday?"

"Yes," Rachel answered warily. "Why?"

"And you were there because you thought your husband might have gone there?"

"Yes," Rachel repeated, still wary. "But there wasn't any sign of him." A sudden thought struck her. "Has he been seen there?" she asked, hope rising desperately inside her.

Seeing the look of near desperation in her eyes, DS Burridge shook his head.

"No, sorry."

He reached into his inside jacket pocket and pulled out a photograph, showing it to Rachel. It was of a professional-looking man in his early fifties, dressed in a tweed jacket.

"Have you seen this man before?" asked the detective sergeant.

Rachel looked at the photograph and then said, "No. Look, what's all this about? What has this got to do with my husband going missing?"

"Are you sure you've never seen this man before? Could you take another look, just to be certain?"

Rachel looked again and shook her head. "I've never seen him before. Who is he?"

"His name is Professor David Underwood," said DC Shaw. "He's the chap leading the project up at Stonehenge."

"And?" asked Rachel.

"He's gone missing too," replied DC Shaw. "Last Wednesday. We wondered whether there might be a connection between him and your husband, seeing as you asked about him at Stonehenge. That's where Professor Underwood went missing. Do you recall your husband ever mentioning his name?"

"No, I don't think so. It's not a name I've heard before."

“Ok, well, it was a long shot, but worth a try,” said DS Burridge, getting up from the table. “If you think of anything, please, give me a call?” He took a contact card from his jacket pocket and handed it to her. Rachel took it and followed him to the front door.

“Thank you for your time,” said DC Shaw as she followed the detective sergeant out. “We’ll let you know if there’s any progress with finding your husband.”

“And I’m sorry for startling you earlier. Goodbye,” said DS Burridge, and with that, he turned and walked down the path towards the garden gate accompanied by DC Shaw.

Rachel closed the door and slumped forward with her head resting on it. She was no closer to knowing what had happened. In fact, if anything, she had more questions unanswered than ever.

# Chapter 5

SATURDAY, 28TH NOVEMBER

LONDON, ENGLAND

Peter sighed and looked up to the top of Nelson's Column, feeling a kindred spirit with the indomitable and steadfast Admiral Nelson as he braced himself for the day ahead. Despite it being early, Trafalgar Square was already crowded. Peter took a sip of his take-out coffee. He just knew it was going to be a long day.

His twin daughters had been looking forward to this weekend for months and were determined to make the most of it. Still, Peter would have preferred to be playing rugby with his mates. He glanced towards his wife, Suzie, who was helping Karen clamber off one of the four great Barbary lion statues at the base of Nelson's Column and smiled to himself.

Peter finished the last of his coffee and went to join the girls. They walked towards the steps leading up to the National Portrait Gallery. Peter noted a slight figure heading towards him, dressed in what could only be described as a hooded cloak. Was this some new in vogue apparel? Strange, he thought, but then, what did he know about young people's fashion, as his girls frequently told him.

They appeared to be on a collision course. The youth, male by his look, wasn't paying attention to where he walked. His head was bowed and hidden deep within a hood. As they drew closer, Peter tried to sidestep to avoid him but, unfortunately, bumped into the youth. It was only a glancing collision, shoulder to shoulder, but Peter felt like he had hit a brick wall. He was sure his shoulder would sport a large bruise the next day.

He turned to say something to the youth, who continued on his way but glanced back. The person was indeed male, but Peter couldn't tell how old he was. He could see a pair of eyes, entirely black, that shone with pure malevolence.

Peter averted his gaze and hurried his wife and daughters along, feeling inexplicably anxious. He paused at the top of the steps, turning to look for the distinctive cloak. He spotted it eventually, on the left-hand side of the square near the statue of Sir Henry Havelock. The youth was gesticulating with his hands. It looked like he was arguing with someone on his mobile, probably using a Bluetooth headset. Remembering the look of cold hatred, Peter felt sorry for whoever was on the receiving end. Those nearby wisely seemed to give him a wide berth.

Peter was about to follow his family into the museum when he froze, bewildered by what he saw. A strange yellowish gas billowed from the outstretched fingertips of the cloaked figure. The gaseous cloud quickly mushroomed across the square and onto the surrounding roads.

Peter stood rooted to the spot. His mouth open in an expression of stunned shock and unable to tear his gaze from the unfolding horror.

The billowing gas engulfed the unsuspecting crowds. People started coughing and retching, clawing at their faces and exposed skin that blistered rapidly and burst, oozing out dark yellowish pus. Coughs quickly turned to laboured breathing, gasping to draw breath into lungs already burnt by the gas.

Like dolls being blown over in the wind, people began collapsing in an ever-increasing outward circle as the gas quickly spread.

Panic spread. Those not already stricken fled before the encroaching yellow cloud, desperate to escape. Some stumbled and fell or were pushed in the ensuing flight. Those too slow to regain their feet were quickly engulfed in a terrible and agonising death.

"Peter, what on earth are you doing? The girls are waiting," said Suzie behind him.

Peter snapped out of his transfixed horror of the scene before him and spun around. His wife stood with her hand over her mouth, a look of horror as she struggled to comprehend the nightmare she witnessed over his shoulder.

“Run!” Peter shouted, forcibly pushing her back through the museum doors.

* * *

PARIS, FRANCE

It was an unexpectedly pleasant day for late Autumn. The sun shone, imparting an illusion of warmth despite the brisk autumnal wind. The area around the Eiffel Tower was packed with tourists – it always was on weekends, especially when the weather was as beautiful as it was today.

An elderly French lady was making her way carefully through the crowds. Madame Duchaine disliked being late and thought she should have taken a taxi instead. She headed towards Rue de Desaix to meet with friends but paused, leaning on her walking stick, when a large group of children passed in front of her. She looked around at the crowds of people, tourists, and Parisians mingled together, enjoying the day.

Her gaze fell upon three people huddled together, looking out of place. They appeared to be women, judging by their height and slender appearance, although it was hard to be sure as they were all wearing dark, full-length cloaks with hoods pulled up. She pondered the strangers briefly, especially considering their strange mode of dress. However, the pressing matter of organising her upcoming ruby wedding anniversary party quickly regained her full attention. In fact, it was the reason for her morning trip to Rue de Desaix – to meet with a couple of her closest friends who would help with the planning. She glanced back briefly, but the women had gone. Madame Duchaine continued on her way, all thoughts of the strangers receding from her mind.

A hundred metres away, under the shadow of some trees along the Avenue Anatole-France, the three figures faced the Eiffel Tower. Slender fingers on their outstretched hands gestured in precise movements. They spoke in barely a whisper, their incantation almost ritualistic. They continued for several minutes until all three stopped suddenly, their outstretched arms pointed towards the tower. Simultaneously, six arcs of pure white lightning shot from their hands, striking the Eiffel Tower a split second later.

The effect was immediate and utterly devastating.

While the tower had been designed to withstand thunderstorm lightning bolts, nobody could have ever contemplated an attack by magic. The bolts hit only two supporting legs, but that was enough. The metalwork, which had stood unyielding for over a hundred and thirty years, glowed brightly, instantly heated to hundreds of degrees. Rivets popped, and the puddled iron beams twisted as the ten-thousand-ton weight of the tower bore down upon its weakened legs. It started to lean ominously to one side as the damaged legs buckled further. As soon as gravity got involved, the outcome was inevitable. Barely 30 seconds after the magical attack hit the tower, it leaned precariously, the angle increasing second by second.

Panic ensued. Those on the ground fled for their lives, many showing little regard for others around them. Some stumbled and fell. Chaos reigned as people screamed in fear. Parents were clinging to their children, couples grasping hands as they ran, determined not to let go.

For those who had climbed up the tower to admire the scenic views of Paris, it was a different story. The buckled lifts no longer worked, and the remaining stairs were jammed with people desperate to escape the tower.

Madame Duchaine had almost reached her destination on Rue de Desaix when she heard the thunderous noise, followed shortly by the terrified screams of many people. It came from the direction of the Eiffel Tower.

She couldn't quite see the tower from where she was, so she made her way back along the road to a point where the tower was in view. She stared, disbelieving. Her mind couldn't comprehend what was happening; it had stood there, unmoving, her entire life. What could possibly have happened to it?

As these thoughts raced through her mind, she heard a sickening, tortured sound of grinding metal. The tower, slowly at first but rapidly gaining speed, toppled over, hitting the ground with an almighty crash. A few seconds of absolute silence followed as if the world itself held its breath, shocked at the horror of what had happened.

* * *

SOUTHAMPTON, ENGLAND

Tyler was happy. It was Saturday afternoon, and he was at a football match with his dad, waiting to watch Southampton play at home against Bournemouth. Another three points in the bag, he was sure. Over 30,000 people eager to watch this local derby match was a capacity crowd. The atmosphere was fantastic.

Tyler was ten years old and had been coming to St Mary's Stadium with his dad for nearly three years. He sat reading the match-day programme and took a bite of his burger. *Perfect, just perfect,* he thought. His mum disapproved of burgers.

"They're not good for you, Tyler," she would say. "You should eat something healthy instead." McDonald's was definitely a no-go area for his family. But this was part of the Saturday afternoon football tradition. You couldn't come to the footie and not have a burger. Anyway, it wasn't a problem as he and his dad had made a pact. They simply didn't tell his mum.

The match started, and the first fifteen minutes lived up to expectations. Both sides were playing well this season and were in the group of clubs jostling for position towards the top of the Premier League table.

Saints started down the left with a promising attack, but the ball was taken following a superb tackle from one of Bournemouth's defenders, who then made an inch-perfect cross-field pass, setting up a counter-attack. It was two on two, and the crowd was on their feet, the Bournemouth fans cheering wildly. A neatly dodged tackle and the player was perfectly lined up for a shot from just outside the Southampton penalty box. The Bournemouth striker, perfectly balanced, leant back slightly as he kicked the ball towards the top corner of the goal. Tyler stood on tip-toes to see past the man before him, praying the ball would go over the bar.

Tyler's eyes widened in shock as the ball caught fire mid-flight, expanding rapidly as it flew through its trajectory. It blazed past the frozen goalkeeper, whose stunned gaze simply followed the fiery ball and over the bar, by which point it was some five metres in diameter. A mere second or two later, the fiery globe burst into the Northam Stand of the stadium, where supporters were still on their feet. It exploded into a thunderous fireball engulfing at least a quarter of the entire stadium and blasting an entire section of the stadium wall outwards.

Tyler clamped his hands to his ears as a deafening explosion swept over him at the far end of the stadium, the blast knocking him backwards over his seat.

The fireball lasted only a few moments, but that was enough to wreak utter devastation. Thousands had been in the stand, but the grotesquely charred remains were barely recognisable as people. Screams and cries from the multitude of those injured competed with the sounds of collapsing rubble and popping steelwork, superheated by the inferno.

Panic erupted as terror swept through the survivors.

Tyler felt strong hands grab him and haul him up from where he lay prone in the next row. His shoulder and head hurt and he felt something wet and sticky on the side of his face. Moments later, his dad was holding him upright on a seat, staring frantically into his face. Tyler stared back at his dad, hardly registering the singed hair, missing eyebrows and reddish glow on his face.

"Are you alright?" he shouted over the furore around them.

Tyler nodded, still stunned by what had happened.

"Are you sure? Does it hurt anywhere?"

Tyler turned his head slightly and touched the side of his forehead.

"Ouch," he exclaimed. His fingers came away covered in blood.

His dad knelt down to look closer and Tyler gazed over his shoulder and gasped at the sight that befell him.

Many not directly in the direct blast area were injured and badly burnt, their cries of pain mingling with the shouts of panic. Those further back still from the immediate impact of the inferno, like Tyler and his dad, had escaped with only minor burns or cuts and bruises. Many people ran across the scorched pitch, heading towards those hurt. Tears clouded Tyler's eyes as he realised it was already too late for those caught in the centre of the fireball.

Tyler's dad picked him up, holding his head gently against his shoulder to protect him from the gruesome sights as much as possible. They made their way outside of the devasted stadium as quickly as possible. Tyler's shoulder hurt even more as his dad clambered his way out, but he didn't cry out. The images he had seen were burned into his mind and he was mute with terror.

* * *

SOMEWHERE IN THE PACIFIC OCEAN

Life aboard the USS *Abraham Lincoln* aircraft carrier was busy but rewarding for Tom. Recently qualified as an Aircraft Director, colloquially known as Bears, he found Navy life suited him just fine. They were currently in the Pacific Ocean on a joint training exercise with NATO, and Tom was gazing over the vast expanse of ocean, watching a perfect sunset.

Suddenly, something completely impossible interrupted his musings. He spotted a faint green glow hovering in mid-air a couple of hundred metres to port. He peered intently, convinced he must be seeing things. He was even more astounded when a figure appeared in the centre of the green glow, hanging in mid-air in total defiance of the laws of gravity.

The figure gestured with his hands as Tom stood there watching, dumbfounded. Suddenly a tiny ball of what looked like fire shot from the person's outstretched arms, moving towards the carrier and increasing in both speed and size as it got closer.

Before Tom could fully comprehend what was happening, the ball of fire passed through the aircraft carrier's hull. A split second later, there was an enormous explosion, buckling the hundred-thousand-ton ship like a mighty beast in its death throes. The blast had ripped the vessel asunder. She started to sink into the depths of the ocean. Soon, random flotsam was the only trace left of the USS *Abraham Lincoln*. Over five thousand souls had been on board, and barely a handful survived, bobbing in the ocean, clinging to whatever wreckage they could.

The figure hovering in mid-air smiled before turning around and disappearing through the green circular glow.

# Chapter 6

ALFHEIM

Camron awoke disorientated. He could feel the sun warming his face, and the air smelt fresh and clean. He opened his eyes cautiously, raising his head slightly to look around.

A woman sat at his bedside, needle in hand, intent on her sewing. Her movements were deft and controlled, the needle flying effortlessly across the garment she was mending. His shirt, Camron noted with surprise.

The woman was slender and fair-skinned, her hair the colour of purest silver, beautifully braided and woven with delicate woodland flowers. He shifted to see her better, but her fingers stopped at the sound of movement; the needle poised in mid-air. She raised her head and looked at him with soft grey eyes and met his stare with a look of her own that was both piercing and captivating. She held his gaze for several moments, and then her entire face lit up as she smiled at him warmly.

Camron had never seen anyone so impossibly beautiful. Or had he? He felt he should recognise her, that he had seen her face before. He looked at her more carefully, trying to recall where he had seen her. Suddenly he noticed her ears. They were pointed and leaf-shaped. Startled, he looked again. Definitely long and pointed.

"Hello, Amr," she said, placing the sewing onto her lap. "I am Nimue."

She paused a moment. "Do you remember me?"

Her voice was as captivating as her looks, soft and musical. Her words tinkled like water flowing through a brook on a lazy summer afternoon. A few images flickered through his mind, random recollections of people and places. He struggled to focus, to pin down these fleeting thoughts, but his mind was clouded and vague.

*Amr? Who was Amr?*

And then, all at once, like floodgates opening, an unrestrained assault of memories crashed down on him relentlessly. Memories that he had been completely unaware of until that very moment. Camron closed his eyes.

He remembered.

In one sudden tumultuous rush, he remembered the previous lives he had lived over the centuries, each one in total ignorance of the others. The sheer volume of memories was overwhelming: wives loved and lost; numerous parents who nurtured him from childhood to manhood; family and friends; enemies and comrades. People who were now long gone. He sat bolt upright, his body rigid and tense with shock as disorderly images tumbled through his mind.

Throughout the centuries, he had lived many different lives. He remembered diverse trades: a blacksmith, a scribe, a serf, a monk, a merchant, a sailor, even a court jester. He recalled toiling in the fields, digging in a mine and working in a shipyard, building great wooden warships.

And he remembered being a soldier. He had been a soldier many times and remembered numerous battles. So much bloodshed, so much death. He remembered the joy of victory and the pain of defeat, the suffering and horror of the battlefield, the look of terror in his opponent's eyes. He felt the pain of wounds and the fear of death. Strangely, however, he couldn't remember ever dying himself.

Nor could he remember having any children.

These thoughts and memories flashed through his mind all at once, threatening to overwhelm him. He remembered it all, but most keenly, he remembered the loss of every person he had loved and cared about over the past fifteen hundred years. He collapsed onto the bed, emotions running through him unchecked. Tears flowed from his eyes, running freely down his cheeks like tiny trickles of sadness.

He remembered.

Amr Pendragon, son of Arthur Pendragon, High King of Briton. He was King Arthur's son. A family connection sprang to his mind. He was also the grandson of Nimue.

His eyes sprang open, staring in shocked remembrance at the woman seated at his bedside. Nimue, Queen of the Elves. His grandmother.

He was unique in the world: part human, part elf.

A howl, torn from the depths of his being, erupted as he cried out in unassailable anguish. His grandmother was there, holding him in her arms, comforting him. How long he stayed like that, he couldn't tell, but at last, the onrush of emotions subsided. He extricated himself from her arms and fell back onto the bed, emotionally drained for the moment.

Nimue looked at him, tears glistening in the corners of her eyes, betraying her regret and sorrow.

"I am truly sorry, Amr," she said. "We never thought you would wander for so long, locked within the *Guardian Spell* we placed on you, or that you would bear so much suffering and anguish when you remembered."

The *Guardian Spell.*

In his mind, he saw a cave next to a spring in the small fiefdom of Ercing. Nimue was there, as was his father, who stood next to him, resolute and determined yet unable to mask the sorrow in his eyes. A third person was also present. Camron's mind clutched briefly at the figure, struggling to put a name to the once-familiar face. Merlin! The person who was both wizard and statesman, druid and warrior warlock to the world. But to Camron, he was a tutor and mentor, guide, and friend. King Arthur had taught Camron how to be a prince. Merlin had taught him how to be himself.

Nimue and Merlin were in the middle of casting a spell, their concentration absolute, focused on the incantation and complex hand movements needed to perform the powerful magic. The *Guardian* Spell had set him on the path of his destiny, ultimately bringing him to this point. That magic had ordained his future. To live lifetime after lifetime, each one as a different person, blind to the knowledge of who he really was. A Guardian, waiting in a cycle of perpetual ignorance.

"Amr?" Nimue's soft voice broke through the tumult of his recollections.

He couldn't speak but simply lay there, dazed and exhausted. He wanted his mind to go blank, to think of nothing, but his new memories would allow him no peace.

Eventually, Camron spoke. "Where am I?"

"You're at my home in Alfheim," said Nimue. "I brought you here after the magical seal at Stonehenge was broken."

"Why?"

"It is time, Amr. Humans have need of magic once more. The task you have been unknowingly waiting for and sacrificed so much for, has finally come."

Camron sat up, a feeling of nausea sweeping across him. He stared at her blankly, struggling to cling to the thread of who he thought he was.

Nimue continued, "The realms are once again connected."

Camron looked at her uncomprehending.

"What do you mean?"

"As you know, or at least once knew, there are different realms that share this one planet. The main realm is inhabited by humans, but there are others. Alfheim and Svartalfheim are the realms of the Elves. These realms are separate from each other but are linked by a web of what we call magic. At certain places along those webs, the magic is particularly powerful. For those with the knowledge and skill, travel between the realms is possible through these portals."

Camron lay back down carefully as Nimue continued.

"After the last War of the Realms, it was decided the only way to prevent future wars would be to place a magical lock on these portals. Stonehenge, being the strongest, would seal them all." Her eyes flickered towards the open window, remembering images from the horrors of that centuries-old conflict. "The most powerful wizards and witches remaining after the war, both human and elf, came together to cast a spell of great magic upon Stonehenge to seal the portal there. As long as the stones remained standing, the magic would hold."

She paused for a few moments, allowing Camron time to absorb all she had said.

"Stonehenge!" exclaimed Camron.

"Yes," replied Nimue. "Stonehenge. But as long as the seal remained intact, we were all sealed within our own separate realms, friend and enemy alike."

"I don't know why, but the stones have been moved. This is why you can remember again. Breaking the seal not only allows the portals to open again but also releases you from the *Guardian spell.*"

Nimue's voice took on a harder edge as she continued. "The Dökkálfar, those Dark Elves whose hatred of us Ljósálfar has remained undiminished throughout the centuries, will be able to travel to your world from their desolate realm of Svartalfheim. And when they do, they will bring death and destruction with them once more."

Disjointed images flashed through his mind. Elves, one of the races of faerie kind, are divided in two. Ljósálfar, whose name meant Light Elves and Dökkálfar, Dark Elves.

Both Dökkálfar and Ljósálfar were similar in size and stature. Light-skinned, slender and beautiful. Only two physical differences could tell them apart. Ljósálfar had golden or silvery hair, whereas the Dökkálfar had black hair, even into old age. More telling were their eyes. One look into the completely dark eyes of a Dökkálfar, and you could not fail to see cruelty reflected. Dökkálfar and Ljósálfar were as opposite in nature as could be, for they were as cruel, vicious and vile as the Ljósálfar were good, kind and caring.

"I know what happened," admitted Camron in a quiet voice, his mind returning to Stonehenge and the disquiet and grumpiness he had so inexplicably felt.

"The stones were moved so they could investigate underneath them. Some scientists thought excavating beneath the stones would provide answers to the mysteries surrounding Stonehenge. I even had an argument with my wife about... My wife! Rachel!" Camron exclaimed. "Where is she?"

Nimue's eyes clouded with the threat of more tears. Of all the pain and hurt her grandson would face this day, this one would be the hardest.

"She is safe. She is still at your home in Dorset."

"Does she know where I am?" asked Camron, worry for his wife giving him purpose and allowing his mind to focus. "Does she know who I am?"

Nimue hesitated before answering. "No, she thinks you have gone missing but has no idea why and for the time being, she cannot know for her own protection. I can watch over her from a distance but cannot intercede directly. The portals are still weak, and it would be dangerous to travel through."

"You brought me through," said Camron, failing to keep the petulance from his voice.

A single raised eyebrow was Nimue's response. "She is safer living in ignorance, even if that ignorance is painful."

"No," said Camron, his voice raised. "I must talk to her, tell her I'm alright. She's my wife." My present wife, he reminded himself with disquiet.

"Amr, my child, listen to me," said Nimue.

"It's Camron," he interrupted her sharply. "My name is Camron!"

Nimue looked at him speculatively for a moment.

"Camron," she said finally. "There are many things you will come to remember during the next few days and many more things I will tell you. But know this, the child your wife carries is the most important person in all the realms of this earth. The best hope of safety for your wife and child is in her continued ignorance of who you and the child really are."

"The child she carries?" asked Camron. "She's pregnant?" Camron usually prided himself on being astute and a keen observer of people, but he'd had a trying morning and allowed himself a moment to state the obvious.

"Yes, she is. Rachel will have your daughter," said Nimue, "and like you, she will be part human and part elf

– with all the blessings and burdens that come with being unique. She will belong to both our worlds and will have the ability to control magic innately, just as you do. Now you must rest," said Nimue, noting that his eyes betrayed his exhaustion. She passed her hand over Camron's face and muttered a brief incantation. Her fingers glowed blue and Camron fell into a deep, restful sleep.

* * *

He had no idea how long he slept, but when Camron awoke, he felt refreshed. He wondered where he was, thinking he had woken from a strange dream. He turned over, expecting to see Rachel lying beside him. Instead, a beautiful woodland could be seen through the window.

He remembered.

Camron groaned. He didn't want this. It wasn't fair. He had agreed to be the guardian centuries ago, but he had been a different person then. He had been a prince, a future king in the making, brought up by his father with the absolute belief that you put your duty to your kingdom and its people above all else, regardless of personal sacrifice. But that had been 1,500 years ago. Since then, the multitude of lives he had lived had been as an ordinary person, not royalty or aristocracy. His duty and loyalty had been to his family and friends during those other lives, not some higher calling he wouldn't have understood. When he, as Prince Amr, had agreed to take on this burden, he could never have imagined what it would mean, what he would be forced to endure and forfeit.

He had been happy being Camron. His life was good, and he loved Rachel with all his heart. Still loved Rachel, he told himself determinedly.

His mind, so full of newly discovered memories, wandered. He had so many questions and thoughts buzzing around his head, each one skittering and eluding his attempts to grasp hold.

But one thought kept recurring with alarming frequency. Magic had brought him back, and he was supposed to help win the approaching struggle against the Dökkálfar. He could wield a sword quite well, although the last time he had used one in combat was at the Battle of Waterloo in 1815 when, as a cavalry officer, he had become unseated from his horse and had to fight his way back to the safety of the British lines. Even so, he doubted one swordsman was going to be enough. It would all come down to magic again.

His few scant years of tutoring by Merlin in the art of magic seemed pitifully inadequate considering the task he had to do. Camron recalled that his spell casting had been quite good, but after 1,500 years, it was rustier than his swordsmanship.

But what was the task? He had no idea what it was he must do. Defeating the Dökkálfar and their minions seemed to both over-simplify the problem and fill him with terror.

Not only had he grown up in his father's castle and learnt to ride and fight, he had also been schooled in swordsmanship by Lancelot, one of Arthur's most loyal knights. He was a warrior and a wizard. He was a prince, both amongst men and elves.

But that was centuries ago. Camron wasn't sure if he was entirely the same person or someone else. He felt far more like Camron than he did Amr. Who would advise and guide him? His father was dead, so he presumed was Merlin. Indeed, everyone else he had grown up with, who might have helped or guided him, was dead. His grandmother was all he had left.

Thinking of Nimue brought their conversation to mind, and he opened his eyes with a start. Rachel was pregnant. He was going to be a dad, and apparently, his daughter was not only involved but somehow vital to any chance they had of winning the war.

War.

There he had said it. It would be another war.

But this would be unlike any war he had fought in since. This would be the 3rd War of the Realms. He remembered the horror of the last one all too well.

He had been young when it started, still under Merlin's tutelage. Still, the destruction and carnage were vivid in his newly remembered memories. He recalled the horror of the senseless death and destruction, although hand-to-hand combat didn't terrify him. While bloody, each combatant stood a chance against their opponent. No, it was the use of devastating magic. The obliteration of entire families, villages, armies even, with the casting of a single spell. For ordinary people and even many wizards and sorcerers, there was no defence against a powerful spell.

How would the world cope today? Men relied on science and technology, not magic.

But then, men had developed weapons capable of mass destruction at the push of a button? Was that so very different from the utterance of a spell? Was a fireball spell any more devastating than a bomb dropped from an aeroplane?

Camron recalled a speech his father, King Arthur, had made to his knights on the eve of one battle:

*'It is not the weapons we take into a battle that defines the war's outcome. Rather, it is the manner in which we wield those weapons, when and how we choose to use them and, most importantly, when we choose not to use them.'*

He dragged his mind back to Rachel, picturing her in their cottage, humming quietly to herself as she cooked in the kitchen or pottered around the garden. He smiled for the first time since waking in the elven realm.

Regardless of anything else he had to face, he was still her husband. He would find a way back to her and protect her. He had made a vow to love honour and protect her, and he was damned sure nothing as trivial as a war with the Dökkálfar was going to stop him from keeping that promise.

He breathed deeply and felt better. Concentrating on Rachel gave him a renewed sense of purpose. Trying to figure out how to save the entire world was too overwhelming. But working out how to protect his wife and daughter seemed possible.

Painful though it was, he closed his eyes and forced himself to remember each life he had lived, one by one.

Starting with when he was Amr, up to his life now as Camron, he thought he had lived forty-two different lives, although some memories were muddled, so he couldn't be entirely sure.

"Who am I?" Camron asked aloud.

"Whoever you want to be," came a sudden reply. "You have, after all, had quite a few lives to choose from. Surely you can find one you like?"

The voice, pure and lilting, came from the doorway to the room. Camron saw a beautiful elven maid standing there, holding a tray covered with a white linen cloth.

She was beautiful, agile and lithe, with long silvery hair neatly tied back. Her eyes were green and sparkled like sunshine filtering through a canopy of lush woodland.

She beamed a radiant smile, and her face lit up with all the wonder and vitality of youth.

"Grandmother said you would be hungry," the young elf said. "Are you?"

Suddenly the 21st century part of Camron, the bit used to eating three good meals a day that got crabby if denied, took over and made it very clear that he was not just hungry but positively starving. He nodded and watched as she glided gracefully to the bed and placed the tray on a small table. She removed the cloth, and a pleasant aroma of soup and freshly baked bread filled his nostrils. She handed him the bowl and perched herself on the edge of the bed, watching him.

Camron took a tentative spoonful of soup and was delighted. It was delicious, not just delicious but quite possibly the best thing he had ever tasted. He concentrated on the soup, savouring every spoonful. It was several minutes before his stomach allowed his mind to work again.

"Grandmother?" Camron said questioningly, after emptying half the bowl, his astuteness still apparently left behind in Dorset. "You said, grandmother?"

"Yes," replied the woman. "I am Geledhil, and Queen Nimue is my grandmother, well great-great-great-grandmother actually, but she isn't keen on too many '*greats,*' something about making her sound ancient. So I call her grandmother. Which makes us second or third cousins twice removed or something like that. Anyway, I think cousin will do," she finished, smiling warmly.

"Cousin would be nice," he said. "I don't have any cousins, nor any brothers or sisters. At least not as Camron," he added in a subdued tone, eyes misting as he recalled the numerous families who had loved and cared for him.

"So, what's it like then?" Geledhil continued brightly, clearly pretending not to notice the tears in the corner of his eye.

"What's what like?"

"You know, living lots of lives. I can't imagine what it's like. I'm only seventy-five, but sometimes, even being this young, I get bored and think there must be more to life."

"I'm not sure. Until I got here, I wasn't aware of any previous lives. I had no memories of them. And now, suddenly, I have too many memories. Many of them I wish I didn't have." Camron went silent, his face clouding with anguish as his words reminded him of the pain and loss during his previous lives.

"I'm sorry," said Geledhil. "I didn't mean to make you sad. Grandmother wouldn't tell me much about you, but she did say not to pester you. You know, you have caused quite a stir. All my friends are talking about you! None of us has ever seen a human before, and most of us thought you were a myth or a legend, you know, like the stories the elders tell us when we're younglings."

Camron looked at her carefully. His arrival had obviously been the cause of much interest and even some excitement, especially amongst the younger elves. But she didn't show any signs of dread or trepidation about the impending war.

*She doesn't know about the breach of the portal seal!* Camron thought, his eyes widening with surprise at this realisation.

"No, she doesn't," said a voice from the doorway.

Both Camron and Geledhil turned to see Nimue standing there.

"No, she doesn't what?" asked Geledhil, startled by her grandmother's sudden appearance.

"Never mind, child," she replied. "And if you've quite finished bringing Camron his food, I'm sure your other chores are still waiting for you." Her eyebrows raised in a manner obviously all too familiar to Geledhil.

As Geledhil leaned over to take the now empty soup bowl from Camron, she whispered, "Grandmother tries to be stern, but she isn't all that scary, really." And with a smile and a twinkling of her eyes, she picked up the tray and left, calling over her shoulder, "See you soon."

Nimue sighed and shook her head resignedly as she sat on the stool next to the bed. She looked thoughtfully at Camron for a moment before speaking.

"Only a handful of us know about the portal's seal. I saw no point in causing widespread panic, which would happen if I told my people without having both you and a plan to present to them. So far, I have you. All we need now is a plan."

Camron felt the encroaching enormity of his new responsibility again, and the fear and dread threatened to suffocate him. He secretly hoped Nimue had a plan and would tell him exactly what he needed to do.

"Halfway there then," he said with more bravado than he felt.

Nimue narrowed her eyes and looked at him closely for a few moments, scrutinising him.

"So much like your father," she said. "But now you must rest some more, you're still recovering from travelling here, and you will need your strength in the days to come."

# Chapter 7

SUNDAY, 29TH NOVEMBER

It had only just gone 8 o'clock, and George Stanley stood in the middle of what seemed like controlled chaos. He was in the White House Situation Room. This was where he should be. After all, he was the President of the United States of America, and these events definitely counted as a '*situation*'. He thought emergency, crisis or even catastrophe might be a better description.

He thought back to his Inauguration Speech just nine months ago. He had known he would have to deal with any number of emergencies. But he had secretly hoped that his first real crisis would be more manageable. Today did not look like it was turning out that way.

The attacks yesterday in England and France were terrible enough, but overnight the news had come in of the sinking of the USS *Abraham Lincoln.* This morning, reports of a plane crash in Hong Kong, an unexplained explosion at an oil refinery in Russia and unconfirmed reports of hundreds dead in India.

And now, reports were coming in of a wall, apparently made of solid stone, suddenly appearing across all six lanes of the Brooklyn Bridge in New York. Aside from its unexplained appearance, what was remarkable was that it was completely transparent, invisible to the human eye. Dozens of people had died, and many hundreds more were injured during the initial multi-vehicle pile-up before it.

He looked around the room. There were all the familiar faces. James Gordon, National Security Advisor; Paul Barnard, Chief of Staff; Patricia Cole, Secretary of Defence; Meiling Chan, Homeland Security Advisor; plus a half dozen or so others.

The noise was becoming unbearable. It sounded like a few heated conversations were taking place simultaneously. George raised his voice above the din, "Right then, folks, let's get started, shall we?"

The noise abated as everyone's attention shifted to him.

"Craig, what do we know?" George asked, directing the question towards Craig Wallis, Secretary of the Navy.

Craig shook his head. "Not a lot. And what little we do know isn't going to help us. Reports from the other vessels in the task force say there was a single massive explosion, apparently from inside the ship, which literally tore her in two."

"Survivors?" asked the President.

"Only fourteen were picked up from the sea. Plus, the eight pilots who were out flying early morning patrols. Just twenty-two survivors out of a ship's crew of over 5,600."

The President removed his glasses and rubbed his eyes, struggling to grasp the enormity of the loss. "Cause of the explosion?"

"Unknown at present," replied Craig. "None of the other ships in the fleet detected any inbound missile, either airborne or sub-surface. The most likely scenario is a bomb planted on board. But it would have to be one hell of a size or, if a smaller one, then planted with extreme accuracy and very precise knowledge of the vessel."

Craig pulled a piece of paper from the folder before him. "Trouble is, she sank in a lot of water, nearly 7,000 metres. We will struggle to get a deep-sea submersible down to her to perform a useful forensic examination. To be brutally honest, if it's answers we're after, then our best hope is that it was a terrorist attack and someone comes forward to claim responsibility. Otherwise, we're only guessing. Sorry, Mr President, but that's where we are right now."

"Thanks, Craig," said George, trying not to let emotion show in his voice. "Ok, what about this wall in New York? Jim, any updates?"

James Gordon looked up from a sheaf of papers he was perusing. "Well, likewise, we don't know much. At 10:30 am, there was a massive, multi-car automobile crash across all six lanes of the Brooklyn Bridge in both directions. Eyewitness reports say the first vehicles just stopped dead, the front of the cars completely crumpled.

Cars following behind piled into them. Several caught fire, adding to the carnage. It was total chaos. Reports so far state..." He paused, glancing down at the report in front of him. "Seventy-eight dead and a further two hundred and ten injured, some critically. I guess we could count ourselves lucky. The bridge was relatively quiet, with today being Sunday. This one is definitely an attack, but no one has claimed responsibility for it. We know what was done but have no idea how they did it."

"And do we know how this wall is invisible?" asked George.

James shrugged his shoulders, "Not a clue."

"Could it be some form of prototype cloaking system?" asked Paul Barnard, "Cameras projecting the image on the other side, that sort of thing."

James considered a moment before answering. "It doesn't look like it, but it's possible. We've tried hitting this thing with sledgehammers, which is how we know it's probably a stone or rock wall. When we hit it, the thing sounds like stone, and it reverberates like stone too, but it's as tough as granite, tougher even. We haven't managed to chip it with pneumatic drills. If it is some form of cloaking system, these are damn tough little cameras."

George took up the reins again. "And then there are the attacks in Europe, Russia, Hong Kong and possibly India. Thousands of people dead. If these are terrorist attacks, it has been coordinated on a global scale, unlike anything we have seen before. Several groups might be behind this but do we really think any of them would be up to an attack at this level?"

James took a sip of water as he gathered his thoughts. "I don't know, a few organisations have tried to claim responsibility, but I think it's doubtful it is any of them. We are talking about several major incidents, meticulously planned and executed to perfection. This shows a level of sophistication we've never seen before. Plus, we had no intel warning at all. No chat-room messages, texts, emails, nothing. Since 9/11, we have had reliable intelligence and systems in place, and we've had no hint of an imminent attack. Especially not a globally coordinated one. I really can't see how we could be this blind to an attack of this magnitude if it was terrorism."

"What about the Russians or Chinese? Could they be behind it?" asked Meiling Chan.

"It's not impossible, but it is improbable," said Patricia Cole. "I don't see what their motive would be. This would be major-league warmongering if it were either of them. It would be suicide for Russia to attack the West and China simultaneously, plus the oil refinery explosion in Siberia looks likely it's part of this."

"As for China," she continued, "don't forget it was a Chinese flight from Shanghai to Hong Kong with predominantly Chinese nationals on board. And there's been an unconfirmed report that the niece of a high-ranking party official was one of the passengers. Would they attack their own? Just as a bluff or diversion? No, I don't see either of them behind this."

George ran his fingers through his slightly thinning hair. "So, what you're saying is some previously unknown super-organisation is intent on causing global chaos and possibly world war. Plus, we have never had even the slightest clue they exist? This sounds more like something from a James Bond movie than anything based on hard evidence. We need answers, and we need them now. I don't care what it takes. We have to know what we're dealing with and how to stop it. You've all got work to do, so let's get to it!"

# Chapter 8

She sat in the Great Hall surveying those before her. All were silent now, no whispered schemes, no murmured plans. Every eye watched her surreptitiously, wary of any sudden outbursts. They knew well the signs of her anger and could tell that her wrath was barely held in check.

She noted their covert glances at the pool of blood staining the floor where the unfortunate messenger who had delivered news of the attacks had recently stood.

*Fools,* she thought. These attacks had not been part of her plan. The other great houses had acted in haste, seeking to further their own power, and now she must act swiftly to regain control.

She must remind all that only her plan would succeed. There would be retributions against the other houses, not too excessive, for she needed them still. But enough, so they knew her will would dominate all.

# Chapter 9

ALFHEIM

Professor David Underwood awoke to the sound of birdsong. He had never been interested in birds or wildlife; his passions being confined to the historical past. Yet the sound caressing his ears was sweeter and purer than any symphony he had ever heard. He lay quite still, eyes closed, luxuriating in the feel of the impossibly soft sheets. His thoughts drifted aimlessly, allowing the beauty of song to soothe him before slowly opening his eyes. He was in a small room, light and airy, with sunlight streaming through an open window and the faintest of breezes making the warmth deliciously perfect.

Turning his head, he looked through the window. Meadows filled with wildflowers, long grasses swaying like dancers weaving gracefully to an unheard rhythm. Butterflies floated lazily on the gentle breeze, delicate and colourful. Bees flitted from flower to flower, industriously collecting precious nectar. Beyond the serenity of the meadows, he could see a forest of magnificent oak trees. Sunshine covered the landscape like a mantle as he gazed out of the window, his mind entranced by the peaceful tranquillity.

"Grandmother, he's awake," called a voice, breaking into his reverie. *Who was that?* Not a voice he recognised. He struggled to gather his thoughts.

Suddenly he remembered.

He was at Stonehenge and had gone to the stones to escape the party. He remembered falling into one of the holes where the stones had stood. So, what was he doing in bed? Was he in a hospital? Sitting up in the bed, he looked around the room and glimpsed a slender young woman with long silvery hair departing through a door.

He was about to call out but was interrupted as another woman entered. She seemed older but equally slender and with the same long silvery hair. She was also incredibly beautiful, impossibly beautiful even. However, her face was sombre, touched with a hint of sadness. Yet he also detected a hint of anger in the soft grey eyes looking towards him, appraising him evenly.

"Good morning. My name is Nimue. Welcome to my home," she said, a definite note of coolness in her greeting.

"Where am I? Why am I here?" David asked. "Is this a hospital?"

She stood, pondering for a moment before speaking.

"Where you are will take a little explaining. Why you are here is entirely due to your own actions," said Nimue, this last sentence said with a definite accusatory tone. David shifted uncomfortably in his bed, pulling the soft sheets around him as his forehead creased with worry. He was beginning to feel he wasn't welcome here, wherever 'here' happened to be.

The younger woman returned, carrying a tray with an earthenware jug and a wooden cup. She smiled at him, a bright, warm, genuine smile and set the tray down on a small table by the side of the bed. She poured water from the jug into the cup and offered it to him.

"Please, drink," she said. "Apparently, the first time through is the worst, and the portals are not yet at full strength. I'm told you feel terribly thirsty afterwards."

David realised he was indeed thirsty and took the proffered cup with a small smile. It appeared to contain water. He took a small, tentative sip and then took another. The water was pure and refreshing and tasted like nothing he had drunk before. It briefly crossed his mind that he would make an absolute fortune if he could bottle this.

"Thanks," he said, "this is delicious."

The woman continued as he drank, "Grandmother says you were very fortunate being pulled through like you were," she brushed a few stray strands of her long silky hair behind one pointed ear. "Especially as you're not a wizard. You could easily have been killed, or worse, ended up in Svartalfheim."

David had stopped listening and gaped at her, eyes wide in disbelief. The half-full cup fell from his hands onto the bed.

"Your ears!" David spluttered.

"Oh, stop staring," said Nimue impatiently. "Have you never seen an elf before?"

The other woman put a hand up to one of her ears as she looked at Nimue. "Grandmother, you know he hasn't. Please, stop being like this. It's not his fault."

"Actually, it is his fault. It's entirely his fault!" she said sharply. But then her features softened slightly, "Well, maybe not entirely his fault, but he does bear some responsibility."

"Elf? Sorry, did you say elf?" interrupted David.

"Yes, that's right," Nimue replied. "You are a human, and we are elves."

David gasped, pushing himself back in the bed as he sought to unscramble his thoughts, to use his intellect to bring reason to this impossibility.

"Elf?" he stammered, fighting to regain mastery of his voice.

"That is what I said," replied Nimue.

"Grandmother!" said the other elf with a tinge of admonishment.

She turned to David, "I know it's difficult to believe, but we are elves. There hasn't been any contact between ourselves and humans for hundreds of years."

"I don't know what I've done or where I am," David said, his voice barely a whisper, "but I'd like to go home now, please?." His nostrils flared and his eyes widened, becoming bulbous orbs. His earlier worry morphed into full-blown fear.

Nimue looked down at him for a long time, the silence grating on David's already fraught nerves. Finally, she moved towards the bed and sat in a nearby chair.

Addressing her granddaughter, she said, "Would you leave us, please. I would like to speak to this man in private if I may?"

"But... grandmother?"

“Now, if you would be so kind.” The authority in her voice was unmistakable, as was the expectation of obedience.

“Yes, grandmother,” she acquiesced reluctantly and left, closing the door quietly behind her.

When the young elf had closed the door behind her, Nimue turned to David. “Well, all of you will need to know what is happening at some point, so I may as well start with you.”

She picked up the cup still lying where David had dropped it on the bed. He flinched as her hand stretched out.

“You have nothing to worry about,” she said, “no one here will hurt you. Now, what is your name, young man?”

“Professor David Underwood,” he said in a croaky voice, thinking that it had been many years since anyone had called him a young man.

“Well, David, if you’re a professor, you should be good at listening and learning new things. Are you good at listening and learning? Because if you’re not, this will be much harder to explain than it already is.”

David nodded mutely.

Nimue continued, “Well then, listen carefully. The world is not entirely how you humans think it is. There is more to it, much more. I am a Ljósálfar, an elf of the light in your language.”

David opened his mouth to speak, but Nimue interrupted him. “Remember to listen, please.”

She continued, “You humans are not as alone as you think. It is not just elves. There are also other faerie-kind as well as dwarves and others. And, as in many things, there are two sides. The balance between good and evil. Ljósálfar and Dökkálfar. Humans used to call Dökkálfar elves of the dark. And in league with the Dökkálfar are goblins, orcs and a host of other vile creatures.”

Davids’ academic mind struggled to believe what he was hearing but Nimue’s eyes, fixed on his, bore no hint of untruth.

Nimue paused, allowing David time to absorb her words.

David's mind was spinning. *Elves and dwarves exist. Goblins and orcs are real. Was The Lord of the Rings a true story then?* The scientist in him wanted to refute it as complete nonsense, but he couldn't. For a start, there was an elf sitting opposite him.

His eyes had widened once more, not with fear this time, but in shock. A thousand questions flashed through his academic mind. What he asked was, "How come no one has ever seen elves before?"

*'Oh, brilliant question!'* said a tiny voice in his head. David ignored it.

"The answer to that question also explains why you are here," she replied, her tone brisk, almost in the manner of a teacher speaking to an unruly pupil. "The Earth contains more than just the one physical planet. There are other realms, different planes of the same land that co-exist in parallel with your own. Separate, but in places, joined. It is within these other planes that the Ljósálfar and Dökkálfar live. In fact, right now, you are within the realm of the Ljósálfar. In a place called Alfheim."

"You mean, we're not..." David stammered, his mind struggling to accept her words.

"No. You're not in Kansas anymore!"

David fell back against the pillows, staring vacantly at the ceiling as his mind reeled.

"How did I get here?" he asked.

"We do not use science or engineering as you humans do." Answered Nimue, "Elves, both Ljósálfar and Dökkálfar, are creatures of magic; an ancient power that is all around us and which we can control and bend to our will."

David massaged his temples, the threat of a headache looming.

"As I mentioned, there are points where the different planes touch the realm of humans and, using magic, travel between the planes is possible at these points we call portals. They are sites of enormous magical power. The greatest of these portals is at Stonehenge. 1,500 years ago, by your reckoning, there was a war between those who dwelt in the different realms. The first war was before the time of men, but during this second war, humans fought alongside Ljósálfar and dwarves against the Dökkálfar and those under their control. It was a bitter and desperate struggle, but eventually, we banished our enemies to their own desolate realm."

Nimue paused, getting to her feet and moving to the window. Her gaze swept the meadows outside, but her eyes were focused on memories long past, and a sudden sadness settled on her.

"We could not take the chance of them escaping," she continued in a softer tone. "To keep the realms safe, we set a magical seal on the greatest of the portals, at Stonehenge, thus preventing anyone from travelling between the different planes. The magic locked the Dökkálfar and their allies in the realm of Svartalfheim forever. But it locked the other realms too, including Alfheim."

Nimue paused with her explanation, regarding David intently before continuing, "Well, that was until you removed the stones and broke the seal!"

# Chapter 10

ALFHEIM

Camron awoke to feel refreshed. Opening his eyes, he saw sunlight streaming through the window, but he didn't know whether it was the same day or the next. He saw a bowl and a water pitcher on a small table and fresh clothes laid out on a chair.

He got up, washed and dressed. The clothes weren't his usual style. There were no jeans, t-shirt or trainers. Instead, he had a simple shirt and a pair of trousers, plain and unadorned but exceptionally well made and exceedingly comfortable. He pulled on soft leather boots and then left the room, his steps making barely a noise on the flagstones. He made his way along a corridor as light and airy as his room. A smile creased the corners of his mouth as he recalled his grandmother saying he was in her house. Her house was, in fact, the elven palace.

Camron set off through the vast, sprawling royal residence, navigating the maze of winding corridors. Flashes of memories surfaced briefly; forgotten images and glimpses from his youth left him with a strangely disconcerting feeling of *deja-vu.* His meandering reminded him of just how remarkable his grandmother's palace was. The palace was the product of expansion over the centuries, seemingly without any architectural plan yet always in harmony with nature and the surrounding landscape. The result was genuinely unique.

Most of the palace was only a single storey high, mainly of wood and other natural materials, with just a few towers thrusting skyward. Only a handful of rooms, such as the kitchens, were built of stone. Each blended harmoniously with the natural environment, so it was hard to tell where the building stopped and nature started. There were even some parts that were underground, using the roots of the great oak trees as supports for both the walls and ceilings.

Camron wandered, quite content to re-explore the place where he had spent time during his childhood. After a while, he came across an open courtyard surrounded on all four sides by the palace walls. A small stream meandered through the middle before disappearing through a hole in the far wall. Sunlight glistened on the water. The sound of its tinkling was like an echo of faraway laughter, filling the courtyard with a sense of peace.

A memory tugged at his mind, and he remembered being here as a young boy, sitting with his mother by the brook, listening to her stories he so loved to hear. She had died when he was eight years old, and those few memories of her, which he had only recently re-acquired, were already very precious to him.

His mother had been half-human and half-elf. Her mother, Nimue, was elvish, but her father had been human. She had inherited the best of both; the grace and beauty of her elven heritage combined with the human focus and determination that comes from a race whose lifespan was measured in decades rather than centuries.

He was still lost in reminiscences when the smell of freshly baked bread caught his attention. Crossing the courtyard, he followed the aroma down a corridor and came to a wide oak door, slightly ajar. Peering through the gap, he saw an enormous kitchen with a fire burning in the hearth at one end and a long trestle table running down the middle of the room. Garlic, onions, brightly coloured peppers and an assortment of herbs dangled from the ceiling. Gleaming copper pots and pans hung on one wall. The room had an air of efficiency and quiet confidence, almost as if it knew it was the heart of the palace.

Camron remembered this kitchen from his childhood, seated at this very table, a platter before him. Warm bread straight from the oven, spread with thick golden honey, sticky sweetness covering his fingers. He would spend hours here, enjoying the quiet company of the elf who ran the kitchens. Arantolthiel had run the kitchen efficiently and with calm authority but always smiled and often had a treat for the young human prince.

* * *

Nimue, sleeves of her elegant gown rolled up to keep the flour off as she kneaded bread, watched her grandson enter the kitchen. She noticed the way he looked at her and guessed his thoughts.

"Arantolthiel returned to her rest many years ago," said Nimue, looking at Camron.

"I'm sorry."

"Don't be," she replied. "She was happy and had a fulfilling life. She was content when she passed from us."

Camron smiled at her words

"Salendal," Nimue called, and a young elven girl preparing vegetables looked up. Nimue nodded towards Camron.

The girl smiled at him.

"Are you hungry?" she asked. "There's bread, honey and some fruit if you are." She didn't wait for an answer but gathered the promised food and a water pitcher onto a platter and brought it to the table, placing it near where Nimue worked. Camron sat down and started to eat.

"You remembered your way to the kitchen then?" Nimue asked, continuing to knead the bread. "Although no surprise. It was always one of your favourite places."

"Well, the food was always much better than at home," he said around a mouthful of bread and honey.

Nimue shook her head ruefully. "I had hoped that after 1,500 years, your table manners might have improved."

"Nope," he said, grinning at her. "Speaking of time, how long have I been here?"

"This is your third day," she replied. "The sudden opening of your memories came as a great shock to you. Many were upsetting and painful. Sleep was the best medicine, so we let you rest."

His smile faded, and he lowered his eyes to his platter and concentrated on breakfast, not wanting to think about everything that had happened to him.

Nimue watched Camron discreetly while she kneaded the dough. When his father, Arthur, was alive, they often came to Alfheim. Her thoughts drifted back to that eventful day when the young Prince Amr had forsaken the life he knew and taken up the mantle of guardian and protector.

*It was about a year after the Second War of the Realms.*

*She remembered the scene vividly. There were four of them; herself, King Arthur, Merlin and Prince Amr. They had travelled to a sacred location in Ercing, a remote place strong in magic.*

*Ercing was a small kingdom, a little to the north of Gwent, and they had travelled under the pretext of visiting Arthur's uncle, Gwrfoddw Hen, who was the king of Ercing.*

*They stood in front of a cave near a stream, making preparations. An old woman lived in the cave. A witch whom the local villages relied on as a midwife and healer. She had lived there for as long as anyone could remember. The old woman had come out of her cave to watch, and Nimue nodded in greeting.*

*"It is time," said Merlin.*

*Nimue looked unsure. She lowered her voice for Merlin's ears only. "How do we know the seal will be broken in the future? Are we condemning Amr to perpetual existence, living one life after the next?"*

*"We have no choice," replied Merlin. "We cannot leave these matters to chance; the risk is too great. If the Dökkálfar breach the seals and we have not prepared, what would befall the world is beyond reckoning. Better to sacrifice one than everyone." His words were true but harsh, yet his eyes betrayed the pain of inflicting the task on his beloved pupil.*

*Nimue nodded and looked towards where Arthur stood by his son and saw there were tears in the eyes of the battle-hardened Dragon King.*

*Nimue started as a hand grasped her arm. The hand was withered with age, the skin paper-thin. Yet the grip belied a strength that the years should have stolen. Nimue's eyes met those of the old woman. They had rolled into their sockets, showing milky white orbs. In a voice crackly with age, she spoke, "Listen carefully, for your deeds this day are necessary. Be warned, for the world will have dire need of magic again one day; the Guardian will be called upon. But heed this well, Queen of the Ljósálfar. Though he shall live many lives through the ages, he shall have just one child. Although this man will be the Guardian of Destiny, it will be his daughter who shall deliver victory to those who would see good triumph. She will be named Gwenllian, the Daughter of Destiny."*

*Nimue and Merlin looked at each other in amazement.*

*Her words of prophecy echoed that of another – a warning given at the end of the First War of the Realms. They turned to look at the woman again, but she was shuffling towards her cave, leaning heavily on a stick for support.*

*"What did she mean?" asked King Arthur.*

*"I don't know entirely," replied Merlin, "but if her words are to be believed, and I am inclined to think they are, then it would seem we are doing the right thing. One day, Amr will be called upon."*

"Grandmother?" His words echoed through the kitchen's silence and brought Nimue back from her memories. "You're the queen. Why are you kneading bread rather than ruling?"

Nimue's laugh was musical and a tonic from the pain of her own memories and the guilt that accompanied them.

"I can rule as well from the kitchen as I can from any throne room. I enjoy making bread. It gives me time to think. They know where to find me if there's a problem, and anyway, you never know when a queen may need to know how to make bread. And also, the most important tasks I have to do today involve you, and here you are, in the kitchen with me. So I am precisely where I should be, am I not?"

Nimue cast a meaningful glance towards the elven girl, and she quietly left the room.

"Now, how much of your life do you remember?"

"Which one?" he answered, pushing his empty plate away.

"The one you were born to, your life as Amr."

Camron's eyes furrowed in thought. “I remember my father’s castle and being trained to fight by his knights. Practising and becoming proficient with the sword, spear and bow. I also remember Father trying to teach me how to rule. Attempting to understand people and get them working together. I guess it would be called statesmanship now, although I was never much good at reading people.”

“Anything else?” prompted Nimue.

“I think I was a good fighter back then. At least I remember being able to fight well. I guess I was better at hitting people than understanding them. I don’t have my father’s way with diplomacy. He always knew the right thing to do and could get people to follow him to the ends of the earth with only a few words.”

“Yes, he could,” said Nimue. “I think that is one of the qualities your mother loved about him most.”

“I also remember Merlin tutoring me in the art of magic, learning about the world's natural elements. How to be a wizard. How to cast spells and control the forces of magic.” Camron paused. “Merlin’s dead, isn’t he?”

“Yes,” replied Nimue quietly. “He died over a thousand years ago. Even though he was a powerful sorcerer and lived for several centuries, he was still a human. He did not have the lifespan we elves have. He was a good friend.”

“My father is dead, and my teacher is dead. It’s only you and me left now, isn’t it?”

“Yes, it’s just the two of us from that time. But then you knew that would be the case when you volunteered. We have to get on and do our best,” her tone was crisp and matter-of-fact. “Now then, your stay here won’t be too long before you must return to your world. We need to make sure you’re ready.”

“You mean, can I remember how to use magic?”

Nimue nodded.

“I don’t know. I remember a bit about the theory about magic, but I don’t remember any actual spells.”

They sat in silence for a short while, each lost in their own thoughts, Camron picking at his breakfast distractedly.

"Is Rachel alright?" he asked suddenly. "Have you been able to keep an eye on her? If I've been here three days already, she must be worried sick."

Nimue's voice softened, "Yes, she is well and safe, and yes, she is worried. But that is better than the alternative." She paused. "Camron, it hasn't been three days for Rachel. Do you not remember that time in Alfheim passes differently from that of your world? You have been with us for three days, but twelve days have passed for Rachel."

He stood up quickly, the realisation on his face clearly showing he had forgotten about how time passed differently.

"Sit down, Camron and listen," said Nimue quickly. "I know you're worried and want to get back to her, but you need to know what has been happening in your world. A handful of the most powerful Dökkálfar managed to get through the portal. They attacked a few days ago, only a few small groups, but they killed thousands in just one day!"

Camron sat back down, the shock he felt clearly reflected in his eyes.

"So, the war has started then?" he asked.

"No, I don't think so," said Nimue carefully. "These attacks were fairly random and had an uncoordinated feel about them. Also, don't forget that the portals haven't recovered their full power yet. For the Dökkálfar to launch a full-scale attack, the portals will need to be at full strength. This gives us some time at least," she said, "but they will attack again and in greater numbers next time. And when they do, we have to be ready for them."

"Thousands dead!," Camron murmured to himself, still staring at Nimue in disbelief.

Nimue could read in his eyes that the enormity of what lay ahead was beginning to dawn on him.

"Come with me," she said after a moment's thought. Nimue led Camron out of the palace and into the forest. They walked in silence for about ten minutes, branches creaking overhead and fallen leaves carpeting the sun-dappled path. The vast oaks gave way to a grove of hazel trees, leading to a small clearing. The creaking of branches had given way to the slightest susurration of the wind and a faint tinkling of water.

In the middle stood a marble pedestal upon which rested a stone basin. Intricately carved vines and branches flowed around the edge of the basin.

Nimue walked over to the basin and waited for Camron to join her.

"You remember what this place is?" she asked.

"I vaguely remember being here but can't remember what it's for."

"This is the scrying grove," said Nimue. She picked up an earthen pitcher from the ground by the pedestal and walked over towards a little pool fed by a small brook at the far side. Nimue filled the jug and, returning to Camron, poured water into the basin.

Looking up, Nimue saw Camron watching her expectantly.

"Yes," she answered the unspoken question, "we can scry on Rachel and check that all is well."

Nimue saw relief spread across Camron's face as he bent to peer intently into the water. Nimue began to cast the spell that awoke the enchantment of the scrying basin.

The image of two women seated at a small table swam hazily to the surface, becoming clearer as Nimue completed the spell. A weak winter sun shone palely into the conservatory at the back of their cottage. Rachel was pouring tea for the other, an older woman who bore a striking resemblance to Rachel.

"Who is Rachel with?" Nimue asked.

"Stephanie, her mother," said Camron, his voice catching. "She lives in New York, where she works for a news network. She must have come over to stay with Rachel."

"Clearly," said Nimue, watching Camron closely. She had had doubts about the wisdom of letting him scry on his wife, wondering if seeing her would be too much and whether he would insist on returning home.

However, as his eyes drank in the image of his wife, safe in their cottage in Winterbourne Cerne, Nimue saw his shoulders relax, his grip on the basin's edge lessen.

Nimue let Camron watch the mother and daughter for nearly half an hour before ending the enchantment. Camron took a deep breath before looking up at Nimue, who saw a tear glistening in the corner of one eye.

"Thank you," he whispered.

She smiled and nodded. "I have called a meeting of my most trusted councillors for this afternoon," Nimue said. "We can discuss what to do and plan for the coming conflict. I would like you to attend."

"Yes, of course," he agreed.

"Good. One more thing. Only a handful of us can speak your language, so the council will be in the elvish tongue. Do you think you can remember enough to get by?"

"I'm not sure. I guess I'll have to try."

"Well, if you are struggling, let me know and I can cast a *tongues* spell to enable you to understand and speak Elvish, but it would be better if you could manage by yourself. I will send someone to collect you when it's time."

# Chapter 11

ALFHEIM

Camron left the scrying grove and meandered aimlessly through the forest, vaguely heading back in the direction of the palace but not really taking much note of where he was going. He tried to focus his thoughts solely on the scried images of Rachel, but they kept getting interrupted by all that Nimue had told him.

Part of the city was a little way inside one of the great forests of Alfheim. The trees were predominantly mighty oaks, old and majestic, standing steadfast through the centuries. Many of the elves had made their homes within the boughs of these trees, blending them harmoniously, so they were part of the tree and at one with the forest. A series of interconnecting walkways, made of branches and vines, linked many trees so the elves could travel to their neighbours without descending to the forest floor.

He wandered amongst the trees, gazing up as they towered above him. The peace and tranquillity of the place eventually seeped into him. Despite his anxiety and the perils he knew were coming, a sense of serenity flowed through him.

His presence attracted the attention of the elves. While they were naturally curious about who he was and what he was doing in Alfheim, they were all very polite. They greeted him with a smile and a quick word or two. Camron hadn't spoken Elvish since his life as Amr. His memories of the elven tongue had returned to him with his other memories, but putting it into practice was quite another thing. He couldn't be entirely sure of what he said to those elves who greeted him. He could only hope he wasn't being rude. He had been walking for almost an hour when he heard someone calling his name. Turning, he saw Geledhil racing towards him.

When she reached him, she threw her arms around him and, almost sobbing, said, "Oh, Camron, I didn't know. I'm so sorry."

Camron, his arms around her somewhat awkwardly, said, "Sorry for what?"

“Grandmother told me about everything that has happened.”

“Oh, I see,” he said, the sense of peace dissipating from him.

“I’ve told Grandmother I’m going to help you. I’m a good fighter, one of the best archers, and my magic isn’t all that bad.” Her voice faltered, “But she said no. She told me I was too young and didn’t understand the dangers I would face.”

“Look, it's ok,” he said, releasing her awkwardly from their hug and looking intently at her. “It will be perilous, and I wouldn’t want you getting hurt. If I didn’t have to, I wouldn’t want to do this either. You should listen to Grandmother and stay here. Protect Alfheim if it should come to it.”

“You sound just like her,” she said crossly. “We’re cousins, and you’re going to need help. You aren’t going to be able to do it all by yourself, are you? It doesn’t matter who your father was or how powerful you think you are!”

“I don’t believe I'm powerful,” he said in a quiet, sombre voice. “I have no idea how I will do everything expected of me. But I do know it will be perilous, and there’s a good chance I might not survive. I don’t want anyone getting hurt because they wanted to help me.”

Geledhil looked into his eyes, matching his intensity.

“This isn’t just your fight. We are all involved. And you’re right, many people will die, humans and elves. All we can do is find the strength and courage to fight for what we know is right.”

He saw the determination in her eyes and was grateful for her words.

“Thank you,” he said. “You don’t know how much that means to me. To be honest, I’ve been terrified since waking up here and finding out who I was and what has to be done.” He looked down, scuffing his boots across the forest floor. “I’m not sure how much of the brave warrior Prince Amr is left. I’m just an ordinary person, and most of the time, I feel like I haven't really got a clue what is happening."

Geledhil put her arms around him and hugged him. Camron stood feeling awkward. When Geledhil finally let go, she looked at him, smiling, her grave face replaced by her usual cheerful exuberance.

"Well, this might help cheer you up," she said, taking him by the hand and pulling him along the path. "We can save the world later. Right now, there is someone who simply can't wait to see you."

"Who?" asked Camron, almost having to jog to keep up with her.

"You'll see," she answered mischievously.

"OK," he said. "But can we speak elvish? Grandmother says there's a meeting this afternoon, and we are all speaking Elvish. I could do with some practice beforehand."

Camron rounded the trunk of a vast tree and saw a golden-haired elf maid a few metres away. However, he barely noticed her, for she had a short length of rope in her hands, on the other end of which, now straining to get free and barking with excitement, was Flint.

"Flint!" he exclaimed. Suddenly the dog pulled free of the elf and bounded towards him.

With everything that had happened over the past few days, he had forgotten entirely about his dog. He vaguely remembered grabbing hold of Flint just as he had lost consciousness on the Cerne Abbas Giant. Somehow, Flint had come through the portal with him.

Flint reached Camron, and nearly sixty kilos of enthusiastic canine leapt at him, bowling him to the ground. Flint pinned him down and greeted him, licking him all over his face.

"Flint! Flint, get off me, boy. You're crushing me," said Camron. Flint, being an obedient dog, completely ignored this instruction. The past few days had been traumatic for him. Reunion with his master was too important to let anything as trivial as doing as he was told get in the way.

Camron could hear laughter from the other elf and knew she enjoyed the spectacle.

Eventually, he extracted himself from underneath the dog and sat up. The other elf came over and joined Camron and Geledhil, who introduced her to him.

"Camron, I'd like you to meet my life friend Xankira."

She said in Elvish, "Xankira, this is Camron, my cousin," said Geledhil as the two elves sat down next to Camron and Flint.

"Do you think he missed you?" Geledhil said playfully.

"Whatever gave you that idea?" Camron replied. He was much too pleased to see Flint to be even the slightest bit chagrined by his lack of dignity. Camron draped his arm over Flint's back as the dog leaned against him, trying to get as close as possible.

"Where has he been?" Camron asked.

"My friends and I, well mainly Xankira, have been looking after him. It was a pleasure. He's adorable, and the other girls love him too. We don't have dogs in Alfheim, only wolves, so we weren't too sure what to do, but grandmother told us. I hope we did it right?" Geledhil sounded a little anxious, but one look at Flint showed Camron that not only had he been well looked after but had probably been spoilt rotten.

"He looks great. Thank you so much." Both elves smiled at the compliment.

Geledhil jumped up, grabbing Camron's hand and pulling him up after her.

"Come on," she said enthusiastically. "Why don't we show you around Alfheim? I bet a lot has changed since you were last here?"

The two elven women gave Camron a guided tour of Alfheim accompanied by Flint, who alternated between remaining at his beloved master's side and dashing off to explore something new.

Xankira grew gradually quieter as they continued walking around Alfheim. Attempting to draw her into the conversation, Camron asked, "So, do you live in the palace as well?"

Her demeanour changed in an instant. Before she had been quiet, even a little shy or reticent, but Camron felt a hint of hostility in her tone as she replied, "No, I don't live in the palace. That isn't for the likes of my family."

"Xankira," admonished Geledhil gently.

"I'm sorry, I have to go. I have a lot to do." And with that, Xankira headed away from them at a brisk pace.

Camron stood, slightly dumbfounded. "I'm sorry," he said to Geledhil. "Did I upset her?"

"Don't worry, it isn't your fault," she replied. "I've known Xankira since we were young. We became life friends the moment we met. We're close, almost like sisters. The only thing that comes between us is money."

"Money?" asked Camron, completely lost. He didn't recall elven society placing too much importance on monetary wealth.

"Yes," answered Geledhil, "her family are of modest means. While it doesn't matter to me, Xankira sometimes gets jealous that I'm royalty and, I suppose, quite wealthy. It doesn't affect her too often, and I'm careful to keep things equal and normal. Still, occasionally she lets it rise to the surface. She'll be okay by tomorrow, you'll see."

Camron watched the dwindling figure of Xankira as she disappeared into the forest. He realised that while the two elves dressed similarly, Xankira's clothes were older and the cloth and leather of a noticeably lesser quality than Geledhil's.

"I didn't think elves were bothered by wealth and station?"

"We're not normally, but a few are more aware and concerned than others. Some end up with more than others in every society, and there will always be those with less who crave more."

They made their way back, their mood subdued by Xankira's reaction.

# Chapter 12

ALFHEIM

Later that same afternoon, Camron was resting in his room when Geledhil reappeared.

“Grandmother says it is time.”

Camron wasn’t sure if Flint was invited but didn’t want to leave him behind, so the three of them set off through the palace's corridors.

When they arrived, Geledhil knocked and waited for an answer before opening one of the double doors. Camron entered with Flint by his side, Geledhil following close behind and closing the door with a soft thud.

The room was bright and airy, with high ceilings supported by stout oak beams darkened with age. A large oak table occupied the centre with a dozen high-backed wooden chairs around it. Sunlight poured through the open windows, and a couple of small birds flittered about the arched beams overhead.

Nimue arched an eyebrow at seeing Geledhil enter behind Camron.

“I sent an invitation just to Camron. But I see a menagerie of dogs and little monkeys has arrived!”

Camron glanced over his shoulder and saw the imploring look Geledhil gave her grandmother. He hoped she wouldn’t be banished from the meeting.

A flicker of a smile crossed Nimue’s face. “Very well, you can stay and look after the dog, but do try to keep quiet.”

Geledhil took Flint off to one side and sat on a chair against the wall. Nimue beckoned Camron to a seat on her left-hand side.

“Let me introduce you to everyone,” she said. “In fact, why don’t you each introduce yourselves to Prince Amr?”

“It’s Camron, please,” he said to the room at large, “just Camron.”

The elf sitting to the right of Nimue introduced herself first.

"Greetings, Prince Camron and well met. My name is Haldamir Anwarünya. I am Queen Nimue's First Councillor."

Next to Haldamir sat an elderly looking elf dressed entirely in black robes with intricate silvery runes interwoven throughout. His silver hair was long, in the usual elven fashion, and his face wrinkled with age, but his eyes were still bright and sharp and his movements firm and steady.

"Greetings, young prince," he said. "I am Findecámo Nénharma, the Royal Wizard."

Tanidaer Felagund introduced himself next. He was head of the elven army. A serious-looking elf dressed in brightly polished chainmail armour. Alongside Tanidaer and dressed in exquisitely crafted chainmail armour, was the Captain of the Royal Guard, Celaena Meldiron. She was the youngest of this august company but seemed comfortable and at ease with her peers, confident in her abilities. The final person was a dour-looking elf whose face had the demeanour of one who very seldom smiled. She nodded briefly, introducing herself as Lenwë Carnesîr, the Royal Treasurer.

When the introductions were complete, Geledhil tiptoed to an ornate table alongside one wall, on which was a tray with some empty golden goblets intricately inscribed with elvish runes. She picked up one, clasped it in both hands and closed her eyes for a few moments. She opened her eyes and took a sip. The goblet was suddenly full of a light amber liquid.

Seeing the look of surprise on Camron's face, Nimue said, "They're magical goblets. Hold one and concentrate on whatever drink you desire, and it will fill with it. Although I suggest avoiding anything too strong, we have important matters to discuss." Nimue uttered this last statement while directing a pointed look towards Tanidaer, who adopted an air of innocence.

Camron took a similar goblet from the table before him, closed his eyes and concentrated. The cup shook of its own accord, and after a few moments, he opened one eye a fraction but saw nothing in the goblet save for some bluish smoke. *I'm not concentrating. Geledhil's goblet filled without the smoke and shaking.* He closed his eyes again, forcing himself to focus on the drink he wanted. It shook more forcefully and what felt like steam, only cold, not hot, touched his face. He heard a gasp from the other side of the room but refused to give up. After what seemed an age, he felt the weight of the goblet increase. Opening his eyes, he saw black liquid with bubbles rising gently to the surface. He looked around the room and saw the startled expressions on the faces of the elves.

"I fancied a Coke," he said with an apologetic shrug.

"Amazing, absolutely amazing!" exclaimed Findecámo. "I would never have considered that a drink from one of the other realms could be invoked." He began pulling out a sheaf of parchment. "I must make some notes. This is fascinating, truly fascinating."

"Later, Findecámo, please?" said Nimue. "We have much more important things to discuss than whether we can create a magical Coke machine in Alfheim."

"Yes, of course, sorry, Your Majesty," he said, rolling up the parchment and putting it away with a wistful look towards the goblet in Camron's hands.

Nimue waited for everyone to settle and then looked around the room at her assembled councillors.

"As you all know, the seals on the portals between the planes have been broken, and the Dökkálfar have attacked the world of humans. Even though we won the Second War of the Realms centuries ago and sealed the portals, I, Merlin, and a few others knew that the Dökkálfar would never accept defeat. They would continue their millennia-old obsession to gain absolute domination over all others. Their hatred of us Ljósálfar has remained unabated for aeons, and they won't stop until they kill every last one of us."

The room was silent, and images of that war he had been barely old enough to fight in flashed across Camron's mind. Vicious battles, screams of rage and screams of terror and blood. So much blood everywhere!

“This is a day that I wished would never come.” Nimue’s words cut across Camron’s nightmarish memories.

“Sadly, we are at war again!” Despite the sadness in her eyes, her tone was commanding, reminding Camron that his grandmother was the elven queen.

“Camron and I are the only ones who remember the last war, but I’m not sure how much help that will be. Things will not be the same this time. Humans now use science and technology instead of magic. Both are powerful but different, and neither has come up against the other before. Also, we no longer have the likes of Merlin and the other human sorcerers to fight on our side.”

“We must look to our strengths and understand our weaknesses. Making use of the first and minimising the latter,” interjected Tanidaer.

“Indeed,” continued Nimue. “Humans now rely on guns and missiles as their primary weaponry, which can be easily defeated by any number of different spells. I would imagine both a *Shield* spell and a *Protection from Missiles* spell will render most bullets and small missiles useless, and I am sure the enemy has thought of many more inventive uses of magic over the intervening centuries.”

Silence settled over the group as the full realisation of just how long the Dökkálfar had been preparing for this moment sunk in.

“Of course,” said Findecámo brightly, trying to remain positive, “we can enchant weapons which would then work effectively against them.” He paused. A frown creased his forehead before he continued more quietly. “But an enchantment spell will only affect a single weapon and would only last for thirty minutes or so. Permanently enchanting a weapon is feasible but takes weeks of work by a powerful sorcerer, and we don’t have enough to make any real difference within the time we have.” He trailed off, despondency replacing his earlier optimism.

“So,” said Nimue. “Apart from Camron, we have no human sorcerers. And whilst every elf receives training to be a wizard or witch, there aren't that many of us who are powerful enough to face a Dökkálfar battle-mage. Alas, I fear our long years of peace have left us unprepared for the task ahead. We have books and scrolls containing these spells but no experience of casting them. Unfortunately for us, I imagine the Dökkálfar have been practising and creating little else over the past centuries. They will have a distinct advantage."

"And let us not forget," said Haldamir, "that after the last war. The Dökkálfar numbered less than one hundred thousand, not that many less than our current Ljósálfar population. However, we have no idea how the enemy has fared during this time or how large their army could be. We can only guess and plan for the worst."

"Why can't we magically scry their world as you do with ours?" Camron interrupted.

"We can't, unfortunately," Findecámo answered. "It's because of how the planes are connected. The plane you humans live in is the hub in the centre. The other planes connect to it but not to each other. For instance, to get from Alfheim to Svartalfheim, you would have to travel via your world. A few of us can scry on your world, but not Svartalfheim. Likewise, the Dökkálfar can scry your world but not ours, which gives us some degree of privacy and protection but no advantage."

"So, the Dökkálfar have probably been studying us for years. That explains how they knew where to attack!" exclaimed Camron. "They can also tune into whatever plans are being made and know what's going on. It's like having a webcam wherever they want."

"I don't know what a *webcam* is, but you're right in saying they can scry on your leaders and listen to their plans," said Findecámo. "But remember, Your Highness, magical scrying requires that you know where you are looking."

"Which they probably do after all this time," said Camron.

"On the plus side," said Nimue, bringing the conversation back from its meanderings. "The human population has grown considerably over the past 1,500 years. Do you know how many live there now, Camron?" she asked.

"About seven billion, I think."

Nimue continued, "Seven billion. Which means we have the potential for a much larger army than last time."

"And," said Findecámo encouragingly, "we also have time on our side, at least for a while. Maybe a few months. The seals on the portals have been broken, but the power of the portals has lain dormant all these centuries, and they are still weak. I believe the initial attacks on the humans consumed much of the portal's power. It will take some time before they are strong enough to allow sufficient enemy numbers to travel through to launch a major attack."

"Her Majesty and myself have been discussing the attacks on the humans," said Tanidaer. "They really don't make any strategic sense. Sad though the death of those thousands of humans undoubtedly is, we cannot see it has gained them any advantage. Indeed, they have actually helped us by forewarning us and announcing their presence to the humans."

"I was wondering the same thing," said Celaena. "This doesn't seem well planned at all."

"I don't think it was planned," said Nimue.

"No," said Tanidaer, "Her Majesty and I think these attacks were random, possibly carried out by some Dökkálfar from one of the minor houses, hoping to make a name for themselves."

"And this gives us an advantage," said Nimue. "The heads of the ruling houses will undoubtedly tighten their grip on the other houses to enforce their own plans. I don't think there will be any more attacks like this. At least, not until they are ready to fight in force."

"But when they are ready," said Tanidaer, "when the portals are at full strength, then we believe they will bring through a much larger army. They will seek to gain a foothold in the human realm."

Nimue looked saddened but nodded her agreement.

"How long until the portals regain their full strength?" asked Camron.

"We cannot say for sure," answered Findecámo, "sealing the portals was magic that had never been used before."

"Your best guess then," said Camron impatiently.

"A few months, with luck."

"Well, that sums up where we stand right now. Does anyone have anything to add before we continue?" Nimue asked the group at large.

Nobody had anything further to add, so she continued. "Well, I believe we need a plan."

"You mean, like me doing something heroic to single-handedly save the world?" Camron piped up. He realised as he said it how puerile he sounded.

"Actually, no," said Nimue a little brusquely, "it isn't your destiny to save the world. It is through your unborn daughter that the world would be saved. All you need to do is stop them from winning until she can do so."

Camron looked at her but said nothing.

Nimue continued, "Eons ago, at the end of the First War of the Realms, a mystical seer delivered unto the elven royal family a prophecy that has been carefully protected and guarded through the ages." She paused, withdrawing a roll of ancient parchment from her robes which she began to unroll. It was yellowed and cracked with age, the beautiful flowing script faded and barely legible. Carefully, she passed the scroll to Camron, who looked at it for a few moments before handing it back.

"Merlin never did manage to teach me much High Elvish, despite his best efforts," said Camron by way of apology.

Nimue picked up the scroll and read. "*When the son of the Dragon King returns at last, then by his courage and sacrifice shall he hold back the tide of evil, even as his daughter holds the fate of all the worlds in her hands.*"

"Nobody knows what task your daughter is destined for, only that it has to be her who does it. We have to fight the Dökkálfar long enough to allow her to grow up and discover what it is."

Camron wasn't sure he approved of his daughter facing untold dangers and being responsible for saving the world, but now wasn't the time to raise his parental concerns.

Instead, he said, "So, does anyone have any idea how we can *hold back this tide of evil*?"

"Actually, yes, we do," Nimue replied matter-of-factly, "and it's quite simple. We will use the same plan Merlin came up with at the beginning of the Second War of the Realms. You will use your father's swords."

"You mean Excalibur?" exclaimed Camron.

"Not just Excalibur. But also, its' twin."

"Excalibur?" asked Geledhil, forgetting she was not supposed to be there.

Nimue looked towards Geledhil and said in a long-suffering yet grandmotherly tone, "Seeing as you are incapable of pretending not to be here, you can bring that wooden box over," indicating a plain wooden box on the side table, unadorned but expertly crafted.

Geledhil brought it over and went to place it in front of Nimue.

"No, give it to Camron, please. It belongs to him now."

Geledhil did as she was bid, placing the box in front of a bemused Camron.

"Open it," Nimue said.

Cautiously, he lifted the lid.

Inside lay a sword. He recognised it. It was his father's sword, Excalibur. Carefully, he lifted it out. It gleamed as if new. Down the length of the blade, Camron could make out the intricately carved runes in High Elvish. Camron held it up, and the others around the table leant forward eagerly.

"Behold Excalibur!" said Nimue, who then smiled to herself. "Arthur always hated me saying that. This is the sword we elves call Caledfwlch."

The sword was similar to a medieval one, but the craftsmanship and metalworking far exceeded anything humans had ever made. It had a perfectly straight, double-edged blade, about eighty centimetres long, with a single-handed cruciform hilt. The sword was beautifully made and perfectly balanced, the edge as sharp and keen as when it was first forged.

Camron gazed at the mirror-perfect surface and examined the beautifully flowing runes meticulously engraved into the blade. Holding the sword up, he felt a magical tingling course through him. He glanced enquiringly towards his grandmother.

"The sword is bonding with you, Camron," she said. "Although the bond won't be complete until you have its twin."

Camron frowned. "Grandmother, you keep saying Excalibur has a twin, but I don't remember father having two swords. He only ever carried this sword into battle."

Nimue continued, "Yes, your father only carried Excalibur into battle. But he had both that one and its twin, Clarent. Ancient blades with separate powerful magic imbued into them when they were forged together aeons ago. However, while Excalibur is purely a combat weapon, Clarent has additional enchantments that make it far more powerful. Clarent is often referred to by humans as 'The Sword in the Stone.' Your father was required to obtain both swords. Clarent he obtained when he drew it forth from the stone. I gave him Excalibur some time afterwards, though not until I was sure he deserved it. But remember, you cannot wield Excalibur and command the sword's full powers until you have first claimed ownership of Clarent."

Camron's eyes roved over the blade in his hands, memories of his father wielding the sword surfacing in his mind.

Nimue continued. "Clarent is often thought to mean '*Cowards Sword,*' but the translation has altered subtlety over the centuries. Its actual name means '*Sword of Fear,*' When combined with Excalibur, it becomes a powerful force that can overcome any enemy."

"How?" said Camron, dragging his gaze from the sword to his grandmother.

"By forcing the sword's opponents to overcome their worst fears. All pretence and lies are stripped away, and they are forced to view themselves with complete and utter honesty. This may sound easy to do, but remember, the Dökkálfar and their allies are creatures of evil and hatred. They have built their entire lives on deceit and wickedness. To be faced with the stark truth of their own existence will be devastating to them." Nimue's visage hardened. "Some may even be driven mad with the knowledge of who they are. But know this, in the midst of a battle, having our opponents forced into a brutal self-assessment of their lives will be disastrous for them. Their protection spells will fail, and most of the enemy will be unable to concentrate sufficiently to use magic. Confusion and panic will spread through their ranks." She looked directly into Camron's eyes. "No spell can protect them from the power of Clarent. This is our one hope to defeat their army."

There was silence around the table as they all absorbed this knowledge.

"Grandmother, it didn't happen that way during the Second War of the Realms. It ended with a terrible battle. If my father had both swords, why didn't he use them?" asked Camron guardedly.

Nimue sighed, her eyes looking at him compassionately.

"There is one thing about Clarent I haven't told you. To bond with the sword properly, you must draw it forth from the stone wherein it lies, which your father did. Control of Excalibur is through a magical bonding between the sword and its wielder and, if successful, the sword will accept the new owner's authority over it. But with Clarent, it is more of a partnership. Before its power can be fully controlled and used, Clarent will test the union by forcing the new wielder to undergo the same *Trial of Truth* as you would have your enemies face. This will lay bare all your fears and weaknesses and force you to acknowledge and accept the dark side of your nature. Through passing this arduous and spiritually painful test, the sword will accept you as an equal and bestow its magic and abilities upon you. Your father was an exceptional man, a brave warrior, kind, intelligent and a just king. But he couldn't overcome the fears revealed to him. He wasn't able to control the full power of Clarent."

Once again, there was silence around the room, all eyes looking at Camron this time.

"And I thought doing something heroic would be the tricky bit," he said with a half-hearted attempt at humour.

"Don't worry, Your Highness," said Tanidaer. "As Her Majesty has said, we do have some time still. Your training will start immediately."

"Training?"

"Yes, you need to learn to fight with two swords, rather than a single sword and shield as your father taught you. That shouldn't take too much time, though. I understand you have been a soldier during many of your human lives, so you should be adept already," Tanidaer replied.

"It is using magic that worries me most," cut in Findecámo. "Your training with Merlin had only just finished when you embarked on this role as unknowing guardian. It will take at least a year to re-teach you everything from your time with Merlin, plus all the other battle spells you will have to research, learn and practice. You know as well as I the rigorous demands magic makes on both our dedication and time. I'm afraid you're going to be rather busy."

"A year!" said Camron in shock. "You said we had only a few months before the Dökkálfar started attacking again. Is that right?" he asked, directing the question towards Nimue.

"No one can tell for sure," she replied. "But probably only a few months, yes."

"And what happens to the world when the Dökkálfar attack? Are we supposed to sit here safe and sound, training and planning? While at the same time, innocent people are killed because no one can protect them?" he replied, anger starting to rise within him. "My wife and unborn child are there without any protection except ignorance and blind luck."

Findecámo was about to respond, but Nimue held up her hand.

"Camron," she said, "I know this is difficult for you, but..."

"Wait," exclaimed Camron, interrupting Nimue, "why can't you just bring Rachel here through a portal? Just like you did with me."

Nimue looked into Camron's eyes, meeting the look of determined hope with one of compassion.

"Camron, we can't bring Rachel here, or I would have done it already."

"Why not?" he said tersely.

"Because it would, in all probability, kill her and your unborn daughter. You survived because you are part-elf and have inherent magic in you. It is just too dangerous for a human to come through the portals until they have regained more of their power. And even if Rachel did manage to survive, the baby definitely wouldn't."

"But she's part-elf too, isn't she?" The question left Camron's lips pleadingly.

"She is," answered Nimue, "but she is still in the womb and is too small and weak to survive traversing a portal."

Camron's shoulders slumped, the small glimmer of hope at being reunited with his wife extinguished.

Eventually, taking a breath to calm himself, he said, "I'll train for a few weeks, but that is all. After that, I must go to protect my family," he said in an uncompromising tone.

"A few weeks is nowhere near long enough," exclaimed Findecámo.

Nimue held up a hand, but Findecámo continued, "Your Majesty, he may have learnt to fight with two swords by then, but he will barely have scratched the surface with his magical studies. He will need to study for a year, ten months at the very least."

"No," said Camron forcefully, his thoughts on Rachel and their baby. "Remember, for every day I spend here, four passes back home."

"Eight weeks, Camron, eight Alfheim weeks," said Nimue in a conciliatory manner. "I don't think the Dökkálfar will be able to attack before then, and I will do what I can to keep Rachel safe in the meantime. But you must be ready and prepared for the fight ahead."

Camron looked down at his goblet, considering.

"Very well," he agreed reluctantly. "Eight weeks, but if they start attacking sooner, I'm going back straightaway."

Nimue nodded in assent. She looked around the table at the assembled elves.

"Well, I think that is enough for today. I'm sure there will be much more to discuss later, but I think this meeting is over for now."

The other elves stood and bowed to Nimue, who nodded her head in acknowledgement as they turned to leave.

Camron was about to place Excalibur back in the box when he felt Nimue's hand on his arm. "You must get used to wearing it now."

She reached into the box and lifted something else, an object wrapped in dark silk that Camron hadn't noticed. Unwrapping it, Camron saw it was a scabbard. He recognised it as the one that had belonged to his father.

"Excalibur will aid you during battle," Nimue said. "But the scabbard is also magical and will preserve and protect you from grievous wounds, as it did your father many times." She handed the scabbard and belt to Camron, who carefully slid Excalibur into place and attached it to the belt at his waist. It felt awkward and yet reassuringly familiar to be wearing a sword again. He had been a soldier many times in the past and felt comfortable wearing the blade.

"You look so much like your father," said Nimue approvingly. "Now come with me; I've somebody I would like you to meet. You too, Geledhil," she said over her shoulder as she turned to leave the room.

# Chapter 13

ALFHEIM

David was sitting on the luxurious grass, leaning against a small elder tree in what was technically a courtyard but looked more like a small meadow. Enclosed by the palace walls, an abundance of wild flowers brought vivid colour to the green canvas of the grass. The setting should have inspired tranquillity, but David's mind was as far from peaceful as was possible. Today was the first day he had felt well enough to leave his bed, having spent most of the past couple of days asleep. He glanced over at his companion as she sat a little distance away. The person, he couldn't bring himself to use the word elf, had aided him from his bed to this courtyard with care and consideration, but he had also noticed the sword at her side.

He closed his eyes, resting his head against the tree trunk. The sheer absurdity of it all threatened to overwhelm him. His academic mind rebelled at the notion of accepting that creatures such as elves and other faerie-kind existed. These should be simply the fanciful creations of fairy-tale authors, consigned solely to the pages of children's books, not walking and talking and acting in a disconcertingly real manner.

*This is all just a dream,* he had told himself repeatedly. Yet, the bruises on his arm gave testament to the number of times he had pinched himself in an attempt to awaken from it.

His latest explanation was that maybe he was in a coma. A fleeting image of falling was his last memory before waking in this nightmare, albeit a nightmare set in delightful surroundings and with exceedingly good food.

He heard a door open and looked up. His companion was on her feet and was bowing as three people and a white dog entered the courtyard. Two of them he recognised; Queen Nimue and her granddaughter. He didn't know the man, but he was conspicuous by his height, towering over the elven women.

David got to his feet hesitantly as they approached, unsure what new twist this nightmare would take.

"Hello David, how are you feeling today?" enquired Nimue.

"Er, fine, thanks."

"Good, I am pleased to see you up and about at last. Now," said Nimue, "I would like you to meet Camron." Turning to the man at her side, she continued, "Camron, this is David Underwood."

"Hi," said the man, holding out his hand in a very familiar human fashion.

David shook it and saw his own curious look refected in the others' eyes.

"David is a Professor from Oxford University. He was leading the project at Stonehenge when he, shall we say, accidentally stumbled across a portal."

"Ah, I see. I was wondering," said Camron.

"Wondering what," said the younger elf. David cast about for her name. Geledhil.

"Wondering what another human was doing here?"

David glanced at Camron's ears, and an almost palpable relief flooded through him.

"You're human!" David exclaimed.

"Yes, I am," Camron replied.

"What are you doing here?" David asked, "Did they…" he shot the briefest glance towards the elves and leant in to whisper, "bring you here too?"

"Sort of," Camron replied, "but I've been here before. A long time ago." Looking over at Nimue, he continued, "Queen Nimue is my grandmother."

"But…" stammered David, "you said you were human!"

"I am, mostly. My father was human, and my mother's father was human, but her mother was Queen Nimue. I guess that only makes me three-quarters human."

David stared alternately between Camron and Nimue, confusion and disbelief once more threatening to overwhelm him.

"Camron is the name he likes to use now," said Nimue, a faint flicker of amusement in her tone, "but his real name is Prince Amr Artorius Pendragon."

Camron shot her a disgruntled look. "I really do prefer Camron," he muttered.

"Pendragon?" asked David.

"Yes, Pendragon. That was his father's name also. Arthur Artorius Pendragon," Nimue said.

"King Arthur? You're kidding, right?" said David struggling to grasp reality as a drowning man gasps for air.

Camron sighed. "No, actually she isn't. I am the son of King Arthur," he said as he gave Nimue a look. She smiled serenely in reply.

"But that was in the 5th Century," exclaimed David, staring from Camron to Nimue. "Which would make you over 1,500 years old!"

Camron nodded.

"But... I mean, that's impossible," said David.

"Not impossible," said Camron, "but it is confusing. I only started remembering who I really was when I travelled through the portals a few days ago, and it's been difficult for me to accept. I can't imagine how hard this must all be for you?"

"Look, I'm sorry, but this is all too much. I'm obviously dreaming or in a coma or something." David backed away until the tree prevented him from retreating further. He had studied the Arthurian legends over the years and had a basic familiarity with most of the characters, both those based loosely on fact and those believed to be fictional. He recalled Amr was the son whom Arthur had supposedly killed. And, according to legend, the Lady of the Lake was Nimue. Now it turned out they were real people and very much alive.

"You're not dreaming. I wish you were. I wish we all were," said Camron somberly.

The two men looked at each other, and David saw a hint of fear in the others' eyes.

Camron sat and beckoned David to join him. Nimue sat demurely on a chair that David could have sworn wasn't there a moment ago.

Geledhil came and sat with them. "Don't worry, I am seventy-five years old, and I still get confused by it all."

David looked at her in disbelief. "You're seventy-five?"

"Yes," she said, smiling. "Even though you look the oldest one here, you're actually the youngling. I'm seventy-five, Camron is over 1,500 years old and grandmother..." Geledhil glanced at her grandmother and decided to change course rapidly. "Well, Grandmother is just Grandmother and as beautiful as ever," she added with unusual tact.

"Very well recovered, my dear," Nimue said sweetly to Geledhil.

"David," said Camron, "I know this all sounds impossible. Until a few days ago, I wouldn't have believed any of it either. It's a bit complicated to explain, but during my father's reign..."

"King Arthur?" interrupted David.

"Yes, King Arthur. Anyway, there was a terrible war, the Second War of the Realms, and..."

"I've already given David a brief account of the war and what the portals do," interrupted Nimue.

"Oh good," said Camron. "So, after the Dökkálfar were defeated, it was decided there should be a safeguard put in place. Just in case the Dökkálfar ever managed to escape, and magic was needed once more."

"But why?" David asked. "Why would they start another war?"

"You must understand," said Nimue, "that the hatred the Dökkálfar have for all other races, especially Ljósálfar, is deep-rooted in Dökkálfar society. Before a child can even walk, it receives a continuous bombardment of hate-filled rhetoric, indoctrinated into the endless struggle for power and dominance. For an individual, this means climbing to power over his peers. For a people, it means subjugation and enslavement of all others. In Dökkálfar society, strength and power are paramount, with any show of weakness mercilessly eliminated."

Horror filled David's face. "That's terrible. Isn't there any kindness at all?"

"Occasionally, but not often. In every people, there are those who are good and those who are bad. And just like there are some Ljósálfar who can be nasty and malicious, there are a few Dökkálfar who are kind and compassionate. It is just that they don't tend to survive very long," said Nimue sadly. "Being nice is a trait likely to get you killed as a Dökkálfar. Love is regarded in their culture as the greatest weakness of all."

"You mentioned some sort of safeguard," said David after a few moments of silence.

"Yes," replied Camron. "Well, sealing the portals prevented both the Dökkálfar and the Ljósálfar from getting to our world. So, it was decided that a human was needed, someone trained in using magic."

"I thought the queen said humans couldn't do magic," David interrupted.

"I said humans can't do magic anymore," interjected Nimue.

"But they were able to use magic once. In fact, I was trained in the art of magic by Merlin, but humans now rely on science and technology. And anyway, as I've said, I am also part-elf. My magic is innate and comes from the elven part of me."

"So they chose you?" David said.

"No, actually, I volunteered."

# Chapter 14

ALFHEIM

Training began the following morning. Shortly after dawn, Geledhil led Camron and Flint along a well-trodden path into the forest, meandering past the oak, beech and ash trees until they came to a small meadow.

The Captain of the Royal Guard, Celaena Meldiron, was waiting for them, along with a nervous-looking David. He looked very out of character, wearing a protective leather jacket and holding a short wooden sword clumsily in one hand.

Just as they had finished saying hello, another elf arrived, two huge wolves trotting obediently by his side. Flint was usually friendly when it came to other dogs, but he kept close to Camron's side at the sight of the wolves.

Camron looked at Celaena enquiringly, who smiled back at him.

"Her Majesty thought it wasn't only you who needed some training. Geledhil will go through some basic swordsmanship with David, while Taldaeron, our Wolf Master, will work with your dog and train him as a war dog."

Taldaeron came over, appraising Flint with a professional eye.

"I'll need to keep him for a few days if that's alright?" he said. "The start of their training is intensive, but Corm and Yarl are experienced battle-wolves and will help settle him in."

Camron looked warily at the two enormous wolves who dwarfed even Flint's impressive size. Nevertheless, he gave Flint a pat and said goodbye to him as Taldaeron led the dog away with the two wolves. Flint, tail down and ears flat, looked back anxiously.

"Shall we start then?" said Celaena. Geledhil led David to the other side of the ground to begin his training.

"Now, eventually, you will have both Excalibur and Clarent, so you need to learn how to fight with two swords. It requires far more control and coordination than sword and shield fighting," said Celaena.

She handed Camron a second sword, similar in size to Excalibur.

"This sword is close to Clarent in size, weight, and balance. It isn't magical, but it's an exceptionally well-made blade and should serve you well until you have Excalibur's twin."

Camron went to draw Excalibur but Celaena stopped him.

"First, we need to get you in better physical shape," she said, looking at his physique with a professional eye.

"I'm not in bad shape," Camron said, feeling a little put out by her comment, but after several hours of exhausting fitness training, he had to concede she might have a point.

Training with Celaena finished at midday, and Camron had time for a brief rest, during which he had lunch with Geledhil and David. They seemed to be suffering from the physical exertion as much as he was. Then, all too soon for his weary muscles, Geledhil led him through the palace to his next training session with the Royal Wizard.

"Findecámo has his rooms at the top of the Sorcerers Tower," said Geledhil.

"What's he like?" asked Camron, eyeing the steep, narrow steps unhappily. "I didn't really get to talk to him much at the council meeting."

"Well, I am not sure he ever thought much of me. I never excelled at spell-casting, and I didn't pay much attention to his lessons," Geledhil confessed as she led Camron up the stairs. "But, apart from Grandmother, he is the best wizard in Alfheim."

Geledhil stopped before a large wooden door at the top of the stairs.

"Here is his room. Good luck!" She smiled and headed back down the tower steps.

Camron paused, trying to catch his breath. Before he could knock, the door swung inwards silently. Camron took this as an invitation to enter. The room was large, with a high ceiling supported by wooden arches. It was a busy room, cluttered and untidy with vials, scrolls, and half-completed experiments strewn across benches and shelves. An air of chaos permeated the room.

“Well met, young prince,” said the wizard without looking up from his bench. “One moment, please. I need to finish this.” A golden ring was held firmly in a small vice on the bench. Findecámo was inscribing minute runes around the inside edge with extreme patience and care. After a few minutes, he unbent from his task and looked up.

“There, all done,” he declared. “Now, if you would be so kind as to come over here, we can begin our first lesson.”

Camron walked towards the cluttered bench. Apparently, neatness and order were not high priorities for Findecámo.

“Well then, let us begin, Prince Amr.”

“Please, call me Camron,” said Camron. “I was a prince for only a couple of decades, but for the past 1,500 years, I have lived as an ordinary man. I may technically be a prince, but I definitely don’t feel like one, so please call me Camron?”

“Very well,” replied Findecámo. “Camron it is. And you may call me Master Wizard, at least within the confines of our lessons. You are here to learn and learn rapidly at that. I find that keeping a proper sense of order between a teacher and pupil helps tremendously, especially when the pupils’ efforts fall somewhat below my expectations.” Camron met Findecámo’s stern gaze.

“Now,” he continued, “I don’t know how much you remember of your tutoring under Merlin, and I suspect you probably don’t either. So, let us start with the basics of how magic works, and we can take it from there.” Findecámo adjusted his robe and clasped his hands behind his back. “There is a force that abounds within the world which we can manipulate and control to perform certain actions. The manipulation and bending of this force to our will is what we call magic, and the use of magic in this manner is called spell-casting. No one fully understands this force. Suffice to say it is there, and we know how to use it."

The wizard paused, peering intently at Camron, keen to confirm his words received the proper attention they deserved.

Satisfied, he continued. "Magical spells are usually cast by a combination of two components. The first is the vocal utterance of the spell, recited in the arcane language of magic. The second element is through specific hand gestures, which are both precise and complex. The combination of these parts is required to cast a spell."

As he warmed to his subject, Findecámo began pacing up and down.

"Even amongst us elven-folk, who have magic as an innate part of our nature, not all are sufficiently skilled to control and use magic. As for humans, only a tiny number ever became witches or wizards."

Findecámo paused and looked at Camron. "Fortunately, through the blood of your elven grandmother, you are not entirely human, so this will give you an advantage in your magical studies."

Camron wasn't entirely convinced anything about his studies would be easy but kept quiet.

Findecámo resumed his pacing.

"Magic is not for the weak-willed. Only a small handful will ever have the intellect to understand magic, the manual dexterity for the hand gestures and the total commitment and dedication wizardry commands of its devotees. To be able to cast a spell, you must first have memorised it, both the words and the gestures. The spell must be remembered perfectly and not merely the words. The exact tone and inflexion are vital. For simple spells, this can be a matter of a few minutes. For more powerful spells, this can take several hours."

An image of tedious hours spent in Merlin's hut, hunched over a spell-book trying to read by the guttering light of a single candle, sprang into Camron's mind.

"Unfortunately," continued Findecámo, "once a spell has been cast, part of the process of manipulating magic is that the spell is erased from the spellcaster's memory, thus requiring them to re-learn that spell before it can be cast again. This is why every wizard or witch needs a spellbook, so they can relearn a spell once it has been cast." Findecámo tapped a long narrow finger against the side of his head.

"Of course, you can learn each spell more than once. So, for instance, if you thought you might need to cast two fireball spells, you would need to learn the spell twice so that two copies are magically etched in your memory until they were cast. There are, of course, some exceptions to the above. Truly powerful sorcerers can cast spells silently, simply by reciting in their minds the words of the spell. Similarly, hand gestures are a means of controlling the force that is magic and, as such, the more powerful the wizard, the simpler the hand gestures can sometimes be. And do not forget, everyday objects can be enchanted with magic. For example, swords can be imbued with magical properties, as is Excalibur, plus rings, armour, and wands. In fact, almost anything can be enchanted."

Suddenly, the old wizard stopped his pacing.

"That reminds me," he said, turning to face Camron. "Queen Nimue asked me to give you something; I must confess I'm a little jealous. I would have very much liked to have had it myself, you know. Now, where did I put it?" he mused, wandering off to a corner of the room and opening a large cupboard. He rummaged inside, muttering to himself for a few moments before declaring, "Ah, here it is."

He turned back to Camron, holding a six-foot-long wooden pole, twisted and gnarled with an egg-sized diamond-like stone clutched in a reptilian claw attached to one end.

Camron recognised it immediately.

"Merlin's staff!"

Findecámo handed it to Camron, who held it transfixed, lost in memories of the innumerable times he had seen it in Merlins' hands.

"Now, to business, let us begin your lessons." Findecámos voice cut through his reminiscence.

Camron had thought the morning training sessions were challenging and tiring. Still, they turned out easy compared to his magical education. Findecámo was a mighty wizard and an excellent teacher, but his standards were exacting.

And so began the repetitive cycle of Camron's days. Weapons training in the morning, magical tuition in the afternoon and evenings spent on the demanding and laborious task of memorising spells for the lesson the next day. Camron threw himself wholeheartedly into the intense regime, partly because the burden placed upon him demanded no less than total focus. However, the concentration needed and the sheer physical exhaustion left him little time to dwell upon the implications of the responsibility thrust upon him. The mantle of hero was not one he was at all comfortable wearing.

# Chapter 15

ALFHEIM

Camron's training had been going well for a week, and he was beginning to feel less exhausted with his lessons. He had even reached the point where he had enough energy left in the early evening to join the others for a meal before he had to start memorising spells for the following day.

One evening at the end of supper, he found himself in the kitchen with only Nimue and David, who leaned towards him slightly conspiratorially.

"You don't happen to have a razor, do you?" he asked, stroking the ever-lengthening beard he was growing. "It's just that I've asked a few of the elves, and they laugh when I explain what I want and why I need it. I really don't understand. They must have razors or something; I haven't seen a single elf with a beard, so surely they must shave."

"Actually, they don't," said Nimue, putting down her cup of herbal tea. "Elves don't have facial hair. In fact, they have hardly any body hair."

Nimue laughed as David spluttered his wine. His face coloured to match the contents of the goblet he held.

"I think they laughed because the notion of shaving is not one they've ever encountered," Nimue said. "I'm sorry, but you will have to get used to a beard unless you want to try with a dagger."

David looked startled.

"Anyway, I think it suits you," she said, picking up her tea again.

Camron felt his own beard. He had tried to trim it a couple of times but had only made it look worse.

David sighed. "Ah, well, never mind." And with that, he got up to leave, bidding them both goodnight.

Camron waited until David had left the kitchen.

"Grandmother, there's something I meant to ask," he said hesitantly. "You've given me Excalibur, but when will I get Clarent?"

"I don't have it," Nimue replied simply.

Camron looked shocked. "But where is it then?"

"Where it has been for all these past centuries; exactly where it belongs and where it is entirely safe," Nimue replied cryptically.

"But where is that?" Camron continued, wondering whether his grandmother expected him to know the sword's location.

"Well, Clarent is the *Sword in the Stone,* is it not?" Nimue answered. "Where else would you expect to find it but in its' stone."

Camron's look was still uncomprehending, so Nimue continued.

"Amongst humans, the story of the Sword in the Stone depicts a stone with a sword protruding from it. However, that is not correct. The stone in question is *Lia Fàil.* It's a magical stone and acts as a gateway to another realm, a tiny realm. In fact, one that is just big enough to hold a sword."

Nimue took a sip of tea and wrinkled her nose in distaste.

"Cold," she muttered.

Camron smiled as he uttered the words of a very basic spell, waving his hand over her cup. Steam began to rise from the tea.

"Thank you, dear," said Nimue with a smile as she blew gently on the now hot tea before continuing. "The popular Arthurian legend states that '*whoso pulleth out this sword of this stone, is rightwise King born of all England.*' This has come down through the ages from the original translation of the Elvish runes on Clarent's blade and has been subtly but wrongly altered over time. The elvish runes actually say, '*whoso calls the sword from the stone shall persuade this land to unite.*' At some point, the elvish runes were translated into Latin. The words *to persuade* were translated to *adduco,* which means *to persuade,* but can also mean *to rule.* Hence, the mistranslation."

“Lia Fàil. I’ve never heard of it. Is it here in Alfheim?” Camron asked.

“No,” she replied. “Actually, it’s in London. The stone goes by various names. We elves call it the *Stone of Destiny*. In Scotland, it’s called the *Stone of Scone*, but the stone is usually called the Coronation Stone in England. It sits at the base of the Coronation Throne in Westminster Abbey.”

“Really?” Camron exclaimed. “Well, that’s one bit of good news. For once, it sounds like there’s something that might not be impossible to achieve.”

“Hopefully,” said Nimue. “While we’re on the subject of things you will need, I’ve put together some items I think will aid you immeasurably. Would you come with me, please?” Without waiting for a reply, she led him out of the kitchen and down some long, winding corridors of the palace, many of which he didn’t recognise.

Eventually, they came to a sturdy door covered with elvish runes. Nimue spoke a phrase, and the door swung silently inwards. They entered the small chamber, completely unadorned save for a large table in the centre upon which sat a wooden chest.

“Over here,” she beckoned, walking to the large chest.

As Nimue uttered a single word, the chest lock momentarily glowed blue, followed by a loud click as it magically opened. Nimue leant in and began retrieving its’ contents.

“Firstly,” she said, “here is the scabbard for Clarent. It should fit the sword Celaena gave you, so you won’t have to carry three scabbards.”

“Thank you,” said Camron, removing the now surplus one from his belt.

“I think you will probably need this,” she said, holding up a suit of finely crafted chainmail armour. It was made from small metal rings, each one linked to four others in a distinct weave pattern to form a strong, flexible mesh. The design covered the entire torso and the arms and groin area. Each individual ring, perfectly made, shone with a bright sheen.

"Is that alfaril?" Camron asked in amazement.

"Yes," replied Nimue, handing the armour to him.

Alfaril was the legendary and extremely rare metal from which the finest weapons and armour were made. It was a metal alloy, lighter than modern carbon fibre yet, at the same time, much tougher than titanium. Next, Nimue passed over a pile of ancient, leather-bound books, which Camron instantly recognised.

"Merlin's spellbooks," he exclaimed in awe, placing the stack of books onto the wooden table.

"Yes, he wanted you to have both his staff and his books of magic."

Camron opened one reverently, his hands brushing the leather cover as he had done countless times during his lessons with Merlin. He recalled the hours spent hunched over these very same books, transcribing some of the simpler spells into the meagre spellbook he had as a youngling.

"And finally," Nimue said, interrupting his reverie. "You will need these," she said, holding out a pair of gold rings in the palm of her hand.

"Enchanted?" asked Camron.

She nodded. "They are part of a set of rings called '*Family Rings*.' They have several magical properties. One provides a basic level of protection from magical spells. More importantly, they allow a rudimentary form of communication between those wearing them. The more magically powerful you are, the easier the communication. But even non-magical wearers can impart basic thoughts or needs, sort of like an empathy link. However, their most important feature is allowing those who wear them to know when the other wearers are in danger."

She held out her other hand to show Camron, "I have one myself. Geledhil also has one. These two are for you and Rachel; she is, after all, my granddaughter-in-law. They will help protect her and let you know if she is in danger."

"Thank you," said Camron with heartfelt gratitude.

Nimue said, "Put your ring on when you give Rachel hers. Recite the incantation on the ring, and the magic will bind your rings to you both."

"Oh, I almost forgot," she said, reaching inside her cloak and pulling out a small, brown leather bag with drawstrings resembling a medieval purse. "You'll need somewhere to put all of these things. This is a magical *bag of holding* and will hold a considerable number of items, far more than would seem possible. In fact, it will hold several hundred pounds of weight but feel as if it weighs hardly anything."

Camron sat down at the table and looked at everything he had been given. He raised his gaze up to his grandmother, who was watching him with curiosity.

"Thank you," he said simply, although there was no mistaking the sincerity in his tone. "But I'm not sure I really deserve them."

"Nonsense," she admonished, then smiled. "The task before you will be difficult enough. These are gifts freely given, which we hope will aid you in your success. And now it's getting late, and I have a busy day tomorrow, so I'll bid you goodnight, Camron." She kissed him briefly on the forehead, reminiscent of how she used to kiss him goodnight when he was a child and then left him alone in the room.

He continued to stare at the pile of items arrayed on the table before him. Little by little, the enormity of the responsibility bestowed upon him was becoming very real. He held his head in his hands and let his doubts and despair wash over him. The Dökkálfar were threatening the entire world, and according to his grandmother and the others on the elven council, it was ultimately down to him to defeat them. No, he corrected himself, not to defeat them; just stop them. Assuming he was capable of this impossible feat, it would be down to his as yet unborn daughter to defeat them. It was ludicrous. He was a management consultant from Dorset, hardly the most dynamic or adventurous of professions. How could anyone think he could accomplish this impossible feat?

He had been a fool, Camron told himself. Why had he agreed to undertake this impossible role? Despite his grandmother's belief, he wasn't the right person for the job. Camron sighed and got to his feet, gathering up the items his grandmother had given him. He made his way through the meandering corridors to his room, his mind deeply troubled. His self-doubt threatened to engulf and completely overwhelm him.

His thoughts inevitably turned to Rachel. He missed her so much that it was almost a physical pain. The logical part of him agreed wholeheartedly with his grandmother's reasoning that Rachel was much safer living where she was in obscurity and anonymity. But the emotional side of him didn't care. He wanted to be with her and protect her, even though he knew his ability to keep her safe was incomplete.

That night, he lay awake for many hours, staring unseeingly at the wooden ceiling. When he finally drifted into a fitful slumber, his mind remained unresolved. But it was thoughts of Rachel and his unborn daughter that prevented him from giving up entirely.

# Chapter 16

ALFHEIM

Camron's fears and doubts weren't as private as he thought. Nimue had been watching him discreetly for a while and grown increasingly concerned. She understood the burden of responsibility bestowed upon him better than anyone, even Camron himself. After all, she had been the Queen of the Ljósálfar for several millennia.

After another week or so, Nimue decided to call a second meeting of the elven council. There was more to consider, and it was time to discuss the rest of the plan.

She sent for Geledhil.

When she arrived, Nimue said, "Would you ask Camron to attend the council meeting in the Great Hall this afternoon, after his training with Celaena, please?"

"Yes, Grandmother," she replied, turning to leave. Geledhil hesitated and slowly turned back, hoping her grandmother was in an agreeable mood.

"Grandmother," she began in what she hoped was her best *'please may I have'* voice.

"You do realise I will say *no,* don't you, child?" Nimue interjected before Geledhil had a chance to finish.

"But that's just it. I'm not a child anymore. I want to help. I am better than anyone else in Alfheim with a bow, and I can fight well with both sword and dagger. I can even do some magic, not much, I know, but some. My English is good, and I can speak Dwarven and High Elvish. Camron is going to need help." Her tone increased in confidence and determination as she spoke. "And you've always said a sorcerer was at their most vulnerable when they are in the middle of spell-casting. They need a warrior by their side to protect them."

She paused, holding her breath and looking at her grandmother, her eyes pleading.

Nimue considered her granddaughter intently. She was right. She was no longer a child. At seventy-five, an elf was considered a young adult. And Camron would indeed need help. He had the strength and courage to succeed in his given quest, but he would need assistance along the way to discover this for himself. After what seemed an eternity to Geledhil, Nimue spoke.

"Very well, you may accompany Camron and help him in his fight against the Dökkálfar."

Geledhil let out a sigh of relief, unaware she had been holding her breath, tremulously waiting while her grandmother pondered her request. Her eyes lit up, and a broad grin spread across her face, delighted she had received permission.

Nimue looked at her sternly.

"This is not a jovial matter, young lady," she admonished. "You do realise there is a high chance you will be hurt or even lose your life aiding Camron."

The smile faded from Geledhil's face, but the determination remained.

"Yes, I know, my Queen," Geledhil replied formally.

Nimue continued, "I love you dearly, child, but you must always remember it is Camron and his daughter who are important. The rest of us, myself included, are simply here to help them succeed and, if necessary, die helping."

Geledhil looked at her grandmother with wide eyes.

"I understand," she said solemnly.

Nimue nodded in approval.

"Very well. Now, would you please go and inform Camron about the meeting?"

* * *

Camron and Geledhil arrived together at the appointed time, Flint obediently following along. The elves seated around the table were those who attended the first meeting. Camron noted that Geledhil also sat at the table rather than loitering at the back. He shot her a quick smile as he sat in his own place.

"During our last meeting," Nimue said, bringing the meeting to order, "we came up with a plan to allow Camron to keep the Dökkálfar at bay. Since then, his training has progressed well." Both Celaena and Findecámo nodded in assent.

"And he has unexpectedly started to gather companions to assist in the quest. I have decided that he will be aided by my granddaughter, Geledhil, and the other human, David and, of course, the ever-present Flint." Flint looked up and thumped his tail enthusiastically against Camrons chair.

"Now, we need to plan in detail how we will accomplish this. Can I have your thoughts, please?" Nimue asked, looking around the table.

Haldamir, the First Councillor, cleared her throat and spoke.

"Well, one of our strengths is that the human population is so large, giving us a numerical advantage. But we need to get the humans working together. We have a chance to galvanise them into a single fighting force. Unfortunately, this won't necessarily be straightforward. They have a tremendous capacity to fight amongst themselves; no offence meant, my Prince."

"None taken," said Camron. "We do rather excel at fighting each other and starting wars, often without any real reason."

"So we need to get them working together." Haldamir continued.

"That is going to be nearly impossible," interrupted Camron. "There are simply too many differences between the countries. You only have to look at our history. We've never achieved much in the way of global unity."

Nimue looked at him. "Camron, it will not be me, nor any other elf, who must convince men to join together to fight the Dökkálfar. That is something for another human to do."

"Who?"

"You."

"Me?" he gasped in a startled exclamation. "How can I convince the world to put their differences aside and work together? Nobody would even listen to me."

"You are a prince, both of the realms of men and of Ljósálfar, and you also command magic; that gives you all the authority you need," Nimue replied sternly.

"I was a prince 1,500 years ago. I can't just turn up saying I'm King Arthur's son, and can I please have a crown. I'd get committed for being insane."

"We cannot fight the Dökkálfar alone," said Nimue, "without humans as our allies, we will fail."

Camron struggled to cope with his mounting terror at the task and wasn't convinced by Nimue's assurance.

"But what makes you think anyone will listen to me? I'm rubbish at dealing with people. I'm no good at diplomacy or tact. Just ask my wife! I'm not the person you need for this. I'll go out with a sword and staff and fight the Dökkálfar to the very best of my ability, but I can't do this."

"You can do this," Nimue said gently. "Your father had exactly the same doubts, but he united the warring lords across Briton. He got them to fight together under his banner, eventually being named king by them. Arthur did it, and so can you."

"I'm not my father, and I'm not asking to be king!" he responded stubbornly. "I might have spent a couple of decades in his court being raised as a prince, but I've spent fifteen hundred years living as a common person. I'm not anybody special, just an ordinary man."

"Nonsense, you are special whether you accept it or not," Nimue said with an air of finality. "Nobody thinks you should be king. Clarent confers your right to unite the people, *not* rule them!"

Nimue sat in silence before she spoke again, her tone softer and more placating.

"Rather than trying to convince several countries all at once, why don't we start with Britain? Suppose you can persuade the Prime Minister that you are genuine and convince him of the need for unity. In that case, he can help persuade the other nations."

"I would still need to get him to see me, and then there's the small matter of persuading him to listen to me instead of having me arrested!"

Nimue smiled. "I can probably help you there."

"How?"

"You remember I told you the Stone of Destiny is in the base of the Coronation Chair? Ever since Edward II, all British monarchs have sat in that chair during their coronation, which happened for a purpose. The stone has a secret power that allows me to speak directly into the monarch's mind at the point of their inauguration. From Edward II onwards, I have spoken thus to each king or queen and told them who I am and issued the same warning; at the time of Britain's greatest peril, you would reveal yourself to them."

Those assembled around the table were silent. None of them had known about this.

"Many were sceptical. Some thought they were mad hearing voices or put it down to the day's stress, but they all heard what I had to say, and they all remembered," Nimue continued. "I last spoke through the stone during the coronation of the present Queen of England. She knows of you, but I am not sure how readily she will believe you. However, she is the closest thing you have to an ally amongst the humans. I understand the Queen and Prime Minister hold a weekly audience. I believe that would provide an ideal opportunity to make contact and convince them both of who you are and what perils we all face."

# Chapter 17

SATURDAY, 5TH JUNE (THE FOLLOWING YEAR)

It was a glorious weekend. The sun was shining, and not a single cloud marred the bright blue sky. This could be the best Glastonbury music festival in years. It was late Saturday afternoon, and the crowd anticipating the next act on the Pyramid Stage was buzzing. An estimated seventy-five thousand festival-goers were eagerly awaiting the on-stage arrival of one of the most celebrated bands in the country. TV cameras were already rolling to broadcast the act as a live event, part of the BBC's *'Summer of Music'* programme.

A lone figure walked on stage. Many of those in the front few rows looked taken aback by his appearance. The person was short and slender. He, for the person most certainly looked male, was dressed entirely in black leather, wearing mid-calf black leather boots and had a mane of black shoulder-length hair that contrasted sharply with his pale skin. His features were angular, and his eyes were large and oval and completely dark, like looking into the depths of a bottomless hole.

Gradually, moving from the front towards the rear, the crowd gave its attention to the lone figure. Even the stage crew stopped their preparations for the next act and looked up, somewhat bewildered. Many people assumed this was some interval entertainment or a warm-up act and listened eagerly.

"I require your attention," the figure called out, his voice carried, as if by magic, to the very back of the crowd. The accent was cold and sharp. The words seemed forced as if English were a strange language for him to speak.

"Let me introduce you to some of my friends," he continued.

Two more people, both looking similar to the speaker, walked onto the stage and stood on either side of him.

"We are Dökkálfar," he announced, sweeping his arm to include the other two, "and these..." he paused as around two dozen other figures trooped out onto the stage, looking like they had walked off the set of a *Lord of the Rings* film.

They were man-shaped, about two metres tall, with short black hair and porcine faces. Those in the front few rows experienced the overpowering odour of these creatures, smelling strongly of sweat and rancid fat. They were dressed in a mismatched assortment of armour, mainly leather or rusting chainmail. They all carried wicked looking blades, made with jagged or saw-tooth edges. These weapons were crudely made of iron. The creatures were obviously reliant on sheer brute force, using muscle-power to wield these weapons and injure their opponents.

The television director sitting in the BBC broadcast van outside tried to decide what was happening. This wasn't in the programme schedule. She already had her team scurrying around to determine if this was a genuine part of the performance.

"Mandy, what's happening? Is this part of the act?" asked one of the technicians.

"I don't know. It's not on our list. Go and look for Paul and see if you can find out."

Mandy was reluctant to cut the broadcast and decided to continue until she was sure this was either genuine or a prank.

"These," the figure on stage continued eventually, "are my orcs," gesturing with a sweep of his arm towards the row of creatures standing at the front of the stage.

The other two Dökkálfar chanted softly, making subtle hand gestures in unison, as the first Dökkálfar continued, his voice menacing, "They really only have two redeeming qualities. Firstly, they are easy to control. Secondly, they are excellent at killing."

He paused for a couple of seconds and then said, "Kill!" in a loud voice, sounding as hollow and devoid of life as death itself.

At this, his fellow Dökkálfar thrust their hands outwards and finished chanting; bolts of lightning shot into the unsuspecting crowd. Rows of death and destruction were carved through the innocent spectators in a single second, killing dozens instantly.

Many people were rooted to the spot in shock. They were unable to comprehend what they had witnessed. Others panicked and turned, desperate to escape the carnage; chaos and pandemonium quickly ensued.

The row of orcs held their wicked-looking blades aloft and let out guttural screams. As one, they leapt from the stage, snarling and grunting, into the front rows of the crowd, bringing their weapons down to hack into the unprepared and defenceless spectators. As the blades cut into flesh, hewing limbs from bodies and hacking mercilessly, the victims' screams drowned out the shouts of the orcs.

Panic swept through the crowd. People desperate to escape the cruel onslaught of destruction barged and shoved their way through, heedless of others. Many fell, tripping in haste or simply knocked over in the scramble to escape.

The Dökkálfar remained on stage, content to randomly cast fireball or lightning bolt spells into the fleeing crowd. Their primary purpose was to instil terror into the humans. The actual death toll from their actions was inconsequential. However, they enjoyed killing and tried to cause as many innocent deaths as possible.

The cameras were still rolling, and the production crew in the outside broadcast van sat open-mouthed, watching in horror as carnage ensued outside. The orcs strode through the crowd, cutting them down in swathes as they tried to flee. There was no combat, nobody could stand against them, and most of those killed had their backs to the orcs, trying in vain to escape.

After a short time, one of Dökkálfar cast an enchantment. A burst of intense red light flashed briefly, and upon seeing the signal, the orcs ceased the relentless carnage and trotted back towards the stage, blood dripping from their blades.

They were heedless of the bodies they trod on during their return. Most were corpses, but the orcs stabbed at the injured as they passed without breaking stride, delivering a blow to end their cries of pain.

As they reached the stage, the Dökkálfar completed casting another spell, and a lurid green circle glowed in mid-air before him. The orcs trotted through the centre of the glowing portal and vanished, followed by the three Dökkálfar. Shortly after they had passed through, the portal disappeared.

Silence descended over the field in front of the Pyramid Stage, broken only by the cries of pain from those left wounded. Most of the crowd had fled in terror, and those who remained stood numb amidst the carnage, unable to take in what had happened. A mixture of horror and fear rooted them to the spot.

"Cut the live feed," said the producer eventually, her mouth dry and her words catching in her throat.

"Cut it," Mandy repeated more clearly.

Her words broke through the horror paralysing the technicians. They quickly moved to switch off the live broadcast, but Mandy knew it was too late. The world had borne witness to this atrocity.

She stared at the monitors in disbelief. The field in front of the stage resembled a battlefield rather than a festival.

*What had happened?* She thought to herself. *What the hell was that?*

Memories of the terrorist attacks from the previous November crept into her thoughts. She wondered whether those responsible for today's atrocity were responsible for the others. She could imagine the media headlines across the world. The enemy was known, and it had a name, '*Dökkálfar.*'

* * *

ALFHEIM

Nimue clenched the edges of her scrying basin tightly, fearful her legs would buckle.

The stone basin rested on a marble pedestal. Intricately carved vines and branches flowed around the edge of the basin. They dug sharply into her fingers as

Nimue grasped the edge forcefully. The silvery liquid filling the bowl swirled. As the scrying spell faded, the faint images were barely discernible on the cloudy surface. She took a few deep breaths to calm her nerves. She had witnessed most of the atrocity at Glastonbury.

A magical warning charm had alerted her to the attack, but she had been unable to do anything other than watch. Even if she had been able to intervene directly, it had been over so quickly that she wouldn't have had time to do anything.

She remained where she was, staring at her reflection in the scrying basin. Her beautiful, ageless face stared back at her, but her grey eyes, usually so clear and bright, were tearful. Her visage reflected a contorted mixture of horror, revulsion and sadness at what she had witnessed.

Nimue finally regained her composure but remained there, deep in thought, for several hours. The shadows in the small grove lengthened as evening came and the sun made its inevitable descent below the horizon. Her eyes were open, but her gaze was far away, her thoughts troubled.

Only when the penetrating chill of the approaching night caused her to shiver involuntarily did Nimue come out of her reverie and look around, almost surprised to find herself still in the scrying grove. She took a deep breath, filling her lungs with the scent of the hazel trees surrounding her. She quickly headed towards the palace, almost at a run, until she arrived at the top of the Sorcerers Tower and knocked on the door.

Findecámo opened it. He looked surprised to see the queen standing before him.

"Your Majesty?" he said inquiringly.

"Is he ready?" she asked without preamble.

Knowing instinctively to whom she was referring, he replied, "Not quite. A few more weeks should be all."

"I don't think we have a few more weeks," she said and, in response to his questioning look, continued, "They have attacked again!"

Findecámo's expression turned to shock, "So soon! What happened?"

"They attacked a musical festival not too far from Stonehenge. The Dökkálfar plan seems aimed at causing terror and panic amongst the humans rather than just outright destruction. But many hundreds are dead, with even more injured." Her eyes clouded with grief as she recalled the devastating scene.

"In that case, your majesty, I don't think he has any choice but to be ready," said Findecámo solemnly.

Nimue nodded in agreement. "We must prepare for him to return to his own realm in a few days at most," she said and, turning to leave, bade the wizard goodnight and withdrew from his chamber.

Camron was asleep in his room, but his warrior senses, honed unknowingly over the centuries, were returning. He awoke instantly at Nimue's gentle knock on the door. His hair looked dishevelled, but his eyes were bright and alert as he opened the door to her, surprise evident on his face.

"Grandmother, what are you doing here?"

"Camron," she replied, then paused.

"It's Rachel, isn't it? Has she been attacked? What's happened?" The note of desperation in his voice was unmistakable.

"No, it isn't Rachel. She is safe and well. But you're right about there being an attack. Dökkálfar and orcs have attacked the music festival at Glastonbury. Hundreds have been killed, many more injured." Nimue brushed the trace of a tear from the corner of her eye, but her voice remained calm and clear. Camron could feel her hurt at this carnage, but she remained focused and resolute. It was time for clear and purposeful action, not emotive reactions.

"Findecámo thinks you are almost ready. I was hoping for a few more weeks, but that isn't to be. We will make the final preparations and return you in a few days."

“I’m not ready though, am I?” he asked. The doubts plaguing his waking thoughts and tormenting his sleep had solidified over the last few minutes.

“Prince Amr, you have to be ready,” she replied formally. “And now you must rest. Tomorrow is going to be very busy.”

She turned to leave.

“Grandmother,” he called.

She stopped and looked over her shoulder, one eyebrow arching enquiringly.

“Rachel is ok, isn’t she? Nothing has happened to her or the baby?”

Her smile as she nodded did more to reassure Camron than any words could. She closed the door behind her as she left, but it was many hours before Camron managed to drift off to sleep.

# Chapter 18

SATURDAY, 12TH JUNE

Despite Stephanie being at her desk early, the newsroom was already buzzing with activity.

All week, ever since the terrible attack at Glastonbury the previous Saturday, reports had been received of a further dozen attacks. Countries targeted included the USA, France, Russia, Japan, Brazil, China and several cities in the Scandinavian countries.

Each followed a similar pattern. A few Dökkálfar wizards supported by many orc warriors appeared suddenly and attacked without warning or provocation. One small glimmer of fortune was that these subsequent attacks were nowhere near the magnitude of Glastonbury's. Nonetheless, they engendered fear and dread amongst people everywhere. The result was a divided world, with many countries looking to protect themselves. Like many other nations, the USA had recalled much of its military resources from around the world.

Stephanies' thoughts turned to her daughter, Rachel. She had spent most of the previous December with her daughter and hadn't returned to New York until after the New Year. It was apparent to Stephanie that, after all these months, Camron had clearly left her and wasn't coming back.

She regretted that she couldn't spend more time with Rachel, but she assuaged her guilt by planning to be there at the birth of her granddaughter and would spend more time with Rachel then.

In the meantime, work consumed the bulk of her time, especially since the Glastonbury attack. Trying to get to the truth, sorting fact from fantasy, was nearly impossible. The sheer volume of social media commentaries, conspiracy theories, and fake news was staggering.

One idea that had quickly gained credibility was that the supposed terrorist attacks of the previous November might have been the work of the Dökkálfar. Using magic would explain how the Eiffel Tower had been destroyed and how an invisible wall appeared across the Brooklyn Bridge.

Acceptance of this fantastical explanation had started slowly but was gradually gaining widespread recognition, even from official government sources.

Everywhere, it seemed, you could find someone who claimed to be an expert in magic and who could give detailed accounts of how magic worked, what the Dökkálfar were really like and how people could become wizards and witches themselves.

It was almost as if history had conspired to produce a society aware of the fictional concept of both magic and fantastical creatures. Centuries of legends, myths and a whole genre of fiction that began with *The Lord of the Rings* epic fantasy. It continued with the popular *Dungeons & Dragons* roleplaying games of the 70s and 80s and, ultimately, to the Hollywood blockbuster movies from the 21st century. It seemed everyone had heard of elves and orcs, but nobody had imagined they could be real.

# Chapter 19

SVARTALFHEIM

Varakenthal paced up and down the room. He would never have revealed any weakness in front of others. But alone, he allowed his anxiety to show. His rise in power and status had been unexpectedly meteoric in the highly rigid and hierarchical Dökkálfar society, especially considering his ancestry. To a Dökkálfar, the house you belonged to meant everything. Loyalty was to that house, after yourself, of course. Servitude was not driven by feelings of love or duty but a simple matter of survival of the fittest. There was strength in numbers, and houses consisted of an extended family structure with one omnipotent person at the head of the house, the Hlyđni-Móđir or *matron mother.*

Many centuries ago, Varakenthal's house had been one of the greatest in Svartalfheim, rising to the lofty heights of the ruling council, comprising the heads of the five most dominant houses. But everything had changed one fateful day during the Second War of the Realms. Varakenthal's ancestor was Chief Warlock for his house. He was to lead an attack on the old Roman town of *Durnovaria* and the nearby Druid stronghold at *Mai-Dun*, a sacred grove on top of a hill that had once been an Iron Age hill fort occupied by the Celtic *Durotriges* tribe.

The Chief Warlock was confident of victory as the Dökkálfar had not lost a battle in the war so far. Yet the following three days had seen some of the bloodiest fighting yet. The magic used by both sides was devastating.

But the humans, Druids and Ljósálfar, had been victorious. They had won their first battle, and when the war was finally over, many had seen this victory as the decisive turning point. The Chief Warlock had staggered back to Svartalfheim with only a few survivors. He knew the fate that awaited his failure. Blame for the defeat had rested solely on his shoulders, and his entire house suffered the wrath of a people who learnt to hate before they learnt to walk or talk. After the savage decimation of their house, barely a handful were left alive.

Varakenthal had ruthlessly clawed his way through Dökkálfar society despite being born into relative obscurity. He had risked much and pushed hard to lead this new attack. He had argued long and relentlessly, and eventually, he had his way. Yet, he was all too aware of the consequences of failure. This time, it would lead to the total annihilation of his house.

He ceased his pacing as the door opened.

"It is time," the newcomer announced before turning to leave.

Varakenthal followed him, the target of their attack firmly in his thoughts. Durnovaria. The town the humans now called Dorchester. The place where his house had once been defeated and humiliated.

* * *

ALFHEIM

Camron was in the middle of a training session, working hard to keep his two swords flowing in perfect harmony. His focus was absolute as he determinedly defended against the concerted attacking play of Celaena. Suddenly a desperate cry cut through his concentration like a scythe cutting through wheat. His ears heard no sound, yet the call resounded through his mind with perfect clarity.

"Arrgh," he cried as Celaena scored two successive hits to his chest due to his loss of concentration.

"Stop," he shouted to Celaena, dropping to his knees and closing his eyes, trying to recapture the diminishing echo in his mind. But it was gone. A single, fleeting call for help. Yet Camron knew with absolute certainty that it had come from his unborn child.

"What is it?" asked Celaena. "Did I hurt you?"

"No, it's my daughter. She's in danger. I must go to her. Now!" Camron ignored the startled expression on the elf's face and hurried out of the training ground.

He ran full speed back to the palace, stopping everyone he thought might know where the queen was. He eventually found her in the library, deep in concentration, an ancient tome lying open on the table before her. She looked up, a flicker of annoyance flashing fleetingly across her face at the interruption. However, it quickly changed to one of concern at the haunted look on Camron's face.

"Grandmother. It's Rachel and the baby. They're in danger."

"How do you know?" asked Nimue.

"My daughter. I heard her cry clearly in my mind when I was fighting Celaena."

Nimue paused for the briefest instant, the moment of surprise in her eyes quickly replaced by a determined look.

"Hurry, grab your staff and the other things I gave you. Meet me in the scrying grove as soon as you can."

* * *

SUNDAY, 13TH JUNE

Rachel didn't like venturing into town on her own. Not only did her pregnancy make her feel tired, but as a community nurse, she knew many people in Dorchester and resented their sympathy concerning Camron. She had been forced to endure the same line of concerned questioning dozens of times. *Had she heard anything yet? Did she know what had happened?* She had heard all these questions and more and disliked having to put on a brave face and answer them politely when all she wanted to do was break down and cry. Camron's absence was like an open wound. She missed him more than she had ever imagined possible. Each day without him was an ordeal she struggled to get through.

She had put off shopping so often that her clothes no longer fitted her. She had tried ordering online, but technology wasn't her thing. She ended up ordering the wrong items. Eventually, she had no choice but to go into town. She had decided she would go on Sunday when fewer people would be around. Hopefully, she could get everything done quickly and be home in a couple of hours.

Once she had made her decision, nerves had set in. She spent the previous day in the garden trying to distract her mind from the shopping trip. Rachel had attempted to make a start on the forlorn-looking garden, which had suffered several months of unintentional neglect, but had soon given up. She had gone to bed early, unable to settle.

Rachel was in town by 10 am on Sunday morning, just as the shops opened. She recalled how Camron had always tried his best to appear enthusiastic about clothes shopping but was never entirely convincing. Even after just an hour, Rachel contemplated giving up and going home, despite not having found everything on her list. Shaking her head, she idly returned the skirt to the rack. *The wrong colour*, she thought and continued to gaze disinterestedly along the row of clothes.

A sudden commotion outside the shop distracted her momentarily, and she became aware of increased activity around her. Looking up, she realised several people were hurrying out of the store. She stopped her perusing and noticed that the clamour was getting closer. Shouts and screams could be distinctly heard outside.

Dorchester was not particularly renowned for rowdiness or noisy protests. Had a fight broken out? She made her way cautiously towards the exit and peered out. People ran past the shop in terror, screaming in fear, pushing and shoving each other in their haste.

Rachel looked towards the direction they were running from and stifled a scream of her own. Five figures were moving down the street, shoppers fleeing before them. The remaining few people came pouring out of the shop, jostling Rachel along as they fled.

* * *

Varakenthal, accompanied by a fellow Dökkálfar and three heavily armed orcs, were having fun. The killing had been gratifying, but not as much as the absolute terror of those who fled for their lives. He would allow them to think they were escaping before throwing a *Fireball* or *Lightning Bolt* spell at them. They had encountered no opposition so far. Even if they did, the *Protection from*

*Missiles* spells the two Dökkálfar had cast upon themselves would render them immune to the pathetic human weapons.

Varakenthal stopped suddenly in surprise. He had detected something magical up ahead, which was impossible. He closed his eyes and concentrated. Yes, there was definitely a taint of magic in the vicinity. Powerful magic, no less.. He cast a *Detect Magic* spell. The force of the power it detected startled him. Concentrating on the spell, he realised that the magical dweomer centred on a human woman, running awkwardly at the rear of a small crowd of humans fleeing them.

Varakenthal noticed she was heavily pregnant.

He pointed towards her and uttered a guttural command to the orcs in their own language. They raced ahead and herded the terrified group against a shop front. At a word from Varakenthal, two of the orcs pulled Rachel from the group, holding her roughly by the arms between them. The remaining orc stood guard before the terrified people.

Varakenthal concentrated on his *Detect Magic* spell, focusing on the female. His eyes opened wide in surprise as the spell informed him the woman did not have magic. It was her unborn child!

"What is it?" said the second Dökkálfar in its own language.

"Something about the child she carries," said Varakenthal, pointing towards the woman.

He began casting a complex spell. His hands wove an intricate pattern in the air before him as he uttered the words of magic that would enable him to complete the *Spell of Knowledge*.

Once cast, the spell gave the Dökkálfar the answer to the mystery of this woman. He stared in amazement, momentarily stunned by the revelation. Then he laughed, a harsh, evil laugh, which sent a chill through the frightened group of people huddled together.

"Oh, this is wonderful," said Varakenthal. "I shall be rewarded beyond my imagining."

“What is it?” repeated the second Dökkálfar impatiently. “What did the spell tell you?”

“That female, she carries his child.”

“Whose child?” insisted the second Dökkálfar, determined to not be at a disadvantage.

“*His* child. Merlin’s Guardian. The child prophesied about. *The DoomBringer.*” His tone portraying the sheer ecstasy he felt at this discovery.

Varakenthal strode up to Rachel, malice gleaming in his dark eyes.

* * *

Rachel cringed in terror, hands clasped protectively over the bump of her unborn baby. Her mind felt numb with dread. She couldn’t understand what was said but could tell by their gleeful tone that her prospects were bleak. She was going to die. She knew it, and so did her baby. For a moment, as the orcs had herded them together, she thought she had heard her daughter’s cry in her mind, but that was impossible. It was her terror playing tricks on her. Rachel was sad. Her fear was mingled with sadness. Sad for her baby, whom she would never see and sad that she had lost Camron.

She knew now, with utter surety, that even if he were still alive, they would never see each other again.

The Dökkálfar stood right before her.

“You!” Varakenthal said in English, intelligible but with a harsh grating accent. The words crawled into her ears like a nightmare. “I know who you are!”

Rachel trembled, unable to respond.

“I shall delight in killing you and your unborn whelp,” he said to her. “With your deaths, so will die the last hope of your kind. You will be defeated. Enslaved or killed. You will all suffer and beg for death.” His laughter rang out, viler and crueller than before. His compatriot joined in.

“I don’t want my baby to die,” pleaded Rachel in a small voice, looking down at the pavement, unable to meet the hatred dancing in the Dökkálfar’s eyes. “Why me?”

Varakenthal cocked his head to one side as he looked at her.

"Oh, this is too perfect," he said. "You don't even realise, do you? You have no idea who the father is or who that unnatural spawn of a brat you carry is! Humans are all so weak and pathetic. It is fitting you die in ignorance."

"Now look here, you ruffian, leave her alone!" said a voice from the side.

An elderly man made his way through the frightened crowd, walking slowly and carefully. He brandished a walking stick in the air like a cavalry officer leading his troops into the charge. An old dog walked by his side, a border collie by its look. Its slow walk showed it didn't think its master's idea of entering the fray was wise.

In his seventies, the man looked slightly stooped with wispy grey hair and an impressive moustache. His clothes were of exceedingly fine quality but had sadly seen better days. His eyes, however, were bright and sharp, and he spoke with a cultured accent.

"Leave her alone. I've just about had enough of you scoundrels rampaging around the place, causing all sorts of uproar and hullabaloo."

He deliberately made his way towards the crowd's front, oblivious to the heavily armoured orcs or the Dökkálfar, any of whom could snuff out his life without a second thought.

The Dökkálfar looked on incredulously. That the old man still lived owed much to their astonishment at his sheer audacity and bravado. Varakenthal shook his head, bewildered.

"The female is going to die. I will, however, happily kill you first. Is that what you want, old man? Do you want to die?"

"I won't stand by and let you kill an innocent woman and her unborn baby. You're monsters, the lot of you, and the sooner you're taught a lesson, the better. If I'd met you in my younger days, I'd have given you a jolly good thrashing!"

"No, you wouldn't. You would have died. As you will now," the Dökkálfar replied. "But, before I kill you, tell me one thing. Why would you sacrifice your own life for someone else?"

"Why? Because we are human. That is why. We protect and look after our own. We care for each other, and when we fall down, we help each other get up and carry on. It's called compassion. But you will never understand why and because of that, I pity you."

The Dökkálfar grinned. "I don't want your pity, human. Just your life!"

The old man continued as if he hadn't heard the death sentence pronounced upon him. "Oh, and one more *crucial* reason why I should protect this woman." He stood up taller, straightening a little, and his face seemed to glow slightly.

"This particular woman and her unborn baby happen to be my wife and daughter," he announced in a younger, more commanding voice.

And with that, his whole body shimmered like a mirage in the desert. The illusion vanished, and the man who stood before them was much younger, tall and strong and dressed in a dark grey cloak. The walking stick had become a two-metre staff, topped with a large crystal held in the clutches of a reptilian claw. In the same instant, the *Illusion* spell on the dog at his side had also ended. In its place was an enormous and powerful white dog.

Varakenthal looked stunned. His mind reeled with incomprehension. *How could this be happening?* Moments before, rewards and untold power had been in his grasp, but now King Arthur's son stood before him.

* * *

Merlin's staff was still held aloft by Camron. He took full advantage of the stunned confusion, bringing the staff down two-handed to smash into one of the orcs holding Rachel, hearing the orc's skull crack beneath the reptilian clawed end of the staff. Dark green blood erupted from the caved-in skull, spattering Rachel, who screamed as she was pulled down by the collapsing orc, his hand still grasping her arm in a death-grip.

Camron risked the briefest of glances at his wife before quickly side-stepping to turn his attention to the second orc. The orc bellowed as it raised a double-headed axe to strike. Camron's staff was still extended before him, and with a swift jab, he thrust the end into the unprotected throat of the orc. The orc stopped, mid-bellow, dropping the axe and clutching its crushed windpipe. A streak of white shot past Camron as Flint leapt at the orc, who stood little chance as sixty kilos of canine muscle barrelled into its chest, sending it sprawling to the ground. Flint was on him in a second, and the time he had spent with Taldaeron and his wolves learning to fight paid off. Powerful jaws clamped around the orc's throat, and Flint bit hard. It wasn't a good way to die. The orc struggled in vain until it succumbed to the inevitable, and death took it.

The remaining orc took flight. Flint, muzzle covered in dark green blood, bound after it, quickly sending the orc sprawling as he lept at its' back.

The unmistakable sound of steel swiftly drawn across leather caused Camron to spin, releasing the staff and drawing his own two swords as he did. He faced the two Dökkálfar, a savage hatred burning in the depths of their black eyes. The leader was beginning the incantation for a spell, but the other had drawn its sword, a vicious looking curved scimitar of black steel.

Camron's glance swept between the two and his briefest moment of indecision nearly cost him dearly. The Dökkálfar leapt forward.

Camron jumped back, barely avoiding the sword's tip that swept across his chest. The Dökkálfar immediately reversed its swing, aiming for Camron's neck, but he was ready, bringing up his sword to parry the blow. Their eyes met as their arms strained to overpower the other. Suddenly the Dökkálfar's eyes shot wide as he realised Camron had shifted his stance slightly. Excalibur, held in Camron's free hand, was poised, ready to strike. That moment of realisation was its last as Camron thrust, feeling only the slightest resistance as the magical sword penetrated the dark-elven armour and was buried deep in its chest. The Dökkálfar screamed, twisting away as it fell, dragging Excalibur from Camron's grip.

Camron took a step forward to retrieve the sword when he heard a crack and felt a sudden pain around his neck. He was spun forcibly around to face the other Dökkálfar. Between them was a whip-like cord that shone with a deep red magical glow. The Dökkálfar held one end whilst the other was wrapped tightly around Camron's neck.

Camron brought up his other sword to severe the magical whip, but it merely bounced off, sending a jolt down his arm. He tried to begin speaking the words of a spell, but the Dökkálfar twitched the whip, causing it to constrict tighter around Camron's throat, cutting off his words. Camron glanced behind to Excalibur, protruding from the chest of the dead Dökkálfar just a few scant steps away. He needed the magic of Excalibur.

The Dökkálfar had seen the direction of his glance and shook his head as Camron tried to take a step toward it, but the magical whip held him fast. Camron tried to move towards the Dökkálfar, but the cord was as rigid as steel, holding him in place. As the noose around his throat slowly constricted, he felt his throat beginning to crush. Every breath became its' own hard-fought battle.

The Dökkálfar smiled wickedly, the certainty of his victory etched across his face. "What will you do now, pathetic guardian of these pathetic humans?" The Dökkálfar said in Elvish.

*Nothing,* he thought despondently. *I'm caught and can't do anything.* His eyes sought Rachel, who struggled to her feet, disentangling herself from the dead orc. Flint was still battling the remaining orc. Camron's death would also mean Rachels. The Dökkálfar would kill her once he was dead. He felt helpless and frustrated. He couldn't die in his first fight. He wanted to shout and scream, rage and throw things. *Throw things!* He felt the weight of the sword still clenched in his left hand.

"I'll do this..." Camron said in Elvish and threw the blade at the Dökkálfar's head with all his strength.

The startled Dökkálfar threw up his hands instinctively to protect himself. His concentration on the spell wavered. Camron felt the whip relinquish its vice-like grip, and he rushed for Excalibur. Withdrawing the sword from the dead Dökkálfar's chest in one swift motion before facing his opponent once more. The Dökkálfar had recovered and sent the magical whip towards Camron once more, but Excalibur easily sliced through it.

Camron strode towards the Dökkálfar, who started chanting a new spell. As Camron swiftly covered the distance between them, the air suddenly shimmered between the two, the Dökkálfar only just completing his *Shield* spell as Camron reached him. The Dökkálfar drew his black-bladed sword, facing Camron with the magical protection shimmering between them.

Camron saw a disparaging look flash across the Dökkálfar's features as Camron raised Excalibur above his head in a two-handed grip.

"This is Caledfwlch," said Camron in Elvish as he swung Excalibur towards his opponents' neck. The Dökkálfar's expression turned to horror. Excalibur passed through the *Shield* spell as if it were merely vapour and neatly severed the head of the elf.

Silence settled over the terrified crowd, broken only by a few frightened sobs.

Camron stood breathing heavily. Excalibur held loosely in his hand, dripping dark red Dökkálfar blood.

Flint reappeared at his side, his white fur spattered with blood. *Green* thought Camron with relief. None of it Flint's.

Camron looked around and saw many of them looking at him with fear and trepidation.

"Is everyone okay? Is anybody hurt?" he asked the crowd in general. No-one answered.

"It's alright, you're safe now," he said in what he hoped was a reassuring tone, all too aware of how terrifying he must look.

"Who are you?" called a man from the crowd, a note of tremulous fear apparent in his voice.

"A friend. I'm here to help," Camron answered calmly. Flint gave a warning growl, and Camron looked up the High Street. "The police are coming. Don't worry. They will take care of things now."

Camron turned towards Rachel. She was staring at him open-mouthed, shock plainly etched on her face. He walked towards her, sheathing Excalibur.

"Hello, darling," he said.

A few minutes ago, she was convinced she would die along with her baby and never see Camron again. And now he was here in front of her, more substantial than she remembered. His chest was broader, and his arms muscular. And with a beard. Not a neat, fashionable beard, but a full-faced affair, suffering from a poor attempt at trimming.

Relief, love, anger and disbelief rose within her, each clamouring for pole position. Anger won, and she slapped him hard across the face.

"You left me!" she screamed and immediately threw her arms around him and burst into tears. "Oh, Camron, is it really you? I thought I'd lost you and was going to die."

"It's me. I'm really here."

They stayed that way until Camron gently extracted himself from the embrace and held her arms, looking into her eyes.

She was about to speak when he said, "Look, I know you've got a ton of questions, and we need to talk. Actually, I need to talk, and you need to listen. A lot has happened to you, And to me. But here is not the place." He put his arm around her shoulder. "Come on, let's go home where we can talk in peace."

Camron looked around at the sound of running feet. Flint started a low warning growl as a commanding voice called out.

"Stop. Armed police. Drop your weapons and lay down on the ground."

Four guns were pointing at them.

“Do it now! Lay down on the ground,” repeated the police officer loudly, his manner commanding and forceful.

Camron edged Rachel behind him as he faced the armed police.

“Officer…”

“Drop your weapons and lay down on the ground. Both of you. Now!”

“Officer, my wife is heavily pregnant and can’t lay down anywhere. Look around you. I’m not the enemy here. Do I look like a Dökkálfar or an orc? I’m human, just like you.”

The armed police officer looked like he was about to repeat his earlier commands but glanced at the dead bodies instead, slightly less sure of the situation.

Before the police officer could say anything, Camron continued, “Look, we’re all on the same side. The only difference between you and me is that I’ve actually killed two Dökkálfar and three orcs. Technically, my dog killed two of them, but you get my meaning.”

Camron paused to let this sink in for a moment.

“This fight is over. I’m tired and hurt. I haven’t seen my wife for several months, and she wants to know what’s been happening. I’m sure you do as well, but she takes priority. So, I’m going to leave now, and you and your fellow officers will lower your weapons and let us go without any trouble. In fact, what would be really helpful is if you would provide some assistance to the rest of these people. They have all been through hell and definitely need some help.”

He paused again, calming himself despite the rising anger he felt.

“And if you don’t like this idea, then I humbly suggest you have a close look around and see what happens to people who threaten my wife or me.”

The armed officers kept their weapons raised, although they cast nervous glances towards both their commander and the dead bodies around them.

Camron repeated, "Drop your weapons, please? Now!" He wove a subtle *Command* spell into the last word. Unable to resist but not really understanding why, the officers lowered their guns and stepped aside.

# Chapter 20

SUNDAY, 13TH JUNE

"Where's the car parked?" Camron asked as he, Rachel and Flint started walking along the high street.

Rachel told him, and they headed towards one of the side streets. Once out of sight of the police, Camron stopped and cast another spell. Several glowing spheres of darkness appeared, hovering above his upturned palm. When Camron uttered the final word of the spell, they shot out in different directions. Each headed towards a different CCTV camera, obliterating any view the camera may have had.

Camron was quite pleased with this spell. He had created it himself to help protect his anonymity in a technological world, combining a *Protection from Scrying* spell with a *Darkness Spell*.

He glanced at Rachel, who was looking at him in shock. He grinned awkwardly. "One of the things I need to tell you is I can do magic. But I guess you've already figured that out," he said. "Come on, I'll explain everything when we get home."

When they reached the car, Camron discovered a problem. Their vehicle was of modest size, economical and eco-friendly. The German designers had spent thousands of hours researching, analysing and debating the various features and layouts for this particular model. Unfortunately, they seemed to have overlooked the need for a wizard to have somewhere to put a two-metre magical staff.

Rachel eased herself into the driver's seat.

"Are you going to help?" said Camron pointedly.

"Pardon!" replied Rachel, shocked.

"Not you," he replied apologetically. "It!" He nodded towards the staff.

Rachel looked and saw the crystal at the tip of the staff flash briefly. Suddenly, the staff shrunk until it was only a metre long and could fit in the car perfectly.

"Thank you," said Camron and got in.

Rachel started the engine, her mind glossing over what the staff had done. She was about to pull away from the kerb when she stopped and looked towards Camron. "Why the beard?"

Camron looked back at her, amazed. Then he burst out laughing. Out of all the hundreds of questions she must have for him, she had chosen that particular one first.

"Well, there weren't any razors where I've been," he replied. "I'll explain everything when we get home."

Neither spoke during the short drive home, each immersed in their own thoughts. Camron used the time to try to control his nerves. Adrenaline was still coursing through his body, but since the battle had finished, he couldn't control the slight tremor in his left hand. He ran through the events in his mind, from the moment he had discovered Rachel was in danger, less than half an hour ago, until now. He hadn't had time to be afraid or let doubts hamper him. Rachel had needed him, and that was all that had mattered. In fact, thinking about it, Camron realised he felt quite calm and controlled during the fight and, strangely, everything had seemed to happen in slow motion.

Once the threat of the Dökkálfar and orcs was over, time seemed to return to normal, almost as if it was rushing to catch up. All his doubts and fears had returned. Camron felt a little guilty for the way he had spoken to the armed response unit, none of whom knew what was going on, but he wasn't about to admit his anxieties had caused him to talk so brusquely.

When they arrived back at the cottage, Flint immediately raced around the garden, checking that nothing had invaded his territory during his absence. His recent encounter with the orcs appeared all but forgotten.

Camron felt a profound sense of relief flood over him. He stood there for a moment, soaking in the view. He was home at last. Rachel locked the car and went to hug Flint, careful to avoid the green sticky blood. Camron called Flint to him and used the garden hose to wash off the worst of it.

They returned to the front of the cottage where Camron stood, looking expectantly at Rachel.

"I don't have my key anymore," he said awkwardly.

Rachel unlocked the front door, and Camron followed her in. The TV was on in the kitchen. Camron grabbed Rachel's arm and pulled her back protectively.

"Is anyone here?" he whispered urgently.

"No," she answered, a little startled. "I've got into the habit of leaving the telly on. I didn't like coming home to a quiet, empty house."

Rachel picked up the kettle and went to the sink to fill it. Camron was surprised, considering everything that had happened in the past couple of hours, that one of his main thoughts was how much he would love a coffee. Rachel sat at the kitchen table and looked at Camron expectantly. He sat down opposite her, looking deeply into her eyes, revelling in the joy of simply seeing her again.

"Well?" Rachel asked.

Camron took a deep breath. "Well, I have quite a lot to tell you, much of which will be hard for you to take in," he began. "But I need you to remember that I love you. That I am still Camron, the man you married, despite how far-fetched some of this may sound."

He paused, collecting his thoughts before plunging onwards.

"I am still Camron, but I recently discovered that I am more than just the Camron you know. You remember my parents aren't my biological ones, that I'm adopted?"

She nodded in acknowledgement.

"Well, I found out who my real father is. I was born a long time ago, a very long time ago."

He paused for a moment, deciding how best to phrase his next words.

"The name I was given at birth is Amr Artorius Pendragon. My father was Arthur Pendragon, King Arthur."

Camron looked into her eyes. She looked back at him, dumbfounded, her mouth agape.

“This is where it gets a bit complicated, a little weird even,” he said, conscious of how bizarre his last few sentences must already have sounded.

“I was born 1,500 years ago. My father, King Arthur, was a human, and my mother’s father was a human, but my mother’s mother was an elf. Actually, she’s still alive. My grandmother’s name is Nimue, and she is Queen of the Ljósálfar Elves. As my mother was half-human and half-elven, I believe that technically makes me one-quarter elf…” he said, rambling slightly

Rachel’s face betrayed her astonishment.

He continued. “This isn’t the first time attacks like today have happened,” Camron told Rachel about the Second War of the Realms and using Stonehenge to lock the portals.

Rachel sat, her posture stiff, mouth open, and a hand clutched at her chest. The kettle on the stove began to whistle as it came to the boil. Camron rose, returning to the table shortly after with a cafeteria of coffee and two mugs.

He took her hand in his, feeling a slight tremble as he continued his explanation, telling Rachel about the Guardian Spell that Nimue and Merlin had cast on him.

“Merlin?” interrupted Rachel. “What… *the* Merlin?”

“Yes, *the* Merlin. He was my tutor. He taught me how to use and control magic when I was young. Anyway, they were worried that something might go wrong and came up with a backup plan. Me! Because of my elven heritage, I would always be able to command and use magic, so I volunteered to act as a sort of sleeping sentinel in-waiting. They cast the *Guardian Spell* on me, which meant I would live my life many times over.”

Rachel pushed back from the table.

“You knew this would happen and never told me?” Her eyes blazed as a wave of anger welled up inside her.

“No, no, I didn’t. I didn’t know anything about this. Every time I came to the end of my natural life or was about to be killed, the spell reverted me to being a baby again. Each time I began a new life, I had no memories of who I was. Nor of any of my previous lives. I lived each life as an ordinary person, the same as anyone else. It was not until the stones were moved at Stonehenge and my grandmother transported me back to Alfheim that the memories of my previous lives came back." He paused as the pain of those memories briefly flashed across his face.

"And that's where I've been for the past seven weeks or eight weeks. In Alfheim relearning magic."

"What about the other five months?" exclaimed Rachel, still on her feet.

"Seven weeks passed for me. But seven months have passed for you. Time flows differently in Alfheim; for every day spent in Alfheim, four pass here."

Rachel refilled their mugs, stirring her coffee absently, trying to absorb all he had said.

"It can't be true? Everything you've said? Please, Camron, don't lie to me. I've been so miserable and hurt these past few months. I have to know the truth."

"It's true. I swear on my love for you. I've missed you so much. The only thing that's kept me sane through everything I've been through is you. I wanted to come back, but it wasn't safe for you or the baby."

"You've noticed I'm pregnant then," Rachel said sarcastically, hands clasped around her bump.

"Yes, but I already knew," he admitted. "My grandmother told me about our daughter."

"You knew!" she exploded, frustration bubbling over. She strode over to the sink, clutching the porcelain edge and breathing deeply. "Why Camron? Why did you let me go through all that? Especially knowing I was pregnant."

"You've seen how the Dökkálfar are. My magic is a real threat, and that scares them. If they knew about you, they would try to get to me through you. Grandmother said the best way to protect you was to keep you ignorant of who I am."

"But they did get to me!" she exclaimed.

"Yes, they did. But I think that was pure coincidence. There's no way they could know about you."

"Are you so sure?" Rachel asked.

"No, but Grandmother is."

"And if she's wrong? I've spent all this time in a living hell for nothing. You've no idea what I've been through." Rachel sobbed.

"Yes, I do. It hurt to see you that sad and worried and not knowing what had happened to me. Not being able to help you. Or hold you."

"You saw me?" Rachel cried incredulously, turning to face Camron.

"Once or twice," admitted Camron. "Grandmother has been keeping a protective eye on you. She allowed me to look in a couple of times when she was magically scrying on you. I could know you were safe, at least."

Rachel's mind was a whirlwind.

"More coffee?" she asked, needing to do something mundane.

"Tea, please?" Camron replied.

She put the kettle back on and got out two fresh mugs.

"If you had all these different lives, does that mean you have hundreds of children scattered across history? How do you know I'm not one of your own great-granddaughters?"

"I may have lived through forty-two lives, including this one, but the daughter you are carrying will be the first child I have ever had. Something about the Guardian spell's magic prevented me from becoming a father. "

Rachel's eyes narrowed slightly. "Forty-two lives and no children? What about wives?"

Camron briefly thought about lying, but he had never lied to Rachel and wasn't about to start now. "Yes, I've had other wives. They're all dead now," he replied in a hushed voice, eyes downcast.

"How many exactly?" she asked, missing the sadness in his voice.

"I'm your second husband, but... well, you're my fortieth wife," he said nervously.

"Forty. You've had forty wives," she exclaimed, her voice rising to a higher pitch.

"I only found out about the others a few weeks ago. With each new life, I thought I was marrying for the first time," Camron said in his defence. "Look, this has come as a bit of a shock to me as well. One minute I was happily married to you, living a perfectly ordinary, normal life and the next, I find out I'm centuries old, the son of a legendary king, and that I'm expected to save the world from monsters out of some sort of Dungeons & Dragons story."

Rachel was quiet for a few moments, thinking that perhaps he might have been through as much as she had. She finished making the tea and handed a mug to Camron, leaning against the worktop as she sipped hers.

"So what's with the beard?" she asked, remembering her question from earlier.

"Oh, that," he answered, relieved to change the subject. "Elves don't have any facial hair, so they don't need razors. I didn't fancy trying to shave with a dagger."

"Well, you're home now, so it can come off, okay?" she said in a tone that brooked no disagreement. "I don't mind the toned body, but I'm not putting up with a beard," she added in a softer tone.

Camron nodded. "Of course. I didn't think you'd like it, but Geledhil said it suited me. She thought it made me look distinguished." Camron spotted his mistake the instant Rachel's eyes flashed.

"Who's Geledhil?" she asked suspiciously.

"She is Nimue's great-great-great-granddaughter, but they shorten it to granddaughter. She's my cousin, second or third cousin several times removed, but still my cousin."

"And she's nice, is she, this new cousin of yours?" Rachel asked acerbically.

"Yes, she is," he replied. "She has been really kind and looked after Flint. And she hasn't only been kind to me; she's been very helpful to David as well. And anyway, she's seventy-five years old." Camron wasn't sure why he added her age but knew it would avert any further questions from Rachel, at least for the time being.

"Who's David?" Rachel asked.

"Professor David Underwood, he's the chap who was in charge of the team at Stonehenge. Moving the Great Trilithon Stone started this whole thing. It triggered the portal to activate, and unfortunately, he fell through it. He's been in Alfheim too."

Rachel paused. "I went looking for you at Stonehenge, and the police came to the cottage afterwards asking some questions. He was trying to find out if there was a link between your disappearance and this David person."

Camron put his mug down and took Rachel's hands, letting himself fall deep into her eyes.

"Enough questions," he said, pulling her close.

"But..." Rachel's words were cut off as his lips found hers.

# Chapter 21

MONDAY, 14TH JUNE

Camron awoke the following morning to the smell of coffee wafting up from the kitchen. He turned over to greet his wife but found her side of the bed empty. *That explains the smell of coffee,* he thought, his mind still fuzzy with sleep and struggling to function. He knew he should get up and start re-learning the spells he had cast during the battle the day before, but memories of his energetic reunion with Rachel last night kept interrupting his thoughts. He lay in the warm bed, a smile playing on his lips as he recounted their lovemaking.

The smell of bacon joined that of the coffee, eventually enticing Camron from the comfort of his bed. Glancing at himself in the bathroom mirror, he stroked his beard. He was used to it now but decided it might be time to shave it off.

Mid-morning found Camron sitting at the kitchen table, having only just finished his breakfast and lingering over a second cup of coffee. He was dressed in the elven clothes he had gotten so used to over the past few months.

"I have something for you," he said to Rachel. Camron pulled a silver bracelet from his pocket.

"It's a magical dagger. You just pull the bracelet apart like this," he said, showing her as he spoke. The bracelet came apart effortlessly, instantly straightening and transforming into a slim silver dagger. Camron took Rachel's hand and folded it around her wrist. As soon as the two ends touched, it turned into an innocuous-looking bracelet.

"How romantic," she said dryly.

"More important," he continued, "there are these." He reached into his pocket again, retrieving the rings given to him by Nimue. "We have one each. They're magical and will help to protect us. The ring will let me know if you're in danger and if so, I'll come straight to you, no matter what. I promise."

Rachel took some reassurance from this as Camron took the two rings, placing one on his finger and the other on Rachel's. She could see a faint inscription around the outside, delicately engraved, but didn't recognise the language. Camron took hold of her hand, their rings touching and raised them to his face. In a strange, almost ethereal voice, Camron recited the engraved phrase. Both rings shone a bright blue, the ring feeling warm against Rachel's skin. Camron finished, and the rings returned to their typical golden hue. Rachel, slightly worried by the ring's unnatural warmth, went to pull it off.

"You can't do that," said Camron.

"Why not?" asked Rachel.

"Part of the magic binds the ring to your finger. They're permanent but perfectly safe. Mine's done the same. Even grandmother has one."

"More coffee?" he asked.

"Please," she murmured absently, staring at the new addition to her finger.

Camron placed the two fresh mugs of decaf coffee on the kitchen table and sat down.

Suddenly, he stopped the mug partway to his lips. He heard a strange calling in his mind and closed his eyes in concentration. After a few moments, he realised it was Geledhil trying to contact him through his magical *family ring.*

*That was quick,* he thought, concentrated again. This time the image of a large stone circle swam hazily into focus. Camron recognised it as the Avebury stone circle, about twenty miles north of Stonehenge. Focusing again, he felt the presence of both Geledhil and David and realised they were there, waiting for him. He projected a feeling of patience back to Geledhil and hoped that she got the message he was on his way to her.

"Darling," Camron ventured, glancing at Rachel munching on a piece of toast. "I don't suppose you fancy a drive?"

"Where to?"

"Avebury."

"That's miles away," she replied. "No. Actually, I'd like a quiet day at home, just the two of us, if possible."

"Ah, well, I've arranged to pick someone up from there."

"Who?" she asked around another mouthful of toast.

"David and Geledhil."

Rachel looked suspicious and took a sip of coffee before continuing.

"How did you arrange to meet anyone? You haven't used your phone or anything. Is this a magic thing?"

"Yes," he admitted. "It's the family rings. Geledhil has one too. As well as providing protection and a warning of danger, they allow a rudimentary method of communication. She sent me an image of the pair of them waiting for us. There's a portal at Avebury. They must have travelled through this morning."

"Why have they come?" asked Rachel.

"I don't know. I guess we can ask them when we pick them up?" Camron said hopefully.

A couple of hours later, they were driving into the village of Avebury. The road cut through the middle of the henge, and they could see the remaining standing stones in the fields to either side. Camron saw two familiar people standing by the roadside just a little way ahead.

"Seventy-five?" said Rachel acidly.

"Pardon," said Camron, confused.

"You said your cousin was seventy-five years old." A definite hint of accusation in her voice. "She can't be more than twenty."

"Actually, she really is seventy-five," Camron replied, maintaining an air of complete innocence. His best defence, he thought. "Elves have much longer lifespans than humans, many centuries in fact. So for an elf, seventy-five is considered a young woman."

"You told me her age to stop me getting cross, didn't you? You didn't mention that she was utterly beautiful."

"Not as beautiful as you," Camron said sincerely. "And anyway, as I recall, you were having a hard time coming to grips with everything that had happened. I didn't want to make it any more difficult. And don't forget, she's my cousin, more like a long-lost sister. Hence, you have absolutely nothing to worry about," he said with an air of finality, hoping to put an end to the issue. They stopped the car and got out.

"Hi, what are you two doing here?" asked Camron.

"We're here to help, remember?" Geledhil replied.

Rachel shut her car door somewhat louder than necessary.

"Sorry, Geledhil, David, I'd like you to meet my wife, Rachel."

"Hi," said David, shaking Rachel's hand.

Geledhil was a little more forward, throwing her arms around Rachel and giving her a big hug, smiling delightedly.

"I'm so happy to meet you. Camron's told me all about you, but he never said how beautiful you are."

Rachel's crossness melted away as she beamed and hugged her back.

Camron could have kissed Geledhil for what she had said but thought it would undo her good work, so he refrained from doing so.

"So what's the plan?" asked Geledhil when she finally let go of Rachel.

"Well, I'm going to Buckingham Palace tomorrow, and then we'll take it from there. I left in a hurry, so I didn't get the chance to finalise things with Grandmother. Did she give you any further advice?" he asked.

"Not really, pretty much what you've said. Start with getting Britain on board and hope the other countries join in."

"I guess you're both going to need somewhere to stay tonight?" Camron said to them. Turning to David, he added, "Unless you were planning on going home?"

"Well, I hadn't really thought about it," David replied truthfully. He hadn't really considered what he could do until this point, only that he felt a deep sense of obligation to help, almost a desperate need. How to be of use was a quandary. However, he was here with the others, and the thought of returning to an empty house neither appealed to him nor seemed a sensible way to help.

Camron came to his rescue and said to Rachel, “If it’s okay with you, could they stay at ours tonight until we get our plan sorted and know what’s happening?”

Still slightly overwhelmed by Geledhil, Rachel nodded, saying, “Yeah, I guess. I’m sure it will be fine.”

As Camron and Rachel climbed into the front of the car, David held the back door open for Geledhil. She looked apprehensive as she clambered in and slightly shuddered as David closed the door.

“Are you alright?” asked Camron as he watched her with concern in the rearview mirror.

She nodded unconvincingly.

“Travelling in a car isn’t scary or dangerous. Well, actually, it can be, but I’ll drive carefully, I promise.”

“That’s reassuring,” said Rachel, her tone heavy with sarcasm.

As Camron started the engine, the car beeped, warning that someone hadn’t done up their seatbelt.

“You need to put on your seatbelt, please?” Camron said to Geledhil. “David, can you help her?”

“Why do I need a... seatbelt did you call it?” asked Geledhil.

“In case we crash, it will..um help er...protect you...” his sentence faltered. Camron didn’t need to look at Rachel to know the look she was giving him.

“Any more helpful comments?” Rachel asked acerbically.

Camron fell silent and started driving. He kept an eye on Geledhil in the mirror and saw her eventually relax slightly as her natural curiosity overcame her apprehension. The sheer scale of technology and urbanity they passed was overwhelming for her, coming from a land where the overriding principle of life was co-existence with nature, not dominance. Geledhil, like most Ljósálfar, had a naturally inquisitive nature, and she was soon bombarding the humans with questions about everything she saw.

However, as they headed cross country towards the main A37, Geledhil lapsed into silence, looking out the car window.

"Geldhil," asked Camron, "are you alright?"

"What happened to the trees?" she asked.

"The trees?" said David, who sat next to her.

"Yes," said Geledhil. "Where are all the forests?"

"Oh, they've all gone. Thousands of years ago, the country was covered in forests, but now only a handful exist." David answered, getting into his stride. "As mankind became less nomadic and started settling into small communities, they cleared away the forests for land to grow crops and eventually raise cattle and sheep."

Tears glistened in the corners of Geledhil's eyes.

"Cleared away the forests? You mean," she paused, looking at him, desperately hoping she had drawn the wrong conclusion, "you cut all the trees down?"

"Well, not me personally," replied David, a little confused. "But yes, our ancestors cut down most of the forests."

Geledhil sobbed and looked out at the patchwork of fields forlornly. They were neatly bounded by hedgerows, with a scattering of trees here and there and occasionally a small copse on a hilltop.

"Are you alright, Geledhil?" asked Rachel.

Camron looked in the rear-view mirror and saw David looking at him bemused, unsure how he had upset Geledhil.

"Elves are one with nature," Camron explained sombrely. "Whereas humans have always sought to dominate and shape the land to how we want it to be, elves live in harmony with the world around them. They don't even think of it as their land. They consider it a privilege to share it with the other creatures who live there. What small areas of agriculture and cultivated plots there are in Alfheim were not due to clearing the forests but simply using what nature had provided for them. Nature is in charge, and crops are grown naturally. And if I'm honest, they taste an awful lot better than anything we produce."

The car's occupants were silent, the humans wondering whether the elves may have made better choices throughout history. Geledhil continued looking out of the window in dismay, appalled at how the land had been shaped purely to serve the needs of humans.

She recognised the basic layout of the land but not the land itself. Across the different planes, the lands were fundamentally the same. The seas were in the same place, and if there was a hill in Alfheim, then there was a hill in the world of the humans, unless they had levelled it to make way for a motorway or a housing development.

But Alfheim provided for only about two hundred thousand elves and a similar number of other faerie creatures, such as sprites, pixies and sylphs. The majority of the realm was left to nature, which had had millions of years to work out how to look after things and managed to do it very well indeed.

It was late afternoon when they finally got close to home. Rachel had been idly thinking what Camron might like for dinner when she suddenly realised the cupboard was bare, literally. She had lost her appetite with Camron's disappearance and had only eaten out of necessity for her baby. As such, there was hardly any food at home and definitely not enough to feed guests. What little she had in the fridge had gone on their cooked breakfast that morning.

"I wasn't expecting any visitors, so I haven't had a chance to go shopping yet. Who would like a takeaway for dinner?" she asked.

David, who had been feeling guilty again, but this time on behalf of the entire human population throughout history, brightened visibly.

"That's an excellent suggestion. I could murder some chips!"

Geledhil gasped, and Camron hurriedly said, "He doesn't mean he is actually going to murder anything. It's just an expression we use when we're famished."

"Oh," she replied, still feeling sensitive about this strange realm.

They made a slight detour into Poundbury, on the outskirts of Dorchester and pulled up outside a favourite local chip shop. David felt embarrassed about Rachel having to pay, seeing as none of the others had any money. As Camron and Rachel got out of the car, David called out, "I'll pay you back." He wondered what had happened to his belongings, including his wallet, since he had left Stonehenge.

When they returned to the car a short while later with their food wrapped in layers of paper to keep it hot, the smell of vinegar and cooking oil assailed Geledhil's nostrils. Her palate was used to fruit and vegetables, and human cooking techniques were anathema to her. Back at the cottage, Rachel briefly showed them around, and then they sat around the kitchen table to eat.

"I think these are the best fish and chips ever," said David.

"They're pretty good," agreed Camron.

Geledhil had broken open the golden batter and sat staring at the fish inside.

"Do you like it?" Rachel asked.

"I'm sorry," Geledhil said after a moment, her eyes not leaving the cooked white flesh inside, "I don't eat fish."

Rachel looked embarrassed, but Camron interjected before she could say anything, "It's my fault, I should have said. Elves don't eat meat or fish. They're vegetarians."

"Not all elves," said Geledhil, pointedly looking at the half-eaten fish on Camron's plate.

"It's the human part of me eating the fish. The elven bit is enjoying the chips," he replied, then grinned. The others laughed as the mood lightened.

Rachel noticed Geledhil had hardly eaten the chips either.

"Have you ever had chips before?" Rachel asked. "They're potatoes which have been deep-fried."

"Deep-fried?" asked Geledhil.

“Cooked in boiling hot oil,” supplied Camron helpfully.

“No,” replied Geledhil. “We have tubers and other root vegetables, but nothing like this. I have never heard of anyone cooking food in oil like that before.”

“Can I get you something else?” said Rachel, thinking she was failing miserably as a hostess.

Geledhil looked at the contents of the fruit bowl in the centre of the table, “Would it be ok if I had some fruit, please?”

“Of course, help yourself,” replied Rachel, ashamedly nodding towards the bowl of slightly over-ripe apples and bananas.

After the meal, Rachel suggested they sit outside to enjoy the early evening sun. Camron carried out a tray of mugs and a large pot of coffee, which he placed on the small wooden table.

Rachel noticed that Geledhil looked less anxious now that she was outdoors.

“Coffee, anyone?” Rachel asked.

“Oh, yes, please,” replied David. “I haven’t had a coffee in weeks.”

“Black or white?”

“White without, please,” he replied, sipping it appreciatively when Rachel handed him a steaming mug.

“Geledhil, would you like to try some coffee?” Rachel asked.

“Yes, I’d love to,” she replied, as anxious to be a perfect guest as Rachel was to be a perfect host.

“Black or white?” Rachel asked.

“I’m not sure,” she replied. “David asked for *white without*, but the coffee you gave him was brown and looked to be with coffee, not without.”

Camron chuckled. “Black or white means would you like your coffee with or without milk. Adding milk makes it taste a little milder. It’s probably best to have milk, although we use cows' milk here, not goats. The ‘with or without’ means would you like sugar in your coffee. Sugar makes it taste sweeter. I would suggest having your coffee white with one sugar for your first cup and see how it goes."

"And remember to sip it slowly. It's very hot," David added.

"Ok, white with one, please," Geledhil said to Rachel with an air of confidence.

They sipped their coffee, and the conversation flowed with ease as the shadows lengthened and the sun eventually set over the hills. Camron fetched candles and wine, and the evening meandered into the night.

The cottage only had two bedrooms. David insisted on Geledhil having the spare room, even though she said she would be more than comfortable sleeping outside under the trees. Rachel made up a bed for David on the sofa, who maintained it would be very comfortable and thanked Rachel profusely for her kind hospitality.

It was gone midnight before Rachel finally closed their bedroom room, leaning against it in a state of pleasant exhaustion, her hand unconsciously caressing her belly. Yawning, she turned and saw Camron already in bed. One look into his eyes dispelled all thoughts of sleep, and a few moments later, they were locked in a passionate embrace.

Rachel extricated herself from a longing kiss and whispered, "Remember, we have guests."

"Well, you're mine. They can't have you," he replied with a wolfish grin. "And anyway, I'm more worried about you." He glanced at her protruding belly.

"Don't worry about me," she replied, pushing him down onto the bed and jumping on top.

A long time later, Camron was fast asleep, but Rachel still lay awake, staring into the blackness of the night. Her mind reeled with all that had happened. Yesterday morning, she had thought herself a widow. And today, she discovered she was married to King Arthur's son and could count elven royalty amongst her relatives.

It took a long time for sleep to come to her.

# Chapter 22

TUESDAY, 15TH JUNE

Her Majesty, the Queen, had attended literally hundreds of these weekly meetings with her Prime Minister, the present one being James Beresford. Over the decades, she had covered virtually every possible aspect of government, including several wars. But never anything so strange as the recent worldwide attacks.

When James Beresford was shown into the room, the Queen noticed he looked greyer and more pallid than a fortnight ago. The strain clearly showed in his eyes. They had lost their sparkling lustre and the bright hazel was now dull and weary. The demands had clearly sapped his usual abundant energy and his purposeful stride was little more than a tired shuffle.

He had only partially updated the Queen concerning the current situation and their plans to tackle the aggressors when there was a discreet knock on the door. Both the Queen and the Prime Minister looked towards the ornate double doors but quickly realised it had come from the opposite direction. A single door on the far side of the room opened, and someone walked in.

The person was tall and wore a dark grey woollen cloak with the hood pulled up, face hidden within the depths of the cowl. Protruding from the top of his shoulders were the hilts of two medieval looking swords. He carried a wooden staff in his hand, about as long as he was tall, twisted and gnarled with an egg-sized stone clutched in a reptilian claw attached to the tip. The stone glittered like an enormous diamond as it reflected the bright spring sunlight.

"Please excuse this interruption," the stranger began in a friendly manner.

"Who are you? How did you get in here?" said James, jumping to his feet.

"Please don't be alarmed. I'm sorry, but I must speak to you."

"Security!" shouted the Prime Minister, concerns for the Queen's safety paramount in his thoughts. He stopped, startled. His voice had come out as a whisper. He took a breath and shouted again, louder this time, "Security!"

His voice came out even softer.

"My voice!" he said, startled that it had returned to its usual volume.

"Please, don't panic. It's just that the louder you shout, the quieter your voice will be," said the stranger by way of explanation. "The effect will wear off in an hour or so. Please, I don't mean you any harm, but I need you to listen to what I have to say. It is imperative."

"Who are you?" asked the Queen, showing far more composure than James had.

The stranger pulled back his hood, revealing a man in his mid-forties.

"I am hoping you already know who I am, Your Majesty?" he said. "My grandmother told you about me many years ago."

The Queen showed no signs of recognition.

"She spoke to you during your coronation in 1953," he continued. "You may not have given it much credibility at the time, but she told you that if Britain were ever faced with a grave and unimaginable threat, her grandson would come to its aid."

The Queen's face, customarily a mask of calm and understanding, looked startled.

"It is true then?" she asked in wonder, more to herself than anyone. "I thought I had imagined it."

"What's going on, Your Majesty?" interrupted James, who was almost at the double doors, intending to summon assistance. "Who is he?"

"Please, Prime Minister, come back and sit down. We need to hear what he has to say."

James hesitated, his hand reaching towards the handle of the door.

"Mr Beresford," the Queen said quietly but authoritatively. "He means us no harm."

She looked again at the stranger. "Was it you who came to the aid of those people in Dorchester?"

He nodded.

"So you really are..." She trailed off.

"Yes, I really am." He waited until James had sat back down before continuing. "My name is Prince Amr Artorius Pendragon. I am the son of King Arthur. As promised by my father, I have come back to help Britain in her hour of need."

James looked from him to the Queen in disbelief.

"King Arthur?" he stammered questioningly, his controlled demeanour failing him completely.

The Queen was silent for many long moments. She recalled the extraordinary occurrence decades earlier during the middle of her coronation ceremony while sitting on the Coronation Throne. She had heard a voice in her head, speaking to her as clearly as if somebody stood beside her. A woman's voice, pure and soft, yet equally commanding and impossible to ignore.

*"Greetings, Your Majesty. Please don't be alarmed. My name is Nimue. You may have heard me referred to as the Lady of the Lake in Arthurian legend. I am not a legend; I am real, and my warning is too. I have given this very counsel to every king and queen of this land since Edward II first sat upon the Coronation Stone. Should Britain ever be faced with dire peril, and you will surely know what that is if it happens, then my grandson will come. The aid he gives will be invaluable beyond measure."*

*"Who is he?" thought the Queen, unsure she should be entering into a conversation with a voice in her head but curious to know more.*

*"His name is Amr, and he is King Arthur's son. Heed this warning well, Your Majesty and pray you never have need of his help."*

*With those final words, the voice faded from her mind.*

"Ma'am?" the Prime Minister prompted, interrupting the Queen's reminiscences.

"One remembers your grandmother's warning," she said to Camron. "You have come to help us then, Prince Amr?"

"Yes, Your Majesty," replied Camron, relief flooding through him. "And please, call me Camron. It's a long story, but I prefer Camron."

For the second time in as many days, Camron recounted the tale of who he was, how he came to be there and what was happening in the world. He described the other races and briefly recounted what had happened during the Second War of the Realms. He told them about the vile nature of the Dökkálfar and others whom they held dominion over.

He warned them that war was upon them in plain and stark terms, and both humans and Ljósálfar would have to fight for their survival. The Dökkálfar would settle for nothing less than total subjugation of humans and complete obliteration of every last Ljósálfar. He told them most of it, but not all. He kept Rachel and his daughter out of the story, still wanting to protect them as much as possible. Both the Queen and the Prime Minister sat in absolute silence, stunned, trying to absorb all they had heard.

The room was silent, save for the ticking of a grandfather clock in the corner. His tale sounded incredible but Camron, though he had spoken quietly, had told them with such surety and conviction that the truth of his words brooked no disbelief.

James eventually broke the silence. "So, these elf creatures...."

"Dökkálfar," Camron supplied helpfully.

"Yes, right, Dökkálfar. You say they are the ones in charge and the orcs and goblins are their minions. Foot soldiers if you like?"

"Yes, that's right," replied Camron. "The Dökkálfar are the ones who are capable of performing magic. There are vastly more orcs and goblins than Dökkálfar, but they control them."

"And they can cast spells to protect themselves from our bullets and missiles?" continued James.

"Yes, which is why we need to fight them with both magic and modern weapons," said Camron. "What's more, it is vital to realise that, even now, the Dökkálfar will be trying to recruit humans to their side; terrorists, extremists, warlords and criminals. In fact, anyone they can bribe, coerce or threaten. If they manage to get their hands on modern technology and weaponry, they will be almost unstoppable. If they were to get hold of nuclear or chemical weapons, they would have no compunction about using them! Your Majesty, Prime Minister, please understand that you are at war whether you want it or not."

The room was filled with stunned silence for the second time that morning.

"Is there anything we can do?" the Queen said in a quiet voice.

"I think so.," answered Camron. "My grandmother, Queen Nimue, has come up with a plan. There is a powerful magical artefact that will help tip the balance in our favour."

He told them in brief terms of the twin swords. He explained that their combined magical power would help defeat the enemy. However, he didn't go into any detail as to how the magic would help.

"I already have Excalibur in my possession, but I don't yet have Clarent. The sword was magically hidden during my father's reign to keep it safe. I know it sounds strange, but I will need access to the Coronation Throne to get the sword. Would you be able to arrange this, please?"

James nodded automatically, still deep in thought, trying to put some order to all he had heard.

After a few moments, Camron spoke again, "Your Majesty, there are a couple of other people I would like you to meet if that's alright?"

The Queen looked at Camron. "Who are these people, may one ask?"

"Companions of mine who are helping me. They're in the next room if you would permit me to fetch them?"

"You may, although one is curious how you all got into the palace?" replied the Queen.

"We simply walked in under cover of an *invisibility* spell, Your Majesty," explained Camron before opening the door through which he had initially entered the room.

"You can come in now," he called inside, addressing the unseen people beyond. A middle-aged man and a beautiful young woman appeared. At her heel trotted a large white dog, tail wagging enthusiastically.

"Your Majesty, may I present Professor David Underwood and my cousin, Princess Geledhil," said Camron.

David gave a formal bow. "Your Majesty."

Geledhil had never met human royalty before but had spent decades around her grandmother who, while being the most regal person imaginable, was informal and relaxed about her position.

"I'm not really a princess," said Geledhil, lowering the hood of her cloak as she spoke.

"My grandmother is a queen like you are. But the children and grandchildren of an elven queen aren't usually called princes or princesses. Except Camron of course, but that's because he's and human prince and an elven prince."

"Elf," stammered the prime minister, spotting Geledhil's sharply pointed ears. "You're an elf!"

"Yes, I am," she replied. "My grandmother is Nimue, Queen of the Elves. She sent me to help Camron."

"It's alright," interrupted Camron quickly. "She isn't a Dökkálfar; she's a Ljósálfar, one of the light elves. Geledhil is on our side." He smiled at her.

"Oh, thank goodness," said James. "For a moment, I thought…" he trailed off, not finishing his sentence.

"One recognises your name but cannot quite place you?" inquired the Queen, addressing David.

"I was in charge of the excavation project at Stonehenge, which started this war, Your Majesty," he replied dejectedly. "Unfortunately, I think all this is my fault."

"Nonsense," said Geledhil quickly. "You weren't to know what would happen."

"Indeed," said James. "No one could blame you. None of us could possibly have known what would happen."

"Your Majesty, Prime Minister, I will need your help, please?" said Camron.

James looked at him enquiringly. "What assistance do you require?"

"To stand a chance of winning this war, we need to join together with the other countries and fight the common enemy. And for that, I'm going to need your help in convincing them," said Camron.

"Well, I suggest we begin with the rest of the Cabinet," said James. "I will set up a COBRA meeting this morning, followed by a full Cabinet briefing later."

He looked towards the Queen, seeking her consent more out of courtesy than any constitutional requirement. She nodded in agreement.

James turned to Camron. "I'm not sure how readily they will believe any of this, but if you can speak to them as you have to us, then I'm sure you will convince them."

"You want me to address a COBRA meeting?" Camron asked. This time it was his turn to sound disbelieving.

"Naturally," James replied. "What you have to say will be far more believable coming from you."

Camron blanched. This was what he had been dreading most. How was he supposed to convince people who were used to making decisions? Admittedly, both the Queen and Prime Minister appeared to believe him. However, convincing two people by talking to them directly was one thing. Addressing a room full of people, all of whom would be sceptical at the very least, was an entirely different matter.

Camron baulked at the thought. His mind worked overtime, desperately searching for a way out. And there was one, Clarent.

"I'm sorry," he said, "but it's imperative I retrieve Clarent as soon as possible. Getting the sword is of the utmost importance."

"But I thought you said it had been safely hidden for centuries. Surely delaying a few more hours won't hurt?"

Camron thought quickly and grasped, desperately, at another straw. "Well, actually, it might," he said. "It is possible the Dökkálfar are magically scrying us this very minute. They may have heard everything we have said. They could be planning to retrieve the sword themselves. Admittedly, there is only a slim chance of this, but getting the sword is too important to take any risks."

"Well..." said James.

"Look, can you speak to them and tell them everything I have told you? Once I have Clarent, I can talk to them if they are still disbelieving."

"Okay," said James, realising this was probably the best compromise he would achieve. Getting to his feet, he pulled out his mobile phone. "If I may, Your Majesty?"

"Of course," she replied, and he bowed to her before leaving the room.

The Queen studied her uninvited guests. "May one suggest you don more conservative clothing if you intend to travel incognito around London? One would think wandering around London looking like characters from a film set might cause a degree of consternation. As will your ears, young lady."

The Queen picked up her handbag and retrieved a plain silk headscarf.

"Here," she said, handing it to Geledhil, "you may use this for now." The Queen then picked up the small silver bell from the table next to her and gave it a delicate ring. The door opened almost immediately, and her Private Secretary entered, bowing to the Queen.

"Your Majesty?" the man inquired, showing not the slightest surprise at the scene before him.

"Would you be so kind as to arrange some suitable clothes for this young lady and gentleman, please?"

The Private Secretary studied the pair before saying, "Yes, ma'am."

"And some tea while we wait if you would be so kind?" the Queen added.

"Yes, ma'am," he repeated, bowing again before backing out of the room and closing the door behind him.

The trio stood, looking somewhat awkward at finding themselves alone with the Queen.

"Do sit," invited the Queen. Both Camron and David perched nervously on the edge of their chairs. Geledhil made herself at home, crossing her legs underneath her comfortably. The Queen looked but didn't comment.

"An interesting constitutional dilemma, don't you think, Your Highness?" the Queen said into the silence.

It took Camron a moment or two to realise she was addressing him.

"I'm sorry, Your Majesty, I don't quite understand."

"Well, you were heir to the throne when your father was king. By rights, you should have become King of Britain upon his death. Hence the dilemma. Constitutionally, are you still royalty? Still a prince? The rightful heir to the throne even? I'm sure an entire team of constitutional lawyers will soon be trying to work this out."

"Your Majesty, Britain was a very different place when my father was king. I was a prince for a mere twenty-five years, but I've been an ordinary person for a millennia and a half. I know which life I feel most comfortable with."

The Queen didn't look entirely convinced. "If one's understanding is correct, Clarent is the legendary *Sword in the Stone*, is it not? The one King Arthur pulled out to prove his right to the throne of Britain."

"Almost, Your Majesty, but that isn't quite right," replied Camron. "That particular legend came from a Latin translation that included the word adduco, which translates to 'to lead' but can also be translated as '*to persuade*'. Clarent's real purpose is that when Britain faces dire peril, it will test the character of the person trying to wield it. Clarent will confer its magical powers on them only if they have the right character, strength and ability to unite the country. In my father's time, that meant bringing the regional warlords together to fight alongside the Ljósálfar and the dwarves. His being made King of Briton wasn't anything to do with Clarent."

At that moment, the Private Secretary returned with the tea and also informed them their clothing was ready. He showed Camron and Geledhil along a corridor and into a room where Camron saw a set of clothes laid out for him. Surprisingly they were the correct size for him. The Private Secretary escorted Geledhil to a door leading to an adjacent room.

"You should find everything you need in there, miss. If there is anything further you require, then do please ask. I shall be waiting outside."

Geledhil went into the other room to change.

Camron had almost finished changing when the adjoining door opened. Geledhil stood in the doorway, completely naked. Camron had never gotten used to the elven attitude towards nudity and how uninhibited they were about their bodies. As a race who were at one with nature, they did not get embarrassed by their unclothed state.

She looked at him enquiringly. "I think I have managed to work out the rest of these strange clothes, but I have absolutely no idea what to do with this?" she said, holding up a lacy white bra.

It had been a while since Camron, middle-aged and happily married, had blushed, but he did then. He wasn't quite sure how to explain and didn't think the Private Secretary standing outside would be much help either.

"Um, it's for..." trailing off as he desperately sought the right words. "I mean women wear them to support their, um, you know..." he faltered again, embarrassed.

Geledhil looked down at the bra she held and then glanced at her small breasts, understanding dawning on her.

"Oh, I see. But why would you need to wear something there? That's ridiculous!" she exclaimed, dropping the bra and returning to her room.

Camron breathed a sigh of relief that she had caught on so quickly, saving him the embarrassment of more detailed explanations. He made a mental note to ask Rachel to have a chat with Geledhil, just to let her know some of the things human women did that an elf might find strange. The image of Geledhil naked flashed into his mind again, and he felt guilty and forced himself to think of something else.

He looked at himself in a mirror. It felt strange to be wearing regular clothes again. He was surprised by how quickly he had become used to dressing like the elves. Their garments were remarkably comfortable. He glanced at his swords. Wandering around London carrying them would be asking for trouble. He opened up the magical *bag of holding* and slid both swords inside, along with his staff, elven clothes and armour.

A few minutes later, Geledhil reappeared, this time fully clothed, wearing jeans and a sweatshirt. She also wore a Buckingham Palace baseball cap, discreetly covering her elven ears.

"How are they?" asked Camron, referring to her new attire.

"Strange," she replied.

"If you give me your own clothes, armour and weapons, I can put them in my bag," he said to her. "I have a feeling we will need them before too long."

When they returned to the audience room a short while later, the Prime Minister was back and clearly waiting for them.

"I've arranged for someone from the Home Office to act as a liaison for you. Smooth over any red tape, that sort of thing," said James.

"Thank you," replied Camron. "Do you want my mobile number?"

"No. The chap from the Home Office will be with you. Besides, if I really needed it, I could get it anyway. One of the perks of having MI5 to hand," he said and then smiled.

Shortly afterwards, Camron, David, Geledhil and Flint left Buckingham Palace via a side door, escorted out by the Queen's Private Secretary.

# Chapter 23

TUESDAY, 15TH JUNE

The man was in his early thirties, a little under two metres tall, strong, and very fit. He wore a dark suit, crisp white shirt, and sunglasses. He sat patiently in the vehicle, waiting for his new assignment to come out of one of the side entrances to Buckingham Palace. His hands rested lightly on the steering wheel, the darkness of his suit sleeves blending almost seamlessly with his ebony coloured skin. Although he sat perfectly still, his eyes continually swept the immediate environment, assessing everything. He was ex-special forces, and some habits were impossible to break. He was a seasoned professional, having worked for several government security organisations since leaving the military a few years ago.

He had undertaken many different duties, but it was the minder assignments he disliked the most, what he called *'babysitting jobs.'* He was especially chagrined with his current mission. With all the recent attacks, he wanted to be in the thick of it, doing something to fight the enemy, not looking after these people. But the orders he had received barely an hour ago had been clear and had evidently come from someone high up. Drop whatever he was doing and provide any assistance required, provided it did not compromise national security. His boss told him these people needed something, and getting it was vital.

He had undertaken this minder role numerous times before, but his charges had always been diplomats, government officials, or other important dignitaries. To give *carte blanche* assistance to ordinary members of the public was unknown. His boss had also told him to monitor them. He was to know where they were and what they were doing at all times. Definitely a babysitting job, he cursed silently to himself. The sound of a door opening alerted him, and he glanced over as several people came out of the palace, accompanied by a large white dog.

His usual prowess with observation and analysis of people and their intent through their poise, mannerisms, and actions deserted him at the sight of the only female in the group. She was casually dressed and wore a Buckingham Palace baseball cap, but that couldn't detract from her appearance. She was simply the most beautiful woman he had ever seen. He couldn't take his eyes off her. As the group started walking towards him, he sat open-mouthed, revelling in the sight of her. It was not until they were almost halfway to him that he shook himself from his reverie and brought his mind into focus.

* * *

As Camron stepped through the door to leave the palace, he saw a black Range Rover with darkened windows awaiting them. As they approached, the driver's door opened. A man in his early thirties, wearing a conservative dark grey suit and sunglasses, stepped out. The sunglasses seemed a little redundant to his wardrobe as the overcast sky threatened rain.

"This is Smith," said the Private Secretary, who had escorted them out. "He's from the Home Office and will help smooth your passage with any bureaucracy you might encounter."

"Smith?" said Camron questioningly. "Any first name?"

"No," said the man called Smith, with a crisp, clear accent. "Just Smith. Would you all please get in?"

Flint looked decidedly annoyed at his relegation to the boot and made his displeasure known by turning his back on Camron as he lay down.

Once they were all inside the vehicle, Smith turned around. "Where to?"

"Westminster Abbey, please," answered Camron. "There's something there I need."

Smith raised an eyebrow questioningly, but Camron didn't elaborate. Smith glanced in the rearview mirror, surreptitiously eyeing his new charges. It was only a short drive to the abbey. As they joined the traffic making its way along Birdcage Walk, Camron looked out of the window as the greenery of St. James's Park drifted past but didn't notice any of it.

The doubts and fears that plagued him since first waking in Alfheim and discovering the destiny thrust upon him resurfaced with renewed vengeance. He didn't know how much longer he could keep this up. He had somehow survived his training in Alfheim and convinced both the Prime Minister and the Queen to believe his implausible and fantastical tale, which had been nothing short of miraculous. He was riding his luck and knew it couldn't last much longer. In his darkest moments, when he lay awake at night staring at nothing, he knew he wasn't the right person for the job. Why couldn't his grandmother see that? She should have given the responsibility to Findecáno or even Valandil, anyone but him.

These thoughts were still troubling Camron as they pulled into *The Sanctuary* outside the entrance of Westminster Abbey. The West door was usually the exit by which sightseers left. The usual entrance was through the grand portico on the North Transept. However, Smith chose the West Door to avoid the queues of tourists patiently waiting to get in.

As they exited the vehicle, a uniformed policeman hurried over, intent on enforcing the no parking sign and moving them on. A brief conversation with Smith, who flashed him an ID badge, quickly changed the constable's mind. Instead, the policeman found himself on guard duty, keeping an eye on the Range Rover to ensure it wasn't towed away.

Camron looked up at the western façade. Westminster Abbey, originally consecrated in 1065, was a magnificent structure. The cathedral was a unique piece of English Gothic architecture, drawing on medieval France's architectural style and traditions. The wrought iron gates before the West Door were locked, so the four of them, plus Flint, made their way through the visitor's centre and shop and then up the steps to the abbey.

Stepping inside, the noise and bustle of the modern world evaporated, and a respectful silence abounded. The constant noise of traffic was replaced by the murmurs and quiet conversations of the many visitors.

Like most visitors who stepped across the threshold, their eyes lifted towards the abbey's vast arched ceiling, soaring magnificently overhead. Grey stone columns rose skyward, ascending like the mighty trees of the Alfheim forests, to support the vaulted ceiling more than thirty metres overhead. A long central aisle stood, from the Nave to the Lady Chapel at the far end, a grand processional path stretching before them.

As they made their way down the nave, passing the *Grave of the Unknown Warrior*, one of the abbey's Marshals, dressed in a red gown, came hurrying over.

"I'm sorry, this is the exit. You need to enter through the visitors' entrance in the North Transept. And you definitely can't bring dogs in here; unless it's a guide dog," said the marshal, eyeing Flint sceptically as he was not on a lead.

Once again, Smith interceded, showing his ID and having a hurried but quiet conversation with him. Camron was beginning to think that having Smith around would be decidedly helpful.

"Well, I'm not sure. This is most unusual," said the marshal, clearly flustered and uncertain.

"Please, feel free to call the Home Office. The number is on this card," said Smith, handing over a business card he retrieved from inside his jacket. "In the meantime, we need to get on. This is of the utmost importance to National Security."

Camron smiled at the flustered man in a friendly manner. "We just need to see the Coronation Throne. If you could show us where it is, please?"

"Yes," said the marshal absently, his voice reciting a sentence from the guided tour while his mind was trying to decide what he should do. "It's in the enclosure within St George's Chapel at the west end of the Nave."

"Whereabouts is that, please?" asked Camron, looking around.

"Sorry," he said. "It's over there," pointing behind them, in the direction they had come.

St George's Chapel was in a small alcove to one side of the West Door, protected by elegant black and gold wrought iron railings almost six metres high. They approached, hopping over the rope barrier that kept the public away from direct contact with the railings.

"The stone's missing," Geledhil exclaimed in anguish.

"What stone?" asked David.

"The Coronation Stone. The Stone of Destiny. It isn't here!" Camron said, looking aghast. "It's supposed to be there," he said, pointing to the empty space underneath the Coronation Throne.

"Oh, that stone?" replied David nonplussed. "Well, of course, it isn't. It's in Scotland."

"Scotland?" said Camron urgently. "What's it doing in Scotland? It's supposed to be part of the throne."

"It is, well, used to be," David said. "But there has always been a strong sense of outrage amongst many Scots. The stone was originally a spoil of war, taken from the monastery at Scone by Edward I in 1296. That's where it gets one of its names from, The Stone of Scone. Anyway, following an increasing level of Scottish pressure for its return, the British government made a symbolic gesture in 1996 to allow the stone to reside in Scotland. It's been there ever since. It's only brought back to Westminster when needed for the coronation of a new monarch."

"And you knew this all the time?" Camron asked.

"Yes," David repeated uncertainly.

"So why didn't you say anything?"

"You didn't ask," replied David defensively. "You said you needed to get to the Coronation Chair. You never mentioned being interested in the Coronation Stone."

Camron looked at David directly. "We need to work on our communication," he said pointedly. He then took a deep breath and collected his thoughts.

"So, where exactly in Scotland is the stone?" Camron asked.

"Edinburgh Castle," David replied, "alongside the Honours of Scotland."

Camron turned to Smith. "That's a hell of a long way to drive. Can you get us plane tickets or something?"

Smith smiled. "I can do better than that. Leave it to me," and he walked off a few paces, taking out his mobile phone to make the call.

Camron pulled out his own phone and called Rachel. He told her all that had happened so far, ending by telling her he was going to Edinburgh.

"I'm not sure how we're getting there yet or how long it will take," he said. "But there's a chance we won't be home tonight."

"Why can't you magic yourself there?" Rachel asked.

"Well, I've never been to Edinburgh Castle, so casting a *Teleport* spell would be risky without first-hand knowledge of the area you're teleporting to. Plus, I can only take one other person with me," Camron replied. "Don't worry. We have a government official acting as a guide. He's sorting us out transport."

"Okay, but let me know what's happening, will you?" Rachel asked.

Camron assured her he would call again as soon as they were in Edinburgh.

Smith returned a few minutes later.

"A helicopter will meet us in Horse Guards Parade in fifteen minutes."

"You're allowed to land a helicopter in Horse Guards!" said David in amazement.

"Well, some poor chap in the Royal Parks department will probably be having kittens right now, but yes, my assignment gives me quite a lot of authority."

They got back into the Range Rover, and Smith drove the few hundred metres towards Horse Guards, parking on the road by the parade ground. They got out and milled around, waiting for the helicopter.

A memory, unbidden, slipped into Camron's mind. He had been here before, many centuries ago. The south bank of the River Thames had been mainly marshland until London, with her voracious appetite and greed for more land, had finally ventured across the river to claim that as her own. Back then, the poor eked out a pitiful existence, battling to raise a few tired crops on the sparse sections of land that wasn't marshy bog. Chickens scratched in the bare earth. Children played, dressed in rags. He had lived in one of the small clusters of hovels he and his neighbours called home. He had been a boatman, making a meagre living ferrying people back and forth along the Thames.

Another image sprang into his mind, catching him unawares. The face of a woman.

She looked in her late thirties, although she was only twenty-five. Long brown hair, tied in a bun, surrounded a careworn face, weathered and tanned by the long hours spent working outside. Her hands were strong and calloused, her skin rough. She wore simple clothes, old and made of cheap material. Still, they were clean, and she had meticulously mended them over the years. She had been his wife all those centuries ago. He struggled to recall her name but couldn't. He did remember he had loved her very much.

A further memory unfurled in his mind. He was hauling his ferry onto the beach one late afternoon and then standing there, watching his wife wrestle with their small plot, using a makeshift hoe to till the soil. It was hard, relentless work, but she refused to give in, determined to supplement his paltry fares, paid in coppers, with food she had grown herself. She had glanced over and spotted him. Her face broke into a smile that had melted his heart every time. She had only lived a few more months, disease and the overwhelming hardship of life finally claiming her.

Why could he remember all that and not remember her name? His eyes misted slightly, the sadness of his loss hitting him anew.

A light touch on his arm broke his reverie.

"Camron, are you alright?" asked Geledhil, her concern evident in her tone.

"Yes," he replied, but his voice came out in a high-pitched squeak.

He coughed and cleared his throat. "Yes," he said again, this time in a normal tone. "I'm alright. Memories, just memories. Sometimes I think I have too many now."

Geledhil smiled, her hand still resting lightly on his arm. She looked as if she was waiting for him to say more, but then they heard the dull *'thud thud'* of a rotor blade, signalling the imminent arrival of the helicopter.

# Chapter 24

TUESDAY, 15TH JUNE

Geledhil's concern for Camron quickly turned to trepidation as she watched the helicopter slowly descend onto Horse Guards. She braced herself. The noise was deafening, and, as it touched down, a door slid open. The others moved quickly, bent over as the rotor blades whirled above their heads, and clambered into the belly of the monstrous beast.

She jumped as a hand gently touched her arm.

"Sorry," said David. "It's quite scary the first time, isn't it?"

Geledhil just stared, unable to vocalise her fear.

"Come on," he said with a reassuring smile. "Best to duck under the blades. Not sure why but everyone does it, so better safe than sorry, eh?" Hand on her arm, he guided her to the waiting helicopter.

Geledhil's face was even paler than usual, and she sat rigid as Smith strapped her into her seat and placed headphones on her head. The door was closed, and the helicopter rose into the air, London spreading out beneath them as they gained height.

"Geledhil… Geledhil!" Her name sounded muffled with so much noise. She turned to David, who was sitting next to her.

"Can I have my hand back, please?" he asked, a pained expression on his face.

She glanced down, surprised to see that she was gripping his hand in hers, years of archery practice giving her a vicelike grip.

"Sorry," she mouthed, releasing his hand, which he rubbed gingerly, coaxing a flow of blood into his fingers.

Any conversation was almost impossible, so Geledhil looked to see what the others were doing. Smith was dozing, and Camron looked out of the window, lost in thought by his expression.

Geledhil decided to follow his example and spent the next three hours gazing down at the familiar landscape that was, at the same time, entirely alien to her.

* * *

The helicopter landed at a small private airfield just outside Edinburgh. Another ubiquitous black Range Rover was there to meet them. Camron assumed it was a regulation issue, along with the sunglasses, for whichever government agency Smith reported to. He had a feeling it wasn't a regular Home Office department.

The driver of the Range Rover nodded in greeting as they approached. He was wearing the predicted attire of a dark grey suit and sunglasses. Camron purposefully strode up to him, hand outstretched to shake his. The driver shook it tentatively, unused to this level of familiarity from those he usually dealt with.

"Smith or Jones?" Camron asked.

"Pardon?" the driver said in a strong Scottish accent.

"Smith or Jones?" Camron repeated. "I was wondering whether you were called Smith or Jones. It's just that we already have a Smith, and it might get confusing if you were also called Smith."

The driver said nothing, appraising Camron from behind his sunglasses. He was used to blending in and being unobtrusive.

"Maybe it's Brown?" continued Camron amiably. "That would fit quite nicely too."

"Jones, his name is Jones," interrupted Smith, with what might fleetingly have been the faintest flicker of a smile.

"Um, that's right, Jones. My name is Jones," said the newly christened Jones.

"Very well, Jones it is. We need to get to Edinburgh Castle, please?" asked Camron.

Jones nodded, getting back into the vehicle. Smith got into the passenger seat beside him. It was a little snug in the back seat with Geledhil squeezed in between Camron and David. Flint jumped into the boot, turned a complete circle and lay down, his head resting on his paws.

"You enjoyed that, didn't you?" murmured Geledhil in elvish, a slight trace of disapproval in her voice.

"Yes," replied Camron, also in elvish. "I've grown to dislike secrets recently. If we are going to work together, we should be honest with each other."

Geledhil raised an eyebrow. "So you've told him who you really are, have you?"

Camron looked away and saw Smith looking at him in the rearview mirror, a frown on his forehead. Smith was apparently confused as to what language they were speaking. Camron realised that elvish would sound almost musical to him, especially when spoken by Geledhil. A feeling of guilt crept over him. Geledhil was right. He was keeping just as many secrets from Smith, more probably.

The blue flashing lights discreetly integrated into the Range Rover aided their journey through Edinburgh. After a while, they turned into the Royal Mile, home to an eclectic mix of picturesque old buildings and proceeded along its entire length towards Castle Hill at the far end.

They stopped at a row of automatic bollards blocking the road into the castle. A security officer came over to enquire as to their business. Jones spoke briefly and showed him his official credentials, which seemed just as effective as Smith's. The bollards lowered, and they proceeded towards the Esplanade at the front of the castle. Only a handful of other vehicles were there, and they pulled up at the end of the short row of cars and clambered out.

The small group headed towards the entrance, looking at the impressive, awe-inspiring fortress standing atop Castle Rock. It looked as imposing now as it must have to the numerous adversaries who had tried to conquer it over the centuries. Much of the castle dates from the 14th and 15th centuries, although one or two buildings dated to the early 12$^{th}$ century.

Camron reached a decision. Turning to Jones, he said, "Look, would you mind giving us a bit of privacy, please? There's something we need to talk to Smith about."

Jones looked at Smith quizzically, but he responded with a shrug.

"Okay, I'll go and arrange your entry," said Jones and, looking a little put-out, headed towards the entrance.

"What have you been told about who we are?" Camron asked Smith once Jones was out of earshot.

Smith paused as he considered his answer. "Not everything, I think, but I believe you are something to do with the recent attacks," he replied, meeting Camron's look.

His astuteness impressed Camron, who then explained who they were and what they were doing.

Smith made a remarkable attempt at remaining composed but was clearly sceptical about their story.

Camron sighed, realising a little proof was needed.

"Geledhil, would you mind taking off your cap, please?"

Smith looked from Camron to Geledhil, confused.

Geledhil removed her baseball cap, flicking her long silvery hair behind her distinctly pointed ears. Smith gasped in astonishment, removing his sunglasses to make sure he saw clearly.

Camron continued, "As I said, Geledhil is an elf. One of the Ljósálfar, a *Light Elf*." She replaced her cap, once more covering her ears, but Smith continued to stare at her. "They are the complete opposite of the Dökkálfar, just so you know."

Smith's face changed expression more times over the next minute than it probably did in a week.

Eventually, Smith looked at Camron and said, "So you're a wizard?"

"*Aye, and a thumping good one at that,*" said David in his best West Country accent, a mischievous grin spreading across his face.

Camron shot him a look. "Very funny!"

Turning his attention back to Smith, he said, "Yes, both myself and Geledhil can command magic. That is why I am here. Since then, I have lived many different lives, unknowingly waiting for a time when magic would again be needed by men."

"So you're an insurance policy?" asked Smith, who seemed to be playing catch-up quickly.

"Well, the elves refer to me as a guardian, but yes, I suppose you could say that." A little chagrin peppered his tone.

"So, who's David?" Smith asked, turning his attention to the professor.

"David is an ordinary university professor," answered Camron, unthinking.

"Not ordinary," interjected Geledhil forcefully. "He is as much a part of this as anyone." She glared at Camron reproachfully.

David sighed. "I was in charge of a project to excavate beneath the stones at Stonehenge. I started all this by moving the stones." He held up his hand before Geledhil could speak, "I know. Everyone keeps saying it wasn't my fault. But I'm helping Camron any way I can. I don't think I could live with myself if I didn't try."

Camron nodded. "So now you know. You are travelling with a wizard, a scholar and an elf. Not your regular company, I would imagine. And our quest to get the Coronation Stone is of the utmost importance if we are to have any chance of avoiding all-out war with some very nasty creatures. Any questions?"

Smith looked at them all intently for quite some while, digesting everything.

"We'd better get on then, hadn't we?" he said, replacing his sunglasses. He turned and beckoned to Jones, who was waiting for them.

"That went surprisingly well," remarked David.

Geledhil grinned at Camron. "Better than secrets, don't you think?"

They could see Jones heading back towards them.

Looking up at the castle, David said, "You know, the last time I was standing here was for the Edinburgh Military Tattoo about four years ago. It's very impressive. The castle is lit up at night, and the military displays were fantastic. Definitely worth a visit if you're in Scotland in August."

"The last time I was here was in 1571," said Camron quietly, images rising from the depths of his memories, "during the siege of Mary, Queen of Scots. The military displays were real at that time. A far bloodier display as I remember."

They all looked at him astonished, reminders of his previous lives still coming as a shock.

They were a surprising number of tourists visiting the castle. Admittedly, it was early summer, and the season was beginning to get in full swing, but equally, this was a time of crisis. Camron shook his head in amazement. It never ceased to astonish him how people simply got on with their lives, continuing to do ordinary things despite any adversity.

They re-joined Jones and headed towards the Dry Ditch and Drawbridge and into the Bridge and Gatehouse. Geledhil looked up at an inscription carved above the main entrance, puzzled.

"I can read English quite well but don't recognise what it says."

"It's Latin," answered David. "*Nemo Me Impune Lacessit*. It means *No-one attacks me with impunity*."

"Or as a Scot would translate, *if you hit me, I'll hit you back harder,"* added Jones with a deadpan look.

Jones gained them access to the castle. A somewhat perplexed official, who introduced herself as Amy, was soon escorting them past the gift shop and other tourist paraphernalia towards the Portcullis Gate. They headed up the Lang Stairs, thus avoiding wending their way alongside the visitors moving along the prescribed tourist route. At the top of the stairs, Amy guided them towards Crown Square and the buildings that had once been the residence of the Scottish Royal Household. Upon their arrival, they discovered a couple of hundred tourists already there. Some milling around while others queued to get into the various buildings; the Great Hall and the Royal Apartments were two of the most popular destinations.

Geledhil checked her baseball cap. Now was not the time to declare her elfishness to the world. The Royal Palace occupied the eastern edge of the square. Dury's Battery was opposite, and the Great Hall formed the southern edge. The Scottish National War Memorial was located on the north side. The usual entrance to the Crown Room was through the door located at the foot of the Clock Tower. The queue of people waiting, patiently in most cases, was lengthy and stretched halfway across the square.

"This way," said Amy. "There's another entrance we can use to get to the Crown Room. It will also allow us to bypass the one-way system for visitors.

She led them across to the northeast corner of Crown Square to an entrance adjacent to David's Tower. The queue here was considerably shorter, and they squeezed past without much difficulty. Jones remained at the bottom, dealing with complaints from unhappy visitors as the others ascended the stairs.

As they entered the Crown Room, the large glass cabinet in the centre drew Camron's eyes. An unimposing block of yellow sandstone rested within the display case alongside the other Honours of Scotland; the Crown, the Sceptre and the Sword of State.

About a dozen people were already in the room, making their way through the one-way system, stopping to admire the exhibits. Several of them looked up at the unexpected arrival of the newcomers, who were obviously not run of the mill tourists, especially with a large dog padding alongside.

Camron turned to Amy. "I'm afraid we're going to have to clear the room. We can't have the general public in here with us."

"I wasn't told anything about clearing the room, only that you needed to see the Coronation Stone," Amy answered, a frown creasing her forehead.

"Please, it's vitally important that we can access the stone uninterrupted," said Camron.

"Look," said Amy, "we can't simply throw everyone out. For a start, it's a one-way system. It'll be chaos if they can't come through here." Flint ambled over to her, and she absently patted his head.

"No, I'm sorry," she continued, "I know we were told to help you, but there is absolutely no way we can clear everyone out of this room at a moment's notice."

"Actually, we can," interrupted Smith. "I can make a call to Downing Street if you like. Get them to explain what the term *'full co-operation'* means." The implied threat in his words was thinly veiled as he removed his mobile phone from his jacket pocket.

Amy looked ashen. Her eyes flickered from the cold, stern visage of Smith to the mobile phone. Uncertainty clouded her eyes.

"I need to check with my manager," she said, turning away with a two-way radio in her hand.

Camron could only make out occasional words from her call, but at one point, Amy had clearly been told to hold for a minute.

Amy turned back to them. "He's just checking."

Camron glanced at Smith, who was watching Amy with the calm assuredness of one who was used to usurping others' authority.

A minute later, Amy ended her call and returned to where they waited.

Shaking her head, she said. "They're sending some help to..." She stumbled over her words, "to clear the room."

"I'm sorry," said Camron.

"Don't be," answered Amy, her gaze fixed on Smith. "Apparently, your friend here carries a lot of clout in the name of National Security."

She beckoned to a colleague on the far side of the room who provided visitor information and assistance. The steward came towards them. His name was Duncan, according to the name badge he wore. Amy conferred with him, during which time another colleague arrived to help. Despite their incredulous expressions, they quickly cleared the room, apologising to the visitors profusely for the inconvenience and reassuring them the exhibit would re-open as soon as possible. The third colleague ushered the last visitors out and guided them down the stairs, leaving Amy and Duncan in the room.

"So what is it about the Coronation Stone you need to look at?" asked Amy.

"Not look at precisely," replied Camron. "This will sound a bit odd, but I need to place my hands on the Coronation Stone."

"Look, clearing everyone out of here so you can have the place to yourself to look at the artefacts is one thing, but getting the stone out of its case for you to handle is something else. I'm sorry. I cannot let you do this."

"But you must," pleaded Geledhil, "this is vital."

"Look, you've come here without any warning, flashing security IDs from some department I've never heard of and citing *National Security* as the reason you can't say anything. And now you expect me to allow you to handle the stone. No, it's out of the question. I don't know who you are and by what authority you think you have the right to do this!"

"This comes from the very highest level of authority," said Smith in a cold, hard voice. "But if you want, I can have you both arrested and held in a very inhospitable place. Now, unless you..."

"Put the threats away, Smith," said Camron commandingly, cutting him off mid-sentence.

Smith glared at him, not used to taking orders from a civilian. Camron met his look with a stern resolve of his own.

"Okay," Smith said eventually. "Do it your way." A tinge of disdain added to the hardness in his voice.

"Anyway," continued Camron in a warm, genial tone, "we don't need to threaten or bully anyone. I'm sure Amy and Duncan are more than willing to help us in any way they can, isn't that so?"

Surprisingly, astonishingly even, both Amy and Duncan nodded their heads, smiling at Camron.

"Aye, of course, we will. That's right, isn't it, Duncan?" said Amy.

Duncan agreed, nodding even more vigorously.

The others looked astounded at the sudden change of heart. All except Geledhil, who had detected the subtle *Charm* spell Camron had woven into his words.

"Now, I need to get to the Stone of Scone. I promise I'm not going to damage it, but I must touch it. Could you do that for me please, Amy? Could you open the cabinet?"

The magical charm had worked on Amy, who didn't hesitate but nodded and again picked up her mobile radio.

"Hi, it's Amy. Look, I need you to switch off the alarms on the Honours of Scotland cabinet."

There was a pause as Amy listened to the voice at the other end of the radio.

"Aye, that's right, the Honours of Scotland."

Another pause.

"Because I'm telling you to, that's why!"

There was yet another pause, considerably longer this time.

"Look, Stewart, I know this sounds very irregular, but I can assure you there is nothing untoward going on. As you know, our guests are here on a matter of national security. Here, speak to Duncan. He'll confirm everything is above board." Amy passed the radio to Duncan.

"Hi, Stewart. It's Duncan. Listen, everything's alright. Just do as Amy says, okay?"

With that, Duncan signed off and handed the phone back to Amy.

"He's turning it off now," he said.

A minute later, a small red LED started to flash in the bottom corner of the cabinet.

"Okay, the alarm is deactivated. We can open the cabinet now."

A few moments later, they had removed one side of the cabinet, allowing free access to the stone within.

Camron turned to Amy and Duncan. "Would you two mind checking the door for me, please? I'd rather avoid any unexpected interruptions if possible."

“Sure,” they replied, eager to help and walked towards the entry door.

With their backs turned, Camron reached into his *bag of holding* and drew out Excalibur, still in its scabbard.

Smith, standing in the background out of the way, gasped audibly.

“Oh, it’s ok. That’s just the legendary sword, Excalibur,” said David, brown eyes twinkling mischievously.

Smith stood stunned, eyes darting from David to the sword Camron drew from its scabbard.

Camron threw David a look, which he returned with a grin.

Holding the sword in his left hand, Camron placed his right hand, palm down, on the top of the stone. His grandmother had told him that when he called the sword, it would come through the stone if it acknowledged him, and he would feel the hilt touch his palm. At that point, he would be able to grasp it and pull the sword out. Camron took a deep breath and concentrated as Nimue had instructed. He focused his thoughts on an image of his father and thought of all he had stood for and how he had united Briton under his leadership. He sent his thoughts into the stone, beckoning the sword to heed his call.

He could feel Clarent. It was in there, somewhere. He could also feel Excalibur responding to the magical link, enhancing the power of his call. Nimue had said that the connection with Clarent would be strong, but it felt weak to Camron, tenuous even. He wondered if he was doing it right, but the only guidance Nimue had offered was that he would know what to do, so Camron followed his instincts. For many long minutes, he called Clarent, beads of sweat lining his brow as he concentrated. Excalibur glowed faintly as if in distant recognition of its twin.

“It isn’t working,” said Camron eventually.

“What do you mean it isn’t working?” asked Geledhil, her eyes widening in alarm.

"What I say," he replied, a note of panic creeping into his voice. "I can feel it inside the stone, and I think it's trying to answer my call, but it won't come. It's like there's a barrier between us or something."

"Are you sure you're concentrating?" asked Geledhil.

"I'll try again," said Camron and repeated the process, this time placing Excalibur's blade on the stone as he held the hilt. After several more minutes of pouring everything he could into summoning the sword, he stepped back, exhausted.

"It's no use," he said. "It's almost as if it's broken."

"Broken!" exclaimed Geledhil. "It can't be. You can see it isn't broken, a bit battered and worn maybe, but definitely not broken."

A nervous cough interrupted them.

"Um, actually, it is broken, was... well, used to be," David said guardedly.

"What do you mean?" asked Camron, turning to David.

"It was decades ago, back in 1950, I think. The stone was fragmented into two pieces when it was stolen from Westminster Abbey."

"Stolen?" queried Geledhil. "I thought you said the British government returned it to Scotland voluntarily?"

"They did, but that was in 1996. In 1950, four very patriotic young Scots decided the Stone of Scone, as they preferred to call it, belonged in Scotland. They broke into Westminster Abbey late on Christmas Eve and stole it. They smuggled it across the length of England and into Scotland in the boot of their car. I remember my father telling me about it. The theft was headline news and caused quite a furore at the time. Apparently, as the stone was removed from the Coronation Chair in Westminster Abbey, they were pulling it by one of the metal rings attached to each end when a fault line in the stone gave way. About a quarter of the block broke off."

They all looked at the stone. It seemed whole and intact.

David continued, "Once they were safely over the border, they had the stone professionally mended. If I remember correctly, the repair embedded three iron bars to fix the two sections together. Their point made, the four Scottish heroes left the stone on the altar at Arbroath Abbey and soon after it was returned to London."

Camron looked devastated.

"This is another of those communication moments, isn't it?" said David timidly.

Camron didn't reply. His shoulders slumped, and he ran his hand through his hair.

Geledhil looked aghast. The stone was the only conduit to Clarent. If the stone was broken, Clarent was lost to them, possibly forever.

Smith had been standing in the background, watching and absorbing everything he saw. This was definitely turning out to be his weirdest assignment yet.

"The magic thing you're trying to do with this stone isn't working because the stone was once broken into two pieces. Is that right?" Smith asked.

Camron nodded glumly.

"And presumably breaking the stone in two again won't help?"

Again, Camron nodded.

"So it looks to me as if we need to find someone who can fix the stone properly. Whoever mended it obviously had no idea about magic, so they wouldn't have known how to repair it correctly. And I suggest that it stays with us until we find this person."

Camron looked up at him in amazement. For all the simplicity of his statement, it made remarkable sense.

"You could be right," Camron said, the faintest flicker of hope lighting his face.

Smith strode over to the door and called for Ashley and Duncan to return.

"Look, sorry about being a bit harsh earlier," he said by way of apology.

"That's ok," said Amy, smiling pleasantly.

"By the way, Camron has one more small favour to ask."

"Of course, anything," Amy replied. Turning to Camron, she asked, "What do you need?"

"We need to borrow the Coronation Stone. Not forever, just for a while, you understand?"

The charm spell was still working, but his natural reluctance to something as fundamental as handing over a treasured artefact made him think before agreeing. However, they meticulously wrapped the stone in protective bubble wrap and waited while Duncan found a bag. They carefully heaved the 150 kilos into a large canvas bag. Not wanting a repeat of the events of Christmas 1950, they were extremely careful as they slowly manoeuvred the cumbersome bag down the stairs and back outside to where Jones awaited them. They then made their way out of Edinburgh Castle, nonchalantly carrying one of Scotland's most treasured artefacts.

As they approached the Range Rover, Smith leaned towards Camron and whispered, "Did you use magic on Ashley and Duncan?"

Camron looked at Smith, and, for a moment, the ghost of a smile crossed his features. Smith's eyes widened in amazement.

They loaded the stone into the boot, and Flint, looking extremely disgruntled, had to squeeze onto the floor at the feet of the passengers in the back seat. As Jones drove, Smith made a call on his mobile, informing someone what had happened and explaining why Scotland had just been relieved of the Stone of Destiny yet again. It was abundantly clear that the person he spoke to was not taking this news kindly.

As Camron half-listened to Smiths' call, his thoughts drifted back to 1296, fighting in the army of Richard I, when the stone had first been taken from Scotland.

Jones left them at the chopper, and they boarded for the return journey. Camron made a quick call to Rachel to update her. He tried to keep the disappointment out of his voice, but she knew him too well and would know how he felt.

"Where to now?" asked Smith.

"We may as well call it a day for now. It'll be late by the time we get back," answered Camron. "Can you take us back to Dorchester, please? We may as well go home and get some sleep and start again tomorrow."

"Ok," said Smith, "who's keeping an eye on that?" he said, prodding the bag holding the Coronation Stone with his boot.

"I'll keep it with me," said Camron. "I can use magic to protect, so it'll be perfectly safe."

They all settled down despondently, silence dominating the flight with that decision.

It had been a very long day but exhausted as he was, his mind was a whirl of thought, trying to figure out how they would get the stone repaired. Try as he might, he was out of ideas. The weight of the responsibility he had shouldered felt overwhelming. He could only think of trying to contact his grandmother and let her know he had failed. He clasped his hand over the magical *family ring*. He concentrated, trying to project his thoughts and images of the day. He felt the ring respond with a faint tingling through his hand and was sure it felt warmer. He knew he had activated the magic, but not whether any contact with Nimue had been successful. He sat back, watching the last rays of sunlight fade over the horizon and thought about how it reflected his mood, with all hope fading into darkness.

# Chapter 25

WEDNESDAY 16TH JUNE

Camron was the last down to breakfast the following morning, but his mood was the most buoyant. In fact, compared to the others sitting around the kitchen table, gloomily nursing their coffee, he almost had a spring in his step.

"Who wants a little drive to Glastonbury this morning?" he announced.

"Why? Who are we picking up this time?" inquired Rachel.

"We're not picking anybody up, but we will meet someone."

"Who?" replied Geledhil curiously.

"Grandmother," he announced casually. "She wants to meet with us, all of us," he said, pointedly looking at Rachel.

"How do you know.." asked David before trailing off. "This is another magic thing, right?"

"*Family rings,*" explained Camron. "Nearly as good as WhatsApp but without the emojis. I got the feeling she wasn't as despondent about the broken stone as we were, so I'm hoping she has a plan."

"Your grandmother!" exclaimed Rachel in alarm. "The Queen of the Elves?"

"Yes," answered Camron cheerily, "that's her."

"You don't really need me there, do you? I am feeling a little tired. Maybe it would be best if I just stayed here," she said, a slight terror creeping into her voice.

"Actually, she specifically asked for you to come along. I think she's keen to meet you," replied Camron.

"Your grandmother wants to meet me?" said Rachel incredulously.

"Well, yes, why shouldn't she? You *are* her granddaughter-in-law, and you're carrying her great-granddaughter. Well, another one anyway," he said, smiling over at Geledhil.

"Grandmother's coming through to Glastonbury?" Geledhil asked. "Won't that be a bit conspicuous?"

"We're meeting her in Avalon. She daren't risk coming through the portals just yet."

"Avalon?" exclaimed David. "*The* Avalon?"

"As far as I know, there is only the one," Camron replied.

"But I thought it was a myth..." he trailed off once more, realising how ridiculous he sounded, sitting around the table with someone born 1,500 years ago and an elf.

"Sorry, I keep forgetting that myth means *probably true* now," David said.

"I'm with David on this one," said Rachel, trying to distract herself from the thought of meeting Nimue. "If Avalon is real, how come nobody's found it?"

"Well, it's another one of those dimensional plane things, a bit like Alfheim or Svartalfheim. Avalon was the isle of the druid priestesses once, sitting at the top of Glastonbury Tor. Back then, the Somerset Levels and the area around what is now Glastonbury were mainly fens and marshland. A permanent mist shrouded the base of the Tor. Those wanting to go to Avalon only did so by permission, travelling by barge. A select few knew a secret path through the fens. However, as the old religions declined in Britain, Avalon faded from men's realm. Remember, Avalon is unique. It touches both our world and the realm of the faerie. Not through portals, but by an older, more primaeval magic, understanding of which has long since disappeared. Only a few know the secret of how to pass through."

"So we travel to Avalon from Glastonbury Tor, and Queen Nimue travels there from Alfheim?" asked David.

"Exactly, and if we don't want to keep her waiting, we had better get going."

They decided to leave Flint at home as the car would be cramped enough with the four of them, and anyway, Camron wasn't sure how he would fare travelling to Avalon. As they left the cottage and walked up the drive to Rachel's car, Geledhil tugged on Camron's sleeve.

“We have company,” she said, nodding towards the familiar black Range Rover parked in the lane outside the cottage.

“What’s he doing here?” Camron asked, a little annoyed. He strode towards the vehicle, and the window wound down as he approached. A familiar pair of sunglasses appeared as Smith nodded in greeting.

“There are laws against stalking,” said Camron testily.

“Not for me, there aren’t.”

“What are you doing here?”

“Waiting for you lot,” he replied. “I’m your personal liaison and red tape bypass enabler, remember? And anyway, you do currently have a priceless historical artefact in your house. It wouldn’t do if someone stole it, would it?”

“It’s fine. I have safely hidden it under the bed,” answered Camron. He laughed at Smith’s startled expression.

“Don’t worry, it’s also protected by some very impressive magic. I am the only one who could touch it, even if someone could find it.”

Smiths' expression relaxed, and he looked past Camron at the others.

“So where are we off to then?”

“We?” Camron looked at him for a moment before deciding. “We’re going to Glastonbury Tor. But if you come along, you do as I say without question when we get there. Okay?”

“Why?” asked Smith.

“Because it will involve magic and could be dangerous. Plus, I thought you were here to help us, not get in the way.” Camron regretted saying the last statement immediately. Smith had already proven more than helpful.

Smith took a moment to consider before nodding his head in agreement. After introducing Rachel to Smith, they clambered into the Range Rover, Geledhil sitting in the passenger seat next to Smith.

Geledhil, while she hadn't entirely gotten over the upset she felt at how humans had treated the land, was at least able to control her feelings. She bombarded Smith with a torrent of questions about virtually everything they saw during the drive. Smith almost regretted being so insistent on accompanying them. The drive to Somerset was pleasant enough and took just a couple of hours to get to Glastonbury. They parked the car on the west side of the Tor and got out. The slope of the hill was much gentler on this side, which would make the climb easier for Rachel.

"This is as far as you go, I'm afraid," Camron said to Smith.

"I'm supposed to stay with you at all times," Smith objected.

"Remember, you agreed to do exactly as I said. Plus, your brief is to smooth our passage in your world. Well, what we're doing here involves my world, magic and wizard stuff. I don't think you'd be able to help even if you could come with us."

Smith wanted to argue further but was still wary of the whole magic thing. He wasn't sure how much he really wanted to get involved. Reluctantly, he agreed to wait in the car.

"Are you sure you'll be okay?" asked Camron, glancing at the considerable bump protruding from Rachel.

Rachel looked up the path towards the summit, over ninety metres high.

"I'll be okay," she admonished. "If we take it easy, I'm sure I'll manage."

The four of them set off up the hill, heading towards the tower situated at the top of the Tor. It was slow going, and they often stopped to allow Rachel to rest, but they eventually reached the summit. There, on top of the tor, stood St. Michael's Tower, a square 14$^{th}$ century stone tower, all that remained of the chapel of St. Michael de Torre. Being a Wednesday morning and still during school term, the only other people on the Tor were a small group of tourists starting to make their way back down. Camron waited for the sightseers to get partway down before reaching into the *bag of holding* and withdrawing his staff.

"This will take some time," Camron said. "It's a tricky bit of magic to perform. I need each of you to place a hand on the staff."

Camron started reciting in a language Geledhil recognised as some form of elvish but wasn't any dialect she understood. After several minutes, a dense fog descended on them.

"Don't let go of the staff," came Camron's warning out of the mist, although by this time, none of them could see the others or even the staff they held. The incantation continued, with Camron's voice coming from far away.

The mist lifted slowly, and Rachel gasped. The chapel had disappeared. They were still on top of the Tor, but the group found themselves in the middle of a ring of standing stones. These were similar to Stonehenge, but each stone was much smaller, about the height of a man. There were several dozen, intact and standing upright, forming a complete ring.

"Is this Avalon?" Rachel whispered in awe, looking around.

"Yes, this is *Ynys Witrin*, to give it its proper name," Camron replied, memories of his previous visits washing over him.

They stood before the remains of several buildings, which had once been home to the Priestesses of Avalon. Time had taken its toll on this mystical place. Many of the buildings were only recognisable by the flagstones that had once formed the floors. A handful of timber supports, now little more than rotten stumps, could be seen, and some were simply overgrown holes where the beams had once stood.

A small number of the buildings were of stone rather than wood and had survived the ravages of time a little better. The most evident and prominent of these had once been the Great Hall. The roof had long ago collapsed, but the walls, while not entire, were recognisable as such. What would have once been a well-tended apple orchard was off to one side, but centuries of neglect had given free rein to the trees to grow and die as they chose. The apple trees were now mixed with alder, ash, and hazel in the overgrown and chaotic orchard.

Camron had not come to Avalon very often when he was young. Still, he did have some vivid memories, including a great feast held in the hall he had attended with his father and Merlin. The Great Hall had been light and airy on those bright summer days. With the shutters thrown open, sunlight streamed through the tall windows, motes of dust caught in a sunbeam, dancing with seemingly pure delight.

The fire in the enormous hearth had warmed the entire hall. Loose rushes strewn over the large flagstones on the floor and wooden torches coated with pitch lit the evenings. Smoke would rise from the torches, mingling with that from the fire and coalescing in the rafters, vying to escape through the small hole in the roof. Two rows of long trestle tables had run down the length of the hall, with the top table nearest the fire being reserved for the High Priestesses and distinguished guests.

Camron's memories were sharp. He could almost taste the delicious food from the feast. His taste buds reignited memories of tasty platters of meat and fish; the delightful aromas of fresh-baked bread and newly churned butter; heaped bowls of fresh-picked wild berries. Lost deep in his memories, Camron started, his thoughts broken like glass shattering on the flagstone floors. Two people had appeared from around the corner of the remains of the Great Hall. He looked surprised. He had been expecting his grandmother but not Findecámo.

"Greetings and well met," said Queen Nimue formally.

"Hello, Grandmother," said Geledhil, rushing forward to give her a hug.

Rachel hung back as the others moved forward to say their hellos.

Camron walked back to her, took her by the hand and headed over to Nimue.

"Grandmother, I would like you to meet my wife, Rachel."

Nimue smiled at Rachel, radiating warmth and genuine pleasure.

"Hello, my child. I have been looking forward to meeting you."

"Hi," Rachel stuttered nervously, almost lost for words in the face of Nimue's beauty. She had thought Geledhil beautiful, but she almost paled to plainness compared to Nimue. Her beauty was ageless and ethereal. She tried a little curtsy, but the combination of pregnancy and nerves made the attempted homage look somewhat akin to a graceless stumble.

Nimue resolved the awkwardness by pulling Rachel towards her in a grandmotherly fashion and giving her a hug while asking, "How are you? I'm so sorry you had such a terrible time not knowing about Camron. That's entirely my fault. You must forgive me. But I believed your ignorance was important to keep you and the child safe. But I was wrong. I didn't allow for the random coincidence of the Dökkálfar finding you by pure chance."

Rachel felt tears fill her eyes unexpectedly. She had imagined she would be in awe of Nimue but instead found herself at ease as if Nimue was a favourite aunt whom she hadn't seen for a while.

"Now to business," Nimue said, reminding everyone why they were there. "We have the right plan and the right people with the right strength and courage. But Camron has told me we do have the small problem of a broken stone."

Her optimism seemed slightly misplaced to Camron, who wanted to make some quip but decided against it. Instead, he said, "Yes, but it becomes quite a big problem if we can't mend the stone."

"Indeed," replied Nimue. "Which is why we need to find someone to repair it."

"But who?" asked Geledhil. "Can you fix it, Grandmother?"

"No," answered Nimue. "Whilst we are very good at magic, we are more at home with nature and living things than the inert substances of the earth like stone and metal."

"Which leaves us at square one with a broken stone and no one to fix it," exclaimed Camron.

"Not quite, young prince," Findecámo said, joining in. "There are others who are very adept at working with stone."

"Who?" asked Geledhil, getting a little exasperated at having to tease the answer out of her grandmother and Findecámo, both of whom clearly already knew.

"The dwarves," Camron burst out, the answer finally dawning.

"Correct," said Findecámo with a certain sense of satisfaction.

"Dwarves," exclaimed Geledhil in surprise. She knew of the dwarves, of course. All elves learnt about them as part of the histories of the realms from a young age, but no one had had any contact with a dwarf for many centuries. In fact, nobody could be sure the race hadn't died out.

"Yes dear, dwarves," responded Nimue. "You remember from your lessons, short, stocky hardy folk, long beards and much taken with strong mead and ale."

"I know what a dwarf is, Grandmother," she replied, slightly more crisply than intended. "How can they help?"

Findecámo answered, "Dwarves are creatures of the earth, at home with stone, metal and all things that come from the ground. Dwarves don't use magic in the same way we do, casting spells and the like. But they have an innate sense of the magic imbued within the earth. Combined with their knowledge of stonework and their skill as masons, they are our best hope."

"Isn't there any other choice?" continued Geledhil. "We've had absolutely no contact with them for, well, forever. How do we even know where they are, let alone if they are willing to help?"

"We don't," Nimue admitted. "But equally, we don't have the knowledge or skill to repair the Stone of Destiny ourselves. Our only hope is to find the dwarves and convince them to aid us. Remember, they fought alongside us during the last war. I'm hoping they haven't completely forgotten about the old alliances."

"So, where will we find them?" asked Geledhil.

"They retreated underground soon after the last war," said Findecámo, "and adopted an attitude of isolationism. They chose to stay in the realm of mankind, believing that humans, with their shortened lifespans, would come to forget about the dwarves and hence leave them alone. They call their realm below the surface Niðavellir."

"But they sealed all the entrances to the under realm, didn't they? Collapsing miles of tunnels and making it impossible to get to or from the surface world," said Camron.

"Not quite all," said Nimue.

"There's still a tunnel?" Camron gasped.

Nimue nodded.

"And do we know where it is?" asked Rachel, caught up in the moment's intensity.

"Yes, my child," said Nimue smiling at her. "Fortunately, we do. It is at a place now called Dunsinane Hill."

"Where Macbeth's Castle was?" exclaimed David. "In Scotland?"

Nimue nodded. "It will be an arduous journey. The dwarven capital was once a vast underground city called Varðasteinn, which literally translates to '*the land of stone.*' We have no idea if it is still there, but we have to start somewhere. It is several days' travel from Dunsinane to Varðasteinn, and the route will be treacherous, not to mention completely dark. Remember, it isn't only the dwarves who inhabit Niðavellir. There are other creatures down there as well. Everything you encounter will be either a hunter or prey."

There was silence as everyone absorbed what Nimue had said.

"Before you say anything," said David, looking at Camron, "I'm coming with you." So far, he had been very much an ancillary to the group, but his voice was steady and determined, as was the look in his eyes.

“Okay,” said Camron without argument. “No problem.”

Nimue smiled briefly, and Camron could tell she was slowly growing to like this academic turned unlikely hero.

“It looks like we might need some extra help. Do you think Smith will come along? Maybe he has some friends who could help?” asked David, who was now feeling much more confident about contributing.

“The tunnels in Niðavellir are often narrow. Most hunters there rely on hearing to find their prey. I agree you need help, but I would limit the group size to no more than seven or eight,” Nimue answered.

“Okay, that makes sense,” said Camron. “I’m sure even if Smith doesn’t come, he can arrange suitable help for us. We should see if we can get organised to leave tomorrow.”

“If I may suggest you aim to leave in, say, three days hence?” Findecámo said. “There are some spells that will be of particular assistance, and you will need time to learn them. Plus, I have one or two items back in Alfheim that will help. It will take a short while to gather them together.”

Camron looked unconvinced, eager to get on and fix the stone.

Findecámo continued, “Remember, time travels differently in Alfheim, so it will take longer than in this realm.”

“I also think your wife would not welcome your leaving quite so soon after unexpectedly getting you back,” said Nimue and smiled pleasantly at Rachel. “Is that not so, my child?”

“Yes,” replied Rachel. “I’d rather he didn’t have to leave me at all, but if he must, I would like some time with him before he goes.”

Camron nodded in acquiescence, capitulating to the logic of Findecámo and the sagacity of Nimue.

“Okay, we’ll travel up to Scotland on Saturday,” Camron declared.

Nimue said, “I will get the items Findecámo mentioned on Saturday morning.”

"How long will it take?" asked Rachel in a quiet voice.

"They should be gone for no longer than a month and back in plenty of time before the baby is born," said Nimue astutely.

Rachel smiled thankfully.

"If I may, Your Highness," said Findecámo, beckoning Camron to one side and lowering his voice to speak to him. "I have made a list of the spells I mentioned; *Stone to Mud, Rock Wall, Heat Vision*, that sort of thing." He and Camron soon became engrossed in their discussion of spells as they wandered through the ruins of Avalon.

"Might I have a word with you also, my child?" inquired Nimue, turning to Rachel, who was still absorbing the fact that her husband had just been addressed as '*your highness*'.

"Of course," she replied a little nervously, not sure what Nimue wanted.

Geledhil squeezed her hand briefly as she passed, whispering, "It's alright. She's very nice really and hardly ever gets cross."

"Except with you, Geledhil dear," said Nimue sweetly, her exceptional elven hearing as acute as ever.

Geledhil smiled and led David off to look around the ruins.

"So you're really Camron's grandmother?" Rachel said, unsure what else to say to the elven queen.

"Yes, I am. I am sorry your world has been turned upside down these past few months. I have watched over Camron's many lives from afar and had hoped this would be a normal, happy life for you both. But his time has come. He willingly chose this path all those centuries ago, and now he must walk it. Unfortunately, too much has changed. We never envisaged the world of humans would be so different and devoid of magic. He was only supposed to be the catalyst that brought people together to fight as one against the Dökkálfar. He was not meant to be the only human left who could fight them on an equal basis."

Rachel stood open-mouthed in shock. She understood Camron was important to the war, vital even, but she hadn't for a second comprehended the enormity of the responsibility.

"He will need you, now more than ever before," Nimue said, interrupting her thoughts.

"But how can I help? What can I do?" she asked helplessly.

Nimue held Rachel's hands and looked into her eyes, stripping away the layers of her emotions and delving into the depths of her soul.

"More than you think possible, my child. He needs strength, courage and belief. These are things Prince Amr had in abundance. Camron has them too. This is what you can do for him. Love him and support him unconditionally. Give him a reason to face his challenges and the belief that he can succeed."

They faced each other, hands clasped together. Rachel became lost in the beauty of Nimue's eyes. The calm and serenity she saw within washed over her, filling her with a sense of peace.

"You are also much stronger than you think," said Nimue reassuringly.

"Will he be okay?" Rachel asked.

"I don't know," replied Nimue honestly. "But like you, he has the strength to do what needs to be done."

Rachel looked again into Nimue's eyes and saw only love and compassion staring back at her. She stood there, gazing transfixed into the depths of those bright grey eyes, wondering at all they had witnessed over the millennia, yet also feeling a sense of strength and comfort.

A noise broke the moment, and, glancing to one side, Rachel could see Camron and Findecámo were making their way back over to them.

"Thank you," said Rachel to Nimue before they arrived.

Nimue smiled and gave Rachel a brief kiss on her forehead.

Geledhil and David also returned. Geledhil noticed the look of worry on Rachel's face had been replaced by a sense of calm determination.

"See, I told you," Geledhil whispered to Rachel, giving her a quick hug.

Nimue turned to Camron. "We will provide you with a map of Niðavellir, such as it is. It will show the way to Varðasteinn but will just be a rough guide. Our records are patchy at best. Also, we have no idea how much the terrain would have changed over the intervening centuries."

"That should make finding the dwarves nice and easy then," said Camron, his tone holding just a hint of sarcasm.

Nimue ignored him and continued, "The map will provide some help, but your best guide will be this." She held out her open hand towards him.

Nestled in the middle of her palm was a plain silver ring. It had a distinctive and unusual shape. While still circular, the ring was serpentine, almost as if designed to entwine around something else.

"This is a *ring of friendship*," she continued. "Not entirely dissimilar to your *Family Ring*. They are magical and exceedingly rare. Each is made of two entwined rings, normally of differing metals. One part of the ring is held by one person, and their friend has the other part. I created this ring shortly after the end of the Second War of the Realms when the Dwarven King told me of their intention to retreat and isolate themselves from the other races. I gave him the other part of the ring as a sign of friendship and our gratitude for everything the dwarves sacrificed during the war."

"So, how can this help us?" asked Camron.

"The ring's magic will allow you to know where its twin is."

"If that is true, couldn't you use it to know whether the dwarves are still in Varðasteinn?" interjected Geledhil.

"No, unfortunately, I can't. Firstly, the rings can't work between the different planes. You have to be in the same realm as the ring. More importantly, the rings' powers of direction get stronger the closer you get to its twin. This is why you will need a map to get you started.

"When you first descend into Niðavellir, you will get the faintest sense that you are going in the right direction. This will get stronger as you get closer. You will eventually get to the point where you can sense the exact direction."

She handed the ring to Camron, who placed it on his little finger. Nimue's fingers were considerably more slender than his own.

"Until Saturday then?" said Camron, giving his grandmother a hug goodbye.

"Oh, I almost forgot. I have something for you," cried Findecámo suddenly, taking off the brown leather backpack he carried.

Camron waited, expecting Findecámo to get something out of the bag but instead, he handed the backpack to Camron.

"Um, thanks," said Camron, unsure what the gift was.

"It's a *bag of lightness*," Findecámo informed him. "It's for the Stone of Destiny."

Camron still looked puzzled.

"Come now, Your Highness, surely you've realised the problem with the stone?"

Camron's look clearly indicated he hadn't.

Findecámo sighed. "The Stone of Destiny is heavy, almost 150 of your kilograms in weight. It's also a dimensional plane designed to hold one specific item, Clarent. But fundamentally, it uses the same magic as your *bag of holding*. So, suppose you put the Stone of Destiny into your bag of holding to make it easier to transport to the dwarves. In that case, you will create an interesting paradox. What happens when you put a dimensional plane inside a dimensional plane? As a wizard, I would be fascinated by the outcome. As a person who wants to enjoy a long and fruitful life, I wouldn't want to be anywhere near it when you tried.

"The *bag of lightness* works differently. It simply reduces the weight of whatever object you place inside. Although it remains the same size, the stone should feel about a tenth of its actual weight."

"Thank you," said Camron, slightly chagrined he hadn't thought about the problem with the *bag of holding* himself and relieved he hadn't put the stone in there. However, he had been thinking of doing just that to make it easier to carry. The four of them returned to the middle of the standing stones to return to Glastonbury Tor. Nimue and Findecámo stood watching them.

"Grab hold of the staff again, same as before," Camron said and started the complex incantation to return them.

Again, the fog descended, and an eerie silence permeated around them. After a minute or two, they noticed a faint glimmer of sunlight, gradually brightening until the mist dissipated. They were once again standing next to St. Michael's Tower.

# Chapter 26

WEDNESDAY 16TH JUNE

Smith was waiting for them. His composed and self-assured demeanour had vanished, replaced by a startled look, mouth open and eyes wide in astonishment.

"Glad to see you waited in the car," admonished Camron mildly.

"You missed all the fun," called out Geledhil teasingly. "Grandmother says *hi,* by the way."

"Geledhil," Camron chided, walking over to Smith.

"Where did you go?" stammered Smith.

"Avalon," answered Camron truthfully. He observed Smith, giving him a few moments to let this sink in.

"We now have a plan to repair the Stone of Destiny so I can get the twin sword from it. But we're going to need your help if that's ok?" asked Camron

Smith returned Camron's gaze and finally gave a slight nod.

"Good, thank you. To repair the stone, we have to find some people who have specialist skills with stone craft. It will take quite a while to travel to where they were last known to live, and the journey is likely to be dangerous. Is there any chance we can get some more help?"

Smith paused for a moment, taking all this in.

"That won't be a problem. But who are these people?" he asked.

"Dwarves," Camron said.

"Dwarves?"

"Yes, dwarves," replied Camron. "Short, stocky hardy folk, much taken with beards and strong mead."

"I thought all these creatures were the enemy?"

Camron decided it was time to fill in some of the gaps in Smith's knowledge. He spent the next few minutes explaining more about magic, *The Second War of the Realms* and the inhabitants of the different realms.

Camron concluded, "But, when the stones were moved at Stonehenge, the seal was broken. Travel between the different realms is possible once more, which includes the

Dökkálfar. Our best hope of avoiding another *War of the Realms* is by using the magic of Excalibur and her twin. The sword you saw me use in Edinburgh Castle was Excalibur."

"*The* Excalibur?" exclaimed Smith. "I thought David was joking in Edinburgh Castle?"

"He wasn't," said Camron.

"That was really the sword in the stone?"

Camron sighed. Popular culture had a lot to answer for.

"Yes, *the* Excalibur. My father's sword. But no, the *sword in the stone* is actually its twin, Clarent. And the stone in question is the Stone of Destiny, currently hidden by magic under my bed at home. We need to fix the stone so I can call Clarent from it." Camron stopped, giving Smith some time to digest this new bout of information.

Smith nodded for him to continue.

"Ok, so you know about the races attacking us; Dökkálfar, orcs and goblins? And on our side, we have us humans and the Ljósálfar." Smith glanced automatically at Geledhil.

"Well," continued Camron, drawing Smith's attention back to him, "there is another race we hope might help us. Dwarves. They helped us fight the last war. If we can find them, we're hoping they will help us again. They retreated underground many aeons ago. There has been no contact with them for well over a thousand years. But they're our only hope of repairing the Stone of Destiny, so we have to find them and ask if they will help us again."

Smith was silent for many moments, absorbing everything he had heard and repeatedly glancing at Geledhil.

"It's Jason," he announced suddenly, unexpectedly removing his sunglasses.

"Jason?" Camron questioned.

"My name is Jason, but I don't like it all that much, so you can still call me Smith."

There was a tentative look on his face. The corners of his mouth twitched upwards, almost as if he were trying to smile but not sure if he was doing it correctly.

"Your surname isn't Smith either, is it?" Camron said, smiling back at him.

"No, but I've gotten used to it. I quite like it – in fact, I like it better than being called Jason."

"Now that we're all such good friends, do you think we can get on and save the world?" asked Geledhil, linking arms with Rachel. The pair of them started down the hill.

Smith returned his sunglasses to their customary position and followed the others as they headed down the Tor.

They hadn't gone very far when Rachel stumbled. She would have fallen if Geledhil hadn't been alongside supporting her.

"Let's rest a minute," Camron said. He was worried the trip had taken its toll on Rachel. Geledhil was staring into the distance, shading her eyes against the autumn sun.

"Dökkálfar," she cried out urgently, outstretched arm pointing to the northeast.

"How far?" asked Camron. Being part elven, his own eyesight was excellent but was no match for Geledhil's.

"About three miles, I think," she replied.

"Five kilometres," translated Smith, who couldn't even see the vague dots in the distance.

"There are four of them," Geledhil continued, "and they are flying towards us quickly."

"Flying," exclaimed David. "How?"

"Magic. Maybe a magical ring but more likely a spell," answered Geledhil.

"And that means they're good, possibly even battle-mages," said Camron. "They must have detected the magic we used to get us to Avalon and have come to investigate. We'll never make it down the Tor in time," he said, glancing down the hill, "I think we're going to have a fight on our hands," he said.

"Let's get back to the tower," said Smith, "it's roofless but will provide us with some protection at least."

They raced back up the tor towards St Michaels Tower, Camron and Smith either side of Rachel, helping her. As they arrived, Camron reached into the *bag of holding* and withdrew his weapons.

"Are you armed?" he asked Smith.

Smith nodded, removing his jacket and withdrawing a SIG Sauer 229 pistol from its holster under his arm.

Camron handed Geledhil her sword and longbow and gave David the short sword Celaena had given him. He looked around. The entrance to the tower was a large arched opening that went all the way through to the other side.

He motioned to David. "You and Rachel in there. I need you to protect her for me, please?"

David cuffed the sweat from his forehead and nodded, his dry mouth unable to speak, but the grip on his sword firm and steady.

As Camron placed his still sheathed swords on the ground near his hand, he glanced at Geledhil next to him. Her face was pale, the fear in her eyes mirroring his own.

*This is her first real fight,* Camron thought.

He tried and failed to control his apprehension and stared as Geledhil took up her longbow. It was made of yew, the wood unblemished, the grain true and straight, the pale creamy sapwood offsetting the honey-coloured heartwood.

Camron stood transfixed as, from around her waist, Geledhil unwound a silk bowstring, taking care not to twist it. She placed one loop of the bowstring over the upper end of the bow, allowing it to slip a few centimetres down the stave, then secured the lower loop into the bottom nock before planting it against the thick leather pad on the inside of her right boot to stop the bow digging into the ground. She placed two fingers on either side of the bowstring, careful to avoid trapping them should she slip and then pulled down on the bow, bending it slightly. In a controlled and practised manner, she slid the loop of the string upwards until it slipped into the upper nock.

She gradually relaxed the tension in the bow, alert in case the bottom loop slipped from the other nock.

She looked up determinedly and forced a brief smile as she saw Camron watching her.

"They're getting closer," said Smith, levelling his sidearm.

In the distance, way up in the air, Camron could make out the bizarre sight of the four Dökkálfar hurtling towards them, each upright but leaning slightly forwards as they flew.

Camron couldn't speak. He couldn't move. Rooted to the spot, indecision gripping him. He couldn't defeat them. He knew it. These were trained battle-mages, powerful and ruthless. What could he possibly do to beat them?

What would happen to the others when he failed? What would happen to Rachel? He had sworn to protect her, but now, faced with the enemy, he knew that promise to be false.

"Camron!" Smith bellowed as he fired three shots in quick succession.

The sharp crack of bullets penetrated the fog of his mind. He blinked and looked around.

Geledhil held the bow up before her as she withdrew an arrow from her quiver. She closed her eyes and chanted a brief incantation. The arrowhead glowed bright orange as she nocked the arrow and drew back. At full draw, the bow was straining, desperate to speed the arrow on its way. Uttering the final word of the spell, the arrowhead burst into magical flame. Taking precise aim, she shot.

Camron saw her aim was true as the arrow flew towards its target, and one of the Dökkálfar stopped suddenly in mid-flight, the arrow protruding from its chest. Seriously wounded, the Dökkálfar could no longer maintain the concentration needed to sustain the flying spell and hurtled towards the ground.

With barely a glance at their fallen compatriot, the other three continued onwards.

Still frozen in inaction, Camron watched the elf plummet to the ground.

Slowly he raised his staff before him, pointing it towards a Dökkálfar bearing down on them, but his mind was blank. He couldn't recall the incantation for a single spell. He watched fixedly as a silver glow emanated from the Dökkálfar's outstretched hand. Suddenly a crack rent the air, and a blinding bolt of lightning arced towards them.

Smith saw it too, and, as the raised hand pointed towards Geledhil, he reacted instinctively, diving at her, the pair tumbling to one side just as the lightning struck the ground where Geledhil had stood.

Two of Dökkálfar headed towards them whilst the other headed to the tower, where Rachel's only protection was David.

"NOOOOO." The anguished cry exploded from Camron.

Suddenly he knew what to do and, like a fog lifting, his mind cleared. He began to cast a spell, his staff pointed at the Dökkálfar approaching the tower. Camron finished casting his spell when it was only a hundred metres away but still high in the air. The *Dispel Magic* spell hit the Dökkálfar, immediately breaking the *Flying* spell and sending him plummeting to the ground.

Camron paused just long enough to see David, sword held aloft, hurtle from the tower towards the fallen Dökkálfar before he turned to face the remaining foe.

Smith and Geledil were back on their feet. They sent a steady stream of arrows from Geledhil and bullets from Smith's gun shooting at the two Dökkálfar. Despite their accuracy, neither seemed to do more than irritate them.

"What's wrong?" called Smith.

"*Protection from Missiles* spell," yelled Geledhil, knocking another arrow.

"Enchant your arrows again," yelled Camron, and Geledhil paused before releasing and began to cast an enchantment on her arrow.

One of the Dökkálfar drew a slender wand and pointed it at Camron. A yellow cloud issued forth from the tip, rapidly billowing towards the hilltop. Camron recognised it as a *Gaseous Cloud* spell, the same one that had caused such devastation in Trafalgar Square all those months ago. He stopped the incantation for the *lightning bolt* he had started and began another. This spell called on one of the natural elements; the wind. Soon the gaseous cloud was battling against a stiff breeze, trying to push it backwards. The Dökkálfar was at a disadvantage; not only was he fighting a wizard, but he also had to maintain his flying spell so as not to drop out of the sky.

Both wizards—one human, one Dökkálfar—concentrated. Beads of sweat formed on Camron's forehead as he focused on controlling the wind spell to push against the yellow cloud of certain death.

A sharp cry of pain almost shattered Camron's concentration. In the periphery of his vision, he saw Smith topple forward.

He smothered his cry of rage and used the anger to fuel his own spell. Slowly, inexorably, the cloud of yellow gas receded towards the increasingly desperate Dökkálfar. He struggled with all his might, but at last, the cloud enveloped him, the poisonous fumes entering his lungs with the inevitable conclusion. Coughing with paradoxical spasms, he lost control of his flying spell and fell to his death, hitting the ground with a bone-crunching thud.

The remaining Dökkálfar had been battling Geledhil, hurling *Magic Missile* spells at her whilst attempting to dodge her magically enchanted arrows. Upon seeing that all his comrades had fallen and being true to the nature of his kind, he decided self-preservation was his best option. A circular green glow appeared in mid-air beside the Dökkálfar, who flew into it and disappeared.

"I think he's gone!" said Camron, but suddenly cried out in pain and slumped to the ground, clutching his shoulder. Protruding from his shoulder blade was a short black crossbow bolt.

Rachel screamed.

* * *

David, who had been returning to where Rachel waited by the tower, whirled around when she screamed.

The Dökkálfar, whom he had checked just a minute ago and thought dead, had knelt up, slowly trying to reload a small hand-held crossbow, his breathing coming in ragged gasps as pain wracked his broken body.

"Nooo..." David let out a bellow of anger and charged towards the enemy.

As he approached, the figure toppled forwards, succumbing at last to its' wounds. Trembling with fear and dread, David swung his sword downwards, partly severing the neck and firmly wedging itself.

Rachel ran towards Camron and, abandoning his stuck sword, David hurried to join her.

"Mörk-Korsbom!" swore Geledhil as they approached.

"Pull it out," said Camron hoarsely.

"No," cried Smith, slowly getting to his feet and holding his hand against his scorched and bleeding forearm.

"You'll bleed too much. It's better to leave it in until we can get you to a hospital."

"No, it has to come out," insisted Camron, teeth clenched in pain, "it's Dökkálfar, so probably poisoned!"

Rachel gasped, tears brimming her eyes.

Camron looked at her. "I need you to pull the bolt out. Can you do it?"

The fear was evident in her eyes. "I can't."

"You're a nurse. You can do this."

"I work with children, not in ER."

"You've been promoted," Camron replied, doing his best to smile.

"I'll help," said Smith. "I've had some experience with wounds."

"Are you alright?" asked Geledhil, looking at Smith's blood-soaked shirtsleeve.

"Just a scratch," Smith answered as he reached into his pocket for the car keys, throwing them towards David. "You'll find a first aid kit in the boot. Bring it quickly."

"I'll go," interrupted Geledhil. "I'm faster. How do these work?" she asked, taking the keys from David. Her lithe figure was bounding down the hillside as fleet as a deer a few moments later.

Between Rachel and Smith, they managed to slowly and carefully withdraw the bolt from Camron's shoulder. By the time they laid the bloody quarrel on the ground, Geledhil had returned with the first aid kit. Rachel took out a couple of sterile dressings and applied a reasonable field dressing to staunch blood flow.

"We need to get you to a hospital quickly. Do you know what type of poison it would have been?" Smith asked as Rachel turned to attend to his arm.

"None that any human doctor would have heard of," Camron replied through clenched teeth as a spasm of pain coursed through him.

"Excalibur," he said suddenly, "pass me Excalibur."

Confusion clouded their features as Smith said, "Camron, you're in no condition to hold a sword."

"Of course!" David exclaimed suddenly, relief flashing across his face. He rushed to where Camron had left his swords on the ground and picked up the scabbarded Excalibur.

"Catch," he called, hefting the sword towards Geledhil, who caught it deftly in mid-air.

"Give it to him to hold," David said.

Still baffled, Geledhil started to withdraw Excalibur from the scabbard.

"No, not the sword, the scabbard. It's magical. Legend states that Excalibur's scabbard holds magical healing properties. So long as King Arthur had it, he could not be killed in battle. Quickly, now!"

Geledhil looked at Camron, who nodded weakly, sweat coating his face. She gently placed the scabbard, with Excalibur inside, into Camron's hands. The scabbard glowed with a faint golden hue, and Camron's face immediately lost a little of its sickly grey colour. He closed his eyes, resting for a few moments.

"Why didn't he tell us about the scabbard?" Rachel asked, desperation still clouding her face.

"I don't know," answered Smith. "It would have been useful to have known."

"Sorry," said Camron faintly, opening his eyes and looking into midnight blue eyes staring down at him.

David, also looking far less worried than a few minutes ago, smiled weakly. "Another communication moment, I think."

Smith shook his head and chuckled softly. He was beginning to feel a sense of camaraderie with this unlikely band of would-be heroes.

Camron sat up slowly, grimacing in pain. He gripped Geledhil's arm urgently. "Did we kill them all, or did the last one get away?" he asked.

"No, he got away. Why?" she replied.

"Dammit," he said forcefully.

"What's wrong?" asked Smith, picking up that something had gone amiss.

"They will know now," Camron replied. "About us, I mean."

The others looked at him questioningly, not realising what he meant.

Camron lay back down, wincing slightly. "Up until now, all they knew for certain was that two of their attacks had failed. But probably didn't know why. Now one of them has got away. They will know we have at least one wizard on our side."

He looked at Geledhil. "They will also know the Ljósálfar have joined us."

"They were bound to find out sooner or later, weren't they?" asked David.

"Yes," replied Camron. "But I was hoping for later. The longer I kept hidden from them, the safer we were. At least until we could get hold of Clarent." He avoided looking at his wife, but she understood where his primary concern lay.

"We'd better get a move on then," said Smith. "Do you think you can walk back to the car?"

"I think so," Camron replied, and very slowly, they made their way down to the car park.

Smith increased his pace ever so slightly until he walked alongside Geledhil, who was helping Rachel.

"That was exceptional bowmanship," he said awkwardly. Giving compliments wasn't a particularly comfortable area for him.

"I know," she replied in a matter of fact manner, barely glancing at him.

Smith stammered for something to say, but in the end, he simply stopped walking and watched as she continued alongside Rachel.

"You know he was trying to pay you a compliment, don't you?" Rachel said to Geledhil.

"Was he?" she replied. "I wondered why he said something so obvious."

Rachel smiled to herself and glanced over her shoulder at Smith. He had resumed walking, but she thought he looked a little crestfallen.

The fight with the Dökkálfar had been brief, but, predominantly due to the gunfire from Smith, it had attracted the attention of a group of tourists, who had promptly called the police. As they neared the bottom of the hill, two armed response police cars hurtled into the car park and screeched to a halt. Three officers jumped from one of the cars, each carrying a sidearm. They raised their guns and issued the standard verbal warning.

Smith expected this. He already had his hands raised, one of which held his ID badge. He faced the three policemen, calmly stating who he was and that he worked for the security forces. Taking no chances, the senior firearms officer approached cautiously as Smith slowly knelt on the ground, hands still raised. A check of his ID had the desired result, and they put their guns away, much to Rachel's relief.

It proved rather difficult to explain the fight's circumstances to the police officers. If not for the three dead Dökkálfar strewn around the tor, Camron would have been inclined not to divulge any details whatsoever. As it was, Smith used the *'in the interests of national security'* line and obtained taciturn agreement to retrieve the bodies of the fallen Dökkálfar discreetly and endeavour to keep the incident out of the public eye.

They departed from Glastonbury Tor shortly after but didn't drive far, instead stopping in the nearby town of Street. They made their way to a Starbucks while Smith paced up and down outside, making several calls on his mobile. He eventually joined them at their table, thanking Rachel for his coffee.

"Ok," he began, "I've made some arrangements. A team from *the Regiment* will be joining us."

"The Regiment?" inquired Rachel.

"The SAS. 22 Regiment," Smith replied before taking a sip of coffee, grimacing. He preferred his coffee almost scalding, and this cup had definitely cooled. "You two can obviously look after yourselves," Smith said, nodding in Camron and Geledhil's direction. "But I think you'll need a bit of a crash course," he directed his gaze towards David. "So I've arranged a special HET course for you."

"HET?" asked David.

"Hostile Environment Training. They're usually customised for the local environment you would be operating in – for instance, a civilian specialist working in an unstable African country would be trained in hostage scenarios and basic outdoor survival skills." He drank some more coffee, forgetting that it was now tepid.

"But we can only guess what is down there, so we will cover some unarmed combat, basic firearms skills, survival skills, and climbing. We might even try some CQC, close-quarter combat in the killing house, just to see how well you cope under combat pressure. Once I drop the others back in Dorchester, we'll head up to Hereford, and the lads will cram all this into three fun-filled days."

David looked dubious but knew from the training he had already received in Alfheim how valuable it would be. He also realised that refusing to go could weaken his case for insisting on accompanying them.

"Ok," he said with a resigned sigh. "I'm looking forward to it already."

Geledhil reached across the table and squeezed his hand gently. “You will be okay,” she said. “I’ve worked with you in training, and I know you can do it, even if you don’t believe it yourself.”

He tried to return her reassuring smile but couldn’t quite match her optimism.

# Chapter 27

SVARTALFHEIM

She was not sitting on her throne in the Great Hall. Instead, Sallakray stood stock-still, as silent as only an elf can be, one eye peering through the hidden peephole into the chamber beyond.

She was the Hlyđni-Móđir of House Dukker, the *First House of Svartalfheim*. Hers was the largest and most powerful of all the Dökkálfar Houses, and she ruled it with an iron fist. Her ruthlessness was legendary, and the fear she engendered brutally deserved.

Hlyđni-Móđir was the title given to the ruling matron mother of each House and literally meant *'obedience mother.'* That was what she was and what she commanded. Most of the senior Dökkálfar in her house were her own offspring, though that afforded them little protection should they face her wrath.

She was ancient, old even by the long lifespans of elves. In fact, she was the only Dökkálfar remaining who had been alive during the Second War of the Realms. Her once perfectly smooth skin was now wrinkled and leathery. Her lustrous black hair, while still dark, was thin and wispy. Her eyes, however, were sharp and bright, revealing a depth of cunning and fierce intelligence. Her demeanour emanated an unyielding determination. Her will was the driving force that kept her strong and purposeful throughout the years. She might look frail, but her presence was commanding. Her absolute authority was abundantly clear.

She smiled as she spied into the chamber beyond, noting that despite being on the brink of war with the humans and Ljósálfar, each House still vied for power and position. Like herself, they employed a mixture of politics, stealth and whatever underhand tactics they could get away with within the perpetual struggle for power that underpinned all of Dökkálfar society. Present were the Hlyđni-Móđir from the other four leading Houses. These five comprised the ruling council that directly governed Nakkazeim, the First City of

Svartalfheim. Both Chief Warlock, usually the elder son and First-Daughter of each House, accompanied their respective Hlyđni-Móđirs.

It was her right to arrive last as the ruling matron mother of the most powerful House. She valued that privilege as those few minutes spent observing the power play between her rivals often gave her the edge when she had to bend the council to her will.

The council chamber had a permanent anti-magic spell cast upon it to prevent any *misunderstandings* during their many intense arguments. In times gone by, many Hlyđni-Móđir had met their end due to a spell cast in anger during a council meeting. Now they deemed it expedient to eliminate all magic from the council chamber. This also had the added benefit of preventing magical scrying, and so the other Hlyđni-Móđir believed their meetings remained secret. Sallakray almost chuckled aloud. Her kind had become so reliant on magic they forgot there was often a mundane way to achieve a similar end. The carefully hidden spy-hole in the wall was a perfect example of how the simplest solution didn't require the use of magic at all.

She listened for a few more moments. The conversations were not concerned with plotting her downfall but focused on the strategy and planning for the upcoming war.

She had heard enough. She hadn't expected to glean anything useful from spying on the others, but it was always worth checking. She could not afford any of the leading houses to plot against hers. Dukker was the most powerful, but if they were to combine to contrive her downfall, she would be in trouble. She replaced the spy-hole cover and crept down the secret passageway, entering the central corridor behind an ancient tapestry.

As she carefully put back the cloth, two figures emerged from a hidden alcove where they had been waiting for her, watchful and alert. The first, Ashvilak, was her Chief Warlock. He was one of her grandsons, but she neither knew nor cared which one. The second was Betshar, her First-Daughter, who had inherited many of her mother's characteristics, including ruthless ambition and cruelty. This made her both a treasured ally and a deadly rival. Sallakray maintained a constant vigilance, knowing how impatient Betshar was to assume the role of matron mother. She had already been the instigator of several attempts on Sallakrays' life over the past century.

Both of them took their position in front of her. In Dökkálfar society, it wasn't prudent or healthy to allow someone to walk behind you, especial someone who saw you as an obstacle to their own advancement. As they made their way along the corridor towards the Council Chamber entrance, Sallakray allowed her mind to wander back to when she had assumed control of her House.

*It was at the end of the Second War of the Realms, at the height of what became the final battle. Sallakrays' mother, Aldertakka, was locked in a magical fight with the Ljósálfar Queen. Sallakray had despatched the human wizard she battled and paused to look around, taking in the devastation of the battlefield. She was dismayed. Many hundreds lay dead or dying on both sides, although this wasn't the reason for her consternation. She barely noticed the dead, except to calculate the resources and fighting capability left to her side. No, what caused her alarm was that they appeared to be losing.*

*The reason for this was apparent. Actually, there were two reasons; the human wizard Merlin and the Ljósálfar Queen, Nimue. They were simply too powerful. Neither had received so much as a scratch throughout the battle. Her own mother, Aldertakka, the ruling matron mother of the Third House, was struggling to hold her own against Nimue. The Hlyđni-Móđir of the First and Fourth Houses combined could barely match Merlin and his princeling pup, Amr. She looked over to where King Arthur's son fought alongside his mentor, the mightiest of human wizards. Briefly, their eyes locked, his green eyes meeting her own.*

*She turned away, stepping back from the thick of the battle and thought quickly. She could use the Dökkálfar defeat to her advantage, but she must be decisive and act. She scanned the ground around her and spied what she needed. Bending down, she picked up a spent Ljósálfar arrow. It had missed its target and was fortunately still intact. Carefully, she withdrew a small leather pouch from inside her tunic and untied the draw-string, pulling out a packet securely wrapped in paper. Unfolding it revealed a thick, black tar-like substance. This was the infamous and deadly Dökkálfar poison. She deliberately coated both sides of the arrowhead, replaced the pouch just as carefully and surveyed the scene around her once again.*

*Nothing had changed, so she made her way to where her mother still battled Nimue.*

*Her mother had both arms raised in the midst of casting a spell when Sallakray came upon her from behind. She grasped the arrow firmly, careful to avoid any contact with the arrowhead. Ducking slightly under her mother's outstretched arm, Sallakray thrust the shaft at an angle, through her mother's breast and into her heart.*

*Aldertakka gasped in pain. Her spell was ruined as her concentration was brutally broken. Her head swung towards Sallakray, confusion clearly portrayed on her face. As the fast-acting poison took hold and her limbs rapidly numbed, understanding dawned on her. The look of triumph in her daughter's eyes confirmed her fears. Aldertakka was not shocked. She had gained her own ascendency through the killing of her mother. However, she was astounded that Sallakray would sacrifice the battle and possibly the war for her personal ambition. It was the last thought on her mind as she drew her final breath.*

*Sallakray looked up, her hand still holding the arrow protruding from her mother's breast and met Nimue's eyes. She saw horror reflected in them. Nimue's eyes were wide with horror, and she had paused involuntarily, shocked beyond comprehending.*

*Nimue's pause gave Sallakray the opportunity she needed to complete her plan. She cast a low-level Magic Missile spell at Nimue, easily countered by even a half-competent mage. It was almost insulting to cast one at Nimue. However, Sallakrays' plan only had a few brief moments to work, and she counted on Nimue's shocked pause to succeed. The magical missiles hit Nimue, but even in her present state of torpor, the spells merely wounded rather than caused a severe threat to her life. That was all Sallakray needed.*

*Nimue had dropped to her knees, clutching the wounds in her chest.*

*Cries of consternation and alarm arose from those allies nearby, and several rushed to her aid. The brief hiatus in the battle gave Sallakray the opportunity she needed. Bending down, she grabbed the body of her dead mother. She unceremoniously hoisted it over her shoulder, crying a terrible curse at the unknown Ljósálfar, who had shot and killed her mother.*

*She turned to leave the battle, glancing back towards Nimue briefly. Their eyes met once more; Sallakrays' glittered with triumph. She was now Hlyđni-Móđir of the Third House.*

*Sallakray made her way to the nearby portal at Avebury, from where she returned to Svartalfheim, closely followed by many others from her house. The lull in the battle gave the other Dökkálfar leaders the opportunity they had also been looking for. They were skilled and brave as a race and spent much of their life training for both magical and normal combat. But their self-preservation and self-interest wouldn't allow them to sacrifice their own lives.*

*The battle was over.*

*The careful withdrawal of the Dökkálfar leaders became a general rout. Orcs and goblins, the lowly foot soldiers of the Dökkálfar army, fought with each other, desperate to escape from the front line of the battle. Their Dökkálfar masters, however, had other ideas. These troops were expendable, there to soak up the brunt of the combat and were invaluable during a retreat to keep the enemy from slaughtering the fleeing Dökkálfar. Many low ranking Dökkálfar unwillingly remained behind as a rear-guard, keeping the orcs and goblins in check with threats, violence and random killings, thus ensuring they fought on. This allowed a fair part of what remained of the decimated Dökkálfar forces to retreat to the safety of their portal.*

*Back in Svartalfheim, Sallakray was exultant. Unlike her treachery against her mother, which had gone entirely unnoticed, many on the battlefield had noticed her successful attack on Nimue. Throughout the entire war, she was the only Dökkálfar to have inflicted any injuries on the Ljósálfar queen*

*Her mother lay at her feet, seemingly killed by a Ljósálfar arrow. Sallakray was elevated to head of her house, one of the youngest Hlyđni-Móđir ever.*

*Her peers were wary of her. To injure Nimue through magic showed she was far more magically gifted than anyone had previously believed. Indeed, many had thought her a mediocre witch at best. They wondered if they had underestimated her ability and were mindful of the threat she may pose.*

*Sallakray knew she could not rely on their caution for long. If she were to survive as head of the Third House and ultimately increase her House status to Second or even First House, then she must not only be thought of as powerful, she must become truly powerful. And so, over the coming decades of their enforced imprisonment within the realm of Svartalfheim, she devoted herself to becoming the most powerful leader, both magically and politically.*

She broke from her reminiscences when she realised they had reached the entrance to the Council Chambers. Ashvilak opened the door, and silence fell in the room. All eyes turned towards them. The three of them walked towards the long rectangular table dominating the room. There were high-backed ornate wooden chairs spaced some distance apart along each of the two long sides and another seat at the head of the table, which was closest to the entrance.

This was the only unoccupied seat, and Sallakray made her way towards it, pausing briefly to survey the occupants of the other chairs before sitting down. Betshar and Ashvilak took up positions a couple of metres behind her. Close enough to come to her aid, should the need arise, but far enough away to prevent them from trying anything surreptitious against her.

Sallakray discreetly wriggled, trying to get comfortable, as she knew these proceedings would continue for several hours. She had once been offered a cushion in deference to her age. She had fiercely declined, refusing to allow even the slightest weakness to show. Observing the formalities, she brought the meeting to order. Today, the main business was to discuss the strategy and planning of the upcoming battle.

# Chapter 28

SATURDAY, 19TH JUNE

It was 6:30 am, and Gary was bored, even though he had only been there for half an hour. It was always the same. He had sat in his makeshift hide in Nine Stone Wood every day for the past three weeks. Except for a couple of trips a day to the nearby cafe for a takeaway coffee and a sandwich, he had sat looking despondently at the group of nine standing stones, desperately wishing for something to happen to break the boredom.

Over the past three weeks, all that had happened was a Japanese family of tourists had visited the place for about ten minutes, and a young couple had decided that the clearing within the standing stones, only a few metres from the busy A35 main road, was an ideal location for some energetic intimacy.

His one consolation was that he had the day shift, 6 am to 6 pm, and the summer this year was warm and pleasant. The other guy, who kept watch with him, had the night shift.

It wasn't loyalty or a sense of duty that kept him rooted in his task. It was fear, plain and simple fear. The abject terror at what would befall him if he failed kept him focused. He had even quit his job to make sure he was here every day. He thought back to a few weeks ago when his life had seemed so exciting.

He was a member of the British Anarchy Rules Front, a small group whose sole aim was to promote chaos and anarchy. He had only joined the previous year, but his enthusiasm had seen his rapid advancement through the group's hierarchy. They had big ideas and devised several cunning plans to disrupt society but never acted on them. That particular day, Gary attended a meeting where the leaders discussed stepping up their actions to a more destructive level.

Suddenly, *he* appeared. Literally appeared, from out of thin air, right in their midst. Silence befell the meeting as they stared, open-mouthed, at the newcomer. There was no mistaking who he was.

“You obey me now,” he said, his cold, clipped tones reinforcing the disdain in his eyes.

Mark, their leader, took a few steps towards the Dökkálfar, bolstering his bravado with action.

“We don’t obey anyone, not the government, not the establishment and not you,” he said. He finished his sentence by telling the Dökkálfar he could go do something to himself that was anatomically impossible, even for a dexterous elf.

The Dökkálfar raised his index finger until the tip rested lightly against Mark’s forehead. He spoke a single word. Green light pulsed along the Dökkálfar’s slender finger, and Marks’ forehead glowed the same sickly colour. He let out one short, terrifying scream and fell to the floor. His dead eyes were open wide, betraying the pain and horror of his demise.

“Does anyone else have anything to say?” the Dökkálfar asked coldly.

A few of the group shook their heads. Others kept their eyes downcast. No one uttered a word.

“As I said, you work for me now. If you disobey, I will kill you. If you fail me, I will kill you. If you try to run away, I will find you and kill you very slowly and painfully. Is that understood?”

A few mumbled agreement, and heads nodded. Everyone’s eyes betrayed the fear and shock they felt at the sudden turn of events.

“However, if you serve me well, you will be allowed to live. I will return in exactly three days to give you your orders. Make sure you are all here, without fail.” His tone left no doubt that he expected their obedience.

Pointing to the man standing next to Gary, the Dökkálfar said, “You are responsible for ensuring everyone is here.” The man blanched, and Gary was grateful he wasn’t the one chosen.

He uttered a short, unintelligible phrase and then he was gone, vanishing as suddenly as he had appeared. They all looked at one another and at Mark’s dead body.

The realisation was dawning on Gary that his life had changed for the worst.

Three days later, they were all there waiting. The Dökkálfar returned, and Gary was given the task of watching the *Nine Stones*, a small prehistoric circle of nine standing stones. They were situated a little way outside of Winterbourne Abbas, a small village near Dorchester in West Dorset. He wasn't explicitly told what he was looking for, only to report anything strange or unusual.

Gary started suddenly, his mind rushing back to the present. He blinked and rubbed his eyes, unsure what he was seeing. A faint shimmering bathed the stones in a soft blue glow, coalescing brightly in the centre, within which a golden-haired young woman suddenly appeared.

As the light faded, the woman, dressed in brown, adjusted the bag on her back, hefted a bow and several quivers of arrows onto her shoulder and adjusted a short scabbarded sword on her belt.

She dropped another bag she held and then stood still for a few moments, appearing to speak to herself and her hands made weird gestures. She closed her eyes and turned in a complete circle. When facing the northeast, she stopped, opened her eyes, retrieved the small bag from the ground, and headed off in that direction.

Gary recovered from his initial surprise and pulled out his mobile phone. He only just had the presence of mind to photograph the mysterious person, albeit from behind. He looked at the screen of his phone. No signal. He swore under his breath and clambered from his hide in the tree. With a last glance at the stranger walking away in the opposite direction, he made his way up the hillside in search of a phone signal.

* * *

Rachel was awake early. The baby had been restless, almost as if she empathised with her fears of Camron's departure. She had been the first one up and gazed aimlessly out of the kitchen window while waiting for the kettle to boil.

The garden was in the poorest condition Rachel could remember since they had bought the cottage. She was usually an avid gardener, and there should be an abundance of flowers at this time of year. But with Camron's disappearance and her pregnancy, Rachel had barely spent any time in the garden. She felt guilty but consoled herself that even if Camron hadn't disappeared to Alfheim, he would probably have tried to stop her from doing too much gardening for the sake of the baby anyway.

A faint smile touched her lips as she imagined the state of her beloved garden if it had been left entirely to Camron to look after. *It would probably look even worse than it does now,* she thought to herself. The kettle started whistling, and she busied herself making tea and a pot of coffee.

Suddenly Flint came padding into the kitchen and stood by the back door, tail wagging excitedly. He barked once, but it was a friendly bark and not a warning.

"What's the matter? Do you need to go into the garden for a wee?"

She opened the back door, and Flint bounded out.

She watched him go and saw, to her astonishment, Flint tearing towards a young woman walking across the garden towards the cottage.

*Who is that?* Rachel thought worriedly. Flint was always wary of strangers who came to the cottage, especially since his training in Alfheim.

The woman was short, only a metre and a half tall, very slender with long, unbound golden hair. She was dressed in a close-fitting tunic and trousers, seemingly made from soft brown leather. Seeing Rachel looking at her from the kitchen door, her face lit up with a breath-taking smile.

Rachel gasped and realised she had the same ethereal beauty as Geledhil.

The stranger had a leather backpack on her back and had slung a shortbow, plus four quivers crammed with arrows, over one shoulder. A slender sword hung from the belt at her waist, and she carried another, smaller backpack in one hand. Despite the apparent encumbrance of everything she carried, she walked with an easy manner, graceful and sure-footed.

Flint reached the young woman, who clearly knew him, and she knelt beside the dog, throwing her arms around him in a welcoming hug.

Rachel called up the stairs to Camron before she stepped into the garden, wrapping her dressing gown tightly around her, still slightly wary.

The elf approached Rachel.

"Hello," she said in a lilting musical voice, reminding Rachel of how Geledhil spoke. "You must be Rachel." Her English was spoken with hesitancy as if she wasn't altogether confident with the language.

Before Rachel could utter a reply, a delighted scream came from inside the kitchen, and Geledhil dashed past.

"Xankira!" She threw her arms around the newcomer in a welcoming embrace.

Watching the two beautiful elves in the middle of her garden while standing there in her old but comfortable dressing gown, a pair of Camron's pyjamas and fluffy purple slippers, made Rachel feel very drab and ordinary.

*Why couldn't Camron be a part dwarf?* Rachel thought ungraciously. *I bet dwarven women are ugly, with beards and broad noses.*

She chided herself for being churlish but still felt plain by comparison.

"What are you doing here?" Geledhil asked Xankira in elvish.

"Queen Nimue sent me with the things you need for your journey," she replied, adding in a hushed tone, "It's all so strange here. How do they live like this?"

"I know," Geledhil replied. "But you get used to it. Some of it is okay, but most of it is strange, and some things are horrible. They cut down most of the forests. I nearly wept when I realised."

Xankira looked horror-struck.

"But there is good here as well," Geledhil said. "When do you go back? Can you stay until we have to leave?"

"The Queen wants me to stay with Camron's wife while you are away."

Geledhil squealed in delight and grasped her hand, leading her over to Rachel, a huge smile beaming across her face.

"Rachel, this is my friend Xankira," she said, switching back to English.

"Hi," said Rachel, still wondering what was going on.

"Hello," replied Xankira, also smiling.

"Won't you come in? Would you like some tea?"

"Tea? I'm sorry, I don't know what that is. I've only been learning English for a little while."

"Tea is what they drink here, except when they drink coffee," Geledhil said to Xankira. "It's made from some sort of leaf. A bit like elderflower or camomile, I think. Tea is ok, as long as you don't add milk, but I wouldn't try the coffee. It's really bitter."

The three of them made their way into the kitchen, Geledhil helping Xankira carry everything. Flint trotted happily alongside.

"He seems to like you. You've met him before, I assume?" Rachel asked Xankira.

"Yes, we looked after Flint when he first came to Alfheim while Camron was still recovering. We only have wolves in Alfheim, and they aren't always friendly. It was wonderful looking after him. He was such fun and always so playful."

Camron finally appeared, having spent the past couple of hours deep in concentration learning the spells he thought necessary for their journey.

"We have a visitor," Rachel said to him, "I did call you."

"Well, if it's Smith, you can tell him to make his own breakfast."

"It isn't Smith," she replied.

"Xankira," exclaimed Camron in surprise, walking into the kitchen. "What are you doing here?" he asked in elvish.

"In English, please?" she said. "I need to practice."

"Okay," said Camron in English. "But why are you here?"

"Queen Nimue promised you some things for your journey. She sent me to deliver them," she said, placing the backpack and bag on the kitchen table. "She also wants me to stay here with Rachel while you journey to the dwarves. To help out if I'm needed."

Camron glanced towards the sword, shortbow and quivers full of arrows propped by the still open back door.

He nodded. "Well, I think that's a magnificent idea. Would you be happy with that?" he asked Rachel, torn between underplaying the danger she might be in and his relief at having additional protection for her.

"I'm not sure..." Rachel trailed off hesitantly.

"Xankira is my life friend. We're more than friends. We're like sisters," said Geledhil. "I know you don't know her, but she is a wonderful person. You'll become good friends in no time."

Camron added, "Please, Rachel. I don't have any choice but to find the dwarves. You and the baby are safe because the Dökkálfar doesn't know about you. But they found you by chance once, and there's no guarantee they won't find you again. Xankira can protect you if necessary. She can fight, and she is also a pretty good witch."

Rachel looked from Camron to Xankira. Camron's face was full of genuine concern and showed the apparent anguish over having to leave her again.

"Okay," she said finally, looking over at Xankira. "I could do with some help around the house anyway." She smiled. "So, who would like some breakfast?"

"Bacon and eggs, please?" piped up Camron eagerly, relieved she had acquiesced.

"You can have Eggs Florentine," replied Rachel. "I'm not stinking out the kitchen with the smell of bacon."

Camron knew Rachel loved bacon almost as much as he did but realised she had said this in deference to their elven guests' vegetarianism.

"Sounds great," he said with determined enthusiasm as Rachel busied herself preparing breakfast.

"So, how did you get here?" Camron asked Xankira.

"I used this," she replied, lifting up the necklace Geledhil wore. Camron noticed Xankira wore an identical one. "I came through the *Nine Sisters* portal near Dorchester, then cast a *locate object* spell on the necklace I gave Geledhil last year. It didn't take long to walk here."

"*The Nine Sisters*?" Camron asked inquisitively. "Oh, you mean *The Nine Stones?* At Winterbourne Abbas? I didn't realise there was a portal there?"

"Yes, but it's only a minor one and has only just regained its power."

"So, what did grandmother send us?" Geledhil asked Xankira.

"There's a shortbow and two full quivers of arrows," Xankira said, nodding towards the back door. "Tanidaer thought it would be of more use in tunnels than your longbow."

"And this," she said, handing Geledhil the smaller of the two backpacks. "Findecámo scribed a travel spellbook for you too. He thinks you should be able to handle the spells in it."

Camron thought he detected a trace of superiority in her tone as she spoke to Geledhil. Geledhil, seemingly oblivious to it, pulled out a small leather book from the backpack and flicked through a few pages, her face a mask of concentration.

Turning to Camron, Xankira said, "Queen Nimue has sent these for you." She started pulling some items out of the larger backpack.

She pointed to six small glass vials, each carefully wrapped in cloth, which she had placed on the table. "Those are healing potions. Hopefully, you won't need them, but they will cure most wounds and counteract many poisons."

Picking up a large package, she handed it to Camron, who looked questioningly at it.

"Koymasse," Xankira explained.

"Koymasse?" asked Rachel, looking over and apparently listening to everything despite being engrossed with cooking.

"Elven waybread. Tastes quite dull, but it's great for travelling. Just a mouthful or two will keep you going all day," Xankira replied.

"Yummy," said Geledhil without enthusiasm. "Grandmother knows how much I dislike Koymasse. I bet she was smiling when she gave it to you."

Next, Xankira opened a small leather pouch and took out six metal cones.

"What are those?" enquired Geledhil.

"Lights," Xankira replied, holding one in her hand and gently lifting up a cleverly hinged cover.

Immediately, a beam of bright light shone from inside the cone.

"Each one has a small crystal inside with a *continual light* spell cast on it," Xankira explained. "There are two shutters at the bottom, one metal to block the light completely and a leather one with small holes in it to give you a dim light if you need it."

"Brilliant," exclaimed Camron, clearly impressed. "I was wondering how we were going to see in the dark."

"And lastly, these two," said Xankira, handing Camron two bound rolls of parchment.

"The thicker one is the spells Findecámo said you would need. And the other is a *Finders Map*."

"What's a *Finders Map?"* enquired Camron, unrolling the parchment and examining the rough map drawn upon it, dismayed by the scarcity of detail.

"Findecámo says it starts off as an ordinary map, but as you travel along its path, it will fill in more details and correct any errors until you end up with an exact map of the route you have travelled. Findecámo told me to tell you not to lose it. He was most insistent he gets the map back at the end of your journey with a complete record of your travels."

Still looking at the map, Camron muttered, “What would have been useful would be an accurate map with details on it *before* we start out.”

Everyone ignored him.

They divided the Koymasse and healing potions between Geledhil’s backpack and Camron’s *bag of holding* and then sat down to breakfast.

They were just finishing when Flint barked and headed towards the front door. A few moments later, the doorbell rang, and Camron opened it. Smith stood on the doorstep, looking very un-Smith-like. Gone was the government-issue grey suit and sunglasses, replaced by Kevlar body armour over a black Nomex flight suit.

Camron grinned. “Suit at the dry cleaners?”

Smith smiled back.

“Where’s David?” Camron asked, peering past Smith.

“He’ll join us at Dunsinane.”

Camron nodded and led Smith to the kitchen.

“The cavalry’s arrived,” Camron announced.

“Is everyone ready?” Smith asked, but his eyes alighted on Xankira and noting her elven features, he looked enquiringly at Camron.

“I think so. Smith, this is Xankira. Xankira, meet Smith. She’s Ljósálfar and a friend of Geledhil. She’s going to look after Rachel while we’re away.”

Smith noted the weapons propped by the back door and nodded approvingly. Looking at Rachel, he asked, “Are you coming up to Dunsinane to see us off?”

“No,” she replied, brushing a tear from her eye. “I don’t like goodbyes. We’re going to stay here.”

Smith moved a little closer.

“Look,” he said, “I know it sounds a bit *cloak-and-dagger,* but if any of my people need to get in touch with you, I thought it prudent to have a code word so you can verify they’re genuine. I’m sure you won’t need it, but just in case, they will say they are calling from *Lancelot House.* I thought that name would be memorable, considering... Anyway, hopefully not needed, but better safe than sorry.”

He turned to the others, "Okay, we'd better get moving. If there's any kit to take, I'll put it in the Range Rover."

Camron turned to Xankira and handed her one of his old Nike baseball caps, "You'll probably need this. Only a handful of humans have ever seen an elf. Covering your ears will help you blend in a little easier."

"Thank you," she said, giving him a hug. "Look after my friend and bring her back safely, please?" she whispered before unclasping him.

Camron smiled at her and nodded imperceptibly.

Geledhil embraced Rachel. "I know we haven't known each other long, but you're family, so make sure you look after yourself and the baby."

"I will," replied Rachel. "And please take care of him for me? Bring him back safe," she added, trying her best to stifle a sob.

Geledhil hugged Rachel and then knelt to hug Flint, burying her face in his long white fur. Disentangling herself from the dog, she said to Xankira, "Come on, you can help me with my gear," tactfully leaving Camron and Rachel alone.

He folded his arms around her, and she buried her face in his shoulder, clinging to him. Her tears so determinedly fought back rose within her, and she sobbed quietly.

"I don't want you to go."

"I know," he replied. "I wish I didn't have to, but there isn't anyone else. This is what I signed up for all those centuries ago."

Rachel knew this, but it didn't make it any easier.

"I'm scared," she admitted in an unusually timid voice. "The world has gone wrong. What if they find me again?"

"They won't," he said reassuringly. "You have the *family ring* now. It will protect you, and let me know if anything threatens you. Plus, you have Flint and Xankira to look after you. It'll be okay."

She stepped back from his embrace and looked fiercely into his eyes. "Promise?"

"I promise," he said sincerely.

“Well, you make damn sure you’re okay and come back to me and in one piece. Do you understand? I need you back. We need you back,” she said, placing one hand on her pregnant belly.

“I will come back to both of my beautiful girls,” he said seriously.

They kissed a long, loving kiss that neither wanted to end.

Eventually, they broke apart. Camron turned to kneel beside Flint.

“You look after my girls for me, Flint. I’m relying on you, boy.”

Flint looked at Camron with bright brown eyes that attested to his intelligence and gave a single bark as if accepting the solemn task laid upon him.

Camron stood up, patting Flint. He swung the *bag of lightness,* containing the Stone of Destiny, over one shoulder and the *bag of holding* over the other.

He kissed Rachel tenderly one last time. “I love you.”

“I love you too,” she replied, her midnight blue eyes shining with tears.

He turned away and walked down the hallway to the front door. Turning back one last time, he looked at Rachel, still stood in the kitchen doorway with Flint beside her and said, “See you soon.”

Camron left the cottage and walked slowly to the Range Rover, the sadness evident on his face at their parting.

Geledhil and Xankira exchanged one last embrace before Xankira headed back into the cottage.

“I will look after your wife, Camron. You have my word,” she said, passing Camron.

Camron and Geledhil climbed into the back seat. They drove for about ten minutes, arriving at a field outside Dorchester where a military helicopter awaited them. The three of them clambered aboard with their weapons and kit. Camron noted Smith was putting a heavy black nylon holdall onto the floor. The barrels of three rifles protruded from the partially unzipped bag.

“Got enough guns?” he asked Smith.

“Boy Scout motto, *‘be prepared.’* I didn’t know if you or Geledhil would want a gun, so I brought some spares,” he said.

“No,” replied Camron, patting the two swords laid across his lap. “I’ll stick with what I know best. But thanks anyway.”

The helicopter took off and headed north.

Geledhil pulled out her travelling spellbook and concentrated on committing several spells to memory.

“How long will the flight take?” Camron asked Smith over the noise of the engines.

“A couple of hours,” he replied.

Camron nodded and opened his *bag of holding*. He pulled out his spellbook and the scroll of spells Findecámo had sent him.

Carefully, he began to scribe the spells from the scroll into his spellbook. He could cast the spells directly from the scroll if he wanted to, but that meant they could only be used once. The act of casting a spell directly from a scroll would obliterate it, just as memorised spells disappeared from his memory once cast. Scribing the spell into his magical spellbook allowed him to repeatedly memorise the spells. His concentration was absolute, and as he completed copying each rune, it disappeared from the scroll. One tiny mistake scribing even a single rune would render the entire spell useless. Smith sat back, watching as his two companions were immersed in what he called *wizard stuff.*

# Chapter 29

SATURDAY, 19TH JUNE

Two hours later, the pilot informed them they were on the final approach to Dunsinane Hill, halfway between the Scottish cities of Perth and Dundee. Looking out of the window, Camron wished he had a pair of Smiths' sunglasses as the sun shone brightly in the clear blue sky. The countryside was a rippling patchwork of fields and rugged heathland.

They were flying over the tiny village of Collace. Ahead, a craggy steep-sided hill, part-covered in purple heather, rose three hundred metres above the surrounding countryside. A small quarry was on one side, and a large part of the western slope had been quarried and now dropped almost vertically to the quarry floor.

They headed for a field just to the north and touched down next to another helicopter, retrieving their gear before following a path towards the hill.

At the base of the hill, between Dunsinane Hill and Black Hill to the west, were several diggers, a couple of heavy-duty surface drill rigs, and some other heavy plant equipment that Camron couldn't identify. Some people wearing hi-visibility jackets and hard hats waited near the machinery. Many uniformed police officers were also present, two of whom moved to intercept them as they approached.

"Hello, I'm Chief Inspector Dickinson," one officer introduced herself, directing her words at Smith. "I assume you're the person the Home Office told me about?"

Smith nodded.

She continued, still addressing Smith, "Well, I've been tasked with keeping the public away and providing you with whatever assistance you may need. So, if there's anything you need, just ask."

"Thanks," Smith answered. "Hopefully, this won't take long, but we'd rather avoid any media interest if we can."

"Of course. Your associates are over there, by the small copse to the south-west. Just follow the base of the hill round," said Chief Inspector Dickinson as she turned to rejoin her fellow officers.

They continued as directed, following the gap between Dunsunane Hill on their right and Black Hill to their left. After just a couple of minutes, Geledhil unexpectedly let out a squeal of delight and rushed towards a group of men. All five were attired similarly to Smith, with black flight suits and body armour.

*Our SAS contingent* thought Camron, surprised by Geledhil's reaction. Suddenly he stopped and stared in astonishment. He recognised one of the five as David, and his jaw dropped. Geledhil reached the group and threw her arms around David, hugging him enthusiastically.

"Hey," said one of the soldiers, who had bright ginger hair. "You never said you had such a gorgeous girlfriend."

"Yeah, isn't she a bit young for you?" called one of the others light-heartedly.

"Girlfriend?" asked Geledhil. "What is a girlfriend?"

Camron arrived in time to provide a helpful explanation. "It is part of the human ritual of finding a life partner. In the early stages, the couple is referred to as boyfriend and girlfriend."

Geledhil looked shocked, releasing David from her embrace. Elven society had much greater respect for couples forming life partnerships than humans. There was no such thing as divorce for elves.

"He is not my partner," she said vehemently.

"So are you going to introduce us then, Prof?" asked the still grinning ginger-haired soldier.

"Prof?" enquired Smith.

David shrugged. "It's the nickname they've christened me with."

"Yeah, that's right, Seven," said another of the Special Forces guys to Smith. "We've never had a professor in our midst before."

"Seven?" asked Camron. This time, it was his turn to look questioningly.

"Seven, you know 007, James Bond. Ever since spy-boy here," nodding towards Smith, "left the Regiment to join MI5, he's been officially named Seven."

Camron smiled and was about to say something when Smith gave him a look and said, "Don't!"

The four soldiers laughed.

"Anyway," said Smith, keen to change the subject, "this is Sergeant Craig Harper, the Troop Leader."

A large, burly man stepped forward and shook hands with them, his grip firm. He was in his early thirties and carried himself confidently. Bright, alert eyes assessed Camron as they shook hands. His dark ebony-skinned hand enveloped Camron's in a firm, almost testing grip.

The next soldier introduced to them was Trooper Mark Tregainne. He was nearly two metres tall, broad-shouldered and heavily muscled. He held out a hand, the smile reaching his brown eyes, the colour almost perfectly matching his short-cropped hair. At only twenty-four, he was already an expert marksman. Arguably the best in B Squadron and an excellent weapons specialist. That, combined with his surname, had almost mandated the nickname '*Trigger.*'

The ginger-haired man was introduced next. Corporal Pete Hamilton was a short, wiry Scot in his late twenties. Raised on a Glaswegian housing estate, he was as tough as they come. He had passed Selection at the same time as Craig. They were close friends and had been through a lot together over the intervening years in the SAS.

Last was Trooper Brian Grant. He was tall, lean, extremely fit, and the newest member of the patrol, having passed Selection just eighteen months earlier. He was a black belt in several martial arts disciplines, earning himself the nickname Bruce after the famous martial arts legend Bruce Lee.

"They're all members of Red Troop, a good bunch of lads to have if it should come to a fight," said Smith.

"We may as well get this over with. How much do they know?" Camron asked Smith.

"Some of it," he replied. "But not the, you know, complicated stuff."

"Well, if they're going to be coming along with us, they'll need to know the rest before too long, so it may as well be now."

Camron took a deep breath as he prepared to introduce himself and the others to the SAS troopers. It seemed that just recently, all he did was tell his story again and again.

Before Camron could be bombarded with questions, they were interrupted by two men, both similarly attired in dark grey suits, although work boots, hi-viz jackets and hard construction hats completed their attire.

"Friends of yours?" Camron asked Smith.

"Acquaintances," he replied. "From the Home Office. They're here to make sure things are organised and go smoothly." Smith went to greet them.

"So," said David gazing up towards the top of the hill, "where's the entrance?"

"Not entirely sure," answered Camron, who had already studied the *Finders Map*, which indicated the entrance was on the rocky south-eastern side but not precisely where.

"Can't you, you know..." asked David, wiggling his fingers in a poor imitation of magical invocation.

"Not sure, worth a try, but Dwarves are inherently resistant to magic, and they went to great lengths to protect themselves from spells."

Camron closed his eyes and began to cast a *Detect Magic* spell. As he had expected, it revealed nothing.

A chuckle behind them made both Camron and David turn round. Smith stood there smiling.

"Well, if all else fails," he said, grinning, "we could always resort to good old fashioned technology." He pointed to where several people were pushing what looked like a bright yellow lawn mover up to the top of the hill.

"Ground Penetrating Radar," he said in answer to Camron's questioning look. "It will allow us to map the underground features and look for subterranean caverns and such."

After just a couple of hours, they had pinpointed a narrow cavern nearly twenty metres behind the south-eastern rockface. The heavy machinery moved in, and the crew set to work.

"Right," said Craig, "equipment check-in five," and he turned to inspect his own kit one more time.

Smith and the SAS soldiers each had a twenty-five kilo Bergen backpack with a large coil of climbing rope strapped to the top and a nine-kilo belt kit called webbing. This contained ammunition, water, food, trauma-care equipment and an emergency survival kit. Their weaponry consisted of a Heckler & Koch G36k carbine short-barrel assault rifle plus two SIG Sauer 229 handguns, one strapped to each leg.

"Who's got the extra batteries?" Craig called out.

"I do," replied Bruce. "You can have them if you want? They're bloody heavy!"

"What do you need all the batteries for?" asked Camron curiously.

"Our helmet torches. It will be pitch-black down there."

"I think I can help you out there," said Camron, remembering the magical lights Nimue had provided for them.

"Can I borrow your helmet, please?" Camron asked Bruce.

"Sure," he said but kept a very close watch on what Camron was doing with his kit.

Camron removed the head torch attached to the helmet and pulled out one of the triangular *continual light* cones. Etched along the edge was a single magical rune. Placing the cone on the top of the helmet firmly, Camron recited the rune, and the cone glowed briefly.

"There you go," said Camron, throwing the helmet back to Bruce, who caught it deftly.

The light cone hadn't fallen off the helmet.

"It won't budge," said Camron as Bruce tried to twist it off. "Open the little catch and lift up the base."

Bruce did as Camron asked and was startled when a bright light shone from inside the cone.

"There's a second cover with little holes that acts as a filter and reduces the brightness if you need it," Camron said.

"How long does it last?" Trigger asked, intrigued. He had been watching what Camron was doing.

"Indefinitely," Camron replied.

"Got any more?" asked Pete eagerly.

Soon they had replaced their standard head torches with magical ones, and a considerable pile of now unnecessary spare batteries lay on the ground.

After that, there wasn't much to do except wait for the digging crew to do their stuff. The city of Dundee was only a few miles away, and Smith arranged for a delivery of pizzas for them all.

They sat by their gear, munching pizzas and chatting amiably. David announced to the group in general, "You know, the original spelling of this hill is Dunsinnan. It's Gaelic and means *'the hill of ants.'* Probably referring to the large number of people it would have taken to build the fortress at the summit."

"Actually," Camron interrupted, "the literal translation means *'the hill of the little folk'* and refers to the fact this was once one of the main entrances to the realm of the dwarves. The village of Collace used to be much larger and prospered through trade with the Dwarves."

"But this was the site where Malcolm Canmore defeated Macbeth in the 11th Century?" countered David.

"Dunno, that's more your area of expertise than mine. It wasn't one of the battles I fought in," answered Camron.

The digging crew seemed to be making real progress, and the tunnel into the hillside deepened with each hour that passed. Sometime later, Camron and David sat alone by the pile of gear, David on his Bergen and Camron perched on the *bag of lightness* with the Stone of Destiny inside. David was stripping and cleaning his H&K rifle with something approaching familiar ease while Camron was sharpening his second sword with a whetstone. Being magical, Excalibur never needed sharpening.

"You look like you've taken to military life quite well," said Camron. "How was Hereford?"

"Tough," said David. "To be honest, I didn't think I'd be able to handle it, but the training beforehand in Alfheim helped. I think I've learnt to look after myself a bit better and hopefully be of some help, but it wasn't easy. The lads helped, though. They're a good team to have with us. Mind you, I'm knackered now. I'm looking forward to a little stroll through the dark just to get some rest."

Camron grinned.

"You do realise you need to be a king to sit on that, don't you?" said David, gesturing to the *bag of lightness* in which sat the Coronation Stone.

Camron smiled. "Well, I would have been king after my father if I hadn't volunteered for all this, so I guess I can get away with it on a technicality."

"Do you ever think about how different your life would have been if you hadn't volunteered?"

"No, not really. I imagine I would have become king and be long dead by now, which would have left everyone in a mess, wouldn't it?"

David nodded but was quiet for a while, lost in his own thoughts.

"You know," he said suddenly, "I've been doing a bit of reading up on the Stone of Destiny."

"And?" asked Camron.

"Well, there's a theory that what you're sitting on isn't the genuine stone. In 1296, after King Edward I defeated the Scottish King, John Balliol, he wanted to remove any chance of someone else making claims to the Scottish throne. He seized the Scottish regalia and much of Scotland's historical records, and he took the Stone of Destiny from the abbey at Scone."

David paused. "Stupid thing," he muttered, struggling to replace the pins in the trigger group of his MP5. Using the hilt of his dagger, he gave the pin a hefty whack, and it slid into place.

Satisfied, he continued, "However, some say the monks at the abbey weren't too happy with this. When King Edward's troops arrived, they presented them with a replica, a piece of local sandstone. None of the English had seen the real stone, so they didn't know any different. The interesting bit is this. The legend states the genuine Stone of Scone was hidden right here on Dunsinane Hill. It is quite a coincidence, don't you think? We have to take the stone to the dwarves, and the entrance to the dwarven realm is where some say the real stone was hidden."

Camron looked at him, concern etched across his features.

David continued, "Sorry, I just thought you ought to know. We need to be sure we have the right stone, don't we? I didn't want to get all the way to the dwarves and have another one of those *communication moments!*"

Camron sat, still looking at David, his mind reeling with even more doubts. *Did they even have the right stone?*

Camron thought for several long moments, his mind returning to the Crown Room in Edinburgh Castle.

"No, I'm sure we have the right stone," he said eventually. "I definitely felt the presence of Clarent when I tried to call the sword from the stone."

"Well, that's alright then," said David.

They both fell into silence, neither entirely convinced but unwilling to voice their concerns further.

As boredom threatened, early in the afternoon, the supervisor from the digging crew approached, his face looking worried.

"We've got a problem," he said. "We've hit a seam of granite that's tougher than any stone I've ever encountered. We've broken the drill rigs trying to punch through."

"Show me?" asked Camron

The team had dug over a dozen metres into the rocky hillside. As the foreman had said, Camron saw a flat granite seam forming a solid wall at the end of the short tunnel. It wasn't completely smooth, but there were no jagged edges or protrusions either. Instead, the granite rock face seemed slightly rippled and undulating with numerous smooth flowing bumps and indentations. The surface was patterned. Shadows and shades of greys and blacks merged in subtly blending gradients.

"I think this might be it," said Camron excitedly.

Smith turned to the supervisor. "Maybe you should withdraw your team to a safe distance?"

The foreman left to round up his men. Camron and Geledhil moved forward to examine the rock surface.

After a few minutes, he turned to them despondently.

"Well, if there is an entrance here, I can't bloody find it."

"What about explosives?" asked Smith.

"I don't think they would work. I imagine the dwarves would have had some sort of magical protection."

"Well, why don't we detect for magic again?" asked Geledhil.

"It didn't work earlier, but I can't think of anything else to try," said Camron. "Have you memorised the spell? I'd only memorised it once."

Geledhil nodded and started the incantation for the *Detect Magic* spell.

Suddenly, writing appeared towards the top of the wall, chiselled into the rock. The words were still legible, as clear and precise as the day an unknown dwarf had carved them.

"That's Dwarvish," exclaimed Geledhil. "It says '*seek not the masters of stone lest you incur the wrath of stone itself*'."

"That must be the dwarven way of saying *sod off,*" said Pete.

"Well, it definitely looks like this is the entrance," said Camron and moved forward to examine the wall again.

Geledhil joined him. After many minutes of meticulous searching, Geledhil's sharp elven eyes noticed something ever so slightly strange with one of the rippling patterns running across the surface of the granite. Carefully, running her fingers across the stone, she discovered a small hole in the granite, about a metre up from the ground. Excitedly, she showed the others.

"It's a keyhole," said Camron in wonder, amazed at both the simplicity and brilliance of the natural camouflage that had hidden it from their first inspection.

He mused, "It couldn't be that easy, but maybe a simple *Unlock Door* spell could be used to open the entrance. It can't hurt to try."

Raising his hands, he commenced the complex series of gestures that accompanied the words of the spell, directing it towards the keyhole.

Nothing happened.

Well, nothing happened to the granite rock face inside the tunnel. But outside, they heard a loud crack. An ominous noise sounded like a piece of rock breaking off a cliff face. They hurried out and saw, just to the right, a massive granite boulder had broken away from the craggy face of the hill and was coming to a halt on the grassy slope below.

Astonishingly, although the rock stopped rolling, it didn't stop moving. The boulder unfurled itself, revealing a smaller stone on top of the larger one, looking like a snowman's head placed without much care atop its round bulbous body. Then, two long tubular pieces of rock swung out from either side, looking like a pair of arms. When it slowly rose up on what could only be described as legs, the dumbfounded spectators realised that what looked like arms and a head were, in fact, arms and a head.

The rock creature ponderously stood up. It was enormous, over six metres tall. Atop its body, the large rough-hewn head was featureless. As they all gaped dumbfounded, two jet black holes appeared on its flattened face, exactly where its eyes should be. A dull orange glow, starting as a pinprick in the centre of each eye, rapidly expanded until its eyes were shining brightly, the warm orange turning to a harsh fiery red. A thin crack opened beneath the eyes, revealing a handful of black obsidian teeth that were unevenly spaced.

“Fucking hell!” exclaimed Trigger.

“Is that an Earth Elemental?” Geledhil asked nervously.

Camron nodded, eyes wide in fear.

Geledhil swore more colourfully in Elvish.

The ground shook as the monstrous creature took its first lumbering step, the glowing red eyes fixed on the small group before the rock doorway.

“Come on,” yelled Craig. The other soldiers were already sprinting towards their pile of equipment and weapons.

Camron tore his eyes from the elemental and followed.

# Chapter 30

SATURDAY, 19TH JUNE

The soldiers clipped on their webbing and hoisted their weapons as Camron arrived. He strapped on his swords and grabbed Merlin's staff.

"Look out!" yelled Geledhil, and Camron saw her throw herself at David, knocking him over despite the difference in size.

A piece of rock, the size of a wheelbarrow, thudded into the ground right where David had stood.

"Thanks," stuttered David to Geledhil, who had landed on top of him.

"No time for that, prof," said Pete grinning as he passed the prone pair.

Geledhil jumped lithely to her feet and began to string her bow. David clambered less gracefully to his, his face flushed. Camron wasn't entirely sure it was due to the shock of nearly being pulverised.

Fifty metres away, the Earth Elemental ponderously stepped over the hole from which it had pulled the thrown rock.

"Ok, let's put down some fire and see if we can hurt this oversized statue," said Craig.

The SAS soldiers and Smith started firing. The noise was deafening. Geledhil clamped her hands to her ears, her eyes wide in shock.

David raised his own weapon, but nothing happened.

"Safety catch," bellowed Bruce. David sheepishly flicked the fire selector to semi-automatic fire. His bullets joined the others.

Despite the hail of gunfire, the creature continued to advance. The bullets hurt it, but not much. Each hit was like a pinprick, chipping off a tiny fragment of rock. It was going to take an entire battalion to kill it with guns.

Geledhil seemed to have recovered from the shock of the staccato cracks of gunfire and raised her bow.

Camron put his hand on her arm. "Don't waste your arrows. They won't make any difference."

Dropping her bow, Geledhil began to chant, her fingers following the precise movements required for the spell she was casting. As she uttered the final words of the incantation, the ground under the elemental's feet turned white. A sheet of ice, several centimetres thick, had magically appeared.

The creature's right foot slipped to one side, threatening to topple over for one moment.

But it didn't. Regaining its' balance, it brought one colossal foot crashing down onto the ice, shattering it.

"This isn't working," called Smith over the sound of gunfire.

Camron stood, rooted to the spot. Not in fear but in doubt. He didn't know what to do. What if the Earth Elemental killed those around him. It would be his fault.

As the elemental took another step towards them, Camron saw several police officers, including Chief Inspector Dickinson, come to a halt away to his right. Even at a distance, their shock was evident.

The creature noticed them too. They were closer to the granite door it protected, and it changed direction towards them.

"Run," bellowed Smith, gesticulating wildly. Like Camron, the police officers remained frozen in place. Shock and fear rendered them immobile.

Geledhil sprang forward, sword drawn. Smith, overcoming a moment's surprise, followed, as did David. All three yelled as they ran.

Camron watched, still anchored by uncertainty.

Geledhil reached their opponent first, darting between its massive legs, sword swiping as she passed. The metal scraped against rock but caused no damage. She swept past again, leaping aside to avoid a massive stone fist.

Smith and David knelt side-by-side, aiming for its head to avoid hitting Geledhil.

Camron, forcing himself, began to drag his feet forward.

Geledhil darted in again, sword tip thrusting at the creature's knee. The blade slid aside just as a rock fragment from a bullet hit her temple. Losing her balance, she fell.

"NOOOO..." cried David, springing up and firing wildly as he ran forward.

The creature turned ponderously towards the prone elf and raised an enormous foot. David dived, dropping his gun, pulling Geledhil just out of reach.

David's cry had penetrated Camron's torpor. His laborious plod became a sprint at his friends' peril.

David lay protectively over the unconscious Geledhil, his horror-struck gaze fixed on the arm that began to swing towards him.

Sunlight flashed off Excalibur as it sliced through stone, severing the crude rocky hand. The elemental, silent until now, let out a roar.

But the momentum of its swing hadn't halted, and the arm smashed into Davids' side, sending him hurtling away

"Take her, go!" commanded Camron, no trace of any indecision in his voice.

Smith lifted Geledhil effortlessly and hurried back to the others.

Camron saw Bruce and Trigger run towards David, but he had no time to check if he was ok. Ducking under another punch that would have crushed him, he swung at the elementals' leg. Excalibur bit deep into the stone, but the leg was much thicker than the arm, and the sword caught, stuck partway into the limb.

Pure instinct saved Camron. Diving to one side, he avoided a second bone-crushing blow by a mere hands-breadth. He scrambled away, coming to his feet a few metres distance.

Camron watched dumbfounded as the Earth Elemental, Excalibur firmly embedded in its' leg, reached down and picked up the severed hand. The eyes shone a brighter red as it placed the hand against the stump of its' arm. Magically, hand and arm were reunited.

"You ok?" asked Craig as Camron rejoined the others.

Camron nodded, breathing hard. "How's David?"

“Not good,” said Trigger. “Bruce is trying to patch him up now.”

“We need a way to put this thing down,” said Craig. He pulled the pin on a fragmentation grenade and lobbed it at the creature, yelling, “Frag out.”

Two more shouts followed quickly as Trigger and Pete also hurled grenades.

The first grenade exploded just by the elemental, quickly followed by the other two. Smoke obscured their view for a few seconds.

As the smoke cleared, they saw the creature bent over double. Cheering broke out but was quickly stifled as it straightened up, holding a massive rock.

“Tough little bastard, ain't it?” said Pete as the elemental raised the rock above its’ head, preparing to throw.

“Take cover!” yelled Camron.

“Where,” said Trigger, glancing around at the grass-covered hillside, broken only by occasional patches of purple heather. “I’ll just find a rabbit hole big enough for all of us, shall I?”

The elemental hurled the rock towards them at considerable speed. Watching its trajectory as it arced towards them, Craig and Pete just managed to dive aside in time.

“How do we kill it?” asked Smith, approaching from behind.

“Is Geledhil ok?” Camron asked anxiously.

“She’ll be fine. She’s come round now,” said Smith. “Now, how do we kill this bloody thing?”

“I don’t know,” Camron replied truthfully. The fears and doubts he thought he had dispelled were threatening to creep back.

“Is it solid rock, or does it have an inside?” asked Craig.

“Solid rock,” answered Camron, watching the creature. It appeared to have taken up a defensive position, standing a little distance protectively before the doorway.

An idea suddenly came to Camron.

"I need Geledhil," he said

"She's injured," said Smith, "I'm not sure she can't fight anymore."

"Yes, I can," said a determined voice behind them. Geledhil's beautiful silver hair was streaked with blood, and a field-dressing wrapped around her head. But her visage was grim and determined.

Camron looked at Geledhil. "Can you cast a *Fireball* spell?"

"Yes, but not a very powerful one."

"It will be if you use my staff. Merlin's staff amplifies the power of any spell cast through it." He handed her his staff.

"Will a *Fireball* spell stop it?" asked Geledhil

"Not on its own, no."

"So, what's the plan?" she asked.

"You heat it. I'll freeze it."

Geledhil nodded and furrowed her brow in concentration, focusing on recalling the exact words of the incantation. Camron listened carefully. He needed to time his own spell to happen just a few seconds after the *Fireball.*

As Geledhil uttered the final words, the *Fireball* flew from the tip of the staff, starting as a small glowing ball of fire but rapidly expanding as it approached its target. It hit the creature in the centre of its chest with an almighty whoosh, detonating with a loud bang. The fire engulfed the elemental and much of the immediate vicinity. The heat was intense, the magical fire making it hotter than a furnace. Even from their safe distance, they could feel the fiery heat singeing their skin slightly.

The creature staggered under the force of the explosion and roared once more but regained its balance and started moving again, its stony body glowing red.

Geledhil stood there, clearly shocked. She had never cast such a powerful spell.

A few seconds later, Camron finished his *Cone of Ice* spell. A narrow slither of ice shot from his outstretched hand, quickly expanding to form a wide solid cone of ice.

The ice struck just where the fireball had, instantly cooling the still glowing creature. Ice from the cone melted, shrouding it in steam.

Suddenly, they heard several sharp, loud cracks above the creatures' roars. The elemental emerged from the cloud of steam, bellowing anew but still moving. Several cracks had appeared across its chest, two of which looked long and deep.

"Shit," said Craig, "won't Stoneface just die!"

Camron's shoulders slumped. He just didn't know what to do.

"Do you think that quarry will have dynamite?" Trigger asked.

"Probably," answered Craig, "but we've already tried grenades."

"Only on the outside," replied Trigger with a grin.

Craig looked at the deep cracks in the elementals' chest.

"Well, what are you waiting for?" Craig bellowed at Trigger. "Get the bloody dynamite."

Trigger sprinted off in the direction of the Collace Quarry.

"Let's keep it busy," said Craig.

Smith and Pete moved forwards alongside Craig, and a steady stream of bullets pounded the elemental.

Camron and Geledhil ran to where Bruce still tended David. He lay on the ground, his chest wrapped in a blood-soaked bandage, his torso a mass of purple swelling.

"How is he?" asked Camron.

Bruce gave Camron a look he had seen on dozens of battlefields over the centuries. He knew what it meant.

Geledhil grasped his arm, "Can't you use Excalibur's scabbard? Like you did on Glastonbury Tor."

Camron shook his head sadly, "It only works for me."

"There must be something?" she insisted.

"I can try a *Healing* spell," said Camron, "it might at least take away the pain and make him more comfortable."

The *Healing* spell did ease David's breathing, and the swelling subsided just a little. But his injuries were just too much for a normal healing spell to mend.

Camron looked into David's battered and bruised face. Guilt and helplessness threatened to overwhelm him once more.

Suddenly, Geledhil swore in elvish and darted towards their pile of packs. Mere seconds later, she returned, carrying a small vial carefully wrapped in cloth. Unstoppering it carefully, she gently lifted David's head and poured the liquid into his mouth.

"You're a genius," said Camron, relief and gratitude beaming across his face. "I'm sorry, I should have thought of the *Healing Potions* myself."

Bruce gasped as a soft silvery glow emanated from David as his injuries magically began to heal.

A shout from behind interrupted them. Trigger had returned.

With a last look at David, Camron, Geledhil, and Bruce rejoined the others. Trigger was attaching the blasting caps and fuses to the dynamite.

"Who gets to stick this into Stoneface?" Pete asked.

"I will," said Bruce. "I'm the quickest."

"No, you're not. I am," interjected Geledhil. "I'm faster and nimbler, and we don't have time to argue."

Camron hesitated for a split second. He loathed having to allow his cousin to undertake an exceedingly dangerous task, especially considering her injury. But she was right. Elves were inordinately more fleet of foot and agile than any human.

"Geledhil does it," he said, but his eyes clearly showed concern.

Passing the dynamite to Geledhil, Trigger said, "You've got three minutes before it detonates."

She nodded, taking the explosive and ran swiftly in a wide arc, coming upon the earth elemental from behind. As she approached, she placed the dynamite between her teeth and, without breaking stride, leapt high upon the creature's back, gripping its shoulder with one hand. Her feet planted into what should be its waist.

It roared at this unexpected incursion and reached to swat her away. Geledhil ducked the clumsy attempt and swung around to the front. Her fingers sought purchase in one of the smaller cracks in its chest. For a second, she hung there, swinging freely, her feet scrambling for support. Her foot hit something. Glancing down, she saw Excalibur still stuck in its leg.

Then, through the soft, supple leather of her boot, she felt a tiny indentation in the creature's thigh and wedged the tip of her toe in. It was the slenderest support, but to the elf, it was enough. She grabbed the dynamite from her teeth and wedged it into the largest crack in the creature's chest and then flung herself backwards, landing lithely on her feet.

"One minute," yelled Craig.

The elemental's arm came crashing towards her. She ducked, narrowly avoiding the massive fist that would have killed her instantly. The scorched ground was now slippery from the effects of the *Cone of Cold* spell. Still, she sprang away agilely, racing for the safety of the others, who were calling to her to hurry.

Craig was counting down the seconds on his watch. As Geledhil arrived, he bellowed, "Fire in the hole!"

They threw themselves to the ground, and, a split second later, the dynamite detonated in a loud explosion. The shock waves from the detonation were devastating, contained as they were within the confines of the crack in the elemental's chest.

The group covered their heads as a multitude of small rock fragments showered them. After a few seconds, Camron looked up and saw the elemental staggering backwards, struggling to retain its balance. In the centre of its chest was a large gaping crater. With a final roar, it toppled back, the holes that had been eyes and had burned so brightly gradually fading to a dark granite.

Gingerly, the group got to their feet, brushing off the dirt and debris and looking around in awe. They made their way cautiously to where the creature lay on its back, their weapons still trained and ready, alert for the slightest sign it still lived.

But it lay there, lifeless and unmoving.

"Well, that was fun," said Bruce. "Are there any more?"

"You're a nutter," answered Craig, laughing. The adrenaline that had coursed through their bodies dissipated, leaving behind a feeling of nervous relief.

"What did I miss?" said a voice behind them.

They spun around. David stood beside Pete, looking pale but clearly healed.

Geledhil rushed to hug him.

"I gather I owe you my life," he said, smiling at her.

Camron felt a sense of hope replace a small amount of the responsibility he shouldered. This oddly mismatched band had faced and defeated a potent foe and, importantly, had achieved this through the combination of modern science and ancient magic. Could combining the strength of modern technology with the power of magic prove to be the deciding factor in their ultimate victory? Would this mean that winning the war wouldn't rely solely on his ability to bond with Clarent? That the world wouldn't have to rely on him to wield both swords in union on the battlefield.?

"What exactly was that thing?" Craig asked,

"It's an Earth Elemental," answered Camron. "A magical summoning of the raw elemental power of the earth encompassed within solid rock. The dwarves must have conjured it as a guardian when they sealed the entrance. I think our attempt to open the entryway triggered it."

"What now?" asked Geledhil. "We aren't any closer to opening the entrance."

A loud noise, like rock cracking, made them jump. They spun around, fearing another Earth Elemental, but Geledhil stopped and pointed at the dead creature.

"Its head has fallen off," she said.

Sure enough, the head was on the ground, lying to one side. As they watched, a second crack sounded, and one of its arms fell off.

"What's happening," David asked urgently.

"I'm not sure," replied Camron, "but I think the magic that has held this elemental into its body all these centuries has been broken. The body is reverting to ordinary rocks."

A third crack sounded, and this time one of its lower legs separated, broken off at the knee. Excalibur came loose, falling to the ground.

A fourth crack announced the separation of the lower jaw from the rest of its head. Within a few minutes, nothing resembling a body remained, simply a pile of rocks. They moved closer to investigate, Camron retrieving Excalibur from where it lay.

"You don't see that every day," quipped Bruce, idly prodding one of the stones with the toe of his boot.

"But we still don't know where the key to the doorway is. We may have neutralised the guard dog, but we haven't got in yet," said Craig.

"Aye, where do you think they might hide a key so it couldn't be stumbled upon by accident?" added Pete.

Everyone looked around, taking in the hill and the barrenness of the landscape as if hoping to notice a sign saying *'Key to dwarven underground here!'*

"They're not teeth," said Geledhil slowly, almost to herself, staring intently at what had recently been the creature's head.

"They're not teeth," she repeated more excitedly.

"What?" asked David, bewildered.

"Look," she said, eagerly pointing at the single row of sparse black teeth adorning the upper jaw of the Earth Elemental's mouth.

"The teeth are only on one side, and there are gaps between each one," she continued.

"So it had bad teeth. I doubt it could find a toothbrush big enough and probably hasn't seen a dentist for centuries," said Trigger.

"The gaps are unevenly spaced, and they don't match the width of missing teeth," she said, slightly exasperated. "They're not teeth. It's a key!"

They all stopped, staring at her and then at the set of teeth.

"You're right," exclaimed Camron. "That's it. That's where the dwarves hid the key."

Camron bent down and grasped what would have been the gums of the elemental. He pulled firmly, and a thin section of stone came away, with the black rock-teeth at one end. Holding it up, the others could clearly see that it did resemble a key.

"Come on then," said Pete enthusiastically. "Let's see if the wee thing fits."

"Not yet," said Camron, causing some of them to look at him bewildered.

"Why not?" asked Craig.

"Well, for a start, we don't know how the key works."

"It's a key. You stick it in the lock and turn it," said Pete, a little sarcastically. "How else would it work?"

"Oh, I don't know," replied Camron, with equal sarcasm. "Maybe instead of physically opening the door, it magically transports us through it. At which point, we would be on one side of the door, and all our gear would be on the other. So, just a suggestion, but before we do anything else, we should get our equipment together to get ready to go."

"Good thinking," said Craig before Pete had time to think of a suitable retort.

"I brought spare weapons and ammo in case Camron or Geledhil wanted them," said Smith. "They're in a black zip-up holdall by our gear. Let's replace the ammo we've used up."

They headed over to collect their equipment.

Camron and Smith went to update a still bewildered Chief Inspector Dickinson.

A few minutes later, the group of eight unlikely adventurers stood before the entrance to the short tunnel. It was mid-afternoon, and the sun shone brightly. Still, even a few short metres into the tunnel, the light was dim and gloomy, as if the darkness dared any to encroach upon its territory.

“Well, here we go,” said David, trying to sound more confident than he actually felt.

They moved forwards until they stood before the granite wall. Camron took the key and, very slowly, inserted it into the lock. It appeared to fit perfectly.

He tried to turn it clockwise. It did not move.

Not wanting to exert too much pressure, he stopped turning the key clockwise and instead tried turning it anti-clockwise. It made a quarter turn with ease and then, suddenly, glowed a bright orange. Camron let go, stepping back. The key slid further into the lock of its own accord. Once it had completely disappeared, they heard a distinctive click. The doorway, which had stood immobile for one and a half millennia, swung silently inwards, with a gust of stale air and dust escaping from the gloom inside.

The group looked at one another.

“Ready?” asked Camron. They all nodded.

Camron grasped his staff and muttered a magical word. The tip erupted into light, and, holding the staff up, he stepped over the threshold into the realm of Niðavellir. The others, except for Geledhil, uncovered the magical lights attached to their headgear and followed Camron into the dark tunnel.

# Chapter 31

SATURDAY, 19TH JUNE

The light from outside didn't penetrate far, almost as if the darkness resented its intrusion. The party moved further into the tunnel.

Camron's feet became the first in centuries to disturb the layer of dust covering the smooth floor. Like the floor, the walls and roof were smooth and regular, the width and height appearing uniform. The floor sloped gently downwards. This did not look to be a natural tunnel but rather one made by skilled hands.

Camron had taken no more than a few dozen paces when the light started dimming, and he heard the soft scraping of stone on stone behind them. Whirling around, he saw the doorway begin to close. David and Trigger, who had been the last to enter, rushed back. Trigger grasped hold of the door. Yet he couldn't prevent it from closing and only just managed to pull his hand back in time.

Camron used the light from his staff to examine the area where the keyhole should have been. There was nothing but smooth stone.

"The keyhole isn't there," he said.

"It doesn't really matter, does it?" said David. "We don't have the key anymore, so it wouldn't help us very much."

Bruce muttered, "I think this is what would be called *the point of no return.*"

"In that case," said Smith, "shall we proceed?"

"Aye, let's do that," said Pete. "At least we can't get lost. The tunnel only goes one way."

"According to the map my grandmother gave us, there should be a dwarven outpost a few miles away," said Camron. "I'm assuming it's abandoned after all this time, but we won't know for sure until we get there."

"Marching formation?" Pete asked Craig.

"Bruce, you take the point, then Pete and me, Camron and Geledhil, Smith and David with Trigger bringing up the rear," replied Craig.

"If I may suggest?" interjected Camron. "I'm all for Bruce taking the lead, but I think Geledhil should be behind him. Her hearing and eyesight will give us our best chance of being forewarned of anything."

Camron would actually have preferred her at the front. Her unique elven vision could see better in the dark than a human could see with torchlight, but he didn't want to cause animosity with the SAS guys this early on. And if he were honest with himself, he would prefer his cousin wasn't the first to venture into anything dangerous.

"I'll go behind Geledhil," he added. "If there's anything magical to deal with, I need to be up there to handle it."

Craig started to object, but Smith interrupted. "Makes sense. Don't worry, Craig. I've seen these two in action. They can handle themselves."

Craig muttered something under his breath but didn't object any further.

"One day, you'll have to explain what that phrase means," said Geledhil sweetly to Craig, who, unusually for him, looked somewhat abashed.

"I told you her hearing was good," said Camron. He spoke a word of magic, and the conjured light emanating from the tip of his staff dimmed.

"I suggest you cover your torches with the filters to dim them as we don't know what's down here. There's no point in advertising our presence unnecessarily."

They dimmed their torches, adjusted their packs and set off down the tunnel. The going wasn't difficult, and they set a steady pace. The tunnel continued onwards with a slight downward slope.

After a couplc of hours, the tunnel suddenly turned back on itself at an acute angle. A further twenty metres and it turned back again, returning to its original course. After another forty metres, the tunnel again switched back on itself. This time it narrowed to just over a metre wide, and the ceiling height dropped to a metre and a half, forcing them to stoop.

"What is this?" asked Craig.

Camron answered, “I think it’s the outer protection for the dwarven outpost. The tunnel design along this stretch switches back and forth and yes, look there at the tip of each switchback. There’s a narrow slit, about a metre off the ground. I think these are the equivalent of arrow slits in medieval castles. The design of this approach would prevent any enemy from overpowering the dwarves. You could only fight two abreast, and most enemies would have to stoop to fight. Not to mention getting peppered with crossbow quarrels through those slits. All in all, I think anyone attacking the outpost from this direction would have a difficult time of it.”

They rounded a final switchback a short while later. The tunnel opened into a largish cavern about sixty metres wide by nearly two hundred long. Geledhil imparted the dimensions as their dimmed lighting penetrated just a short distance into the inky blackness. A wall to their right, some four metres high, ran along the length of the cavern, punctuated by a single opening near the mid-point. They could see the remains of what once must have been a set of sturdy wooden double gates reinforced with metal bands.

“Do we have to go in there?” David whispered, fearful of the unknown hidden within the darkness.

“No,” answered Geledhil. “The tunnel continues on, almost directly opposite on the far side of the cavern.”

“But this must be the dwarven outpost,” said Smith. “We ought to check it out, though. I wouldn’t like the thought of anything in there creeping up on us later from behind. And besides, if it is empty, this would make a far safer place to rest for the night than the open tunnels.”

They agreed and headed towards the derelict entrance, fanning out in a battle-ready formation,

“This one’s ours,” said Craig and the four SAS troopers, plus Smith moved forward in a practised and smooth manner, each man covering and being covered by the others. Their professionalism and cohesion as a team was impressive, and Camron was happy for them to lead. Besides, Camron remembered dwarves did not typically employ magical traps and enchantments. They were more likely to use ingenious mechanical traps triggered by cunningly hidden footplates and other devices. Craig and his team were as liable to notice these as he was.

The team followed the usual SOP (Standard Operating Procedure), which they used for any type of building clearance. Once through the gates, they cautiously fanned out across the small courtyard before reconvening at the building entrance some ten metres beyond the wall. The SAS team made their way methodically from room to room, checking that each was clear.

The outpost consisted of a large central room with a handful of smaller rooms. Closer investigation revealed the desiccated and rusty remains of a few weapons and an almost unrecognisable shield lying in a stone weapons rack against one wall. On the other side of the main room were several plain, unadorned, but skilfully crafted low stone tables, with long benches on either side. Camron stepped into one of the adjacent rooms and saw a large brick oven, still intact. A further doorway led to what he thought may have been a storeroom.

Back in the main room, Craig was emerging from another side room.

"Some sort of communal sleeping room, I think," he answered to the questioning look Camron gave him. "Probably the barracks."

The last room looked like it might have been an office of some sort, probably for the commander of the small garrison.

The thick perimeter walls segregated the outpost from the rest of the cavern. The outer face was still surprisingly smooth, with only a few areas showing signs of crumbling. Each wall on either side of the entryway had a set of steps carved into the inner face of the defensive wall. Camron ascended one and saw a banquette or fire-step ran the length of each wall, a little under a metre below the top.

Camron stood, looking across the cavern, wondering what he should do.

*Do I need to tell the others what to do? Would they listen to me? What would I tell them anyway?*

Voices cut through his anxious thoughts.

"Looks cosy enough," said Trigger cheerfully from the courtyard. "We can use our hexamine to heat up some food in the old kitchen. The light should be well enough hidden."

"Ok," said Craig. "Pete, you and Bruce take the first watch."

Bruce ascended the same steps Camron had climbed whilst Pete took the other. The others began to settle down for the evening, preparing their meal and sorting out their bedding for the night.

"Just the chap," hailed Craig as Camron re-entered the main room. "Can we have a look at that map of yours, please?" Craig and Smith waited whilst Camron placed the *Finders Map* on one of the old tables

Craig was about to say something when he stopped and stared at the map.

"That wasn't there earlier," he said, pointing to the detailed section between the entrance at Dunsinane Hill and the dwarven outpost where they currently were. "Have you filled it in?"

"No," answered Camron. "The magic of the map fills itself in as we go. Impressive, isn't it?"

"It'd be more impressive if it filled the bloody thing in before we got there," Craig replied.

Camron looked at Smith. "See? I'm not the only one. I said exactly the same thing."

Smith sighed. "It's an awful lot better than a blank sheet of paper, though, isn't it?" he said, not expecting a reply. He turned to Craig. "You were saying?"

"Oh, yes," he replied. "I'm not too happy about that enormous bloody hole in the wall where the gates used to be, but it doesn't look like there's anything we can use to make a barricade.

"Don't worry," said Camron. "I can help. I'll cast a *Wall of Stone* spell, which will block the entrance. It should last long enough to see us through the night."

Craig looked a little startled. After all, he had never encountered any form of magic before today. Talking about spell casting as if it were an everyday occurrence would take some getting used to.

"Okay, thanks," he replied, his tone slightly hesitant. "But we'll still keep a couple of lookouts on the wall. Eight gives us two-hour stints each, not too arduous."

After they had finished their meal, those not on watch duties sat in the main room. Craig and Smith had pulled a few stone tables into a rough circle. The benches were far too low for them to sit on, but the tables were almost the right height.

David blew on his scalding black coffee, sipping it gingerly.

"I've been wondering," he said. "If there have been two previous *Wars of the Realms* and the last one was such a terrible conflict, how come no one knows about it? I mean, there is no history, no folklore, nor any legends about the war. It's as if it has been erased from history."

Camron had been ruefully eyeing his own black coffee, mourning the lack of milk. "Well, actually, that's exactly what did happen," Camron answered.

"What do you mean? How can you eradicate an entire war from history, especially one on the scale you said it was?"

Camron looked around before speaking. Both Smith and Craig were listening intently.

"It was all part of the plan Queen Nimue, Merlin and my father contrived. The idea was really quite simple. Lock the Dökkálfar and their allies in their own land forever and over time wipe all knowledge of them from human history."

"Why?" asked David.

"Well, they didn't think the human race could be trusted," answered Camron ruefully. "Remember, at that time, humans had already developed siege engines, and some parts of the world were using steel to make weapons. Can you imagine if we had combined magic with our ability to develop technologically?"

Camron looked around at his audience. "So, the decision was made to eradicate knowledge of magic and send the Wars of the Realms to myth and legend. Merlin spent much of his remaining life travelling around Britain, Ireland and many parts of Europe, destroying or re-writing the few written records and histories there were."

"But how can you re-write history?" asked Craig.

Camron took a sip of his black coffee and was not surprised that it tasted as bad as he had feared.

"Remember, this was in what we now call *The Dark Ages.* Back then, most records weren't in written form but were stories, folklore, and poems passed down verbally through the generations. The bards were the keepers of these traditions, charged with the memories of the people. They were the custodians responsible for maintaining the accuracy and sacredness of *the Word.* It wasn't good enough to remember the gist of a story. It had to be remembered verbatim, complete word for word accuracy. Otherwise, over time, the histories would change with each retelling."

Camron eyed his mug suspiciously before placing it on the ground. "Merlin's self-appointed task was to convince the guardians of this knowledge to alter these records. Bards and druids had a long tradition of cooperation and working closely together. Indeed, sometimes bards became druids themselves, and many druids were likewise conversant with bardic knowledge. As the most influential druid, Merlin commanded great respect amongst the bards. With the consent of those highest amongst the bardic orders, he set about changing the stories concerning not only the war but everything about the Ljósálfar, Dökkálfar, dwarves, orcs, goblins and the rest."

"You're kidding," exclaimed Craig.

Camron shook his head. "For nearly two centuries, Merlin travelled the lands and brought the plan to fruition. And on the whole, he succeeded. He had a bit of a problem with the Saxons in the Scandinavian countries. They were never that welcoming of bards or wizards, so many of their own stories and legends remained to be passed down. It explains the widespread knowledge of the

Norse legends and myths about elves and suchlike. But on the whole, he did a pretty good cover-up job."

* * *

The following morning, they breakfasted on Koymasse bread and mugs of hot, sweet tea, black of course, but slightly better than the coffee of the previous evening. The magical wall of stone had disappeared while they were finishing breakfast, the spell Camron had cast expiring as predicted. Shortly after, they left the abandoned dwarven outpost and resumed their journey. Once again, Bruce and Geledhil took the lead.

The next few hours passed without incident. Travel was relatively easy, with the sloping tunnel taking them further downwards. None of them lowered their vigilance for even a fraction of a second. This was unknown hostile territory. Once, they had to scramble over rocks that partially blocked the passage due to a section of the tunnel roof collapsing.

Around mid-morning, they encountered a stream that crossed their path, forcing them to wade through it. The water was waist-deep, inky black, and cold as an arctic winter. Their icy, wet clothing diminished their good mood, and the prospect of a warm crackling fire at the end of the day seemed an unlikely prospect. The cold seemed to affect David more than the rest. The earlier spring in his step had gone, although he resolutely put one foot in front of the other.

Camron was beginning to think he might have to do something and was running through his repertoire of spells to see if he could magic a means of drying their clothes. Suddenly, he noticed that both Bruce and Geledhil had stopped, not far from where the tunnel appeared to open out. He caught up with them, and Geledhil said, "The tunnel opens into a vast chasm. It cuts across our path."

"How far across?" asked Craig, who had also reached them.

Bruce answered, "At least fifty metres, I think. But I can't see the bottom. The walls look sheer."

“There was a stone bridge across the chasm once,” Geledhil added. “I can just make out the bridge remnants jutting out from the far side.”

“It was there once,” said Camron, looking intently at the *Finders Map*. It showed the route traversing an arched bridge that crossed the chasm and continued into a tunnel on the far side.

“Great,” muttered Craig.

“It’s not all bad news,” Geledhil said. “There’s a ledge heading off to the left. It’s a bit narrow, but if we’re careful, it should be okay. And anyway, it looks like it’s our only option.”

The rest of the group made their way to the end of the tunnel and stopped. Before them, cutting right across their path, was the chasm, looking as if a vast gash had been gouged through the solid rock by an enormous claw.

Trigger gave a low whistle. “Well, that's a hell of a gap to jump.”

The path continued along the ledge Geledhil had told them about to their left. She had mentioned it was narrow, but the phrase *‘a bit narrow’* meant different things to a nimble elf and a burly six-foot SAS trooper carrying almost thirty kilos of equipment and weapons. It was only a couple of feet wide, less in some parts.

“So this is our route?” asked Craig sceptically. When both Geledhil and Bruce nodded, he continued, “It doesn’t look like we have much choice then.”

“Ok,” said Camron, a slight note of apprehension in his own voice, “let’s go. I suggest we opt for visibility rather than caution, so let’s turn our lights up so we can see where we’re going.”

Bruce stepped cautiously onto the narrow ledge, which clung precariously to the sheer damp rock wall of the chasm. Geledhil was a few paces behind him and was herself followed by Camron, the magically glowing crystal on the tip of his staff giving off enough light for them to see nearly a hundred metres.

The opposite side of the chasm was a sheer wall, unbroken by any narrow ledges of its own. Their progress was slow. They couldn't walk side on with their backs to the wall due to their Bergen's, so they walked facing forward, placing one foot almost in front of the other, resembling a troupe of novice tightrope walkers. Their left hands were placed on the wall to steady themselves, and each footfall was carefully tested before putting weight on it. After a few minutes, the ledge started sloping downwards but only at a very slight angle.

They moved slowly but steadily down. The only sound accompanying their footfalls was the scrape of arms and backpacks against the rock face.

Camron hadn't paid much attention to the *Friendship Ring* his grandmother had given him until now, relying mainly on the sketchy *Finders Map* and the fact their path had been reasonably straightforward. But now, they had deviated from the map onto an entirely blank section of the parchment. As they moved further away from the spot where the bridge once stood, Camron worried about how they would find their way to Varðasteinn. As he thought of the dwarven city, he felt an unfamiliar feeling in his mind. He concentrated and realised the vague feelings were coming from the *Friendship Ring.* It told him he was heading in the wrong direction.

*Great,* he thought, *that's helpful. A useless map and a ring telling me I'm lost!*

They continued negotiating their treacherous path for a further twenty minutes with no end in sight. Camron was beginning to worry about how long they would have to traverse it. Stopping to rest would be difficult and awkward. Unslinging their backpacks would be all but impossible.

Geledhil was thinking the same thing. Being an elf, she was having by far the easiest time. The narrow ledge posed not much more than an inconvenience to her, rather than the ordeal the humans faced. In fact, she was considering suggesting that she scout ahead and see how much further it went.

Camron was straining to look past Bruce to see what lay ahead when a sudden crack split the silence.

The ledge disappeared, and Bruce dropped from sight as the thunderous clatter echoed around them.

Geledhil, with reflexes impossible for any human to imagine, threw herself forwards.

Camron reacted instinctively and dived towards her disappearing body, his arms outstretched as he grabbed her legs.

* * *

Geledhil was still mid-air when her hand just caught the outstretched hand of Bruce. He had been using his left hand against the chasm wall to steady himself, and those fingers clawed against the rock face as he fell, desperately seeking a purchase. Geledhil's slender hand gripped Bruce's bloodied hand, hanging on with a vice-like grip born of a determination to save him from falling.

Suddenly, she felt arms snaking around her legs, grasping tightly as she landed heavily. She lay with the upper part of her body hanging over the missing section of the ledge. Camron had both arms tightly bound around her legs, his face resting awkwardly on her buttock cheek. Geledhil heard Craig shout to Pete to grab hold of Camron's legs.

Her eyes met those of Bruce. She saw fear in his eyes.

"Shit!" he swore. His hand was slick with sweat, his fingers bloodied, and the skin ripped away.

Geledhil's arm felt like it was on fire, the pain almost unbearable. The full weight of Bruce hanging there with all his gear strained her muscles. She felt herself being pulled inexorably forward. Her left hand scrabbled at the rock face for any slight handhold. She slid a little more and started to topple forwards but refused to let go. Geledhil felt Camron's grip on her tighten, arresting her descent.

They had reached an impasse. Pete had Camron, Camron had Geledhil, and she had Bruce. But that was it. No one else could help. The ledge was too narrow to get by.

"Bruce, you ok?" called out Craig.

"Just hanging around," he replied almost casually, although his eyes, still locked onto Geledhil's, betrayed his fear.

"Can you cast a spell or something to float him up?" Smith called out to Camron.

"Not lying on the ground with my arms wrapped around Geledhil's legs, I can't. I need my hands to cast spells. And if I let go, she'll get pulled over the edge," answered Camron.

Geledhil felt something shift under her. A few more centimetres of the ledge gave way, toppling her forward a little more. She felt Camron's grasp on her legs tighten even more. His chin propped in an undignified manner on her backside.

"Don't worry, I've got you. I won't let you go," Camron said in a soft voice.

Geledhil felt comforted by his words, but she had no idea how they would get out of this precarious situation and feared the worst. Camron couldn't use magic while holding onto her, and the ledge wouldn't hold out much longer. It would take her, Bruce and Camron when it finally collapsed.

More rock gave way beneath her, tumbling past Bruce into the darkness below. Geledhil could let go, but she wouldn't, no matter the cost. It seemed their brief adventure had come to an abrupt end. She saw in his eyes that he knew it too. He smiled at her, not his usual mischievous grin, but a genuine smile full of warmth and friendship, although his eyes were sad. Then Bruce took a deep breath, his decision made and his resolve hardening.

"Pete," he called out. "Look after Trigger for me, will you, mate? You know he'll shoot his own foot off if left on his own."

Comprehension dawned on Pete, and he called out, "Don't you dare quit!"

"I'm not quitting," Bruce replied determinedly. "I'm making sure the mission goes on. You lot make sure you finish this thing, okay? And give those evil bastards hell from me!"

"Can't you do something, for fucks sake?" Pete implored Camron.

Camron lay, holding on to Geledhil. Inadequacy and wretchedness threatened to engulf him.

Bruce looked back at Geledhil.

"Thank you," he said. "For catching me and for not letting go. But this is my decision. Mine alone. Okay?"

Bruce held her gaze for a moment longer before releasing his grip on her hand.

Geledhil couldn't hold him. The weight of him and the slickness of his hand was too much. He slipped from her desperate grasp and fell into the inky blackness, the light from his magical torch lighting his way down. He fell for many seconds but didn't utter a single cry.

Finally, the torchlight stopped descending after what must have been a couple of hundred metres. They stared at the tiny beam of light far below, shining like a beacon in the darkness, marking where their comrade had fallen.

# Chapter 32

SUNDAY, 20TH JUNE

Pete swore softly.

Trigger stared in disbelief. They had spent years in combat training, pushing themselves to be the best until they had reached the lofty heights of the Regiment. They were an elite group who belonged to arguably the best Special Forces regiment in the world. The possibility of dying on active duty was something they all accepted. But most expected that to be in combat, not falling off a narrow ledge in a dark chasm deep underground.

After a few moments, looking at the faint beam of light, Craig pulled his thoughts back to their predicament.

"Is everyone else okay?" he asked gruffly.

Pete, Trigger and Smith all replied immediately.

"Camron? Geledhil?" Craig repeated.

"We're okay," answered Camron, disentangling himself from Geledhil and clambering to his feet. The Stone of Destiny in its bag, plus the two swords strapped to his back, made the manoeuvre difficult. His staff had remained upright, magically standing where he had let go of it.

Smith turned to David, who was next in line behind him.

"You okay?" he asked.

David had had minimal experience with death until now. The only people he had personally known who had died were his parents and an elderly aunt he had seldom seen. Now the death of someone he had only known for a short time but had come to like and respect came as an enormous shock.

"I'm okay," he said eventually, his voice thick with grief.

"Good man."

Geledhil stood facing the others, tears trickling down her beautiful face.

"I'm sorry," she said quietly, but the emotion in those two words conveyed the depth of her sadness and guilt.

"It wasn't your fault," said Smith. "None of us would have been quick enough to have grabbed him in the first place."

"He's right," added Pete. "You've nothing to blame yourself for, lass."

Craig glanced past Camron and Geledhil at the fallen section of the ledge. Almost two and a half metres had disappeared. Not an impossible jump if unencumbered, and there was a decent run-up. But, unfortunately, they were two options missing from their present situation.

"How do we get across that?" Craig asked.

Geledhil wiped the tears from her face and took two steps back. She accelerated towards the missing section, leaping gracefully into the air and landing lithely on her feet on the opposite side.

Camron looked at the gap and glanced thoughtfully at his staff, still standing upright by itself where he had let go of it.

He addressed it in a muted tone, "You know you shortened yourself to fit into the car when I saved Rachel? Can you elongate and maybe flatten out as well?" He had bonded with the staff and knew it had a level of empathy and understanding, an enchanted life force of its own. He also knew his next request would demean it, but he had no choice. He continued, hesitantly, "You know, like taking the shape of a plank?"

Trigger said, "Why are you talking to a stick?" but fell silent when the crystal at the tip of the staff started glowing.

It wasn't its usual blue glow. Instead, it was purple. Camron knew he had insulted the staff by asking, but they had to get across, and this was the safest way he could think of. After a few moments, the staff began to stretch, growing in length before slowly expanding width-ways until a solid looking plank stood upright before them. Camron took the plank and lowered it carefully across the missing section of the ledge. One by one, the group's remaining members made their way across the gap. Camron came last, and when he knelt at the far side and grasped the plank, it returned to its previous shape, once more becoming the Staff of Merlin.

The narrow ledge continued to slope gently downwards as they continued their treacherous descent. Every so often, Camron glanced back towards the bottom of the cavern at the slowly diminishing light that marked where Bruce's body lay.

They finally reached the bottom of the ravine towards the end of the day and were now several miles from where Bruce had fallen.

The group was divided, and there had been a heated discussion about going back to find his body to give him a proper burial. However, it would have been almost impossible to do so.

During their slow descent, they had heard fast-flowing water, which they could only presume came from underground rivers flowing through the ravine, any of which might have proved impassable. Camron had also reluctantly pointed out that, even if they could get to Bruce's body, it would have lain there for a long time before they could reach him. The harsh reality was that some other creature who inhabited this world would probably have found him first. Camron didn't need to add that most creatures wandering these tunnels would consider Bruce's body a free meal.

And so, with heavy hearts, the company had crossed the ravine and made an early camp in a tunnel that came to a dead-end after only ten metres. They had taken watch in pairs while the others tried to get some sleep. Most had lain awake, staring at the utter darkness of the tunnel roof above them, straining their ears for any slight noise in the total silence of this strange world.

* * *

They were all up and about early the following morning, each going about their allotted tasks in silence. No one had slept much after the previous day's incident, and the mood was subdued. Added to this was their increasing discomfort as the temperature slowly rose the deeper they delved underground.

After a meagre breakfast of Koymasse bread, they quickly packed up their camp. When all were ready to move off, they consulted the *Finders Map* and held a brief discussion about which way to go. They were many miles off course with no way of climbing back up the far side of the ravine. While the *Finders Map* filled in the detail of the path they had already travelled, there was no indication of which route they should take to re-join their original path. They had been forced to go east, following the ledge to the ravine floor, when they should have travelled south. They decided their best plan would be to find a tunnel leading southwest and hope they could eventually find their way back to their original course. They walked westwards along the ravine floor for almost half a mile before finding a promising tunnel. With Geledhil taking the lead and Camron several metres behind her with his staff tip glowing softly, they moved through the tunnel. Camron concentrated on the *Friendship Ring* and was relieved to feel, albeit faintly, that they were heading in nearly the right direction.

Their sombre mood continued throughout the day, but they remained alert and watchful, mindful that this hostile environment did not tolerate carelessness. Craig reckoned they were probably a little more than two miles underground, and the temperature was approaching 40°C. This added to the increased air pressure, making their journey difficult and uncomfortable. David especially struggled, and partway through the morning, the others insisted on lightening the load he was carrying in his Bergen, sharing some of his equipment amongst themselves, with Camron putting what he could into his *bag of holding.*

Aside from their footfalls and the faint rustling of their clothes, the silence was absolute as they moved through the tunnels. Primordial fear of the dark threatened each of them. The unending blackness surrounded them and the ever-present sense of thousands of tons of rock above their heads, just waiting for the day when it might obey gravity and collapse into the tunnels. If it hadn't been for the light from Camron's staff and their magical helmet torches, the darkness would have been absolute. As it was, their light only extended about fifteen metres. They relied heavily on Geledhil's elven vision and ability to see in the dark. She remained outside the meagre pool of light, walking ahead of them.

Their passage consisted of every type of tunnel conceivable. Some were simple, straightforward passages they traversed with ease, maintaining a reasonable pace. At other times, they had to squeeze through narrow crevices, or the ceiling forced them to walk in a cross between a stoop and a crouch. Even these they came to regard as relatively easy compared to some of the other sections they encountered. Nearly vertical shafts that could only be navigated by abseiling down them. Camron would cast a *Knot* spell on the ropes, binding them to even the smallest outcrop yet releasing the line to be retrieved once they were all safely down.

However, the worst was the maze of slits and belly crawls where they had to push their backpacks in front of them and crawl through gaps so tight that retreat was all but impossible. Their body joints simply would not allow them to go backwards. Geledhil proved an absolute blessing. She would go through the narrowest of slits first to make sure the gap didn't become impossible. Her lithe body allowed her to crawl backwards, albeit with much bruising and scraping of skin, should the gap narrow too much and force them to seek an alternate route.

At times, they encountered small patches of, what appeared to be, a luminescent lichen growing on the walls, which gave off a dim light of its own. These pools of light came as a welcome relief to the endless blackness surrounding them, and they regarded each one as a little oasis.

Each time they encountered a side passage or fork in the tunnel, they consulted their compass and the *Finders Map*. They chose the best route, always southwest, heading slowly back to their original path. They often followed a likely looking way only to reach a dead end as the tunnel petered out. At these times, they retraced their steps, sometimes for several miles and then tried to find another route.

Their journey was exhausting, and if not for their physical fitness, they would have soon faltered. David struggled the most. Despite his age, he had always been reasonably fit, and the time spent training in Alfheim had increased his strength and stamina considerably. However, this was the ultimate in extreme potholing, and it was taking its toll on his endurance. Despite his protests, the rest of the group insisted he get as much rest as possible when they camped each night and often refused to allow him to take a turn at night watch duty, instead just dividing the night into three watches.

They camped in a narrow tunnel one night, one person on guard at either end. After yet another cold meal of Koymasse bread and army rations, they sat with their backs against the tunnel walls, talking quietly. David, who sat next to Camron, thought about their conversation at the abandoned Dwarven outpost. Gathering his thoughts, he turned to Camron and said, "If you look at all the legends, stories and half-truths about your father, then a lot of them make sense if you interpret them correctly. Merlin didn't build Stonehenge, as legend says, but he was part of the group who created the portal seal there. Your father didn't kill you at Ercing and lay you in a burial mound but sacrificed your life as Amr to become this slumbering guardian. Even the tale of the *Sword in the Stone* carries some semblance of truth."

Camron considered David before answering.

"You're right. The important thing was to ensure that humans never knew magic was real and try to regain its' use. Merlin knew he could never completely obliterate the truth, so he went one better. He erased all links between my father and the elves and other non-human creatures. He then obfuscated the remaining facts by subtly altering them and turning them into myth and legend. We have all heard of the legend of King Arthur. But nobody believes it's true. Instead, people believe that if he did exist, he was just a warlord or tribal chieftain who managed to unite the Britons to fight against the Saxons. Who would think to link Arthur and his *knights of the round table* to the legends concerning the Álfar and those of Norse mythology?"

David nodded thoughtfully before continuing.

"Am I right in surmising that your father was originally the warlord chief of the Cornovii? The Celtic tribe who were part of the Dumnonii, in what is now Cornwall."

Camron nodded.

"And he spoke the language we now refer to as Brythonic or Brittonic, the tongue from which both Welsh and Cornish evolved?"

Again, Camron nodded.

"And the literal translation of horn in the Brythonic tongue is *corn*, from where we get the modern name, Cornwall?"

Camron nodded a third time.

"So the legend that states that when Briton is in its direst need, and the horn of Arthur is heard, then shall King Arthur return with his knights, even that is based partly on truth. The horn doesn't refer to a literal horn. It refers to one born of the line of Cornwall. As your father ruled there, so you're of the line of Cornwall, aren't you?"

Camron smiled. "I can see why Grandmother changed her mind about you," he said. "Normally, when she takes a dislike to someone, which is very rare indeed, it can last for centuries. You had to be quite exceptional for her to change her opinion of you in such a short space of time."

David smiled. "I'll take that as a compliment." Privately he felt very relieved, remembering the underlying frostiness he had felt from Queen Nimue when he first awoke in Alfheim.

They hadn't been travelling long the following morning when their tunnel suddenly opened into a vast cavern, wider than it was long. The light from a large patch of luminous lichen cast an eerie green light, which glittered off a small stream running some two hundred metres across the width of the cavern. The light allowed them to see across to the far side, where another tunnel led off almost directly opposite where they stood.

Watchful and alert, Camron stepped into the cavern and was surprised to feel soft loam underfoot, a welcome change from the hard rock they had become used to. However, this wasn't the only surprising thing. Off to one side, they saw many strange plants that looked like enormous mushrooms. A field full of metre-high fungi was the last thing they had expected to find.

"Do you think they're edible?" asked Trigger hopefully, pulling out his knife in eager anticipation of carving off a chunk.

"Dunno," answered Pete, "how do you tell the difference between mushrooms and toadstools?"

"You can't," piped in David. "The term *toadstool* is generally meant as a poisonous or otherwise inedible mushroom. But it doesn't define a particular class of fungi. As appetising as they look, I wouldn't recommend we actually eat them."

"David's right," said Craig. "We're a long way from any help if we get poisoned. Come on, let's keep moving."

With a last wistful look at the fungi, Trigger replaced his knife and followed the others across the cavern floor. They reached the small stream that was less than a metre deep and took the opportunity to refill their water canteens before splashing through and heading towards the tunnel opening they had seen.

They continued their journey through the underworld for a further three days until, late one morning, they reached a tunnel that looked different to the others. This one was not a rough natural tunnel or fissure that varied in height and width. Instead, it had a consistent width and a uniform height. It had clearly been created rather than being a naturally occurring formation. Examining the *Finders Map,* they estimated this was the original tunnel they had started out on. It had been over a week since they had left the world of sun and open spaces above them. By their reckoning, they would have reached their current position within three days had they been able to cross the ravine by the bridge.

They were all tired and dirty, their bodies had suffered cuts and bruises, and their clothes were filthy and scuffed with rips from the sharp rocks they had squeezed past and crawled over. They were weary of this hostile underworld that had already claimed the life of one of them. But each adjusted their pack and determinedly started down yet another tunnel.

# Chapter 33

MONDAY 28TH JUNE

Raknarden clenched his fists, suppressing his desire to obliterate the noxious birds singing so gratingly nearby.

He was a Dökkálfar of House Dukker but, unfortunately for him, not a high-ranking member, merely one of the multitudes of middle-ranking males who served the house. His driving ambition was to gain the power and status he believed were his right. His entire life so far had been in pursuit of this singular goal.

The Dökkálfar were on the brink of all-out war against the humans and their Ljósálfar allies, and yet he was forced to undertake this pointless errand rather than an achievement that would get him noticed. He should be helping with the plans for the upcoming war, using his keen intellect to impress and gain advancement.

But Sallakray's summons could not be ignored. She had sent him into the realm of the humans to find a solitary Ljósálfar and discover what purpose lay behind the elf being there. He couldn't see the importance of this one elf and resented the mundanity of his chore. But he feared Sallakray's wrath too much to complain, despite his vexation being a poisonous cocktail of hatred and envy.

Finally, a few days ago, one of his human thralls found the Ljósálfar. He spoke of a young elf-maid travelling through a portal to the realm of men. Her apparel indicated her to be a warrior, which should have been reason enough to improve his mood, but it hadn't. Rather than following the elf, the idiot human had wandered in the opposite direction to '*find a mobile signal*,' which had something to do with the primitive technology they used to communicate with one another over long distances. The magical punishment he had inflicted on the human would last several more days. During that time, he would endure unimaginable pain and torment, coming to understand the consequences of his failure. This thought brought a faint smile to Raknarden's face.

Thus, Raknarden was now in the humans' realm, hunting the Ljósálfar himself. It had taken some time and required all his magical skill and cunning, but he had finally managed to locate her. Two days ago, he had tracked her down to a cottage in a small village a short distance from the town of Dorchester.

He did not know why the elf was here, apparently living alongside a human woman. But he was sure something important was happening. It could not be a coincidence that this elf had come to the same area where Dökkálfar had been killed two weeks ago. Nor that this town was where his ancestors had suffered their first defeat during the Second War of the Realms.

Humans had found a way to fight back, and he was sure this Ljósálfar and the human woman were involved somehow. He was determined to find out more.

The sun had risen only a short while ago. Raknarden hovered in mid-air, right outside the window where the elf slept. He was perfectly safe from detection, having cast both an *Invisibility* spell and a *Levitate* spell on himself. True to her routine, shortly after arising from her bed, she took off her nightclothes and removed the necklace from around her neck. She placed it carefully on the bed before heading through the door to the adjoining room where she bathed. Raknarden waited, straining to hear the sound of running water through the closed window. After a few minutes, the noise stopped. He heard her soft voice drifting out from the room as she sang to herself. He clenched his teeth tightly, her singing grating on his ears even more than the birdsong earlier.

He drifted to the window and carefully prised it open. With the agility and sure footedness of all elves, he climbed silently through the window, his feet landing noiselessly on the polished oak floor. He crept carefully to the bed, testing each footfall for creaking floorboards until he stood gazing down at his goal. It was a simple necklace comprising a plain silver chain coupled with a silver pendant in the form of an intricately wrought oak leaf. Raknarden took out a pair of soft leather gloves and put them on. What he was about to handle warranted special care, and it would be disastrous if he were to touch it with his bare skin.

He withdrew a small leather pouch from his tunic and untied the drawstrings, pulling out a second necklace. This one was as unlike the one on the bed as it could be. It was, however, similar in size and a similar length chain, which was all that mattered. He placed it alongside Xankira's necklace and took a moment to listen, checking she was still singing while bathing.

His plan would fail if she suspected anything was amiss. Finding a Dökkálfar in her room would indeed count as something awry. Fortunately, she appeared preoccupied with bathing. With a single magical word, he dispelled the *Invisibility* spell. He would need all of his concentration for the magic he was about to cast.

He chanted softly, keeping his voice as quiet as possible while his hands wove an elaborate pattern. While not overly long in its casting, the spell was complex and required precise and absolute incantations. After a minute or so, he completed the spell. Before him, two identical necklaces lay on the bed, both made of silver with an oak leaf pendant. The *Illusion* spell was perfect. The necklaces were indistinguishable from each other.

Raknarden picked up the original necklace Xankira had placed there only a few minutes ago and deposited it into his pouch. He retraced his steps and climbed agilely out of the window. He didn't need a levitation spell to get down from the first-floor window but climbed down the vines, clinging to the wall of the cottage. He reached the ground and ran nimbly across the lawn, his feet leaving no imprint on the slightly dewy grass.

He was elated as he ran fleetly across the fields, his emotions flush with his success. He hadn't thought he would fail, but the ease with which he had accomplished this part of his plan buoyed him. The rest of it would proceed just as successfully. He smiled as he imagined the Ljósálfar girl placing the duplicate necklace around her neck. Only a powerful wizard or witch would be able to discern the *Illusion* spell he had cast upon it.

The necklace he had left her was a powerful artefact with a subtle curse. It would delve into the wearer's innermost secrets and personality, searching for character flaws. Once it latched onto one, it would gradually bring it to the fore, forcing that trait to become a central part of that person's character while at the same time suppressing any good characteristics the wearer may have.

All Raknarden had to do was give the cursed necklace a few days to consume her entirely and then devise a way to meet the elf and speak with her. A straightforward *Detection* spell would allow him to ascertain which trait the necklace had latched onto. Then it was simply a matter of using that, possibly with a *Charm* spell, to gain her trust and coax information from her. He needed to know who she was and what she was doing in this realm. Only then could he plan his next step.

Once he had the information, he could simply kill her or take her back to Svartalfheim for further interrogation. However, his preferred option was to turn her into a spy, totally under his control.

The power and status he would gain by owning and controlling a Ljósálfar spy would be great indeed. No longer would he be looked down upon and ordered about like a common house goblin. He would command respect and fear, his opinions would be listened to, and his counsel sought by his peers.

# Chapter 34

TUESDAY, 29TH JUNE

It was late one afternoon when Camron and the others finally reached their destination. The tunnel ended abruptly on a wide ledge overlooking an enormous cavern. Large patches of the now-familiar fluorescent lichen were dotted across the roof. Even though it amounted to the equivalent of just a few dozen light bulbs, to eyes now accustomed to the dark, the area looked well lit.

The group stood mesmerised by the view before them. The ledge was thirty metres up the sheer cliff face. The wide pathway rose from the cavern floor below and continued up another sixty metres to the cavern roof. Their position afforded them a magnificent view, and they looked in awe at the city spread before them. It was huge and covered over three-quarters of the cavern, protected behind a massive stone wall. It had taken some seconds before any of them noticed what was amiss. The city appeared abandoned. More than abandoned, it looked derelict, unlived in for centuries.

"Where are the dwarves?" David asked, not that any of them could possibly have known the answer.

"Shit!" Craig swore. Pete joined in.

"All this way and the little buggers aren't here," said Trigger.

"They can't have all... well, you know, died out?" Uttered David in astonishment.

No one answered. Each lost in thought, which ranged from pity for the dwarves to disbelief at the pointlessness of their journey and anger at all they had sacrificed to get here.

"Well," said Smith, trying hard not to sound equally despondent, "we've come this far. We may as well have a look round."

They doused their lights and followed the path down towards the cavern floor below. Camron glanced towards the deserted city in the hopes of catching a glimpse of some sign of dwarven life. However, it remained silent and still, just a memory of the hustle and bustle that had once taken place there.

They reached the cavern floor and stared across several hundred metres of open ground towards the city walls. The walls themselves were impressive, reaching a height of ten metres or more and stretching across the cavern from end to end. A single entryway stood directly opposite them, once protected by an enormous set of double gates made of stone like the rest of the wall. One of the gates still stood, silently guarding the city, but scattered bits of rock on the ground were all that remained of the other.

"Ok," said Craig. "Let's stay alert, shall we? It might look deserted, but we can't be sure." Turning to Camron, he added, "There's plenty of light, so we'll go first this time."

Camron nodded in agreement, and they readied their weapons before heading towards the city gates. They passed through the thick outer wall and into the city beyond. A little way inside, they discovered a small river at the bottom of a shallow ravine, running parallel to the wall, like a moat. A single arched bridge spanned the ravine, and they were glad to see it was still intact. They crossed over the bridge and walked cautiously down the broad central avenue that led into the city's heart.

The quality of the buildings and stonemasonry was exceptional. Every part of the city alluded to the enormous care and attention taken in its' construction. The dwarves had clearly been master stonemasons of a calibre unknown to the world of men. Stopping briefly to peer into one of the abandoned buildings, they saw the furniture and contents mainly fashioned from stone, with a few pieces containing rusting metal flakes. There appeared to be nothing made of wood.

In the distance, near the end of the thoroughfare, they saw a much larger building, several stories high with turrets towering towards the cavern roof. The whole complex looked far grander than the other buildings they passed.

“Do you think this was the king’s palace?” asked David.

“Probably,” answered Smith. “Have you noticed the cave walls?”

David hadn’t and looked to one side, peering intently. As illuminated as the cavern was, the walls were some distance away and shrouded in gloom. It took a moment for David to comprehend what Smith referred to. Numerous ledges cut into the walls formed a series of terraces. At the back of the terraces were the fronts of what were probably individual family dwellings, each with a doorway and several windows.

Geledhil stopped mid-stride, her face tilted upwards. Craig raised his hand to signal a halt, and the soldiers dropped to a crouch, eyes alert and ears straining. David likewise fell to a crouch, somewhat belatedly. Camron quietly stepped alongside Geledhil. She glanced at him briefly, the inquiring look in his eyes asking the unspoken question.

In an almost inaudible whisper, she said, “I can smell fire,” She paused, trying to discern the faint smells she had detected, “and meat cooking.” She nodded towards a broad street heading off to their left, perpendicular to their present route.

Camron drew Excalibur, Geledhil nocked an arrow, and the others readied their weapons, safety catches turned off. They set off down the side street, heading in the direction of the smell. After a few dozen metres, they saw a crossroads up ahead. Geledhil nodded to the right.

A sudden noise stopped them in their tracks.

A strange creature came from around the corner to the left, humanoid in shape, barely 140 centimetres tall, dark green leathery skin covered in crude leather armour. Bare, over-large feet slapped the ground as it walked backwards, long gangly arms straining under the weight of one end of a large stone bench. Beads of sweat dripped down its flat, almost ape-like face as it struggled with its burden. The creature continued, unaware, cutting directly across their path.

A second creature came into view almost immediately, carrying the other end of the bench. Unfortunately, this one wasn't oblivious to their presence. Long pointed bat-like ears twitched, and it swivelled its head towards them. Narrow, blood-red eyes registered shock at the sight of the heavily armed group confronting it. It opened its mouth and let out a loud yell, lips pulled back to reveal sharp fangs. Dropping the end of the bench, it turned to dash back around the corner, but not quick enough. A thunderous crack echoed around the cavern as the creature crumpled. The creature lay, clutching its thigh, yells of warning turning to cries of pain.

However, these didn't last long as a Smith fired a second shot into its chest, silencing the creature for good.

Alerted by the cries of its companion, the first creature turned its head, a look of stunned disbelief on its face. It let go of the stone bench but immediately started yelling in pain. The bench had landed on one of its large flat feet, crushing it under the weight.

Craig sprinted towards the creature and knocked it unconscious with the butt of his gun.

"What on earth are those things?" asked David.

"Goblins," spat Camron, the distaste in his tone almost palpable, as if uttering their name was repugnant. Although it had been 1,500 years since he had last seen one, he had recognised them immediately. After the Dökkálfar, goblins were the race he despised the most.

"Run or fight?" asked Pete, noting the assortment of leather armour and the wicked blades the goblins carried.

"Fight, I think," said Craig. "I don't fancy trying to retreat with more of these hounding us." No one disagreed.

"Quickly then, let's move," said Smith. "I think we've lost any element of surprise we might have had."

Smith and the SAS troopers took the lead, fanning out professionally, making sure they covered each other, alert to possible danger. Geledhil followed immediately behind them, her keen elven senses straining to detect the slightest sound or movement. Her bow was held at the ready with an arrow nocked.

Camron came next, struggling to remain focused, battling his turmoil. He had fought goblins before and knew they were cruel and spiteful creatures and highly cunning. He had no idea how many they might encounter. He was afraid that his companions would rely on him and his magic to get them out of danger should they be vastly outnumbered. Beating the earth elemental was thanks to Bruce's idea and Geledhil's dexterity. The magic he had cast to destroy the elemental had been relatively straightforward. What weighed heavily on his mind was his failure to save Bruce in the ravine. The image of him falling soundlessly to his death still haunted Camron's dreams. His utter inability to save him gnawed at him like a canker. If he couldn't even save one man, how was he supposed to help save the entire world? These doubts had dogged his footsteps throughout the many weary miles travelled through the tunnels. But now, faced with the imminent possibility of being responsible for the others, resurfaced with renewed vigour.

Alongside Camron walked David. Whereas Camron was oblivious to his surroundings, David was only too aware of his. This would only be the second time he had been in a proper fight in his entire life. The earth elemental had been a surprise. None of them expected to fight to gain entry at Dunsinane. The others had carried David along, adrenalin compensating for his lack of bravery. He had needed no skill to point his rifle at the enormous creature and empty magazine after magazine into it. In the aftermath of the fight, while the others surveyed the broken creature or re-supplied with ammo, he had discreetly moved off to one side to be quietly sick. His insides were cramped with terror at what had happened. That same fear struck him now, threatening to paralyse him. This time, it was in the full knowledge he was walking towards a fight, and it was as much as he could do to put one foot in front of the other. Sweat glistened on his face, his body felt clammy and cold, and his hands trembled. He tried to release the safety catch of his assault rifle, but his hands were shaking too much. He stuck one under his armpit to keep it still.

They headed right at the crossroads, using what cover they could find by keeping close to the buildings on either side. After a minute or two, they came upon a wide-open plaza. The source of the smells Geledhil detected became evident. A fire was burning, and two carcasses were being spit-roasted above it. Somebody had recently occupied the area around the fire. They moved away from the building and took a few cautious steps into the precinct. Suddenly, from behind various broken columns, piles of rubble and other points of cover, there rose over twenty goblins, each with a crude crossbow aimed in their direction. The goblins unleased a volley of quarrels.

Camron, Geledhil, Craig and Pete were in the direct line of fire. Geledhil easily dodged a couple of bolts aimed at her. Camron instinctively used Excalibur to deflect one heading his way. Both Craig and Pete received hits, the force of the impact from the quarrels knocking them back several paces. Bruised and winded, both gave silent thanks to the invention of Kevlar body armour.

The goblins quickly ducked back out of sight.

"Quick, before they can reload," bellowed Smith and charged forward. The others followed, all except David. He remained standing, statue-like, paralysed with fear. *Move*, he silently screamed to himself, but his body wouldn't respond. Tears streamed down his cheeks as he watched his friends run towards the goblins, straight into the second wave of crossbow bolts, hastily fired by those goblins who had managed to reload quickly.

Their lack of accuracy saved David from his shame. A quarrel cracked into the wall beside him, skidded off and hit him, carving a deep gash in his left arm. His cry of pain shattered his terror like a stone crashing through a glass window. He bellowed again, this time in anger, and rushed forward, adrenalin now coursing through his veins.

One goblin had remained hidden behind some rubble. It stood and took careful aim, planning to strike from behind. Hearing David's cry, the goblin spun around and brought his crossbow to bear on the enraged human hurtling towards him. David raised his gun and fired a long staccato burst. Several 9mm bullets thudded into the goblin, physically lifting him from his feet and flinging him backwards into a crumpled heap, the quarrel flying harmlessly towards the cavern ceiling.

The intended recipient of the goblin's quarrel, Pete turned at the gunfire and surmised the situation instantly.

"Thanks," he shouted at David. Pete had seen the fear on David's face as they had approached the plaza and had wondered if he would be of any use. He was now very glad David had managed to conquer it in time.

The others were doing equally well. Geledhil had moved off to one side and stood atop one of the numerous piles of rubble, still partially protected by a fallen colonnade. Her shortbow was causing havoc amongst the goblins they fought. Every time one stood up to fire their crossbow, Geledhil's arrow would unerringly hit it first. Several goblins had drawn swords and charged, preferring hand-to-hand combat instead of facing elven arrows. Goblins learnt to fight from a young age but had never encountered modern human weaponry. No matter how expertly wielded, a sword or mace was no match for a Heckler & Koch G36k carbine short-barrel assault rifle. The SAS soldiers tore through the goblin ranks.

Like the fight in Dorchester and the battle with the Earth Elemental, Camron found his doubts and fears dissipated once the fighting began. His thoughts were calm and composed, almost as if time slowed to allow him to assess the battle and plan his move. The fact amplified his relief that there wasn't anything he needed to do. There would be no need for Camron's magic today. Geledhil's accuracy ensured that few goblins dared stick their heads above cover to fire their crossbows. The soldiers were moving methodically through the plaza, shooting as they came across the remaining goblins.

And suddenly, as quickly as it had started, it was over. The absolute silence returned as swiftly as it had left.

The rush of adrenalin that had sustained them through the chaos of the fight started to ebb, their heartbeats slowed, and their breathing returned to normal. Both Pete and Smith came up to David, slapping him on the back in a comradely manner, acknowledging his contribution to the fight and affirming his right to be a member of their team. He smiled weakly, fighting his nausea. Geledhil noticed his arm.

"You're hurt," she exclaimed, moving swiftly to David to check his wound.

Pete looked at it as well. "It's only a flesh wound, be right as rain in a couple of days," he said, pulling out his medi-kit and dressing the wound.

"Well, you're definitely a battle-hardened veteran now," said Smith and smiled at him.

Camron looked at the carnage surrounding them. All of the goblins were dead.

"We ought to have kept one alive," said Camron belatedly. "We could have interrogated them as to where the dwarves were."

"We did," replied Trigger. "Remember the first two we saw. Craig knocked the second one unconscious."

"He's right," confirmed Craig. "Pete, you and Trigger come with me." They loaded fresh magazines into their guns and then headed back to where they had encountered the first two goblins, once more alert and professional.

Geledhil tried to get David to take one of the magical healing potions, but he refused. "It's only a flesh wound, and besides, we don't know what else we will encounter. We ought to save them in case they're needed." Geledhil wasn't convinced but didn't press the matter.

Camron privately agreed with David, and anyway, he seemed to be wearing his bandage as some sort of indication as to his right of passage in combat. Camron still battled his own doubts and fears, and he wasn't about to take David's new sense of confidence away from him. He was pleased for David, although he was a little envious of the professor turned hero.

Camron moved towards the fire, curious as to what was fuelling it. This deep underground wood was a rare commodity, and he didn't believe anyone would waste it on something as mundane as a fire. A crude spit had been fashioned out of metal-hafted spears, and on it were a couple of carcasses, slightly overdone by the look of them. One of the carcasses had been the goblin's meal. Gnawed bones lay scattered around.

David prodded the fire with a goblin sword lying nearby. "Some sort of animal dung by its looks," said David. "It explains the smell anyway."

Camron took his knife and sliced a tiny sliver of meat off the untouched carcass. "It tastes like goat," said Camron in surprise.

"Goat," said Geledhil. "But we haven't seen any animals down here. I wonder where they found them."

"I'm not really too fussed where they came from," said David. "But it will make a nice change from that Koymasse bread."

The others returned a short while later, the still unconscious goblin carried between Pete and Trigger. Goblins were short, thin and wiry, so carrying one wasn't difficult. They had taken the precaution of binding the creature's hands but had set a splint on its crushed foot.

"Let's wake it up and see what it has to tell us then," said Smith, bending over the goblin.

"Hang on," said Camron. "Before we wake it, can you speak the goblin language?" he asked Geledhil.

"Sorry, no. I can speak dwarven but not goblin," she answered.

"Ok, I'll need to cast a spell to communicate with it." Camron thought briefly, recalling the gestures and incantation necessary for a *Tongues* spell.

"You can rouse him now," Camron said to Smith when he had cast the spell.

The goblin let out a low moan, the pain in its crushed foot returning with consciousness. It sensed it wasn't alone and opened its eyes slowly, widening in shock at seeing seven strange, ugly creatures standing over it, looking down menacingly. It tried to raise itself into a sitting position but struggled, hampered by both its bonds and the fresh stab of pain coursing up its leg. Looking around for a means of escape, it saw the dead bodies of its fellow goblins and realised its plight was dire. It flopped back onto the ground, prone before its captors.

"Who are you?"

The goblin looked up, clearly surprised at hearing its' own language spoken.

"Who are you?" Camron repeated forcefully.

"Hraaaknar," the goblin replied in its harsh, guttural tongue.

"Are there any more of you?"

"Lots," Hraaaknar answered, his tone trying to show bravado, but his eyes kept flickering to the dead strewn around.

"Nearby?"

The look of fear and desperation that crossed the goblin's face reassured Camron they were in no imminent danger.

"Where are the dwarves?" Camron asked.

The goblin looked uncomprehending at the question.

"The dwarves who used to live here? This is their city?" Camron asked.

"No dwarves," replied Hraaaknar, his tongue twisting around the word with similar vehemence Camron had used for the word *goblin* earlier. "Dwarves go long time ago."

"Do you remember dwarves living here?" Camron asked, trying to gauge when the dwarves left. He recalled that goblins had little concept of the passage of time.

"No," answered Hraaaknar. "Our tribe shaman tells stories of how goblins fight dwarves. Chase away long time ago."

Camron relayed this information to the others before continuing.

"Where are the dwarves now?"

Hraaaknar didn't answer, but his eyes had subconsciously glanced south.

Camron pointed in the same direction, asking more forcefully, "Are they that way?"

Hraaaknar paused before answering, trying to be brave, but he was alone, in pain and fearful for his life. Hraaaknar capitulated and nodded.

"How far?"

Hraaaknar shrugged, "Far, much far."

"Another city?"

The goblin nodded miserably.

Camron turned to the others, switching back to English. "It looks like the dwarves left a long time ago. There's another city to the south, but no idea how far. The goblin's concept of time is limited. So what do we do now?"

"I hate to suggest this," said Craig, "being army and all and used to the chain of command, but I think we should discuss and decide democratically what to do next."

"I agree," said Smith.

None of them wanted to remain around the dead goblins for longer than they had to, and the fire would act as a magnet to any other creatures wandering by. They decided to carry on to the palace and spend the night there.

They gagged Hraaaknar and stuck the shaft of a spear through the crook of his arms and behind his back. Pete and Trigger half-led, half-carried the goblin as he hobbled along on his injured foot. Craig walked behind, his weapon trained on the goblin. Camron stuck the uneaten goat on the end of another spear and swung it over his shoulder. They headed out of the plaza, making their way towards the royal palace, Geledhil taking the lead once more. No further incidents occurred, and they arrived a short while later at the entrance to what had once been the palace of the dwarven king.

"I'll make dinner," offered Trigger, grabbing his Bergen and rummaging around in the bottom. He dug out a couple of plastic packets and several dehydrated vegetable ration packs. A short while later, a wonderful aroma filled the area.

"Curry?" asked Pete incredulously. "You brought curry powder?"

Trigger nodded, clearly delighted with his foresight and ingenuity.

"If anyone else had even suggested the possibility of having goat curry down here, I would have laughed at them. But with you, it doesn't surprise me," said Craig, salivating at the thought of the meal to come.

Compared with what they had been eating since coming underground, the goat curry was sumptuous. Trigger had even remembered to make just a vegetable curry for Geledhil.

After dinner, Camron wandered off a short distance and took out the *Finders Map.* It showed their current location in Varðasteinn. The portion of the map between there and Dunsinane, far to the north, was incredibly detailed. Every single tunnel and cavern they had traversed, each twist and turn and dead-end was magically inscribed. However, below Varðasteinn to the south, the page remained blank, devoid of any clue as to what lay beyond the city. Camron looked at the *Ring of Friendship* on his left hand. He had gotten used to the delicate tickling in the back of his mind, almost taking it for granted as it guided him if they were heading in the right direction or not. He had ignored the faint tugging completely since they had arrived at what they thought was their destination. However, focusing his thoughts on the ring once more, he realised the ring was still guiding him south.

Camron felt mixed emotions at this. Part of him was elated that their quest hadn't entirely failed. There was still a chance they might find the dwarven king somewhere to the south. But that required having to venture into the unknown wilderness of the underworld once more. How far would they have to travel, and what further perils and dangers would they have to face, all without any guarantee of success? Camron sat alone, the weight of responsibility bearing down on him again.

His thoughts turned to Rachel. He had been gone for over a week now. How many more weeks would it take to find the dwarves? And even if they could find them, they still had to convince them to help. And once they had done all that, there would be a long journey back to the surface.

He thought of Rachel and concentrated on his *Family Ring*. He could feel the link, but it was like trying to watch television on an old black-and-white TV with bad reception. He wondered whether being so far underground was causing this but dismissed it quickly. The rings worked across the different planes of existence. Being a few miles underground shouldn't make any difference.

A thought struck him, was the *Friendship Ring* affecting the *Family Ring*? After all, they both worked on similar principles, and the magic involved was probably comparable. He took off the *Friendship Ring, and Rachel's link* became stronger and clearer. He received the vaguest of feelings back, a general sense of well-being tinged with longing for her absent husband and a hint of sadness. However tenuous, he clung to these feelings, revelling in the connection it gave him to his wife.

Using the *Family Ring* reminded him that he hadn't once let his grandmother know what was happening in all their time underground. He felt guilty as he realised she might have felt his emotional reaction to Bruce's death a week ago but would have no idea who had died. He wondered whether she had been trying to contact him.

He switched his thoughts from his wife to his grandmother and concentrated on her image. He felt an immediate connection with Nimue, and the feeling of relief he received almost overwhelmed him. However, it didn't last long. An equally strong sense of anger quickly replaced it. He was left in no doubt that while she was delighted to hear from him, she was equally cross with him. His grandmother's wrath was no trivial thing.

He took a steadying breath and concentrated on getting his thoughts in order. Trying to portray all that had happened through the ring's limited empathic communication wasn't easy. Camron thought he had at least managed to get across the most salient points of their journey so far and that the quest wasn't over yet. He also realised he had conferred the feeling that they would continue. This hadn't been a decision he had made consciously, but, thinking about it, he realised he would make no other choice. Despite his doubts about his ability, he had to try.

He felt his grandmother's ire abated slightly and her sympathy for the loss of Bruce. She also acknowledged his decision to continue and approved of it. He received a final encompassing wave of love for both himself and Geledhil. He returned the feeling to her and bade her goodbye before withdrawing his concentration from the ring.

He sat there a while longer, lost in his thoughts.

He became aware of Geledhil's surreptitious glances in his direction. He realised she was probably dying of curiosity about what he had been doing. He got up and made his way back to the others.

Craig looked up as Camron sat down. "So, the wanderer returns. We've been discussing what to do next. Do we continue or go back to the surface and work out another plan?"

"We continue," said Camron without preamble.

"So much for the democratic discussion," Pete chimed in.

"I'm not going to force any of you to come with me if you don't want to, but I have to go on. My grandmother agrees with me."

"You spoke to Grandmother?" asked Geledhil.

"Yes, sort of, through our *family rings*."

"Yours works? I tried mine, but nothing happened, although I wasn't too surprised as I've never really been much good at magic. Plus, not only are we on a different plane, but we're a long way underground."

"No, the rings work fine, but it worked better once I had removed the *Ring of Friendship*."

"So we continue south to find the dwarves then," said Craig, more statement of fact than a question.

Camron smiled gratefully, acknowledging the unspoken agreement to go with him.

David added his consent, “You know I might enter the London Marathon next year. This fitness regime is doing me a world of good.”

“So when do we leave?” asked Smith.

Getting to the dwarven city had been a long and arduous journey, so they decided to spend the next day in the palace resting. It would also allow time to sort out their gear, mend clothing, and dry out some of the goat meat to help preserve it for the next leg of their journey.

“What about our ugly friend there?” asked Pete, pointing his thumb towards Hraaaknar. “We can’t leave an enemy to our rear.”

“There’s only one thing we can do,” said Craig. “We can’t take a prisoner with us, especially considering he’s injured and would slow us down.” He drew out his knife and stood up. “May as well get this over and done with.”

“No,” shouted Geledhil, suddenly realising what Craig was proposing. “You cannot kill the goblin, even if he is our enemy.”

“Look,” said Pete, “I would rather we didn’t have to either, but we can’t take it with us, and we can’t afford for one of us to take it back to the surface as a prisoner. If we leave it here, who knows how many others it will round up to follow us. Travelling through this underworld is hard enough without a whole bunch of nasties dogging our every step. It’s not nice or pleasant. It isn’t necessarily right. But this is war, and sometimes we have no choice but to do what we have to.”

Geledhil looked at Camron, the desperation evident in her eyes. Camron felt similar to her regarding the sanctity of life, being part elf himself. The thought of having to kill someone, or something, which was unarmed and defenceless, was anathema to him. But he could not think of any other solution to put their safety first. Tears welled up in Geledhil’s eyes, and she shook her head, pleading with Camron. Craig continued towards the terrified goblin who sat off to one side, securely bound and tied to a pillar.

* * *

Hraaaknar had not understood a word of what they had said, but that wasn't necessary. The ugly creature bearing down on him with a knife in his hand and a grim, determined look was all the clues he needed. The skinny female's pleading and the outpouring of emotion only confirmed his fate. He shuffled back as far as possible as if he could sink into the pillar at his back and disappear. He was a fighter but, like most of his kind, had a shallow streak and put his self-preservation above all else. He whimpered in fear, his breathing coming in short, sharp gasps.

* * *

"I've an idea," said David unexpectedly. Every face turned to look at him, except for the goblin whose eyes were firmly fixed on the steel blade Craig held in his hands. David did not return the curious looks but gazed upwards towards the stone towers that rose majestically above the palace. He was looking at one in particular. It was nearly a hundred metres tall, more of a column than a tower, seemingly without windows or doors. Towards the top was a broad ledge running around the outside. Access to this ledge was via a narrow arched bridge spanning from that tower to a nearby one.

"If we put the goblin on that ledge and destroy the bridge, he'll be stuck there for a while, giving us plenty of time to get away before he can summon any more of his kind."

"He could climb down. It looks difficult, but it could be done," argued Trigger.

"Not until his foot heals. It'll be at least a week before his foot is in any condition to attempt the climb."

"He'll starve to death first," said Geledhil.

"Not if we leave him what's left of the goat," countered David. "Remember the other carcass we saw. They eat the bones as well as the meat. Those sharp pointed teeth of his will gnaw through anything."

Craig looked at David keenly, trying to find a flaw in his plan. He couldn't. "I think it might work," he conceded. "But what if it starts shouting for help."

"If we do it as we leave in the morning, we will be long gone before any unwanted attention might arrive. Anyway, I think it's a risk worth taking."

The others nodded. Smith was happy with the solution, not that he was particularly opposed to their first plan. He was a professional and wouldn't have baulked at killing the goblin if necessary. Still, he knew from the reaction of Geledhil and, to a certain extent, the look in Camron's eyes that if Craig had dispatched the goblin, there would be a rift in the group. That could prove deadly in a hostile environment such as this.

Craig sheathed his knife and turned away from the goblin, returning to the others.

The following day, as the others prepared to depart, Craig, Pete, and Trigger made the long, arduous climb up the steps of the tall tower adjacent to the column they had selected as the goblin's aerial prison. Hraaaknar, clearly still in pain, was half-dragged, half-carried along.

Finally, they reached the top. Craig and Tigger led Hraaaknar across the narrow stone bridge while Pete placed an explosive charge on the bridge.

Hraaaknar's groans turned to whimpers, and his eyes widened in fear.

"We ain't throwing you off, you ugly bastard," said Trigger, despite knowing the goblin didn't understand him.

They took Hraaaknar around the far side of the tower. Leaving the gnawed carcass and some water on the ledge, they unbound the goblin and retreated back across the bridge.

The SAS soldiers took cover inside the tower and detonated the charge, sending the arched bridge crashing to the ground.

"Time to leave," said Craig as they emerged from the tower's base and collected their bergens from where the others waited.

“Aye,” said Pete, “if there’s any more of the beasties around, they’ll have heard the explosion.”

The small group paused at the mouth of the large tunnel that headed south. Camron took one last look at the Varðasteinn. This city had offered some semblance of refuge despite the dangers and contrasted sharply with the wilderness of the tunnels. He sighed, hoisted the pack containing the Stone of Destiny into a more comfortable position and uttered a word of magic, illuminating the tip of his magical staff.

Once again, they headed into the darkness of the tunnels, leaving behind the small pretence of civilisation the abandoned city had offered them.

# Chapter 35

SATURDAY 3RD JULY

"It looks lovely on you," said Rachel, walking around Xankira as she stood in the shop wearing a pale green jacket. "I think we should get it. You need a jacket, and my old one just hangs off you."

Xankira wasn't feeling very grateful.

She knew she ought to be grateful, but she felt decidedly grumpy.

Taking off the jacket and handing it to Rachel, Xankira said, "I'll wait outside. I need some air."

"Ok," said Rachel, heading towards the queue at the till. "I'll just pay for this."

Xankira stood outside yet another clothes store, weighed down with several bags, all full of new clothes for her and all bought by Rachel. Xankira hated being poor and hated accepting charity even more. She glossed over the technicality that even if she had any elven gold with her, she wouldn't have been able to spend it in the human world. Rachel had insisted on taking her shopping.

Xankira had been wearing some of Rachel's clothes whenever they left the cottage, but they were a poor fit. She was leaner than Rachel and at least twenty centimetres shorter.

"Hello."

Xankira jumped, startled as the intrusion interrupted her thoughts. She looked up and saw a man standing a few metres away from her, leaning casually against the shop window. He was in his mid-twenties and, she supposed, reasonably good looking for a human.

"Are you waiting for someone as well?" he continued, oblivious to his unreturned greeting. "Somehow, I always seem to be the one waiting outside. My friend is in there buying yet more clothes he doesn't need. I don't know where he gets his money from. I really don't. I know I couldn't afford to spend the amount he does."

Xankira detected a hint of bitterness in his tone, somewhat akin to her own feelings. Despite her reluctance to engage in conversation with anyone, she turned towards the stranger.

"My name's Josh," he said, pausing and raising an eyebrow enquiringly, hoping she would fill in the blank with her own name.

"I'm Xankira," she replied eventually.

"Xankira... what a lovely name. Very exotic and unusual." She smiled at the compliment, despite herself. "That isn't a Dorset accent unless I'm very much mistaken. You're not from around here then, I take it?"

"No," answered Xankira. "I'm visiting a friend for a couple of weeks."

"The one inside with all the money?" he inquired, nodding in the direction of the shop door.

Xankira nodded.

"I have to confess, it isn't entirely a coincidence that I'm waiting outside this shop," he said. "I saw you go in and was captivated by how beautiful you are. I hoped I would get to see you again, and here you are, right next to me. I couldn't believe my luck when you came out just now."

Xankira glanced away, not daring to meet Josh's intense gaze. But, despite her discomfort at his compliment, a small smile crept into the corners of her mouth. She noticed Rachel weaving her way through the shop towards her. Xankira's smile disappeared.

"Is that your friend?" asked Josh.

Xankira nodded.

"Well, I'd better be off anyway. It was a pleasure to have met you, Xankira." He threw her a disarming smile as he turned to leave.

Xankira's gaze was still following him as he walked away when Rachel finally emerged from the shop.

"Come on," she said. "Let's find somewhere to have a coffee. I'm exhausted."

"Okay," answered Xankira unenthusiastically, hoisting the shopping bags more comfortably. She stopped herself sighing just in time, but the thought of Rachel recuperating with a coffee and then wanting to start another round of shopping was maddening. They headed to Starbucks and found an empty table outside.

"You wait here. I'll get us a drink. Coffee alright with you?" asked Rachel.

"Water, please?" answered Xankira as she sat down, surrounded by their purchases. *Yet another thing I can't pay for,* thought Xankira, annoyed she didn't even have the money to pay for a drink.

"Hello again."

Xankira turned, startled at the unexpected voice. She didn't notice the last words of magic drifting away on the breeze.

Sitting at the table behind her was Josh, smiling warmly at her. Xankira smiled back, despite herself.

"She really shouldn't talk down to you like that. It makes you sound more like a servant than a friend," he said.

"She isn't really a close friend," she admitted. "I've only known her for a couple of weeks. Actually, I'm only helping out. Keeping an eye on her as a favour to my best friend. Just until her husband gets back."

"Ah, I understand now. I couldn't quite picture you working for someone like her. So why isn't your best friend helping out instead of you?"

Xankira hesitated. She shouldn't be talking to him, but an insistent tugging in her mind urged her to continue.

"She's gone on the journey with Rachel's husband."

"A journey? Sounds mysterious. I wonder who this intriguing husband of hers is and why the grand journey?"

"I really shouldn't say," answered Xankira tentatively. Part of her was screaming not to say anything and have nothing more to do with this man. But it was a small part, buried in the deepest recesses of her mind, and she was finding it easier and easier to push these thoughts aside. The necklace lay against her skin underneath her clothes, its curse overpowering her good nature and emphasising the jealous streak she had always fought to contain.

"It's a secret journey, is it?" asked Josh.

Xankira nodded.

"I'm good at keeping secrets," said Josh, "I've been keeping them all my life."

*I can trust you*, thought Xankira, oblivious to the *charm* spell he had cast on her.

"Well, you must keep this secret, but it's something to do with the Dökkálfar attacks."

"Sounds dangerous?"

Xankira nodded again.

"You're not in any danger, are you?"

"I can look after myself," she replied defiantly. "And Rachel. That's why they chose me to protect her."

Josh looked impressed. "Well, you seem to be an extraordinary young woman. But there is one thing I don't understand. Why is Rachel so important?"

"She isn't really," said Xankira, her envy wanting nothing more than to diminish Rachel's significance. "It's her husband, Camron. He's the important one. Well, he and their unborn daughter. They're the ones vital to winning the war."

"The war?"

"Yes," she replied, "against the Dökkálfar."

"But how could an unborn child win a war?"

"I don't know. It's to do with some prophecy from the time of King Arthur, I think."

"And Rachel's husband, Camron, did you say he's called? He has something to do with King Arthur, does he?"

"Yes, he's his son," replied Xankira automatically. The small part of her mind still her own howled in anguish, but Xankira did not hear it.

"Xankira?" said a voice behind her.

Xankira turned and saw Rachel approaching.

"Well, it was nice to meet you," said Josh, rising hastily and departing before Xankira could say anything.

"Who was that?" asked Rachel, placing their drinks tray on the table.

"No one," she replied absently, her mind a little foggy. The conversation with Josh was already dimming in her memory.

* * *

Raknarden hurried away, waiting until he found a deserted spot behind some shops before dismissing the *Illusion* spell. Josh's appearance dissipated, replaced by the cruel, handsome features of the Dökkálfar.

His mind reeled with possibilities.

Could Rachel's unborn child be *the DoomBringer*, the one who must die before the Dökkálfar could win?

This was more than he could have possibly dreamed of. He had the wife of King Arthur's son and their unborn daughter in his grasp. The power this would bring him would be almost beyond measure, but only if he played it to his full advantage. He would have to think carefully and plan how best to use this information. His mind was awash with possibilities.

*Should I kill them both now?* He thought but quickly dismissed the idea. *Tumultuous events are on the horizon. Killing the DoomBringer during the forthcoming battle will surely throw the enemy into disarray.* His thoughts returned to his own gain. *Should I tell Sallakray? No, he could not trust his Hlyđni-Móđir not to overlook his part in the event.*

Her image floated into his mind, cruel eyes as hard as adamantine.

*Betshar,* he thought, *House Dukker's First-Daughter. If she could claim the glory of killing the DoomBringer, she would surely depose her mother and ascend to the head of the house?* Raknarden could already see himself standing alongside Betshar, revelling in his craved glory and power.

# Chapter 36

MONDAY, 5TH JULY

It had been four days since they had left Varðasteinn and the morning started much the same as previous days. They ate a cold breakfast of Koymasse bread with the last of the dried goat meat and then broke camp. Geledhil took the lead and moved a short distance ahead, staying just out of reach of the lights of the rest of the group, which allowed her elven vision to work in the darkness but not so distant as to be too far from help should the need arise. She knew Camron worried about her being ahead on her own, but he also knew that being out in front, in the dark, was where she could make the best use of her talents. They travelled non-stop for much of the day, resting briefly around noon, according to Craig's watch, for yet more Koymasse bread.

It was late afternoon when Geledhil stopped suddenly, her keen senses alert. She had heard something up ahead, only the faintest of noises, but it was enough to warn her. It sounded like metal striking metal. She took a few more steps forward, treading silently, as only an elf can. There, she heard it again. Definitely the sound of metal striking metal, a distinctive and unmistakable ringing. She moved forward another few metres until the tunnel began to curve away to her left. She stopped and waited for the others to catch up, her acute elven hearing still picking up the ringing clashes.

"What is it?" Camron whispered as the others reached her. Craig held up his hand, signalling to the others to stop and be silent.

"Listen," she said. They did but could hear nothing. Even Camron's hearing was nowhere near as acute as hers. "I can hear metal ringing on metal. It could be dwarves mining?"

"Or it could be fighting," said Craig in a whisper.

"How far away do you think it is?" asked Smith, his voice barely audible.

"Five hundred metres, maybe more," she answered. "It's difficult to tell in these tunnels."

"Ok, let's stay alert and be ready," said Craig.

Geledhil considered thanking him for his thoughtful advice but settled on throwing him a look instead. In the gloom of the tunnel, Craig didn't notice.

They once again readied their weapons, switching the safety catches to automatic. At the same time, Geledhil fitted a new bowstring and nocked an arrow. They continued on, their pace slowing to a stealthy walk.

Geledhil heard shouts intermingled with the metallic clashes that were becoming louder and more frequent. She had never done any mining herself but had been in many mock battles. The noises she heard sounded more like the latter. As they moved further around the long wide arc of the tunnel, Geledhil became aware of the faintest glimmer of light filtering along the passageway. They soon covered their own lights as a precaution, moving forward in the dim gloom of the corridor. Soon they approached a spacious cavern, lit with now-familiar luminous fungi

Over on the far side, a pitched battle was taking place. The fighting appeared to have been underway for some time, given the number of bodies they could see strewn around.

*Goblins* thought Geledhil.

She realised the other combatants were dwarves. Each reaching no more than 120 centimetres tall, an overly large head sat atop broad shoulders, and barrel-like chests gave them a stocky, burly appearance. Clasps and intricate braids decorated their long, thick beards. They fought with various weapons, predominantly battle-axes, but some with maces and war hammers.

From their position just inside the tunnel on the other side of the cavern, it looked like the goblins had the upper hand. As Geledhil and Camron watched for a few moments, waiting for the others to reach them, another dwarf was struck and fell. Only three dwarves remained standing but still faced eighteen goblins.

"Why are they fighting?" whispered Smith.

“Dwarves and goblins just hate each other. Always have done,” Camron replied.

“Do we go around them?” said Geledhil softly.

“No, time to help, I think,” said Camron quietly.

They stepped into the cavern without delay and fanned out, weapons raised. Geledhil took several arrows and placed them, tip down, into the soft sand of the cavern floor. She took careful aim and loosed. Before her first arrow had reached its target, she had a second one nocked and was taking aim. The first arrow had flown true, hitting a goblin straight between the shoulder blades. It died, never knowing what had hit it.

The goblin next to it didn’t even realise its compatriot had died before Geledhil’s second arrow struck it. A third goblin just had time to turn its head and stare dumbfounded at its fellows as they toppled forward, arrows protruding from their backs. The third arrow passed through its neck, severing its spinal cord.

*She’s good*, thought Pete, and although he would never admit it aloud, he was glad she was on their side.

The rest of the goblins realised they were under attack from the rear, and several turned to face this new threat. The sight of humans that greeted the goblins must have been as surreal and confusing as they had been to the humans. Five figures, dressed entirely in black, each holding a stick to their shoulders, were advancing towards them. Behind them stood two more, not dressed in black but equally strange looking. Six goblins rushed forward to meet them, holding wicked-looking swords aloft with curved blades made of black metal.

Five Heckler & Koch G36k carbine short-barrel assault rifles opened fire, four of them firing two rounds into the first four goblins from the right. The fire selector on David’s gun was set to automatic mode. He delivered a somewhat longer burst of fire than intended. The stream of bullets killed a goblin.

His more prolonged burst of fire had another unexpected benefit. The precise *double-tap* shots from the SAS troopers, while noisy, did not immediately register with the other goblins. However, David’s long staccato burst in the echoing confines of the cavern was unlike anything the goblins or dwarves had heard before. The loud, low-pitched boom of the gunshots resonated around the cavern, echoing off the walls.

The combatants turned towards the sound, momentarily frozen in terror at the deafening noise. All except for one older goblin who, unfortunately for the dwarf he was fighting, was deaf. The goblin didn't hear the gunfire. He merely saw it as good fortune when the dwarf stopped trying to hack him with his axe and gaped dumbfounded over the goblin's shoulder. The goblin took a second to thrust his blade into the distracted dwarf's unprotected throat before turning to see what the fuss was about.

The death of their comrade galvanised the two remaining dwarves. They let out a terrifying war cry and resumed fighting, one of them burying his double-headed battle-axe into the old goblin's neck.

The remaining goblins also recovered quickly. Three of them continued fighting the dwarves while the rest rushed to meet the newcomers, now only a few metres away. Three more goblins died as the troopers continued firing.

Pete, with Trigger following, veered slightly to the left, widening their line of attack and forcing the goblins to separate. The move was well-rehearsed and a standard SOP tactic. However, nobody in the British army, or any military, had devised a standard operating procedure for combating sword-wielding goblins. The ploy was sound. Unfortunately, the outcome wasn't.

Pete had moved no more than twenty paces to the right when he stopped suddenly. Three crudely made black arrows protruded from him. Two had hit his chest, lodging in his Kevlar body armour but not puncturing it. The third arrow was lethal. Aimed at his chest like the other two, it had missed and hit him in the throat instead. Blood gurgled from Pete's throat, his eyes portraying disbelief as he dropped his weapon. He fell to his knees with his hands clutched desperately at his throat. A second later, he toppled forward.

“Man down!” bellowed Trigger. Rushing to Pete’s side, he let out a long burst of fire in the direction of the goblins before turning his attention to Pete. Several more arrows thudded into the ground around them.

Trigger pulled out his first aid kit and tore open an army battle dressing, placing the ABD pad over the wound at Pete’s throat. Blood was everywhere but no longer spurted out. His heart had already stopped beating.

Camron had heard Trigger’s yell and looked up. Three goblins stood atop a small rocky outcrop that had provided them with cover. Armed with short bows, they were busy concentrating their fire on Trigger as he crouched next to Pete. Camron pointed them out to Geledhil. “Keep them busy but be ready when I finish my spell.”

Geledhil took careful aim at the boldest of the goblins who stood slightly to one side of the outcrop. The goblin loosed his arrow a second before Geledhil fired hers. The goblin’s face lit up with glee as his arrow thudded into Trigger’s thigh, causing him to cry out in pain. However, his delight was short-lived as Geledhil’s arrow found its mark dead centre of the goblin’s chest. It toppled backwards under the impact and was dead before hitting the ground. The other two goblins ducked back behind the rocky outcrop.

Camron completed his spell. The tip of his staff shone with a dull brown glow, matching the colour of the surrounding rocks as the magic enveloped its target. The *Rock to Mud* spell hit the rocky outcrop, and it collapsed like a soufflé gone wrong. The two goblins cowering behind toppled into the thick glutinous mud and struggled to free themselves. Their efforts lasted long enough for Geledhil to fire two arrows in quick succession. Both goblins fell face down into the pool of mud created by Camron’s magic. Their bodies were still and lifeless.

Only two goblins were still alive. Realising their situation was dire and, true to the nature of their race, they turned and fled. They ran as fast as their bare flapping feet could carry them, but it wasn't fast enough to outrun bullets. Craig and Smith fired simultaneously, their aim deadly accurate. Two more goblins added to the toll of the dead.

Several seconds of silence followed, each of the surviving combatants surveying the scene momentarily lost in thought as they absorbed all that had happened in the last few minutes.

Trigger's groan broke into their thoughts. Craig and Smith rushed towards him, his own pain etched across his face though he still struggled in vain to aid Pete.

* * *

One of the dwarves turned to face the strangers who had come, suddenly and unexpectedly, to their aid. Blood flowed from a dozen cuts, and several nasty welts and bruises began to discolour his skin. Hreidimar ignored the pain, his eyes remaining alert and his battle-axe, covered in the blood and gore of goblins, held at the ready. His stance poised for action if needed.

His eyes flicked briefly to his companion, the only other dwarf who remained standing. Gurrandig looked in a bad way. He had lowered his axe, resting the head on the ground as he leant on the haft for support. He looked ashen, his wounds more numerous than Hreidmar's, but he was a dwarf. He wouldn't wholly lower his guard until he knew the nature of the creatures standing opposite them.

Hreidmar had never seen creatures such as those he faced but could guess what they were from the books and histories he had learnt as a youngster. They were the first to set foot in the realm of dwarves for almost a millennia and a half.

Humans!

He eyed them warily but noted they had lowered their strange weapons. Those weird *bang sticks* imparted death at such a distance, without arrow or quarrel, and in a loud manner, each crack reverberating around the cavern.

“Please don’t be alarmed. My name is Camron. We’re friends.”

Hreidmar started. The last thing he had expected to hear was his own tongue. The dialect was ancient and spoken with a strange mellifluous and dulcet tone rather than the thick, guttural timbre he usually heard. He was even more startled to realise the one who had spoken was female. At least, he assumed she was female due to her long silvery hair and slim physique. Dwarven women tended to be only slightly less stocky than their male counterparts, and their beards were a softer down than the full wiry beards of the menfolk.

“Are you alright?” the female said, taking several steps forward. Even by the dim light of the cavern, Hreidmar could see the concern in her eyes.

He nodded gruffly. However, he felt anything but all right.

“Who are ye?” he asked, his visage grim and his body still taut and ready for action. Before anyone could answer, Gurrandig collapsed, toppling to the ground. Hreidmar dropped his axe and knelt by his friend. He looked up as footsteps approached, startled to see the female already standing by him. The footsteps he had heard came from two others, who were hurrying towards him. She hadn’t made the slightest noise. He stopped and looked again in astonishment.

“Alfar,” he spat, not entirely with the same vehemence as Camron had previously uttered *goblins*, but with an undertone of loathing nevertheless. Even though dwarves had fought alongside Ljósálfar during the last war, there was no love between the two races. They had always disliked and distrusted one another.

“Ljósálfar,” corrected Camron, also speaking Dwarvish, though his tongue struggled with the words he had last spoken 1,500 years ago. “And she’s here with us. Let us help you and your brave friend, please? We have healing potions.”

“We want none of your Alfar witchcraft here. Get ye gone from these tunnels,” Hreidmar replied, turning his face from them to look at Gurrandig.

“Then your stubbornness will surely kill your friend. He needs urgent help, and we offer it freely and unconditionally,” Camron continued doggedly, withdrawing several of the precious healing potions from his bag.

There was another stifled cry from the injured human. Hreidmar watched as Camron handed a glass vial to one of the humans, speaking to him in their strange language. The human hurried over to the injured one.

“Look,” said Camron, turning again to the Hredimar, who still knelt by his dying compatriot. “We didn’t have to help you. We could have waited until they killed you and avoided a fight altogether. But we came to your aid. We fought the goblins alongside you and shared equally in the risks of battle.” He trailed off, leaving the unspoken words hanging in the air between them. Hreidmar’s eyes flicked towards the fallen humans. His eyes shifted from the still form of the dead human to the injured one. Hreidmar watched as the vial contents were poured down his throat.

“Will you let your friend die because of your misplaced distrust?” ask Camron.

Hreidmar stood up, and he and Camron locked eyes for many seconds, each evaluating the other. Camron was willing the dwarf to see sense.

Eventually, Hreidmar said, “Do what ye can for him.” His voice almost cracked with restrained emotion.

The elf knelt down next to Gurrandig and gently raised his head onto her lap. With nimble fingers, she opened a vial containing the magical healing potion. She poured it down his throat, taking pains not to spill a single drop.

Hreidmar stood. His body may have been motionless, but his eyes absorbed every action in detail, alert to the slightest hint of treachery. His friend’s life was in the hands of these strangers, but that didn’t mean he trusted them.

The elf uttered a word, holding out her hand but not taking her eyes from the Gurrandig. Camron handed her another vial, which she administered just as gently as the first. She laid Gurrandig back down and started to treat his many wounds, staunching the blood flow with the dressings. Her movements were deft and precise.

Hreidmar noted the elf's efficiency in her tender ministrations with professional detachment. He could have done no better himself. The bandages and powders applied to the wounds, though strange, had worked better than the strips of linen dwarves usually used.

* * *

Smith looked down at the strange dwarf. Until less than an hour ago, he had never seen a dwarf, but he felt a comradely concern for him as a fellow soldier. The indefinable *brothers-in-arms* camaraderie crossed nations, creeds and colours. And now race.

"Will he live?" asked Smith.

"I don't know," answered Geledhil, brushing the hair from her face and rubbing her eyes wearily. "His breathing seems a little less shallow, and we've stopped most of the bleeding. But his wounds were grievous. I'm not sure any human or elf would have survived them."

"What about another healing potion? Would that help?"

"No. You can take one for most wounds and a second if they are more severe, but any more would be wasted. If the magic of two potions doesn't work, then nothing will."

Camron approached Hreidmar.

"Your turn," he said in dwarvish, holding out one of the elven vials. "You've got a couple of nasty wounds yourself. Here, take this. It will help. And then we can see to the bleeding."

They spent the night in the cavern. Gurrandig was far too critical to risk moving, no matter how unpleasant their surroundings might be. Camron cast protective spells across the entrances of the three separate tunnels that led from the cave, ensuring they were safe from ambush by more goblins during the night. The others hauled the dead goblins into a pile in the far corner and did their best to ignore them.

A row of dead dwarves was on the ground, carefully laid out, six in total. Hreidmar knelt respectfully by each of them, murmuring soft words over them. His words were choked and his vision blurred by tears that he so seldom shed. But each of them had been a friend of his. He would not allow them to go to their rest without a proper farewell to a brave and loyal companion. He crossed the arms of the last one, closing already stiffening fingers around the haft of their battle-axe, adjusted their helm and straightened it as was proper. Hreidmar stepped back and said a final farewell to his friends.

He wished he could have gotten them back home for a proper burial, but that was impossible. The law of the underworld dictated their fate, scavenged by whatever creature happened upon them first. A fate unbefitting such brave souls. But this was a harsh and unforgiving world, and he accepted the unfairness sanguinely.

Hreidmar's reverie was broken as two humans laid their own fallen warrior alongside the dwarves surprisingly comradely. Hreidmar looked up, staring intently into the eyes of one of them. The visage of the human was strange to him, but within those strangely coloured eyes, he thought he detected a look seeking his approval.

This simple action of unity shocked Hreidmar. He blinked, looking down the row of bodies now numbering seven and realised how fitting it was. They had fought together and died together. It was only right they should rest together. He lifted his eyes and met those of the human again. Hreidmar nodded once and then knelt by the human. He uttered the same words over the fallen comrade as he had over his fellow dwarves and then carefully, reverently, crossed the humans' arms in the same manner. He rose and met the human's gaze, although Hreidmar's eyes held the plea of approval this time. The human nodded, a small, sad smile crossing his face.

With the cave magically protected, they sought to get what rest they could. Despite weariness from the battle, sleep eluded most of them.

Gurrandig died a short while later, a great stillness taking over his body. His wounds had been too grievous even for the magical healing of the elven potions and Geledhil's constant ministrations. The row of the fallen now numbered eight.

"We can't leave them here like this," complained Smith. "It isn't right. We had no choice but to leave Bruce, but we can't abandon Pete."

"We won't," Camron announced, climbing stiffly to his feet. He had spent the past few hours memorising spells for precisely this reason. "We're going to bury them, all of them. And properly too. Nothing is going to disturb their rest." He turned to Hreidmar and explained in Dwarvish what he intended to do. Hreidmar looked down at them and nodded.

Craig knelt by Pete, pulling out his id tags. He also took his rations and spare ammo.

"Stand well back," Camron said. He began to cast the first of the spells. The row of dead dwarves and Pete were against one of the cave walls. Camron cast another *Rock to Mud* spell on the wall, causing it to collapse like a minor mudslide, completely engulfing the bodies.

"Now, I'm going to solidify the mud."

"Wait," called out Trigger. He darted forward with Pete's rifle bayonet in his hand. He placed it in the mud, with the hilt and half the blade still visible. "It's not right to leave his grave unmarked."

Camron then cast his second spell, this one the reverse of the first, a *Mud to Rock* spell. The thick glutinous mud hardened to solid rock, sealing the bodies within a permanent stone coffin. No creature would be able to scavenge them now. The diverse group stood in silence for a few moments, each lost in their own thoughts, saying their private farewells to the fallen.

Camron eventually broke the silence, speaking in Dwarvish. "Hreidmar, we came to your world to ask the dwarves to help us. Will you help us, please? Will you guide us to the dwarven city?"

* * *

Hreidmar stood still, his expression rigid and unfathomable. Inside, however, he was a whirl of emotion. Although humans, Ljósálfar and dwarves may have once been allies, that was in the distant past. And even then, there had been a mutual wariness between dwarves and elves. They were just so diametrically opposite in their natures. Ljósálfar were creatures of magic, at one with nature and all things living and oft given to being erratic and unpredictable. Dwarves, however, were solid and dependable, at one with the earth and rock; stoic in nature, sometimes stubborn and even surly in their demeanour.

They had very different outlooks on life and had been reluctant allies.

Hreidmar knew of the nature of the Ljósálfar from the histories he had learnt growing up. His natural distrust of them was ingrained. But he was also intelligent and reliant on his own judgement, a necessity for surviving in the tunnels. He had witnessed the efforts Geledhil had made trying to save Gurrandig and the tears that had flown freely from her strange oval eyes at his death. This group had come to his aid, unbidden and at considerable risk to themselves. Indeed, one of them had died in the attempt to help the dwarves, and another had been injured.

He felt his own wounds, now almost healed thanks to the magical potion. A gift was freely given by the elf.

Surprising himself, Hreidmar uttered words of agreement. "I'll lead ye to me home, Mortheill. But I can give ye no assurance of how ye will be greeted there. That will be for the king to decide."

"Thank you," said Camron, relief flooding his visage. "How far is it to travel there?"

"We will be there in about a ten-day."

Hreidmar led the way, this was his homeland, and his vision in the darkness was even better than Geledhil's. Several times during that first day, they had to stop and rest. Despite the magical healing of Trigger's wounds, he had not fully recovered and struggled to keep up. Geledhil, walking slightly behind Hreidmar, kept a watchful eye on the dwarf and noticed that he seemed to be suffering from the aftermath of his wounds. He laboured with his breathing and walked with an almost imperceptible limp. Geledhil was glad of the periods of rest on Trigger's behalf. She suspected the dwarf was far too proud to admit the need to stop.

They made camp that night in a large niche off a small cavern. David beckoned Geledhil to come with him and sit by Hreidmar, who had seated himself off to one side alone. The dwarf glowered suspiciously as the pair sat next to him. David offered him a mug of black coffee, smiling and nodding to the dwarf.

"It's alright," said Geledhil in Dwarvish. "It's a drink the humans like. They call it *coffee* and drink it very hot. Personally, I think it tastes quite bitter."

Hreidmar took the proffered mug. If the elf didn't like it, it might be all right. He took a careful sip. She was right. It was bitter, but not unpleasantly so. He took another sip.

David watched Hreidmar for a moment. "Geledhil, I was thinking, if we're going to enlist the aid of the dwarves, then it would be useful for us to talk with them in their own language. Seeing as we're going to be travelling together for a while, would you ask Hreidmar if he would be so kind as to teach me Dwarvish? In return, I can teach him English. If he'd like to learn."

Geledhil recounted David's proposition to the dwarf, who, after some consideration, nodded in agreement. Thus, the pattern for their journey was set. When they stopped for the evening, the three of them huddled together in an informal language class. Occasionally, one or two of the others would join in, picking up a phrase or two of Dwarvish that might come in handy. Camron was also grateful for the lessons. While he didn't directly participate, he listened discreetly. He had last spoken the dwarven tongue 1,500 years ago. Not only was he very rusty, but the dialect Hreidmar spoke was different. A refresher course was precisely what he needed.

Hreidmar made their journey through the underworld to Mortheill considerably less arduous than it might otherwise have been. His knowledge of this world was encyclopaedic, and wariness towards them gradually diminished as he pointed out creatures they had not noticed. Which fungi were edible, and where were the safest places to rest. On one occasion, they encountered a small group of strange, bovid-like animals that loosely resembled goats. Hreidmar called them Groths and said his people had domesticated large numbers of them, providing the dwarves with a bountiful supply of milk, meat, wool and leather. Geledhil had to force herself not to wrinkle her nose in disgust when he told them that Groths' dung was the most common source of fuel for burning.

# Chapter 37

THURSDAY, 8TH JULY

"Rachel," Xankira's call penetrated the warm fluffy fog of her dreams. Rachel opened a bleary eye and glanced at her mobile phone. 6:05 am. She groaned. Did Xankira not realise a woman this close to giving birth needed as much sleep as possible. There was no telling how much she would get once her daughter was born.

"Rachel, wake up." Xankira's tone was more insistent, urgent even.

Rachel grabbed her phone, intending to use it as a prop to point out the unearthly hour of her awakening, when she noticed nine missed calls from her mother. She sat up slowly. Xankira stood in the open doorway of her bedroom, looking anxious.

"What is it?"

"I don't know. You had better come and look. Please?" Her elven eyes, usually so sharp and penetrating, darted nervously.

She realised she could hear Flint's deep growls from downstairs, interspersed with the occasional warning bark. Rachel dragged herself from her bed, the bump that contained her daughter making the process cumbersome. Xankira led her to one of the rooms at the front of the cottage. She stared out of the window towards the narrow lane. Rachel moved alongside her and peered out.

"What the bloody hell is going on?" Rachel exclaimed.

White vans blocked the lane, all with large satellite dishes attached to their roofs. Reporters, camera crew and others festooned her front lawn. Suddenly, one of them noticed the two women looking out the window. Cameras immediately swung in their direction.

They stepped back from the window, and Rachel hastily shut the curtains.

"Who are they? What are they doing here?" she asked.

Xankira couldn't answer. She didn't know herself and actually had less of an idea than Rachel, never having encountered the voracity of the press before. Suddenly

Rachel's mobile, still clasped in her hand, rang, making them both jump.

*'Mum calling,'* the display announced. Rachel hurriedly pressed the answer button.

"Rachel, I'm so sorry. It's all my fault."

"What is, Mum? What's going on?"

"They found out about you and Camron."

"How? You promised you wouldn't breathe a word to anyone, not even to Bob."

"I didn't." The remorse in her voice was evident. Stephanie might be a journalist, but her family always came first. "Well, it wasn't me directly," she continued miserably. "One of my colleagues overheard a bit of our phone call yesterday and got curious. We record all the calls in the office, so he pulled the audio and listened to our conversation."

"But I told you who Camron was ages ago. We didn't talk about that yesterday."

"But we did. You kept saying you couldn't feel him anymore and didn't know if he was safe or even alive. I was trying to reassure you."

"Oh no..." Rachel's hand flew to her mouth as she recalled the previous day's conversation. Her mum was trying to comfort her. Her last sentence. *'He's King Arthur's son, has Excalibur and can use magic; nothing could possibly happen to him.'*

"I'm so sorry, Rachel. I should've been more careful, but I was only trying to reassure you."

At the end of the phone, there was silence as Rachel tried to absorb all her mother had told her.

"Rachel? Rachel, are you still there?"

"I'm here, Mum." Her mind whirled through the ramifications of what this exposure might mean to her and her baby.

"Look, I'm flying over today. Is that okay?" The question was posed in a quiet, hesitant voice. Although she wasn't really at fault, Stephanie hated having put her daughter in this situation.

"Yes, Mum, that's ok. And don't blame yourself. It wasn't your fault."

"Thank you. Look, don't worry about picking me up from Heathrow. I'll rent a car and drive down to Dorset."

"Thanks. One other thing, mum. You might want to tell your colleague to find somewhere quiet to hide this out for a while."

"Why?" asked Stephanie curiously.

"Well, Camron's definitely going to be hacked off with him. So will Geledhil, I imagine. And not forgetting the baby's other grandmother, Queen Nimue. I'm not sure anyone would fare too well should those three take a dislike to them."

Stephanie laughed, the tension easing from her slightly. She had been livid with her colleague at his underhand and disloyal act. But now, Stephanie almost felt sorry for him, though not entirely. She would take a certain amount of pleasure in informing him how much of a hornets' nest he had stirred up for himself.

Rachel and her mum said their goodbyes, and Stephanie told her she would try to catch a flight in the next few hours. It was only 1:30 am in Washington. Rachel sat on the edge of the bed, still in shock. She told Xankira what had happened, brushing over the technical references concerning the recorded phone conversation.

"So everyone in your world knows who Camron is now?"

"Yes, pretty much," answered Rachel.

"This is bad. If the Dökkálfar find out who you are, they will surely come after us."

Rachel nodded nervously, although she felt comforted by the reference to *us*. She had grown fond of Xankira and was relieved she wasn't planning on abandoning her in this time of crisis. Her phone rang again. '*Withheld number*' flashed up on the screen. If this were a newspaper thinking to gain the inside scoop, she would tell them exactly what she thought of them.

"Hello," she answered coolly.

“Hello, is that Rachel?” The woman’s voice sounded friendly and pleasant.

*So this is their ploy, the ‘friendly approach’*, thought Rachel before saying, “Who am I speaking to, please?”

“My name is Clarissa McCarthy. I’m from the Home Office. I understand you’re having a bit of a spontaneous get-together in Dorset right now?”

“That would be one way of putting it,” Rachel replied, still guarded with her responses. “Forgive me, but where did you say you were calling from again?” Rachel stalled for time as she tried to think of some clever way to catch this person out and get to the truth.

“I’m sorry, I should have said. I’m calling from Lancelot House. Hopefully, Mr Smith informed you we might be calling sometime?”

In truth, Rachel had forgotten about the cloak-and-dagger code word Smith had told her about just before leaving, but nonetheless, she felt relieved. Clarissa, it appeared, was genuinely from the Home Office.

“Can you do anything to move the reporters and camera crews?”

“I’m sorry, but it’s gone much further than having the press camped on your lawn. You and your husband are all over the newspapers, TV and the Internet. It’s time to move you to a safe location until your husband returns, and we decide what to do next.”

“Where to?” Rachel asked.

“I’m afraid I can’t say over the phone, but it will be perfectly safe, I assure you. I can get someone down to you within the hour. In the meantime, I’ll arrange for the police to come and keep an eye on things, okay?”

“Okay,” Rachel replied and then suddenly remembered. “Xankira needs to come. She must stay with me.”

“Not to worry, Rachel. We already know about Xankira. I’d suggest you both pack a bag with a few things.”

“My baby is due in eleven days. What about everything for her?”

"I'll tell you what," said Clarissa helpfully. "Why not pack what you can? Anything else you need we can sort out later. How does that sound?"

"Yes, that's fine. Thank you. One last thing, my mother is flying out from Washington this morning; she'll be driving down from Heathrow and won't know we've left."

"Don't worry, we'll arrange to meet her at the airport." Clarissa was obviously used to handling situations and ensuring everything went smoothly. Right at that moment, Rachel was happy she did.

Rachel relayed the telephone conversation to Xankira, and they were soon busy packing. Xankira took less than five minutes to pack her bag, but Rachel intended to bring as many of the new things she had bought for the baby as possible. The police soon arrived and began clearing access down the lane, forcing some larger media vans to move further along. Within the hour, Rachel, Xankira and Flint were all in the kitchen, Xankira wearing a baseball cap to hide her ears. Several hastily packed bags were with Xankira's pack and weapons next to the front door.

Flint barked suddenly, rushing to the front door where he stood, hackles raised, growling menacingly. Xankira followed, peering out of the window discreetly. Two black Range Rovers had pulled up outside, their windows darkly tinted. Six men, all dressed in sombre dark grey suits and sunglasses, stepped out of the vehicles. Two of them proceeded up the garden path towards the front door. One of the others had a brief conversation with one of the police officers. The police, aided by several of the dark-suited newcomers, proceeded to clear the entire garden of the media amid much grumbling and annoyance.

Xankira held Flint's collar as she opened the door to the gentle knock. She was greeted by a large pair of dark sunglasses and brilliant white teeth.

"Rachel?" the man inquired.

"She's in the kitchen. Please come through. Flint, shush, it's ok, they've come to help us. You have come to help, haven't you?" she asked the second man stepping through the front door.

"Yes, miss, we have. We'll get you away from here to someplace safe."

"Rachel?" the first man repeated as he and Xankira entered the kitchen. She nodded.

"We're from Lancelot House."

"Can I see some ID, please?" Rachel asked.

The man nodded approvingly, holding out his ID for Rachel to check.

"Are you packed and ready to leave?" he asked.

"Yes. Where are you taking us?"

"London, miss. You'll be safe there."

Xankira's eyes narrowed in thought. "I'll take Flint into the back garden for a few minutes. It will take us a while to get to London, won't it?"

"Thank you, Xankira," said Rachel, smiling in gratitude.

"Come on, Flint. Let's stretch our legs for a couple of minutes."

Flint looked warily at the two strangers in the kitchen, unwilling to leave his mistress alone with them. "Go on, Flint, go outside with Xankira," Rachel told him, pointing towards the now open back door. Reluctantly the dog followed Xankira out.

Xankira made her way to the bottom of the garden before glancing around and checking that no one was paying any attention. Her mind raced. She had secretly met with Josh in this garden and knew he was an elf. She had to let him know what was happening.

She slipped behind one of the larger trees, hidden from view and began to murmur a chant while at the same time tracing magical runes on the tree trunk. She stepped back after completing the spell. The glowing golden runes on the tree were already fading. After a few more seconds, they had disappeared entirely.

The *Follow Me* spell she had cast could only be detected by a wizard and couldn't be read or seen by someone not versed in magic. When she arrived in

London, she would cast the second part of the spell, which would change the magical runes to give her new location. She wasn't sure Josh would find her secret message, but it was the best she could do at such short notice. Composing herself, she made her way back indoors.

# Chapter 38

FRIDAY, 16TH JULY

Gradually the tunnel became easier to pass, the floor changing from rough, uneven rock to a smooth sandy surface. After weeks of hard travel, it was almost a joy to walk on.

"We near home," said Hreidmar in halting English. "Then I take you see King Throndim." His pace quickened in anticipation of reaching Mortheill.

The others exchanged quick glances, conflicting emotions flickering across their faces. Tempering their relief at finally reaching the dwarven capital was concern at what awaited them. Hreidmar was now entirely on their side, though initially, he had been reticent and unfriendly, despite their wading into the fight and saving his life. But how much harder would it be to convince the dwarven king of their intentions and elicit his aid?

They encountered the now-familiar phosphorous lichen, lighting their way faintly. As they drew closer to the city, the tunnel light grew brighter until it was the equivalent of two or three candles. To the group used to near darkness, it was almost blinding. Coming around the final bend, they saw Hreidmar standing a short way in from the end of the tunnel, waiting for them to catch up.

Geledhil stood by his side, nervously playing with the necklace Xankira had given her. Camron saw the trepidation in her eyes. For a while, he had been the only human in Alfheim, surrounded by thousands of Ljósálfar. But there had never been any antagonism between humans and Ljósálfar. He understood Geledhil's fear of being the only elf in a city of thousands of dwarves.

"Come," Hreidmar said in English, grabbing Camron's arm. "My home, Mortheill." His face shone with pride as he almost dragged Camron the last few paces. Camron stepped into a cavern similar in size to the one that housed Varðasteinn.

Scattered throughout were mushroom groves and fields of strange plants, presumably edible judging by the dwarves' effort to cultivate them. Other areas had been fenced off and contained hundreds of Groth, the weird underground goats they had encountered in the tunnels. The whole cavern was a hive of activity.

On the far side ran a wall about twenty metres tall. An enormous stone gate stood open in the middle of the wall. Camron had taken all this in at a single glance but what startled him was what he saw flanking the entrance. Two huge Earth Elementals stood guard, one on either side. The only sign of the magical life that empowered them was their eyes, which burned with a dull red glow.

"Not again," said Trigger.

"You've seen elementals before?" Hreidmar asked, lapsing into dwarven, unable to keep the surprise from his voice.

Camron hesitated before replying, caught between the indecision of lying to their new friend and admitting they had killed one that had probably been an ally of the Dwarves. "Yes," admitted Camron. "There was one at the cave entrance we came through to get underground."

"It was still there after all these centuries?" Hreidmar said in surprise. "I didn't think any of the old sentinels remained. So how did ye convince it to let yer past? Elementals ain't known for their friendly nature."

"We didn't negotiate with it. We couldn't. As soon as we found the entrance, it came to life and attacked us. I'm sorry, but we had no choice but to stop it."

Hreidmar looked stunned. The two earth elementals protecting the city gates were formidable but a poor reflection on the power of the elementals his ancestors had summoned. The ones who guarded the entrances to their world of tunnels were amongst the most powerful ever conjured.

His eyes reflected a mixture of sadness for the loss of the elemental and respect. Defeating one would have required a great deal of courage and skill.

"Best yer don't mention it when yer meets the king. It might get things off to a bad start. If you think this is impressive, wait until you see the city."

“And the only way in is through those gates?” asked Geledhil, already knowing the answer.

Hreidmar nodded, leading towards the massive double-gates gates, wending through the mushroom groves and Groth paddocks. They drew startled stares from the dwarves tending their fields and Groth livestock. Several of them grabbed weapons kept readily to hand, but Hreidmar called out, reassuring them all was well. A few made for the gates themselves, hurrying in a lumbering run, impeded by thick leather-armoured jerkins and heavy hob-nailed boots.

They were still a couple of hundred metres from the gates when a contingent of several dozen heavily armed dwarven warriors came marching out to meet them. In their midst was an elderly dwarf, judging by the long silver beard, neatly braided with silver ringlets. He was dressed in deep purple robes instead of most dwarves' customary armour. An axe hung from his belt, however.

“Doloric. He’s one of the king’s councillors,” whispered Hreidmar, although, for a dwarf, a whisper was as loud as an elf would shout.

Both parties stopped while still some distance apart. “Wait here,” said Hreidmar. “I’ll talk to them.” He set off towards the elderly dwarf, who stood waiting.

“Wait,” called Camron suddenly, hurrying to catch up. He pulled the *Friendship Ring* off his finger and handed it to Hreidmar. “Show this to the king. Tell him it is half of a *Friendship Ring* which my grandmother, Queen Nimue, gave to King Darlangor at the end of the Second War of the Realms.” Hreidmar nodded, taking the ring and then carried on towards the waiting dwarf.

A short but heated discussion ensued between the two dwarves, of which Camron could only manage to catch a few words here and there. Hreidmar returned, looking downcast.

“Yer to wait here while I go and talk to King Throndim and his councillors. Don’t worry. It won’t take me long to make the numbskulls see sense.”

He shrugged apologetically as he turned and made his way back to the dwarves, who escorted him past the watchful gaze of the elementals and through the gates. A dozen guards remained outside, their purpose none too subtly apparent. Camron and the others spread out and made themselves as comfortable as possible yet remained alert, their weapons easily within reach.

Several hours later, Hreidmar emerged through the gates again, accompanied by a handful of guards. More dwarves followed, each carrying a bundle of some description. Camron could tell by the stamp of his gait that he was in a bad temper and feared the dwarf's meeting with the king hadn't gone as well as expected.

"Stubborn fools," Hreidmar exploded. "They won't let yer into the city. We're to wait out here while they decide," he grunted disgustedly, throwing down the leather bag he carried.

"How long is that likely to take?" asked Craig.

Hreidmar shrugged. "Days!"

"Thanks for trying, Hreidmar," said Smith, slightly dispiritedly. "I guess all we can do is wait. Will you keep us informed of what they decide?"

"I won't have to. I'll be out here with yer," Hreidmar replied with a defiant glance towards the city.

"That's ok. You don't have to, but thanks for the support," said Camron.

Hreidmar ignored him as he picked up the discarded bag and started removing the contents, pulling out a bedroll, food and cooking implements. The bundles brought by the dwarven guards contained more bedding and food.

Camron felt disheartened at their reception but glad for Hreidmar's companionship.

They quickly settled into a routine. Each day, the dwarves provided them with food and drink. The preferred drink for dwarves was mead, brewed from the strange mushrooms they grew and was very potent. However, the dwarves seemed to be able to drink vast quantities of it with little discernible effect. Smith quickly suggested they ask for water and limit the amount of the heady brew they consumed. The language lessons continued each morning, and in the afternoon, they trained. Both Hreidmar and the SAS Troopers were keen to learn about each other's combat techniques and soon explored new fighting methods to complement their respective styles. Even though they were within the jurisdiction of the dwarves and the safety they afforded, the group still maintained a watch each night, just in case.

A few days later, a solitary dwarf came through the gates and approached them late one afternoon. Camron had been cleaning Excalibur simply for something to do and paused to watch the dwarf approach. He was ancient and leant heavily on a staff as he walked. His face was wrinkled with age, giving it a leathery appearance. The dwarf stopped before Camron. He stood there stroking his long grey beard for a moment, his eyes fixed on Excalibur, which rested across Camron's knees.

When he spoke, his voice was deep and gravelly, "Happen I recall a story my old grand-pappy once told me about a battle that his grand-pappy were in. They fought alongside a human king who had a sword much like that one ye 'av there. He was brave, that king. His courage and skill saved many that day. Not just humans but dwarves and elves too. I reckon anyone brought up by a man such as him is alright by me."

He didn't wait for any response but abruptly turned and headed back towards the open gates.

The unexpected gesture touched Camron, and he stood up, intending to go after the dwarf. Hreidmar placed a firm grip on his arm. "Let him go."

"Who is he?" asked Camron.

Hreidmar chuckled. "Not an easy question to answer. His name is Borfdak, and he's one of the oldest dwarves in the city. He ought to be on the *Council of Elders* but thinks they're all numbskulls. He's stubborn and cantankerous but as fierce as he was two centuries ago. You've just been complimented by a dwarven legend. He was one of the best miners and bravest warriors, and he still commands tremendous respect. Having Borfdak acknowledge you can only help."

Camron sat back down, eyes on the ancient dwarf as he made his slow way back towards the city.

# Chapter 39

MONDAY, 19TH JULY

Smith had drawn the monotonous early morning watch from 2 am until 6 am. Not that time meant a tremendous amount in the perpetual semi-darkness of the underworld. His thoughts had wandered to the world above, memories of early morning dew on the grass and watching glorious sunsets, a cold beer in hand. A sudden grating of stone on stone broke his reverie. He looked up and was surprised to see the Earth Elementals had shifted their heads to the right, glowing red eyes intent on one of the far entry tunnels. Smith followed their gaze but saw nothing. He strained his ears to discern what might have attracted their attention. Nothing.

He looked back at the elementals, but they were motionless, attention focused on the tunnel. Then Smith heard it, the sound of several hob-nailed boots dashing towards them, the echoes resonating in the confines of the tunnel. The professional soldier in him kicked in. He reached for his rifle and then, without taking his eyes off the tunnel, awoke each of the sleeping forms around him. Hreidmar was closest, and as he reached down to wake him, Smith saw his eyes were already open and alert. Smith woke each with a shake of the shoulder, indicating with a finger to his lips to remain quiet. In under a minute, the entire group was armed and ready.

Camron looked at Hreidmar enquiringly. “My folk,” answered the dwarf in a barely audible whisper. “Mebbe two or three of them, possibly from the outlying guard-post.” Sure enough, two heavily armed dwarves came hurtling out of the tunnel at full pelt, headed towards the city gates.

A few minutes later, Geledhil broke the silence. “I can hear booted feet. More dwarves, I think. Many more, but these ones are walking.” Alert, senses straining for the slightest indication of what was happening, they stood in a defensive formation, waiting.

More figures appeared out of the tunnel, but these weren’t heavily armed dwarven warriors. Shock and disbelief registered on Camron's face as a few weary and bedraggled dwarves stumbled from the tunnel into the cavern, some leaning on others for support. His grip relaxed on his staff as he watched in astonishment. More and more dwarves appeared. Most looked tired and fearful, fatigue dogging their footsteps. Camron wasn't sufficiently au fait with the subtle differences between the dwarven men and women, but he could clearly see some smaller, beardless dwarves who were obviously children, some carried on the backs of the adults. A frightening number of the dwarves looked wounded, sporting makeshift bandages, slings and crutches. Their clothing was dirty and dishevelled, and Camron guessed they had been travelling for some days.

"Stay here," said Hreidmar. "I'll find out what's going on." He hefted his axe and headed towards the newcomers. Hreidmar had only gone a few metres when the great city doors opened. Many dwarves came pouring out, heading for the new arrivals. Some were carrying jugs, while others had baskets of food. Towards the head of the procession were a group of several dwarves, some dressed in purple robes, Councillor Doloric among them.

"Come on," said Camron. "Let's see if there is anything we can do to help." While he was genuinely concerned about the plight of the dwarves pouring into the cavern, his motives weren't entirely altruistic. Anything that showed them in a good light to the dwarven king might help their mission.

Hurrying, they quickly caught up with Hreidmar, who pointed out one of the dwarves at the head of the group coming out from the city. "That's Throndim, the king. This must be bad if he has come out."

As they drew nearer to the now milling mass of dwarves, Doloric and two other councillors came over to them.

"What has happened? Who are these people?" asked Camron in Dwarven.

"They've come from the outlying settlements and border outposts," said Doloric.

“Only about half the dwarven population live in Mortheill,” Hreidmar added. “The rest live in small settlements and villages.

Doloric continued, “Information is sketchy right now, but it would appear the goblins have risen up and attacked.”

Hreidmar gasped incredulously. “No goblin tribe could overrun this many dwarves.”

“I know,” answered Doloric, his face reflecting the horror of the situation. “The reports are confusing, but it would seem it wasn’t just one tribe.”

“More than one!” the disbelief in Hreidmar’s tone was unmistakable.

“Yes,” said Doloric. “I know. It’s unheard for goblin tribes to work together, even against us dwarves.”

A thought struck David, “Is this connected to those goblins who attacked your mining party?”

“Mebbe,” said Hreidmar. “There’s always the odd skirmish with different goblin tribes. That’s why we have border outposts to protect our homeland. But if the tribes are united. ” He left the sentence hanging, unable to speak of that awful possibility.

“How many goblin tribes are there?” asked Camron, his eyes scanning what by now was over a hundred refugees.

Doloric paused, looking at Camron and seemed hesitant to answer, as if uttering the words would lend credibility. “All of them!”

“All of them?” exclaimed Hreidmar. “That’s impossible. There must be some mistake.”

“I don’t think so,” Doloric replied before looking at Camron. “It would seem they had help.”

Fear gripped Camron, a hard knot in the pit of his stomach. He listened to Doloric’s words, but he knew what was coming deep down. He forgot to breathe, praying he was wrong.

“From who?” asked Hreidmar.

“Dökkálfar.”

That single, terrifying word had not been uttered in the Dwarven world for many centuries, outside of history lessons to the young.

Camron watched disbelief turn to fear in the dwarven faces around him. He understood. The world above ground was as remote and unreal to them as this underground world had been to him. Hreidmar had accepted their account of what was happening, but Camron knew he hadn't fully understood. Now, faced with the indisputable evidence of the misery and destruction they wrought, he knew their world had changed.

"Come with me," said Doloric. "The king wishes to speak to you."

The king was deep in conversation with several of the recently arrived dwarves as they approached.

Camron listened as they recounted their harrowing tales of the attacks and the desperate flight from the goblins. They waited patiently but couldn't avoid attracting considerable attention themselves.

Rumour of their recent arrival had spread through the city. Still, very few of the dwarves had actually seen the newcomers. Even fewer realised an elf was amongst them. Geledhil did her best to be unobtrusive, remaining in the middle of the group, partially hidden by the taller humans around her. But she couldn't conceal herself entirely, and it wasn't long before murmurings and dark looks were directed towards her.

Doloric heard the mutterings and saw the pointed looks. He gestured to several dwarven guards, who came and stood nearby.

The king continued listening to the dwarves, occasionally interjecting with a question. At first glance, there appeared to be very little about the king that would mark him as someone of great importance. He wore armour similar to Hreidmar's, heavy chainmail over a thick leather jerkin. In fact, if anything, it looked like it had seen more use than Hreidmar's, although exceptionally well looked after. Likewise, the battle-axe hanging from his belt was polished and honed to a sharp edge. The handle looked smooth and well worn, the recipient of many hours of careful oiling. The only thing that singled Throndim out was the thick circlet of gold that adorned his battle helm.

Hreidmar mingled with some nearby refugees while waiting for the king. He spoke to them in hushed tones, listening to them recount the last few harrowing days. There were numerous accounts of heroism and self-sacrifice, especially during the flight to the city. The goblins had chased and harangued them continually. Many courageous dwarves, often in groups of as little as two or three, had stayed behind, acting as a rear-guard. Their heroic self-sacrifice bought precious time for the others to flee. Hreidmar listened to these harrowing tales, filled with sadness and horror. He felt pride also. The bravery of those who had fought and the tenacity of those who had fled to the city, not only to seek refuge but to regroup and prepare to fight back. Defeat was not a condition that sat lightly upon the shoulders of the dwarven people.

Finally, the king looked up and beckoned them over. The other dwarves moved away from the king, creating a space around him and his close advisors, into which the small band of humans and solitary Ljósálfar stepped. Camron bowed as they reached the king, and the others followed suit. The king, reaching not much higher than Camron's midriff, looked up at him intently for many long seconds, his eyes alert and penetrating. His armour and weapons bore testament to his prowess as a seasoned and competent warrior. Still, the intelligence Camron saw in his eyes made him realise Throndim was also a clever dwarf. He commanded authority naturally and with ease. His kingship seemed to sit easily on his broad shoulders, although the current events would be a trying test.

Throndim's eyes travelled over the remaining companions in the group, pausing barely imperceptibly as he noted Hreidmar stood with them. His look sought out Geledhil, and his gaze lingered longer over her, the stony expression on his face unreadable.

"Do you speak Dwarvish?" he asked Camron in Dwarvish.

“Yes, Your Majesty.”

Throndim took something from a small pouch on his belt. Camron saw it was the *Ring of Friendship.* “And you are truly the son of King Arthur? The one our legends say will return in time of need?”

“Yes,” answered Camron.

“Then greetings to you, Prince Amr,” Throndim said with a nod.

Camron didn’t object to his formal title but replied, “Greetings to you, King Throndim, from myself, my companions, and my grandmother, Queen Nimue of the Ljósálfar.”

“It is sad that men and dwarves should meet again on a day heralding such terrible events,” Throndim said, still toying with the ring he held. Camron didn’t think it worth mentioning they could have met several days sooner under much more auspicious circumstances. He also didn’t miss the inclusion of men and dwarves and the omission of Geledhil.

“Indeed, your Majesty. I wish our peoples could have been reacquainted under happier times. However, such has always been the alliance between men, dwarves and Ljósálfar that we will come together in times of need to assist each other and fight for the common good.”

Throndim remained silent for several moments, considering Camron and his words. “And yet,” the king said severely, “your arrival seems to have brought others. Niðavellir, our world of tunnels and caverns, has always been a dangerous place. Still, it has suited us dwarves and been our home for centuries.”

He looked around, taking in the mass of refugees steadily growing in number.

“And now many of our outlying steadings and villages have been raided by goblin war-bands led by Dökkálfar. They used their unnatural magic to sneak up upon our warriors and bring death and destruction. Hundreds of my people have been killed over the past few days.”

Camron could see the pain that the suffering of his people caused Throndim. “Majesty,” he said, “the

Dökkálfar would have come regardless of whether we arrived or not. It must have taken the Dökkálfar several months to subjugate the goblin tribes into submission and organise a coordinated attack of this magnitude. This has been carefully planned and would have been initiated many months ago."

"But how is it the Dökkálfar are here at all? How have they managed to escape from their realm after all these centuries?" The accusatory tone in the Dwarven king's voice was unmistakable.

"The great portal seal at Stonehenge was breached nearly a year ago. The Dökkálfar have been attacking the world of men for some months. Many thousands have been killed," said Camron. The sadness in his voice was evident and caused Throndim to pause in thought.

"This is yours, I believe." Throndim held out the *Ring of Friendship* that Camron had sent when they first arrived at Mortheill.

Camron went to take it and then stopped short, startled. On Throndim's little finger, he could see the twin to the ring he held in the palm of his rough, calloused hand.

"Aye, lad. It's the other half of the ring. We have kept our word and remembered. It has been passed down the generations from king to king, though in truth many doubted it was little more than legend." He thrust his outstretched hand further towards Camron, proffering the ring again.

"Thank you," said Camron. "But the ring isn't mine. My grandmother gave it to me as we left to come and find you. She too has kept her ring close through the centuries, keeping faith that the bonds that once brought us together as allies would not be entirely forgotten."

"Queen Nimue is still alive?"

Camron nodded.

Another silence stretched out, the dwarves around them numbering several hundred by now, intruding on their thoughts for the first time since they had begun speaking with the king.

"So," Throndim said eventually, "you've come all this way to ask us to help you fight the Dökkálfar?"

Camron nodded again.

"If you haven't noticed, we have some Dökkálfar of our own to fight," said Throndim. "Not to mention hordes of goblins."

This time, Camron paused, gathering his thoughts and calming his mind before answering. "I won't deny that I seek to re-establish the old alliances between men, dwarves and Ljósálfar. No single army could hope to defeat the Dökkálfar and all their minions. Only by combining our strengths and fighting together as one can we hope to defeat them."

Throndim was about to utter a quick retort, but Camron continued quickly. "But that isn't the reason we have come."

Throndim raised an eyebrow in surprise.

"Your Majesty, have you heard of *Lia Fàil*?" Camron asked. Of all the questions Throndim was expecting, this would have been an incredibly long way down the list. He nodded nevertheless.

*"Lia Fàil?"* queried David, forgetting himself and the company he was in for a moment. Throndim's glare very quickly reminded him.

"*Lia Fàil* is what the elves call the Stone of Destiny," whispered Geledhil.

"And you know the secret it contains?" continued Camron. This time, a glimmer of understanding flickered across Throndim's typically featureless expression. "You are aware of the legend of the twin swords?"

Throndim nodded again.

"Well, we need them. I already have Excalibur, but I need to get the sword in *Lia Fàil*," Camron concluded.

"Well, lad, why can't you or one of the pointy-eared elves simply wiggle your fingers and summon it, or whatever it is you wizards do?"

Camron noted this was the second time Throndim had referred to him as a *lad*. He thought about pointing out that he was probably four or five times older than the dwarf. However, he didn't think this would improve the fledgling human-dwarf *entente cordiale.*

Camron took a deep breath. "I tried, but it didn't work. *Lia Fàil* is broken."

"Broken! *Lia Fàil* is dwarf-made. The earth magic would last for tens of millennia. How can it be broken?"

"Physically broken." Camron suspected what the reaction of the dwarf would be once he had finally teased out the story of the stone's damage.

"An artefact of this magnitude and importance. How could it possibly be damaged?"

Camron looked downcast as he admitted, "It was dropped by the men trying to steal it. It broke in two when it landed on the ground."

Throndim's look was disbelieving. "Wasn't it guarded? Surely every means known to humans should have been employed to protect it?"

*I may as well get this over with,* thought Camron. "It wasn't guarded but left alone in an unlocked church. The thieves wanted to return it to Scotland, where they thought it belonged."

Throndim spluttered, unable to form coherent speech.

Camron continued quickly, "King Throndim, you must remember that Merlin's efforts to obfuscate the truth of the last *War of the Realms* with myth and legend worked only too well. Humans now believe that magic, elves, and dwarves are nothing more than myths and childhood tales. What you and I know is important, men have forgotten. In some respects, humans are like children who need to be taught the truth about the world they live in, and they need to learn quickly."

A sharp intake of breath from behind told him Smith's grasp of Dwarvish was better than he realised. "They tried to repair the stone but didn't have the understanding or skill to do it properly. If it is possible to mend *Lia Fàil,* then it is only the dwarves who possess the ability. The quest we have undertaken is to ask you to repair the stone and enable us to retrieve the sword held within it."

Again, there was a long pause as Throndim considered. He looked up at each of them and then gazed once more over the congregating dwarven refugees.

"You have *Lia Fàil* with you?" he asked eventually. Camron nodded.

"Bring it to the council chambers tomorrow morning. Hreidmar will escort you. You may also bring one of your companions." He paused a moment. "But not the elf. Many of my people retain a mistrust of magic-using elves. It would be unwise to bring her into the city, especially after today. Now, I must see to my people," he said by way of dismissal.

"Very well, Your Majesty," said Camron, trying hard to contain his frustration at the further delay.

# Chapter 40

TUESDAY, 20TH JULY

The following day Hreidmar, Camron and David made their way towards the city gates. Although she would never admit it, Geledhil was secretly pleased Camron was not taking her. Being the only elf in a city of thousands of dwarves filled her with dread.

Over the past twenty-four hours, a makeshift city of tents and temporary dwellings had sprung up outside the city walls. Mortheill struggled to cope with the influx of so many from the outlying villages. By late the previous night, the number of dwarves arriving in the city had dwindled to a trickle. However, from early morning, more dwarves had started arriving. These were from villages that had not yet been raided, but word had spread. The dwarves, true to their practical nature, had packed up their homes and left for the safety of the city. Forming a defensive perimeter around the refugee camp were several hundred dwarven warriors. Apart from the Royal Guard and the City Watch, the dwarves didn't maintain a standing army. However, from a very young age, every dwarf, both male and female, was taught how to wield an axe and use a crossbow. The majority of male dwarves carried a battle-axe with them as a matter of course, especially in the tunnels. The entire dwarven nation was a militia reserve, which could be mobilised very quickly.

Large numbers of dwarves were being organised into military units. Additional armour and weapons were issued from the city armouries, and combat orders were drawn up. Since the first of the fleeing dwarves had arrived, seasoned warriors had patrolled the surrounding tunnels to prevent the goblins from getting too close to the city.

Camron looked up as they passed the two enormous Earth Elemental guardians and walked through the open gates. He could have sworn the dull red glow of their eyes followed the small group.

They emerged into a second, much larger cavern. Unlike Varðasteinn, which had buildings almost up to the wall, inside the outer curtain wall of Mortheill was a wide-open space of barren ground, along which a clearly defined path headed towards a second, slightly lower wall about a hundred metres away. Walking along the wide pathway, David glanced up and saw enormous stone blocks hanging precariously above the roadway. Feeling a little nervous, he made to step away from being directly underneath them, leaving the path in the process.

"I'd stay on the path if I were you," said Hreidmar before David had taken no more than a couple of steps. He stopped immediately. Several weeks in this underground environment had taught him to act first and question later.

"Why?" he asked.

Nodding towards the broad expanse of empty space to the side of the path, Hreidmar said simply, "Traps." David carefully retraced his steps back to the path.

Hreidmar continued, this time indicating the enormous stone blocks above. "If the outer wall were ever to be breached, we would drop these blocks, thus blocking the path. The enemy would then be forced to the open ground. The area is riddled with hidden pits, each one cunningly concealed. Anything heavier than a small Groth would trigger it. They're about ten metres deep with razor-sharp stone spikes at the bottom. If you survive the fall and miss the spikes, you would stay down in the pit. The walls are perfectly smooth and unclimbable. Not a pleasant way to die, but then, killing a goblin isn't supposed to be pleasant. At least, not for the goblin," Hreidmar concluded grimly.

Once through the gates in the inner wall, they were in the city proper. It looked remarkably like Varðasteinn, although on a smaller, somewhat less grand scale. But then Mortheill had initially been the second dwarven city and not the capital. However, the quality of the workmanship of the buildings was as magnificent as any they had seen in Varðasteinn, without any evidence of abandonment and decay. This was a living, vibrant city.

The streets were busier than usual. News of the goblin attacks had spread through the populace, and many had taken to the streets to see for themselves. Bands of dwarves moved through the city in newly formed military units, each group battle-ready and eager. Because of this heightened activity, they were the subject of much attention as they passed and drew many curious and even a few hostile looks. The contrast between the emptiness and silence of Varðasteinn and this bustling city was stark. Despite the interest they triggered, their progress was unimpeded.

Hreidmar led them towards a large building situated in the city's centre. He informed them this had once been the city governors' residence, although it was now the royal palace. As they approached, Borfdak emerged from a doorway and stepped in line to join them, nodding briefly to Hreidmar but otherwise saying nothing.

They gained entrance to the palace without a fuss and were shown to a reception room where Doloric waited. He stepped forward to greet them but stopped suddenly, an eyebrow raised in surprise at seeing Borfdak with them. He paused, considering for a moment, before coming to a decision and allowing the matter to pass. He greeted Camron and the others formally and bade them follow him to the council chambers.

Doloric led them along a wide corridor ending in a pair of large double doors, seemingly made entirely of gold. The group stopped before the doors, and Doloric looked at them, indecision crossing his face. Camron felt that he wanted to say something, perhaps some hint as to what to expect or some insight into how best to deal with the king. Their eyes locked together for several moments, but Doloric turned swiftly and nodded at the two guards stationed on either side. Without further ceremony, they opened, and Doloric led them inside.

They entered a large chamber, windowless but with the walls and columns ornately decorated with masterfully crafted stonework. Where other rooms might have pictures or murals, this one was adorned with intricately carved bas-reliefs depicting battle scenes of heroic dwarves defeating overwhelming hordes of goblins. A long rectangular table, made entirely of stone, occupied the centre of the room. What did surprise them were the dozen or so chairs arrayed on either side. These were all wooden, the largest quantity of wood any of them had seen since entering this underworld. The wood was obviously ancient, but the smell of oil and the dark patina shine attested to the care lavished upon these rare and valuable items.

Seated in a wooden chair richly decorated with gold and precious gems was Throndim. As king, he sat at the head of the table. To his left and right sat more dwarves, many old but each with sharp, intelligent faces that were now directing piercing looks towards the newcomers. One dwarf, seated immediately to the king's right-hand side, was noticeably younger than the others but bore a striking resemblance to the king himself. This dwarf leapt from his chair as they entered the chamber, finger-pointing accusingly at Borfdak.

"What's he doing here?" he shouted, his tone leaving little doubt about his feelings.

Throndim shifted his gaze to Borfdak, who met it with a look of his own, although he did concede a nod of deference towards his sovereign. After a moment, Throndim placed a placatory hand on the still-standing dwarf's arm and bade him sit. Still glowering at Borfdak, he did as the king requested.

"Greetings, King Throndim," Camron announced before any other disruptions could occur. "You have our thanks for allowing us an audience at this council."

"You are welcome, Prince Amr," Throndim replied. However, his demeanour was still wary and not the warm and friendly welcome Camron had secretly hoped for.

"May I introduce my companion?" Camron asked, gesturing towards David. "This is David Underwood, a scholar from the world of men and one who, though he joined us almost by accident, has proven his worth in both combat and intellect."

David flushed at the unexpected praise. He found his tongue had become dry and threatened to stick to the roof of his mouth. "Hello, sorry, I mean greetings, Your

Majesty," he stammered, his nerves not helped by having to speak in Dwarvish.

The king nodded in acknowledgement. "Please, be seated," he said, gesturing towards the empty seats at the far end of the table. There were three spare seats on each side and a slightly more ornate chair at the end. Not as splendid as the king's throne but grander than the other chairs.

Camron took a seat next to a grey-bearded grizzly looking dwarf. He had to stretch his legs out across the entire underside of the table, as the dwarf-sized chairs did not accommodate his six-foot build. Likewise, David slid uncomfortably into the seat next to Camron, wiping the sheen of nervous sweat that clung to his forehead. Hreidmar took the remaining chair on their side and sat next to David. Camron wondered whether Borfdak would sit opposite him next to another dwarf or, considering his reception, opt to sit alone, opposite Hreidmar. Surprisingly, he did neither but casually eased himself into the ornate chair at the far end of the table. Several dwarves looked alarmed, and more than one glanced at Throndim. Again, the king looked appraisingly at Borfdak before nodding briefly in acquiescence.

Before each place was a mug of ale, and Throndim reached towards his, taking a long pull and wiping the white foam from his beard.

"Well, now we are all seated," said Throndim, looking pointedly at Borfdak, "we can begin. Prince Amr, may I ask you to tell us about your quest and why you seek our aid? For the benefit of those present who haven't already heard."

Camron nodded and took a draught of his own drink to buy him a few moments to collect his own thoughts. Over the past few days, he had grown used to the dark, heavy mead the dwarves drank, and he savoured its earthiness as he thought about where to begin. *We need them as allies*, he thought. T*here's no point in lying or keeping secrets.* And so Camron recounted their tale from the beginning, missing out on only one or two salient points, such as the prophecy concerning his daughter and the fight with the earth elemental on Dunsinane Hill. Camron spoke for quite some time. When he had finished, the assembled dwarves were silent for a minute or two, taking in all he had said.

"You have brought *Lia Fàil* with you?" asked Throndim.

Camron stood and lifted the bag easily onto the stone table. With considerably greater difficulty, he and David took the stone out of the bag. Without the bag's magical properties, the stone resumed its 150 kilo weight. Every eye in the room looked at the nondescript block of yellow sandstone, visually unexceptional but for the remarkable magic imbued in it.

"Your Majesty, if I may?" a hugely muscled dwarf said, interrupting their thoughts.

"Of course," answered Throndim, who continued talking as the other dwarf rose and proceeded towards Camron and the stone. "Karatack is one of our most skilled craftsmen."

Karatack lifted the Stone of Destiny with ease, handling it confidently but with great care. He turned the stone over in his rough, calloused hands, the muscles in his arms bulging as he bore the stone's weight. He found the thin crack in the stone where it had been repaired and shook his head, muttering to himself, "Amateurs!"

"Can it be repaired?" asked Throndim.

Camron held his breath, waiting for the answer.

"I don't know, Your Majesty. Possibly. But it won't be easy. We need to undo the shoddy repair work first. Then we can see what's what."

Throndim nodded as Karatack put the stone down and returned to his seat.

*Well, here goes* thought Camron. "King Throndim, will you help us, please? Will you try to repair the stone?" He looked directly at the king and saw the indecision in his eyes, the hesitation before he answered. Camron's hopes deflated. After everything they had been through to find the dwarves, they would be thwarted at the final hurdle.

However, before Throndim uttered any refusal, another voice spoke.

"Throndim. You know that me and your pappy were like brothers. He wouldn't have hesitated to help. He remembered the old alliances and respected them."

"Don't speak to my father in that tone, Borfdak," said the young dwarf at the king's right-hand, once again rising to his feet, this time anger unmistakably replacing his earlier displeasure. "You shouldn't even be here. You're not a member of this council."

"I'm here," replied Borfdak, his tone calm and even, his eyes still on Throndim, "because I see things clearly, and I speak plainly of what I see. Sometimes even the wisest and cleverest amongst us need reminding of a little common sense."

Camron groaned inwardly. This was all going wrong. He had waited to get this opportunity to speak to the king for so long, and now the meeting was deteriorating into a petty argument. One or two of the other dwarves began voicing opinions of their own. One was advocating on Camron's behalf, but most were siding with the king's son, visibly irritated by Borfdak and his rudeness.

"Enough!" bellowed Throndim, slamming his hand on the stone table with a resounding bang. "Is this how we behave in front of guests? Thraidurn, sit down."

The voracious argument was stifled immediately, many participants looking chagrined and casting their eyes downward. Throndim's son, Thraidurn, sat back down, casting Borfdak a baleful look. Borfdak's gaze stayed steady, staring at Throndim.

"For all his other faults," Throndim spoke into the ensuing silence, "Borfdak is right on this matter. My father would not have hesitated to offer his help." He paused a moment. "But these are different times, and I am not my father." He turned his gaze to Camron. "You are an intelligent and shrewd man, Prince Amr. You have only asked us to repair *Lia Fàil* for you. But if we accept this burden and the responsibility that comes with this, then in our hearts and our conscience, we will be obligated once more to the old alliance of men, dwarves and elves. This I think you know or suspect to be the case at least."

Camron met his gaze evenly, giving neither acknowledgement nor rebuttal.

Throndim nodded to himself, evidently having decided something. "What will happen now in the world of men?"

Camron blinked, the unexpected question throwing him slightly. "Well, Your Majesty, the Dökkálfar cannot travel through the portals from Svartalfheim directly to Alfheim. All travel must go via the world of men above. If the Dökkálfar wish to achieve their aims they've craved in the past, that is, the subjugation of men and dwarves and the obliteration of Ljósálfar, then they must have a firm and secure foothold in the humans' world.

"I think," continued Camron, "there will soon be the first and possibly the most important battle. The Dökkálfar will want to win this decisively, quickly and with maximum shock. They will want to make men think twice about attacking them and give them cause for concern. If they can win the first real battle outright, this will buy them the time they need to establish a presence in the realm of men. Once there, they will gain access to humans' weapons and technology and assimilate them into their own battle plans. If they do this, they may well be unstoppable."

There was another silence around the table.

"We have remained isolated from the realm of men for many centuries and with good cause," said Throndim eventually.

Camron started to interrupt, but the king held up his hand, commanding their absolute attention. "But we have seen over the past hours that the Dökkálfar do not seem content to limit their attacks to only humans and Ljósálfar." He met the eyes of each one of his council advisors, not demanding acquiescence but seeking support for the decision he had come to. Despite reservations in some, he saw no opposition.

"We will help repair *Lia Fàil*," Throndim said finally. "As to anything else, we will have to see how our own predicament unravels. As Karatack has inferred, repairing the stone may take some time. We will find you all accommodation within the city. However, I suggest the elf remain discreetly unobtrusive."

"Thank you, Your Majesty. You do not know how grateful we are for your help," said Camron, realising he had been holding his breath and finally allowing himself to breathe again.

"However, we have many weeks of travel just to return to the surface, and I fear we will be needed there. May I ask that we leave *Lia Fàil* with you, and if you successfully repair the stone, could you bring it to us? The *Ring of Friendship* will guide you."

Throndim considered a moment before nodding, "Very well. If you cannot wait, you must begin at once."

Once again, Borfdak interrupted the king, "But you won't need to travel so far to get back to the surface." A slight smile crossed his usually stony face. "Niðavellir does have more than one entrance. There's another one just a few days' travel from here."

The dwarves around the table looked startled; this was obviously news to them. However, their looks of surprise were nothing compared to the shock that flashed across Throndim's face.

"How do you know about that?" he demanded in a low, strained voice. "That knowledge is for the king and the king alone."

"Your father told me." Borfdak replied casually.

"He had no right."

"Maybe not, but I've never told a living soul until today. And, in the circumstances, I think it is information that Prince Amr and his group can make good use of, rather than keep it a dusty old secret of no benefit to anyone."

Throndim made a harsh noise in his throat but said no more.

"Your Majesty," said Camron, "you have already agreed to help us so much, but could we impose on you further by asking that Borfdak show us the way to this exit, please?"

"He can tell me," said Hreidmar, the first words he had uttered since entering the council chamber. "I'll need to know anyhow as I'm coming with yer." Hastily realising what he had said and in front of whom, he added, "That is, if Your Majesty will permit me?"

"And why would you want to accompany these men, not forgetting the elf, up to their world?" the king asked, a hint of his earlier stoniness returning.

"When the goblin war-band attacked me and my fellows, we were greatly outnumbered and sore put. They came to our help, heedless of the risk to themselves. And as for the elf, I watched her battle to save Gurrandig, striving way beyond the point our own healers would have given up."

"So you wish to accompany them to repay a debt you feel you owe them?"

"No, my king, I wish to go with them because they are my friends."

# Chapter 41

SATURDAY, 24TH JULY

It was late morning. Geledhil stood waiting for the rest of them to catch her up. With Hreidmar as their guide, the journey from Mortheill had been straightforward and trouble-free. A small troop of dwarven warriors had accompanied them for most of the first day but had returned once they passed the furthest of the city outposts.

"I think we need to find another way," announced Geledhil as the others caught up. They looked beyond her, down the tunnel.

Camron groaned. This was their fourth day since leaving Mortheill. His anxiety over returning in time for his daughter's birth increased.

"You might be right," said Trigger, slumping against the rock wall to ease the weight of his Bergen from his shoulders. At the furthest reaches of their visibility, they saw the reason for Geledhil's dismay. A massive rockfall had completely blocked the tunnel.

"Would magic shift it?" Smith asked Camron hopefully.

"It depends on how much the tunnel is blocked, but it looks quite extensive. I don't know, possibly not."

"We passed a passageway a few hundred metres back. Maybe we could try that?" said Craig.

"Are ye coming, or were you planning on taking an early lunch?" Hreidmar called to them. He was standing just before the rockfall.

They continued towards the dwarf, but their hesitant expressions were clearly visible. He grinned, a knowing look twinkling in his eyes. He didn't wait for them but started to scuff at the ground near the side of the wall with his metal-shod boot. A minute later, they heard the distinctive clink of metal upon metal. The dwarf knelt down and grabbed the metal ring his digging had uncovered. He gave it a mighty heave, and an entire floor section disappeared before them in a cloud of dust and dirt. When their coughing and astonishment had subsided, they saw a ramp leading downwards underneath the blocked passageway.

Hreidmar's grin was as broad as his barrel-like chest. "Ye didn't think we'd make an exit to the surface world easy to find, did yer?" Not waiting for a reply, he started down the ramp, heavy boots echoing noisily. The others exchanged disbelieving looks before following.

Their route became increasingly tricky, always heading upwards. Sometimes, the gradient was imperceptible. Other times they climbed sheer rock faces. Once or twice, they had to negotiate climbing narrow vertical chimneys, bracing backs and feet against the walls, ascending slowly. Towards mid-afternoon, as they walked along a narrow tunnel, they reached a point where the ceiling started sloping abruptly until it melded into the floor, blocking the passageway entirely.

"What now?" asked Smith. "Another secret path?"

Hreidmar smiled. "Not quite." He withdrew two blood-red rubies from a pocket and walked forward, stooping as the ceiling lowered. His hands felt along the walls, searching for something. After a short distance, he found what he was looking for; two shallow indentations a few centimetres apart in the ceiling. Carefully, he inserted the rubies, pushing each one until he heard a definite *click*. Retracing his steps quickly, he re-joined the others and turned to face the tunnel. Suddenly, the ceiling shifted slightly. By the startled expressions of his companions, the others had noticed this as well. It moved again, this time curving and coalescing into a distinctive shape. There were gasps behind him as the sloping ceiling detached itself, turning into a small Earth Elemental that filled the tunnel. Its glowing red eyes were the rubies Hreidmar had placed into its eye sockets. They could see that beyond the tunnel continued onward.

"The final protection," Hreidmar announced, clearly proud of this dwarven ingenuity. He spoke a word in a strange tongue, and the elemental stepped aside to allow them to pass. Hreidmar went last, reclaiming the rubies as he passed. After they had gone past, the elemental melded itself back into the ceiling, gently sloping down to block the tunnel once more.

"I think we're getting close," said Geledhil. "There is a faint glimmer of light ahead." She was right. The tunnel inclined upwards, and the light increased almost imperceptibly as they progressed.

When they halted for a brief rest, Smith rummaged around in his Bergen and withdrew a small bag. From it, he took out several pairs of thick dark sunglasses. He handed a pair to each of them.

"We'll need these to help our eyes acclimatise to light again." Two pairs remained in his hand, a stark reminder of the two comrades who would not be returning to the surface with them. He handed one to Hreidmar and respectfully placed the remaining pair in his pack.

An hour later, they reached the source of the light. Light flooded through a narrow gap, mere centimetres wide. From beyond, indistinct voices could be faintly heard.

Hreidmar spent several minutes searching, eventually finding a cleverly concealed mechanism. He twisted it, and they heard a soft clunk. Putting his shoulder to the rock, he heaved, pushing it outwards. They were in a narrow passageway. The light, and the voices, were coming from their left.

"Ready," said Smith, donning his sunglasses. The others nodded and did likewise. After fifty metres, the passage turned a sharp right. They stepped out into a small cavern, right in front of a group of what clearly looked like tourists.

Several of the tourists yelled in fright.

"It's okay. Please don't be alarmed. We're British Army soldiers on a training exercise," Smith called out to them. "Bit awkward, really. We got lost and wandered around the tunnels for a couple of days trying to find our way out."

His tone was light, touched with chagrin to highlight his embarrassment. Craig, catching on, discreetly ushered Trigger and David to the front, along with himself, partially shielding those not dressed in military attire. Smith's easy manner worked. The tour guide stepped forward, although still unsure and hesitant.

"Sergeant Craig Harper, ma'am," Craig introduced himself to the lady who seemed to be the tour guide. "Could you point us in the right direction to get out, please? Wouldn't want to get lost again." His slight self-mocking smile was intended to help gain her support.

Katie, the tour guide, was quick to recover from her initial shock. She knew the cave system was extensive and went far beyond the areas the tourists were permitted to visit. In fact, many parts had not been fully explored, so these soldiers might have stumbled into these caves from a nearby cave system. She was, however, confused as to why they all wore dark sunglasses, despite the fact the light in this part of the cave was dim and would have been darker still in the caves they had come from.

"Of course," she said, recovering her composure. "It's that way. Look, I'll come with you. The sight of you lot emerging from the caves is likely to cause even more panic. My name's Katie, by the way." Turning to the tour group, she asked them to remain calm and stay where they were until she returned.

"Katie, sorry, I know this will sound strange, but where exactly are we?" asked Smith.

She levelled him a suspicious look but answered after a few moments. "You're in the Peak Cavern in Castleton." Blank stares greeted her announcement. "In the Peak District. Just how lost did you get?"

He didn't reply but smiled sheepishly.

She led them along the path beside the small river, which ran through the caves, passing under *Five Arches* and over a series of bridges until they reached the bottom of steep steps.

"The *Devil's Staircase*," said Katie, "not far now."

Hreidmar was trailing at the back of the group, head down, shielding his eyes from the intensity of the electric lighting that provided just sufficient light for visitors to view the caves. Despite the sunglasses they wore, the light was like that of a glorious summer's day to the group who had been underground for so long. To the unfortunate dwarf who had spent all 180 years of his life underground, the meagre watts of the electric bulbs were almost unbearable.

They soon reached a broad and spacious entry cavern known as the Vestibule and could see the cave exit some hundred metres ahead. Other tourists were milling around, admiring the natural wonder of the cavern. There was obvious shock and a few startled gasps at their appearance. However, with Katie leading them, the reaction was more curiosity than fear.

It was a bright sunny day outside, and the light blazed through the entrance, the brilliance penetrating every nook and cranny. Yet the group would have preferred the weather to be wet and dreary. At least it wouldn't have hurt their eyes so much. To Hreidmar, it was agony. Even with his sunglasses on, he had to squeeze his eyes shut. The insides of his eyelids looked like fiery orange orbs. The brightness was more intense than anything he could possibly have imagined. He covered his face with his thick rough hands.

"Can't you do something?" asked Smith, wiggling his fingers in what he thought approximated spell casting.

Camron considered before answering. "There is something we could try." Turning to Geledhil, he said, "Can you cast a *Darkness* spell?"

"Yes," she answered, "but he wouldn't be able to see anything if I cast one on him."

"Normally, that would be true, but your magic is weaker than mine. If I disrupt your spell slightly while you cast it, he'll hopefully be shrouded in a gloomy duskiness rather than total darkness. Plus, the innate dwarven resistance to magic will slowly dissipate the spell rather than expiring after an hour or so. It will gradually get lighter for him rather than all at once. It's got to be worth a try at least."

Geledhil nodded in agreement, and Camron looked from Smith to Katie. Smith took the hint, approached her and began talking, distracting her while Geledhil cast her spell.

It worked. Hreidmar looked like he was surrounded by a haze of black tobacco smoke. Still, he was, at least, able to tolerate the light, albeit with some considerable discomfort.

They followed the prescribed footpath, which was suddenly free of tourists. It ran alongside one wall. Most of the cavern was devoted to an impressive display of traditional rope making, the industry that had helped sustain the village of Castleton for several hundred years. They reached the cave exit and could see beyond a narrow, steep-sided gorge with a tarmacked lane leading away to the village. A sign prominently displayed read '*Welcome to Peak Cavern. The Devil's Arse!*'

Hands shielded their eyes as the meagre protections afforded by their sunglasses proved insufficient to shield their subterranean eyes from the relentless glare of the summer sun. Hreidmar, despite the magical *Darkness* spell, suffered immeasurably more than the others. Not only did his eyes feel like they were being scorched by the sun, but the sheer amount of nothingness that was the open sky was genuinely terrifying to the dwarf. He had lived all his life underground, comforted by the millions of tons of solid rock above him. Even the largest caverns were only a couple of hundred metres high. But here, above ground, there was nothing between him and the vastness of the skies above. Hreidmar raised his arms over his head and fought with the courage characteristic of his people to not turn tail and run back into the caves.

He stood stock-still and stoic.

The rest of them also loitered in the cave entrance, giving their eyes precious minutes to acclimatise gradually. Smith was the first to move. Once outside, he dropped his Bergen and began rummaging in the side pouches. He pulled out something and stood up, holding a mobile phone, which he removed from its protective case before turning it on. "Typical, no signal," he announced after a period of waving the phone in the air like some wayward orchestra conductor.

“Well, we are in the Peak District,” said Craig. Turning to Katie, he asked, “Is there a landline phone we could use, please?”

“There’s one in the visitor centre, in the office next to the café.”

“Did you say café?” asked Trigger eagerly. She nodded. “Well, what are we waiting here for? There’s proper grub waiting for us.”

Without waiting to see if the others followed, he set off at a pace only SAS troopers carrying a full pack could manage. Craig was just behind. Their route followed a narrow path running alongside a row of old, slate-roofed cottages. They soon arrived at the Visitor Centre car park. Trigger and Craig were halfway across when Smith let out a loud whistle and beckoned them back. They trekked back to him, their annoyance plain to see.

“You have money, do you?” Smith asked. Their faces dropped disconsolately, and their enthusiasm quashed.

“Bugger!” exclaimed Trigger.

“I thought not,” grinned Smith, holding up a plastic credit card. Craig snatched it.

“Thanks, Seven. What’s the PIN number?”

“2-4-6-8”

“Seriously? No wonder we’re in so much trouble.” Craig and Trigger headed back towards the café, muttering about amateurs being in charge.

“You might as well join them,” Smith said, hoisting his Bergen onto one shoulder. “I may be some time.” He started across the car park, but in the direction of the sign saying ‘Visitor Information'.

Camron, David, Geledhil and Hreidmar entered the café and looked around. A dozen tables were laid out with spotless white tablecloths and handcrafted pottery jugs holding cutlery neatly wrapped in napkins. A small vase of freshly picked wildflowers adorned each table. Several tables were already occupied. A silence settled over the café as the strange group entered.

They saw Craig and Trigger by the counter, discussing their culinary options. A large fan on the counter struggled to fulfil the job the air-conditioning would have been doing if it hadn't been out of order. Trigger's now long hair was blown about haphazardly as he eyed the menu.

"Sandwich, sausage roll or Cornish pasty?" Trigger mused, partly to himself and partly seeking gastronomic guidance from Craig.

"Difficult choice, mate. I'm not sure, in all good faith, that I could narrow it down to a single selection. But," Craig paused, a big grin spreading across his face, "seeing as Seven is paying, why don't we treat ourselves and have the lot?"

Trigger's smile was equally broad. "You see, that's why you're a sergeant. It's being able to think like that and make split-second decisions." Trigger turned to the pretty but nervous-looking girl behind the counter. "Two BLT sandwiches, two sausage rolls and two Cornish pasties, please. Oh, and four Cokes. Plus, whatever they are having," he concluded, indicating where Camron and the others stood.

Geledhil took one look at the food on offer from the refrigerated counter and pulled out her last piece of Koymasse bread. "I'm fine with this," she said.

Camron ordered food and drinks while Trigger and Craig pulled several tables together. The handful of other patrons in the café looked on with either curiosity or, in some cases, unease. One or two of them decided prudence was the best option. They finished their drinks quickly and left.

Camron noticed a large TV attached to one wall, showing a news channel, albeit with the volume muted. On the screen, a reporter stood in a grassy area devoid of all features, save for a strange luminous half-sphere in the distance behind him.

Camron gaped in astonishment. Geledhil caught his expression and followed his gaze. "Is that," she hesitated a moment, "is that a *Sphere of Protection*?" she asked.

Camron nodded, still dumbfounded.

"But it looks huge. It must be what, about sixty metres across. I didn't think they could be that big?"

"They can't," answered Camron, finding his voice. "Not even Merlin could cast one of that size." He stopped talking as the chef came over with their sausage rolls and pasties, which Trigger had insisted on having hot.

"Excuse me, could you turn the telly up, please?" asked Camron. "I'd like to hear what's going on with that."

"You mean the orb?" the chef answered. "Blimey, mate, where on Earth have you been for the past fortnight? Stuck in a cave?"

"That's right," answered Hreidmar helpfully. The dwarven sense of humour was as different from the humans as it could be, revolving around mead and fighting. Irony was an alien concept to dwarves. The chef eyed him dubiously, suspecting he was having the mickey taken out of him.

Camron caught his attention again by asking, "So where is this orb?"

"Stonehenge. It appeared nearly two weeks ago and has been growing ever since." He picked up the TV remote and turned up the volume.

The reporter, who was still on the screen, was speculating whether there was a connection between the orb's appearance and moving the stones last November.

"Well, they got that bit right," said David.

An interview with a very smug-looking man, who purported to represent the druids in Britain, was sanctimoniously saying how he had known all along that moving the stones would cause something like this to happen.

Smith joined them, dumping his Bergen and pulling up a chair. "Apparently, there's a bloody great big orb covering Stonehenge."

"We know," answered Craig, "just been watching it on TV. What do you think it is?" he asked Camron.

"I think it's a *Sphere of Protection.*" Blank expressions greeted this explanation. "It's a form of magical protection that is pretty much impenetrable. It's normally used to protect wizards during a battle. The trouble is, I've never heard of one as large as this one."

"What's it for?" asked Smith.

"Well, considering it's covering the portal at Stonehenge, then if I were the Dökkálfar and planning an attack, I'd need to bring a whole load of troops through the portal. With a *Sphere of Protection* covering it, they're completely safe from attack until they're ready to fight. We can only estimate how many and what they are bringing in but can't do anything to stop them."

Smith swore.

"Ditto," said Craig. "So, what's happening with us now?"

"They're sending a couple of choppers to pick us up."

"Two?" questioned Craig.

"Yes," replied Smith, "you and Trigger are returning to Hereford for debriefing. The rest of us are going to London."

"I'm not," said Camron determinedly. "I'm going to see my wife before I do anything else." He steeled himself for an argument.

Smith smiled. "That's why we're going to London. She's there."

"What?" asked Camron, half rising from his seat, concern quickly spreading through him.

"Apparently, there was an incident with the press. Somehow they got hold of who she is and who you are. It was deemed advisable to relocate her to a safe house. She's with Xankira and Flint, and she knows you're back."

He sat back down, relief quickly replacing his concern.

"So, now we wait for our lift to arrive," said Smith. He turned to Camron, "There's a briefing tomorrow at 11 am. The PM will be there and a few bigwigs from some countries in the coalition. Your presence is requested as well."

"Oh, joy!" exclaimed Camron, his forehead furrowing in consternation. "Do you think you can arrange for a helicopter to take us to Stonehenge first thing in the morning so we can have a look at the sphere close up? Seeing it first-hand might help."

"I'll see what I can sort out," said Smith.

"Thanks. I think I will finish my tea and then see if I can use a phone to call Rachel," said Camron, devouring the last of his sausage roll.

Geledhil glanced around at her companions, a tinkling laugh escaping her lips as she looked to Hreidmar. He was finishing his third Cornish pasty, and his thick wiry beard had become liberally coated with flakes of pastry. He met Geledhil's laughter with an unabashed look of his own. "Are there any more of these? It tastes much better than Groth." The others joined in with Geledhil's mirth.

She got up and went to the counter, politely asking the young girl if they could have a couple more pasties. She nodded, looking slightly less nervous in the face of Geledhil's warm smile and pleasant demeanour. She had started ringing the new order into the till when she let out an ear-rending scream. The fan on the counter had blown back Geledhil's hair, revealing her distinctive elven ears.

"Dökkálfar!" the girl screamed and sprinted into the kitchen to escape whatever wickedness the elf sought to bring down on them. Pandemonium descended as the few other patrons sought their own escape. Chairs were overturned, trays of food and drink scattered with abandon. Within a few seconds, the café was empty of everyone else.

Geledhil's expression was a mixture of sadness, disbelief and horror. How could she have been mistaken for a Dökkálfar? Hreidmar's expression had also changed, but his wasn't one of fear or revulsion. He looked at Geledhil with sympathy and sadness and perhaps a hint of guilt, for his own people also had pre-judged. He felt ashamed on their behalf.

He stood up and walked over to her, taking her gently by the arm and leading her back to the others, "Come on, lass, they didn't mean it. They probably don't know the difference between Ljósálfar and Dökkálfar. Don't let it upset you."

“Yeah,” chipped in Trigger, a lopsided grin on his face. “And anyway, I can’t wait for them to realise Hreidmar is a dwarf. All hell will break loose then.”

Hreidmar grunted in disgust, but a faint smile touched the corners of Geledhil’s mouth nonetheless.

Geledhil realised it didn’t matter quite so much what other people thought. The important thing was the friendship of the people gathered around her.

# Chapter 42

SUNDAY, 25TH JULY

Camron stretched, trying to ease the stiffness in his body and stifled yet another yawn. They travelled in two black Range Rovers, speeding through the dark, near-empty streets on the outskirts of London. His mind wandered back to late afternoon. A helicopter had eventually arrived in the early evening, landing in a small field next to the visitor's car park at Castleton. They said their goodbyes to Craig and Trigger, whose lift back to Hereford hadn't yet arrived.

The helicopter had only just risen when Smith swore loudly and insisted they land again. He had forgotten to retrieve his bank card from Craig. There was much grumbling from the pilot, but, as Smith said, he might trust Craig with his life, but he would never trust him with his credit card.

Camron smiled to himself, recalling Hreidmar's obvious terror at being in a helicopter. He kept up his bravado by muttering continually. *'If the elf can fly, then so can a dwarf.'*

Camron's reverie was broken by the driver saying, "Nearly there."

He was yet another dark-suited anonymous figure, although thankfully minus the sunglasses considering he was driving at night. The clock on the dashboard read 12:15am. He had spoken only briefly to Rachel and hoped she would still be awake. Even with the pressure of responsibility and his own fears, he had missed her terribly. Camron gazed fixedly out of the window as if he might catch a glimpse of her.

They drove through a respectable suburb and turned into a tree-lined avenue before long. Up-market detached properties adorned each side of the street, many isolated from the world by high walls and wrought iron gates. The cars turned into one, imposing solid wooden gates barring their entry. Their driver wound down his window and identified himself through an intercom box, holding an ID card up to the tiny camera embedded in the machine. He listed the occupants of the vehicle and those in the one behind them.

A few seconds later, the gates swung inwards, and they proceeded onto the drive. The house itself was impressive and looked to be Victorian. Gravel crunched under the car tyres as they slowed to a stop before the front door. Another grey suit stood outside, although he wore a light summer jacket to ward off the night's chill. He was alert and watchful, Heckler and Koch MP5 carbine at the ready.

The front door burst open, taking the guard somewhat by surprise, and Flint lept out. Behind the dog came Rachel, moving at an ungainly waddle, encumbered as she was by nearly nine months of pregnancy.

However, Camron noticed none of this; his eyes fixed solely on hers. An enormous smile broke across his face. Her smile mirrored his. Her eyes sparkled with the joy of having her husband safely returned. Camron opened the car door, a difficult feat with nearly sixty kilos of German Shepherd dog jumping up and pushing against it. Camron squeezed out and ruffled Flint's fur.

"Hello, boy. Did you look after my girls for me?"

Flint's frantically wagging tail went unnoticed as Camron hurried over to his wife, their eyes still locked together, devouring each other. He took her gently in his arms, aware of how large her bump had become. They kissed tenderly and then clung to each other, Camron luxuriating in the smell of her hair and the warmth of her breath on his neck. They eventually broke apart, primarily due to Flint's insistence that he get some attention. David and Geledhil clambered out of their car, and each was hugged affectionately by Rachel. Much to Smith's surprise, she also hugged him, and he awkwardly half-hugged her and gingerly placed his hands on her back.

"Xankira!" Geledhil squealed in delight, rushing to embrace her. Xankira's muted response surprised Camron. They weren't the same cries of excitement with which they had greeted each other when Xankira had first appeared in their cottage's garden.

*Maybe she's tired,* he thought, *or possibly she's a bit miffed at being left behind.* Whatever the problem, Camron was still inordinately grateful to her for looking after his wife.

"Going up in the world, I see," said Camron. He smiled as he looked over Rachel's shoulder at the impressive house. Before she could answer, the sound of heavily booted feet on gravel reminded him he had been remiss.

Turning to Hreidmar, he said, "Hreidmar, I'm so sorry, my friend. Let me introduce you to my wife, Rachel."

Turning back to Rachel, he said, "Rachel, this is Hreidmar. He's a dwarf and is going to help us."

Rachel was doing an admirable job of regaining her composure. In truth, what with hugging Camron and Flint jumping about all excited, she had literally overlooked Hreidmar. While dwarves didn't have any unusual features, such as the pointed ears of elves, their stature and broad, compact physique made them very much an oddity to human eyes. She held out her hand to him, the radiant smile once more beaming from her face. Hreidmar raised his thick muscular arm and took her hand gingerly in his rough-skinned stubby fingers. Their brownish ochre colour contrasted with her own slender, pale ones. She squeezed his hand gently as they shook, and he returned the gesture, careful not to hurt her, acutely aware of the power of his own hand, strengthened and hardened in the tunnels through mining and fighting.

"It is lovely to meet you, *Hidemer.*"

"It's Hreidmar," said Camron gently.

"Oh, I'm so sorry. Hreidmar," she pronounced slowly, careful to copy Camron's pronunciation.

Hreidmar beamed at her, his thick bushy beard twitching as he smiled. "It is good to meet yer, Rachel." His accent sounded thick and guttural to her ears.

With the introductions made, they all went inside, where Rachel and Xankira had coffee and homemade biscuits waiting for them.

* * *

They ended up driving to Stonehenge the following morning as all air travel in the vicinity of the dome had been banned. The journey was uneventful, and they spent much of it dozing, catching up on some much-needed rest after the exertion of the past few weeks. They were all dressed, ready for combat. Despite their misgivings, it had been Hreidmar who had convinced them of the prudence of this.

"We don't know anything about the sphere. What if something is waiting inside. I wouldn't want to find anything hostile dressed just in a nice suit with nothing but one of your mobile phone things to protect me."

A military checkpoint blocked the A303 a couple of miles before Stonehenge. They could see the road beyond closed to all traffic with diversion signs directing them another way. Not even Smith's now legendary *'get past anything'* security ID could sway the impassive sentries. The presence of a Challenger II battle tank behind the blockade convinced them to follow the diversion. Soon after, they pulled into the car park of the Stonehenge Visitor Centre, now used as a command centre by the Army. Despite its closure to tourists, the car park was almost full, mainly of military vehicles. However, Camron did notice several of the ubiquitous black Range Rovers. The stones weren't visible from the visitor centre, as it was discreetly nestled in a dip in the landscape a mile and a half away.

However, as they alighted from their vehicles, they could see the top of the sphere as it protruded above the gently sloping fields to the east.

"What's wrong?" Camron heard Geledhil ask. He looked back and saw she stood next to David, who looked around the car park with a questioning gaze.

"Oh nothing, nothing's wrong. I was wondering what happened to my car, that's all."

"Your car?" asked Camron confused.

"Yes. The last time I was here was when we were moving the stones." He paused, a lump rising in his throat as the guilt of his own contribution to this war resurfaced. "Anyway," he continued, pushing aside his feelings, "when I was transported from Stonehenge to Alfheim, my car was left here. I just wondered what had happened to it. Smith got my wallet, phone and other bits back after returning from Niðavellir, but I don't know where my car is."

"Shall we ask the dome nicely if it would stop growing while we look for your car?" said Smith.

David smiled, "No, that won't be necessary. I didn't like that car much anyway."

As they all moved off, Geledhil fell into step beside Smith.

"That was very kind of you to ask the dome to stop growing to find David's car," she said quietly, "but I don't think the magic works that way."

She missed the grins Smith and Camron exchanged.

A military entourage greeted them. The commander in charge of the site, Colonel Kempton, introduced himself. Camron requested a closer inspection of the sphere. The buses that previously ferried sightseers to the stones had been commandeered by the army. During the short drive to the stones, they passed several massive defensive works still under construction, each designed to protect the troops against whatever they might encounter. As the bus pulled to a stop a few hundred metres away, five astonished faces gazed in disbelief out of the windows. An enormous dome, reminiscent of the Millennium Dome on the bank of the River Thames, encompassed the central circle of sarsen stones and extended to enclose the outer ditch.

The group alighted from the bus and stood transfixed, staring at the spectacular sight.

"That's enormous," exclaimed David unnecessarily.

The magical sphere pulsed a dull shade of white, intermingled with swirls of bright colour, like a bizarre hypnotic rainbow.

Camron and Geledhil set to work. Over the next hour, they cast various magical *detection* spells.

“Well,” said Camron once he had exhausted every magical option known to him, “it’s definitely a *Sphere of Protection.*”

“Can we break it,” asked Smith.

“No, I don’t think so,” answered Camron thoughtfully. “It would appear they Dökkálfar have modified the spell to create one so big. This sphere needs to be constantly fed with magic to support its’ size. There must be Dökkálfar wizards inside continually renewing the spells.”

“Bugger,” said Smith.

* * *

Camron remained quiet during the return trip to London, contemplating all he had seen. Their destination was a meeting with the Prime Minister, who wanted Camron’s opinion on what he thought they would be facing. Memories of previous battles with the Dökkálfar a millennia and a half ago resurfaced, the horror and carnage returning vividly. It was impossible to comprehend the world once more entering the maelstrom of killing that a new War of the Realms would entail.

On their arrival in London, they were met by several officials, who led them a short distance from the main Whitehall buildings to the side entrance of a nondescript office block. Camron was pleased they had heeded his warnings about the ability of the Dökkálfar to scry on their meetings. They descended several flights of stairs until they reached a large reception area. The carpet was thick and luxurious. Walnut panels covered the walls, which were polished to a magnificent sheen. Heads turned when they entered, several people stopping to look at the newcomers. Camron thought a few of them appeared to be security officers, like Smith, but he wasn’t entirely sure. None of them spoke. The room was silent save for the hum of the air-conditioning.

A middle-aged woman dressed in a business-like blue jacket and skirt sat behind an enormous reception desk. She didn’t smile, but her look towards them was expectant.

“Good afternoon,” she said as they approached. “The Prime Minister and the others are waiting for you,” she addressed Camron. "You'll have to leave your..." she paused, her eyes roving over the assortment of swords, axes, bows and guns the troop had with them, "your weapons with me. The rest of you can wait out here. There's a restroom through there where you can freshen up if you need to," she said, indicating a door off to one side as her eyes rested on Geledhil's appearance a moment longer than was necessary.

"I'm sorry," said Camron politely, "what do you mean, *wait out here*?"

"This meeting is high-level and classified. You are the only one authorised to attend."

Camron nodded slowly as if only now understanding something that should have been obvious.

"I see. In that case, I would be grateful if you give the Prime Minister our apologies." Camron turned around and headed towards the door through which they had entered.

Clearly flustered, the woman stood and called after him, "Excuse me, I'm sorry, but where are you going?"

"Home," Camron replied directly.

"But... but the Prime Minister is waiting for you. You can't just leave!"

"If my companions aren't permitted to attend, neither shall I." He continued towards the closed door. The two security officers stepped forward to block Camron's exit.

"Could you move aside, please?" Camron asked amiably. One of them looked past him towards the woman, who was clearly at a loss regarding how to handle the situation. She shook her head slightly.

"I'm sorry, sir," he replied, "but I can't permit you to leave."

Camron sighed, but his eyes hardened. "Look, I have no wish to threaten you, let alone fight you. However, in all probability, my companions and I are the single most powerful combat force in the world. If we want to leave, there is nothing you can do to stop us, so please, let's avoid any unpleasantness, shall we?"

“Camron, it’s okay. We can wait here,” said Geledhil in a placating manner.

“No, it’s not okay. We travelled through Niðavellir together. We fought goblins and lost comrades. If it is okay for you to go through all of that alongside me, then it is damn well okay to accompany me here. Anything I’m told I’m just going to repeat to you anyway, so it makes absolutely no difference.”

He had turned and delivered this last line as an ultimatum to the woman, her face a perfect portrait of indecision. The other occupants were all on edge, nervous as to the outcome. Camron’s words had not been a boast but a statement of fact. He and his companions were indeed a formidable force, and no one relished a confrontation.

Though they had not unduly raised their voices, they had attracted some attention. The double doors leading into the meeting room opened, and a man stepped out. He took in the scene with a single glance; Camron facing the tense officers barring the door, the woman stood in the middle of the room looking nervous and agitated. The room’s other occupants were all alert and tense.

“What’s going on?” he asked in a light tone. “We’re waiting for you, Camron.”

“It appears to be a private party,” he replied. “My companions aren’t invited.”

“Well, this is quite important. Your involvement is only due to your, shall we say, unique position. Is there a problem?”

“No problem at all,” Camron replied, “as I said to your colleague here, please thank the Prime Minister for the invitation, but we’ll be leaving now.”

The man looked from Camron to the guards barring the door, assessing the situation. “So, if I understand this correctly, you won’t join this meeting without your companions?”

Camron nodded, meeting the man’s questioning look with a determined look of his own.

“Very well,” the man sighed, “but you will, at least, have to leave your weapons out here.”

“Not Excalibur. The sword stays with me.”

The man nodded in acceptance and turned to the woman, “Rowena, would you please organise some extra coffees?”

It took a few minutes for the group to offload their assorted weapons. Hreidmar was particularly recalcitrant and took some persuading but eventually agreed and removed a surprising quantity of weapons secreted about his person. Not just his battle-axe but also knives, throwing axes and one or two items even Camron didn’t recognise. They were piled onto a nearby table, causing it to creak under the weight. Camron cast a minor spell on the table, causing it to simply glow a dull yellow, but said to the room at large, “I’ve cast a protective spell on our weapons. If anyone touches them, their arm will wither and become useless.” Geledhil hid her smile at the deception, and they all proceeded to the meeting room.

They trooped in through the double doors, except for Smith, who hung back undecidedly, torn between going with the others and understanding that this was a meeting way above his pay grade.

“Come on, Smith,” said Camron. Smith hesitated.

“I said come on,” repeated Camron encouragingly. “You’re one of us, aren’t you?” Smith nodded, still unsure.

“Well then,” Camron said.

Geledhil forestalled any further argument by grasping Smith firmly by the hand and almost dragging him into the room. Camron followed. A half-smile creased the corners of his lips.

Unsurprisingly, the room they entered was just as plush as the reception area outside, with the same burnished walnut panels covering the walls. An imposing dark oak table dominated the room. Around thirty chairs were placed down either side, upholstered in green leather and comfortably padded. About half of the seats were already occupied.

"I've invited the others to join us," said the man who had ushered them in. "If there is no objection, Prime Minister?" Camron presumed this aide, or whoever he was, knew the Prime Minister quite well. He managed to convey enough meaning in his tone that the Prime Minister didn't object.

"No, not at all," said James Beresford. "You seem to stick together quite well, don't you?" The slight tone of his voice was at odds with the hint of merriment sparkling in his eyes as he looked at Camron.

They took seats around the table as Rowena brought in some more coffee. There followed brief introductions. Opposite the British Prime Minister sat the French Prime Minister, Monsieur Balluet, the German Chancellor, Frau Bauer, and the US Defence Secretary, Patricia Cole. Several senior British ministers and ambassadors from Italy, Spain, Canada, China and Russia were present. Several people in high-ranking military uniforms were also present, most sitting alongside their respective government representatives.

"Right," said James, "I think we've had enough diversions for one day. Shall we get started?" There was a general murmuring of assent and a few moments of shuffling as people sought to get comfortable in their seats.

"Good, well, today's meeting aims to discuss our strategy to handle what is clearly now the war against the Dökkálfar and, in particular, how to deal with the orb covering Stonehenge. Camron, I believe you have been down to Wiltshire this morning. What do you make of it? Do you know what it is?"

Camron looked around, aware of every pair of eyes focused on him. His throat was suddenly dry, and he took a sip of coffee before answering. "From the magical detection spells Geledhil and I cast, it looks like a *Sphere of Protection.*"

"Looks like?" interrupted the Frau Bauer before he could continue. "You mean you are not sure?"

"I mean, I have seen these spheres before, but never one so big. They provide powerful magical protection, completely impregnable. Nothing can pass through the sphere. Wizards sometimes use them for protection during a battle or as a shelter if they are tired or injured. Still, the biggest ones I've heard about would only be large enough for a handful of people. The one at Stonehenge would hold hundreds, easily."

"So why is it there?" asked Patricia Cole.

"I think they are using the sphere as cover and protection to bring through enough battle-mages and troops to win the first battle decisively. The Dökkálfar lost the previous two Wars of the Realms because men, Ljósálfar and dwarves united and fought together as allies." He paused, allowing his words to be absorbed by the rapt audience. "If I were the Dökkálfar, I would be desperate to avoid this happening again. They need to attack and defeat each in turn, and it has to be us first as all the portals connect to our realm. They need a firm foothold in our land, and the best way to achieve that is to win the first major battle quickly and conclusively. Suppose they can overwhelm us and devastate our defences with a combination of magic and pure ferocity. In that case, they will then have time to defeat and subjugate the others."

"But what about the attacks that have already happened?" interjected James. "If they need to defeat us in turn, why tip their hand?"

"My grandmother, that is Queen Nimue of the Ljósálfar, thinks that most of the initial attacks were not part of the Dökkálfar's overall plan. Their society is divided into separate matriarchal houses, each vying for power. She thinks some of the smaller houses launched the early attacks to advance their own position."

"So you're saying," said the Monsieur Balluet, "is we can do nothing to stop them assembling their forces?"

"Yes, and no. Enlarging and maintaining a protective sphere of that size must take the magical skills of a considerable number of Dökkálfar wizards. Each of them will have to dedicate themselves entirely to it. The sphere is basically impenetrable. But attacking it might weaken it a little. Suppose we can keep up a constant barrage of tank and artillery fire. In that case, they will have to devote more wizards to maintaining the protective spells. It won't stop it, but the more disruption we can cause, the better."

"And what happens when they are ready?" asked Patricia Cole.

"When they have enough of their army on this side of the portal, they will allow the sphere to dissipate. Then the battle will commence. Orcs and goblins will comprise the bulk of their army. In size and strength, humans are a bit bigger than goblins, but as you have seen, orcs are considerably stronger than men. We will need to ensure our army is substantially larger than theirs. And that's not accounting for the battle-mages the Dökkálfar have. We might have technology on our side, but they have magic."

"Can't we send in an airstrike once the sphere disappears?" asked Frau Bauer. "Have a few squadrons of F-35s on standby?"

"That would be a good idea," said Camron, to which the Chancellor smiled in satisfaction, "apart from one small problem." The smile disappeared from her face. "The Dökkálfar have been magically scrying on us for centuries. While they don't have access to our technology, do not make the mistake of thinking they do not understand its capabilities. They will have devoted a great deal of energy to creating spells and tactics to counter our weaponry. For example, it is almost certain that they have created a version of the *Sphere of Protection* spell that could be cast at a moving object. Imagine a missile fired against them that they can trap within an impenetrable sphere, a smaller version of the one at Stonehenge. When it detonates, the explosive force will be contained inside, the energy confined until released when the sphere is dispelled. They could direct it to go anywhere; ammo dumps, fuel containers, army barracks, cities. Anywhere. Worse, what if it were a nuclear warhead. They could contain it and send it to London, Paris, New York, wherever they wanted. With a single spell, they have rendered our most potent military technology obsolete."

The stunned faces around the table gave testament to the potential devastation this would heap on them.

"There's another spell that would also be disastrous for us. It's called *Control Person,* and it does just that. It allows a wizard to magically control the mind and will of another. Imagine if they cast the spell at the pilots of the F-35s you want to send in. They could command them to turn those same missiles on our own forces."

"But what you're saying," said a general with an American accent, "is tank shells or even bullets could be rendered useless?"

"Yes, possible, but unlikely. The *Sphere of Protection* is a powerful spell that's hard to cast and requires the expenditure of a lot of magical energy. Even powerful battle-mages would only be able to memorise at most two or three instances of the spell. They wouldn't waste it on anything as small as an artillery shell. Likewise, while the *Control Person* isn't quite as complex, it is not a spell they could use to control great swaths of our army. They would reserve its use to targeting those who could cause the most damage; fighter pilots, possibly some tank commanders, that sort of thing."

Camron paused a few moments before continuing. "Please, make no mistake, this battle will be a hard, bloody affair, and our casualties will likely be very high. Very high indeed. It will come down to the courage of soldiers fighting hand-to-hand with the enemy. I do not think we will have seen devastation like this since the Battle of the Somme during the Great War."

"And how can you be so sure?" Monsieur Balluet asked. "How can you possibly compare it to the Somme?" Incredulity clearly showed in his tone.

"Because I was there," Camron replied quietly. His eyes became distant, recalling images from a century before, the death, destruction, and unimaginable horror returning to him anew. Everyone around the table knew who Camron was, but they didn't truly grasp what it had meant to be him until he had uttered those four words. Realisation dawned on their faces as the reality of having lived dozens of lives over the past 1,500 years sunk in.

They struggled to comprehend what it must be like to be Camron. A few still looked dubious, disbelieving even.

“Pah,” uttered Monsieur Balluet, looking away from Camron in blatant dismissal of his assertion.

“He is telling the truth,” said a soft, quiet voice in the corner. Everyone jumped, startled. Some leapt from their chairs. Geledhil and David smiled in recognition, despite having been equally surprised. Camron too recognised the voice, but he looked up slowly, his thoughts far away in a shattered French countryside. An elderly elf stood in the corner of the room. He was dressed entirely in black robes, interwoven with intricate silvery runes. He smiled in greeting, and Camron thought he detected a hint of approval in the bright, sharp eyes that met his own.

“Please, it’s okay. He’s with us. On our side, I mean,” said Camron quickly, hastening to avoid any misunderstandings. “If I may, I would like to introduce you all to Findecámo Nénharma, the Royal Wizard from the court of my grandmother, Queen Nimue.”

Findecámo looked at those assembled around the table. “I must apologise for my unorthodox intrusion into this meeting, but Queen Nimue thought my presence might be beneficial. That I might be able to offer some assistance.” In truth, he had been at the meeting since it started. Rather than being invisible, Findecámo had cloaked himself in magic that rendered him unnoticeable. The corner where he stood had simply held no interest to anyone.

“Very well. Please take a seat, Mr Nénharma,” said James, as disconcerted as the others but making an admirable attempt at normality.

Findecámo took a seat and then, without waiting for an invitation, continued speaking to the French President. “As I was saying, Prince Amr—”

“Camron,” Camron interrupted.

“Camron,” Findecámo continued with a flicked glance at his former pupil, “is telling the truth. He was at the Battle of the Somme. In fact, he fought through some of the worst of it. Not only that, but except for Queen Nimue, he is the only person alive who fought for us in the *Second War of the Realms.* Those two facts qualify him to advise us on what to expect during the upcoming battle."

"Yes indeed, quite so," James said into the ensuing silence. "Now, shall we discuss how we will prepare for this battle? The sphere is continuing to grow. Do you know how big it will get and how many troops they will have?"

Camron looked to Findecámo, who thought for a few moments before answering.

"I estimate they will probably total between 25,000 and 35,000 troops. The bulk of their army will comprise goblins and orcs, with goblins being the more numerous. Like us Ljósálfar, the Dökkálfar do not have a large population, and I would imagine there will be only a few thousand Dökkálfar. However, most of them will be trained battle-mages." Findecámo glanced around the table. The look of shock and dismay was becoming the norm for this meeting.

"But please remember," he continued, "this is purely an estimate. One based on logic, intelligent analysis and a small amount of magical scrying into Svartalfheim. But essentially still a guess. I estimate the sphere will reach a diameter of approximately seven to eight hundred metres."

"That's an area of about five square kilometres!" exclaimed Patricia Cole.

"So, I suggest we need to prepare defences another six hundred metres beyond that. That's about a kilometre from the centre of Stonehenge," mused the general from the USA. "That's going to give us a perimeter of..." he paused, frantically trying to recall the formula for calculating the circumference of a circle from his school days.

"Over six thousand metres," chimed David helpfully. "About four miles."

"Guter Gott," exclaimed the Frau Bauer, "that is quite some undertaking. The amount of concrete alone will be enormous."

"Not concrete," interrupted Camron. "The defences will need to be constructed of soil with wooden supports."

"Why?" asked a Canadian admiral.

"Because even a simple *fireball* spell will turn defences of reinforced concrete into nothing more than a multitude of fist-sized flying missiles. The soil will absorb the impact of many of their spells."

"That will make the task almost impossible," continued the American general.

"I think I may be able to help," said Findecámo softly. "Queen Nimue will be sending a few thousand Ljósálfar archers and mages to assist you. We can create a magical *Wall of Protection*, about thirty metres high and as impenetrable as the sphere. I think we can create one a little over a mile long, and if it is curved, that will allow us to seal a third of the perimeter. Your defences will only need to meet where our magical protection ends."

"Well, that will help enormously," said James. "Not only will it reduce the length of our defences, but we will be able to concentrate our own forces better. Thank you, Findecámo. And please thank Queen Nimue for the promise of elven troops."

# Chapter 43

WEDNESDAY, 28TH JULY

A sharp pain woke Camron, jolting him from his dreams of goblins and Dökkálfar. He instinctively reached for Excalibur, which always lay on the ground beside his bedroll. He rolled to his right, seeking the blade and promptly fell out of bed. The rug cushioned his fall but couldn't save his pride. He got up gingerly, rubbing the soreness in his ribs that had nothing to do with his fall.

Rachel sat up in bed, an anguished look on her face. "Camron, stop messing around."

"Did you poke me in the ribs?" he asked sleepily.

She nodded guilelessly. "I couldn't wake you any other way."

"What did you want to wake me for?"

She presented him with a level look, "Well, I fancied a 2 am chat."

"Really?"

"No, you idiot. The baby's coming." As if on cue, Rachel clutched her hands to her belly. A look of pain crumpled her beautiful face. The hazy fog of sleep departed Camron instantly. Shock and concern vied for dominance.

"What should I do?" he asked.

He received another look.

"Getting me to the hospital might be a good idea." She shook her head in disbelief. "It's a good job you're not responsible for anything important, like saving the world."

Camron smiled, accepting his wife's gentle admonishment. "Technically, it's the baby who will save the world, not me." Then hastily added, "I'll get your bag," seeing the warning flash in her midnight blue eyes.

"And wake Mum," Rachel called after him.

"I'm already awake," Stephanie announced, passing him as she entered the room. "Now, let's get you dressed and off to the hospital, shall we?"

Camron fetched the bag that had already been packed as Stephanie helped Rachel get dressed. They assisted her down the stairs as Xankira waited for them by the front door, looking anxious.

"Can you look after her while I get the car?" asked Camron.

Xankira nodded as he stepped outside. The officer on duty outside the front door looked at Camron enquiringly.

"The baby's coming, Greg. It's coming!" Camron said.

A broad grin split the officer's face. "First one?" asked Greg.

"Yes," admitted Camron, trying to contain his nerves.

"Don't worry, sir, it'll be okay. I have three. I'll bring the car around, shall I?"

Camron's nod was interrupted.

"That won't be necessary," said a voice.

Greg spun around, his gun levelled and ready.

"Put that away, young man," the voice said somewhat imperiously. To his surprise, Greg obeyed unquestioningly.

"Grandmother?" Camron asked, not quite believing his eyes. Queen Nimue was walking up the driveway of their London safe-house. She swept past the astonished Greg and proffered her cheek to Camron for a kiss.

"What are you doing here?" he stammered.

"Your wife is about to give birth, is she not?"

Camron nodded mutely.

"I have been present at the birth of every one of my grandchildren, great-grandchildren, great-great... Well, you get my meaning. I have been present at each birth, including yours. So why would you think I would not be present for your daughter's?"

Camron's blank stare and loss for words were fortunately saved by the front door opening.

"Camron, hurry up, will...." Rachel trailed off as her eyes fell on Nimue.

"Look, Grandmother's here," announced Camron unnecessarily.

Next to Rachel, Stephanie's expression was even more astounded. Her mouth echoed a silent '*Oh*' and her eyes wide with shock and wonder.

"Your Majesty," said Rachel, recovering enough from her surprise to attempt an awkward curtsey. She lost her balance as another contraction swept through her and would have fallen if Xankira hadn't caught her.

"Well caught," said Nimue.

"Thank you, Your Majesty," Xankira replied, strong arms steadying Rachel.

"Now then, child, let's get you inside and see about getting you comfortable."

"She needs to get to the hospital," said Stephanie, still unable to take her eyes off the ethereal beauty of the woman before her.

Nimue turned and bestowed a smile on her. "You must be Stephanie, Rachel's mother?"

Stephanie nodded, Nimue's attention suddenly robbing her of speech.

"Well, normally, I would agree with you, my dear, but this is anything but normal. Your daughter will give birth to the *Daughter of Destiny*, a child who will be of both human and elven royalty. It would be better if she gave birth here and not in a hospital."

"But what if there's a problem?" asked Stephanie.

"I have been attending births for several millennia. I am sure that we will manage between us," Nimue answered, spreading her arms wide and ushering them all back inside. As she turned to close the door, she said to a still astonished Greg, "Please ensure you are all on your guard. If an attack is to happen, it will probably be tonight."

He nodded, and Nimue heard him talking into his radio as the door closed with a gentle click.

"Camron, would you help Rachel back to her room, please?"

"Yes, Grandmother."

By now, the remainder of the group, human, elf and dwarf, were up and loitering around the hall and staircase, wondering what was happening. Nimue's appearance caused a degree of awe and wonder. Findecámo was tasked with explanations and introductions in her absence. Nimue and the other women followed Camron into the bedroom.

"I suppose you will be following the strange human custom of being present during the birth?" Nimue asked Camron. A single arched eyebrow intimated at the expected answer, but he steeled himself before saying, "Yes. I will be present at my daughter's birth."

Nimue glanced at Rachel but, seeing no hint of disagreement, nodded. "Very well, but don't get in the way."

Shortly after, Nimue had Rachel settled in bed, with Stephanie and Xankira calmly and efficiently going about their allotted tasks.

"What shall I do?" asked Camron, feeling surplus to requirements.

Nimue looked at him appraisingly, and then a ghost of a smile flickered across her lips as she glanced at Rachel's hand, protectively cradling her belly.

"It's about time one of them knew," she muttered to herself. To Camron, she said, "Stay next to your wife and hold her hand. She will need all the support she can get soon enough."

Camron stood by Rachel's side and gently held her hand. After a minute or two, she squeezed as another contraction approached. Camron placed his free hand on her brow, his own furrowed in concern for his wife.

A sudden tightening of his lower back was quickly followed by intense pain, like an abdominal cramp, only much, much worse. He jumped back, letting go of her hand and clutching at his own stomach in shock. Rachel, still recovering from the pain of her contraction, hadn't noticed. A soft tinkling laugh drew Camron's attention to Nimue.

"What just happened?" he asked, still shocked and startled.

"You were touching Rachel when the pain of her contraction came. The connection you have with your *Family Ring* is strongest when there is physical contact. You felt the same pain as your wife. Congratulations,

Camron. You are the first man to ever experience the pain of labour. Now, go support your wife and marvel at what the *weaker sex* endures to bear your children."

Camron returned to Rachel's side, taking her hand once more, although somewhat gingerly. She looked at him through pain-filled eyes, her lustrous mahogany hair dishevelled, a few strands plastered to her forehead with sweat.

# Chapter 44

SUNDAY, 22ND AUGUST

Preparations for the impending battle kept Camron and the others extremely busy. He had spent many hours working with Findecámo to provide further insight into the uses of battle magic and the sorts of spells they might encounter. Along with Geledhil and Findecámo, he was also busy running language classes for several dozen army personnel to give them a basic grasp of the Elvish language. Queen Nimue had promised to provide a contingent of Ljósálfar, and these hastily trained interpreters would be required to act as a liaison. Hreidmar and David were also teaching a few people Dwarvish, including the commanding officer in charge, General MacDougall. Just in case, Throndim sent any of his people to help.

They were all having a much-deserved day off. Camron was lounging in the garden of the London house that was now their temporary home, enjoying a few precious moments with his baby daughter. He had cast a minor cantrip, a spell that produced some brightly coloured spheres of light. Thanks to her elven heritage, Gwenllian's eyes were bright and sharp, despite being only a month old. They followed the glowing orbs as they danced before her.

Flint lay alongside her rug, one paw protectively placed on its corner. Since Gwenllian's birth, Flint had designated himself *Chief Baby Protector.* Only a select few could approach Gwenllian without receiving a throaty growl and waiting for Rachel or Camron to approve before moving closer. Even Rachel's mum, Stephanie, who had returned to Washington the previous week, had initially been denied access by Flint.

The rest of the small company was also in the garden, lounging around peacefully. Rachel and Geledhil had cooked a delightful lunch, vegetarian of course, which even Hreidmar couldn't fault, despite the lack of meat and ale.

Suddenly, as Camron's concentration broke, the glowing spheres stopped mid-air.

"What's the matter?" asked Rachel, seeing the visage of contented bliss slip from her husband's face. Flint raised his head at the tone of concern in his mistress's voice.

"Nothing," he replied. "Well, nothing bad anyway." He held up his hand with the *family ring* on it. "Grandmother has sent me a message. The contingent of Elven archers and mages are on their way. We're to meet them before dusk at the portal in Avebury."

Rachel couldn't hide the crestfallen look on her face. She had been hoping to have a few more hours with her husband. Camron smiled, realising the reason for her chagrin. "Don't worry. You get to come along too."

"Why me?" she asked.

"Well, unless you want to be parted from Gwenllian, you'll have to come. The Ljósálfar wish to meet her."

"Why on earth would they want to meet Gwen?"

"Because they have come to fight for her. Remember, it isn't only the Dökkálfar who have prophesied about Gwenllian. The Ljósálfar wish to pay their respects to the *Daughter of Destiny.*"

Rachel was not entirely happy, but Camron was uncharacteristically adamant that their daughter must be there to greet them.

"Smith?"

Smith looked up at the mention of his name, although he had already been paying close attention to the conversation.

"You couldn't rustle up a helicopter for us, could you?" asked Camron.

"Another one? Okay, but you'd think I was made of helicopters!"

"That's ridiculous," exclaimed Geledhil. "You don't look anything like a helicopter."

Hreidmar grunted in agreement, casting Smith a somewhat pitying look. David grinned.

Smith got up from where he had been lounging on the grass, enjoying the sun's warmth. He grabbed his suit jacket, the removal of which was his only concession to the informality of the afternoon and pulled his mobile phone from an inside pocket.

"I've meant to ask," David said to Camron, "why do we travel by helicopter. Couldn't you conjure up one of those magical doorways?"

Findecámo let out a chuckle. David looked from the elven wizard to Camron and saw him blush.

"I'm sure he would if he could," said Findecámo, still chuckling. "But despite my best efforts during the weeks of his re-training, Camron never seemed to manage the *Portal Doorway* spell. He could cast a *Teleport* spell no problem, which in my opinion is the more complex of the two, but that only allows you to take one or two others. I blame myself as his teacher. The failing is entirely mine." Despite his admission of inadequate tutelage, the merriment remained in his eyes.

"Well, you're in good company," said Camron. "Merlin could never get me to master that spell either. Although he was far less gracious and blamed it entirely on me. If I recall correctly, he put it down to a combination of laziness and stupidity."

The light-hearted mood continued while they waited for the entirely non-magical helicopter to arrive.

* * *

It was early evening when they finally arrived at Avebury, a few miles from where the ominous sphere still engulfed Stonehenge. They weren't the only ones awaiting the arrival of the Ljósálfar allies. Quite a few military personnel and several high-ranking government officials were present. Protocols for receiving visiting members of another humanoid species were probably being hastily drafted. While this was not a full state reception, they would be greeted with a level of due dignity and respect.

The handful of houses within the large ring of standing stones stood empty in response to the impending battle. Their owners evacuated some time ago.

They had not waited long before the stones started to glow a bright iridescent blue. Suddenly, from within the midst of the stones, marching four abreast and in perfect unison, came the Ljósálfar. Camron and the rest were used to Geledhil's flawless beauty and only occasionally looked at her in awe. But the other officials had never encountered the beauty of elves before and stood speechless as row after row of Ljósálfar marched past them. The warrior elves, both male and female, were dressed identically. They wore protective leather armour, over which were breastplates and metal greaves made of an unknown golden metal that shone brightly in the afternoon's final rays of sunlight. Each carried a long, beautifully crafted bow in the same style as Geledhil's, plus three quivers packed full of arrows. Scabbarded swords hung in their belts, and atop the head of each elf sat an ornate helm, fashioned of the same golden metal and beautifully engraved with elvish runes. The effect was both awe-inspiring and captivating. Their footsteps were in perfect unison, yet together made barely more noise than a gentle breeze through softly rustling grass.

At their head strode the familiar figure of Tanidaer Felagund, the commander of the elven army. Upon seeing Camron and the others, he detached himself and moved towards them.

"Greetings and well met, Prince Amr," he said formally in Elvish, though his smile lit his face at their reunion.

His gaze slid to the baby girl held in Camron's arms, and his eyes met hers. She returned his gaze with profound scrutiny. Tanidaer took one of Gwenllian's hands in his slender fingers and lowered his head, touching his forehead to her hand.

"Greetings, fabled *Daughter of Destiny*," he intoned solemnly.

Camron held his daughter in his arms.

She watched the procession with an intensity almost disconcerting in one so young. As each row of elves passed the baby girl, they looked towards her, thumping a clenched fist to their breast and nodding in respect.

Rachel watched her daughter's reaction and could have sworn Gwenllian met the eye of each elf.

Findecámo detached himself from the group and moved forward to speak to one of the elves before leading him towards the waiting officials, most of whom still wore expressions of wonderment and awe.

After nearly three thousand warrior elves had come through the portal, Camron noted a change in their appearance and realised Ljósálfar mages were now coming through. These marched in the same perfectly ordered ranks but with noticeable differences in their attire. Many carried quivers of arrows, although no bows. Presumably, they were spares for the archers. The elves were guided towards a prepared encampment of tents in one of the woods to the south, close to Stonehenge.

"Well, that's something you don't see every day," said David, still slightly awestruck by the spectacle.

"I dunno what's so special about a bunch of pointy-ears prancing in their finery," said Hreidmar. "Now, if yer wants to see something impressive, wait 'til my folk gets here. That'll be a sight to tell yer grandchildren about."

"I didn't think we knew whether King Throndim was sending any dwarves to fight," said Findecámo, returning to the group. "We don't even know if they will have Lia Fàil repaired in time."

"They'll be here, don't yer worry your pretty little head about it," growled Hreidmar. "And they'll have the Stone of Destiny with them too." He turned his back and tramped off, ignoring the last few Ljósálfar marching past.

* * *

THURSDAY, 26TH AUGUST

Hreidmar pulled on his heavy boots and left the tent he shared with David. The sphere surrounding Stonehenge had stopped expanding shortly after the elves had arrived. The day before, Findecámo announced that he could detect a definite weakening of the protective orb, which meant that the upcoming battle was probably only a day or two away.

Hreidmar stomped toward the mess tent, thumping his arms against his chest to ward off the morning chill. The dwarf had spent his entire life several miles underground, where the temperature was considerably higher than the surface, and even the mild chill of a bright summer's morning felt icy cold to him. He spied Camron, Geledhil and Findecámo ahead of him and hurried to catch up.

Suddenly he stopped, mid-stride, his face a mask of pure concentration. Hreidmar was at one with the earth. He had spent many long decades listening to the rock and stone of his world and had a deep, innate understanding of what it told him. This morning the ground was resounding with marvellous news.

"They're coming!" he announced in a thunderous bellow, an enormous grin visible beneath his bushy beard.

Startled by the dwarf's shout, the trio ahead of him turned around. Hreidmar reached them and poked Findecámo unceremoniously in the ribs. "They're coming. I told ye, yer great pointy-eared disbeliever. I told yer me folk'd be here, and here they be."

"What are you on about?" asked Camron, cutting off Findecámo's protestations as to his unfair treatment at the hands of the dwarf.

"Can ye not feel the ground?" Hreidmar asked joyously. "Can ye not feel the tremors of the earth? That be the sound of dwarves marching to war."

None of them could feel a thing. Geledhil dropped to her knees and placed an ear to the ground. A smile creased her face, mirroring Hreidmar's. "He's right," she announced.

"Course I'm right."

Geledhil continued, her ear still pressed to the earth. "I can hear marching feet, maybe a couple of miles to the north. It's difficult to tell because the footsteps are so heavy, but I'd guess there must be several thousand."

"See," Hreidmar exclaimed, almost hopping up and down on the spot in glee. "I knew Throndim wouldn't want to miss this fight."

“Well, let’s hope they have Lia Fàil with them,” said Findecámo, still rubbing his bruised side.

Camron and the others headed to meet the dwarves. It wasn’t long before even the humans in the group could hear the rhythmic sounds of hundreds of marching hob-nailed boots. As they crested the rise of a small hill, their eyes met, for the second time, the welcome sight of an army of allies marching to war.

“Here be dwarves,” said Hreidmar, the pride catching in his throat.

The contrast between the arrival of the elves and the dwarves could not have been more different. Where the elves marched almost silently, both in voice and tread, the dwarves trooped with a resounding stomp of heavily booted feet crashing down in unison. A song bellowed heartily at the tops of their voices, accompanied by the regular beat of their step. Rousing and bawdy, Camron realised as he interpreted the vocals. He glanced towards David, whose broad smile gave ample testament to his rapidly growing command of the dwarven language.

At the head of the marching column was Thraidurn, son of Throndim.

Like the elves, the dwarves had come dressed for war. Their appearance was not as uniform as the elves, and they were definitely less brightly coloured. Brown leather armour, most overlaid with a chainmail shirt, was the mainstay of their attire. Strapped to their backs were large round shields. Axes, maces, war hammers, daggers and heavy crossbows hung from belts or backpacks.

A group of high-ranking officials, all garbed in military fatigues, arrived in several vehicles and quickly formed a welcoming party, standing alongside Camron and the others.

“The dwarf on the left at their head is called Thraidurn,” Camron said to General MacDougall, who stood next to him. “He is the son of King Throndim.”

The dwarven column came to a halt in front of the delegation.

“Greetings and well met,” said Camron in Dwarvish.

“Greetings to you, Prince Amr,” replied Thraidurn.

“Call me Camron, please?” said Camron. “Your presence is most welcome. All of you,” he emphasised, looking over the dwarves’ heads at the army behind them.

“If I may make some introductions?” With this, Camron introduced the group. Thraidurn gave a faint hint of surprise when General MacDougall greeted him in a hesitant but understandable dwarvish.

“We have been teaching a handful of humans to speak your language, hoping you would come,” explained Camron.

“As grateful as we are to your arrival with so many warriors, I must ask. Have you managed to repair the stone? Have you brought *Lia Fàil* with you?”

At this question, a slight commotion started several rows back. “Get out of my way, you louts,” a gruff voice bellowed in dwarvish. They all turned and stared as a grizzled, ancient dwarf shouldered his way to the front.

“Borfdak,” Camron exclaimed, smiling at the gruff old dwarf. His smile widened even further when he saw the dwarf had Camron’s *bag of lightness* across his shoulders, the Stone of Destiny protruding out of the top.

“Did yer think we wouldn’t be able to mend it?” Borfdak asked. “Tis made of stone. There ain’t nothing made of stone that a dwarf can’t fix.”

# Chapter 45

SATURDAY, 28TH AUGUST

Their small company stood waiting, expectant in the shadowy greyness of early morning. By dawn's faint light, they could see the brightness of the *Sphere of Protection* surrounding Stonehenge slowly diminish. Vague, shadowy images moved within. The enemy was preparing for battle, as were the thousands of men, dwarves and Ljósálfar.

Nearly four kilometres of earthen trenches hid most of the allied troops, spread out in a wide defensive arc before them. The remainder of the huge defensive perimeter was blocked by the magical, and hopefully impenetrable, *Wall of Stone* created by the Ljósálfar mages. Behind the trenches were massed hundreds of battle tanks, including American M1-Abrams and British Challengers. Each had been fitted with a large switch at the rear, effectively a *cut-off switch*, in case the enemy magically subjugated any of the tank crews. Further back still were the artillery lines, protected by roving troops on the lookout for any ensorceled artillerymen.

The small group was again prepared for combat. Smith and David dressed in black, H&K machine guns slung across their shoulders. David also carried an elven short sword scabbarded on his belt, a gift from Celaena.

*'No point in all that training in Alfheim if you don't have a sword,'* she had said.

Camrons' eyes watched alertly, but his mind wandered to the previous evening. He had said goodbye to Rachel and Gwenllian, not knowing if he would ever see them again. He had clung to his wife as her tears flowed down her cheeks onto his shoulder.

*'Please don't die. We need you to come back to us."* She had repeated it over and over again. But it wasn't his own death that had brought such foreboding. An inexplicable and overwhelming fear had threatened to engulf him that something terrible would happen.

*'Protect them, please?'* Camron had implored Xankira as he left.

*'With my life,'* she replied but lacking the fervour his own plea had contained.

A collective gasp broke his reverie.

As the dawning summer sun peeked over the eastern horizon, the first rays touched the now almost ethereal sphere. Like fog dissipating under the onslaught of the burning sun, the sphere disappeared entirely.

"Bloody hell," exclaimed David.

"Fuck," swore Smith.

Not even Camron knew the dwarven expletive that escaped Hreidmar's lips.

The massed ranks of the enemy began to pour out in all directions.

Geledhil gripped Camron's arm as the enormity of the battle swept over them. Only Camron had ever seen the like before, and he placed his hand reassuringly over hers.

"Is this what it was like? You know, before?" asked Geledhil in a small voice, her gaze sweeping over the massed ranks of goblins, orcs and Dökkálfar. Camron knew she was referring to the Second War of the Realms. He nodded, suppressing a shudder at the horror he knew this day would bring.

The Dökkálfar didn't appear in a hurry to attack. A few moments later, the reason became apparent when the stones, visible for the first time in weeks, glowed brightly, signalling more troops coming through the portal. But as they saw what the enemy brought through, Camron swore himself. Dozens of monstrous creatures, each over three metres tall, lumbered through the portal. Greeted by Dökkálfar and orcs, they were shepherded into position, hurried along with shouted curses and whacks from long crude clubs that seemed to have little effect on their tough, grey rock-like skin.

"Are they..." Geledhil left the question hanging, unwilling to put a name to the creatures who were still growing in number.

"Yes," answered Camron. "Trolls!"

"Big beasties, aren't they?" quipped Hreidmar.

"But incredibly stupid and sometimes hard to control," said Camron. "That's probably why they're only just bringing them through. They can be unpredictably violent and aggressive. Added to their incredible strength, that makes them dangerous opponents."

They watched as troll after troll joined the ranks of the enemy.

"Does this change our plans at all?" The question came from a bald man in his fifties who had made his way towards them. General MacDougall, accompanied by a handful of staff officers, was in overall charge of the battle.

"No, our plan is still the best one we could have. The trolls don't change it. They just make it a bit harder, that's all," answered Camron.

"So we engage the enemy, and while we're busy attacking each other, you do your magic thing with the sword and hope they don't notice until it's too late?"

Camron nodded, not trusting his voice as his private doubts assailed him once more.

"Ok," General MacDougall replied. "Well, no point in wasting any more time."

He turned to speak to his staff when a sudden commotion rippled through the enemy ranks. Turning to look, Camron saw an aged female Dökkálfar rise up above them, literally. She hovered there, a *Levitation* spell keeping her a few metres above the ground. Although she did not shout, the entire battlefield could hear her magically enhanced voice when she spoke.

"Why are you doing this?" she asked in heavily accented English, the words sounding harsh and guttural despite her attempt to sound placating. "I do not wish for you to die. Surrender, and we will spare your lives. Do not listen to your leaders. They know they cannot win and are wasting your lives needlessly."

"Good morning, Sallakray," said another voice, this one softer and lighter, "it's been a long time."

This voice had also been magically enhanced, but all similarities ended there. The two voices could not be more contrasting. Startled, Camron spun around to look into the face of his grandmother. Nimue's eyes fixed on those of the Dökkálfar hovering mid-air.

"Greetings, O Mighty Queen," Sallakray sneered. "So you have come to witness my victory."

"You lost last time," Nimue replied. "You will lose again."

"Oh, but that is where you are wrong, Queen of the Ljósálfar," Sallakray spat the last word as if its utterance left a sour taste in her mouth. "Last time, you had Merlin and Arthur. Now you have only his misbegotten whelp," her eyes flicked briefly towards Camron. "Without human wizards, you cannot possibly hope to defeat my battle-mages with the paltry Ljósálfar that you command. You are no match for my power, Queen of Light." Sallakray lifted her arm. A dark red ruby set into a ring glowed briefly as a jet of blood-red light shot forth, arcing across the intervening space to where Nimue stood.

Nimue raised her arm and uttered a word of magic. From her hand sprang a ray of cornflower blue light. The magic collided midway between the two witches, red and blue, struggling for dominance. They appeared evenly matched for a few seconds, but Camron noted a subtle shift. Nimue's magic was increasing in intensity, whereas Sallakray's was faltering. Inexorably the blue light pushed the red towards its caster. The confident, sneering visage of the Hlyđni-Móđir of House Dukker disappeared, replaced by a mask of pure concentration as she battled to avoid defeat. With a final magical thrust, Nimue's magic overcame Sallakray's, both beams dissipating in a loud boom that threw the Dökkálfar to the ground, bruised and humiliated but otherwise unhurt.

Sallakray screamed her rage, and with that, all hell broke loose. The army of the Dökkálfar attacked. Orcs hurled long spears with wickedly barbed tips as goblins fired crossbow bolts, the volley darkening the skies. The trolls picked up stone blocks, which had once formed part of Stonehenge's great monument. They hurled these enormous blocks effortlessly at the defensive lines. These formidable weapons ploughed through troops and squashed tanks with equal ease.

However, this was nothing compared to the ferocious onslaught of the Dökkálfar witches and wizards who unleashed a devastating sorcerous attack; *fireballs, lightning bolts, cones of ice, magic missiles* and dozens of other spells rained down on the defenders in an overwhelming barrage.

General MacDougall bellowed orders, and the allies opened fire. Shells, mortars and heavy machine-gun fire poured into the enemy. Across the entire line of the enemy troops, protective spells repelled their shells and bullets. But not all of the enemy were protected. Casualties quickly built up on both sides, although the defenders endured most of the early losses.

Camron had turned back to his grandmother in time to see her visibly sag from the effort of her magical confrontation with Sallakray. He leapt forward and steadied her.

"Are you okay?" he asked, concern masking his eyes.

She smiled weakly. "Yes, I am alright. Sallakray has grown immensely powerful since we last battled. I hate to admit it, but that took a great deal out of me." Her smile strengthened as she continued. "It took far more from her, though. Not just magically. A public show of weakness and failure in front of the Hlyđni-Móđir of the other houses will have harmed her greatly."

"I didn't know you'd be here," said Camron.

"Of course I would be here," she admonished gently. "I fought in the last War of the Realms. What made you think I wasn't going to fight in this one?"

Camron shrugged, unable to find a suitable answer but relieved she was here.

"We should move back," said Smith, noting the proximity of some of the Dökkálfar spells. They headed back towards the visitor centre that was now heavily fortified and acting as the forward operating base to support the battle. Within the Stone of Destiny waited, watched over by Findecámo. He had appointed himself its guardian from when the dwarves had returned it.

They waited several more minutes, ensuring the battle was well underway. Clarent's effect would be greatest with the element of surprise, but Camron fretted over every passing minute. The enemy definitely had the upper hand, although it was not entirely a one-sided fight. They were inflicting considerable casualties on the enemy, but nothing compared to what they were taking.

When Nimue announced it was time, Camron closed his eyes, endeavouring to block out the sounds of battle. He took several deep breaths, focusing his thoughts on the sword held within the Stone of Destiny. In one hand, he gripped Excalibur. The other rested, palm down, on the surface of the plain sandstone block before him. He sent forth his mind, calling out to Clarent, invoking the summoning as prescribed by his grandmother.

The last time he had tried this, he had felt only the faintest connection. The sword's reaction to his call was weak, as if a long way off. This time, the response was immediate and powerful. So forceful, in fact, that he jumped back involuntarily, severing the connection.

"What's wrong?" asked Geledhil. "Are you alright?"

"Is the stone still broken?" demanded Nimue.

"No, everything's okay. More than okay, in fact. The strength of Clarent's response took me by surprise, that's all. I'll try again."

Camron stilled his mind and focused once more on the stone. Excalibur reverberated in his hand, almost as if in anticipation. He placed his other hand back on the block, noticing that it felt warm to his touch. He sent out a probing thought, and Clarent responded immediately. Camron called, willing the sword to heed his summons and come to him. He pushed his palm against the stone, exerting pressure and felt the hard sandstone surface give way beneath his touch, becoming soft and malleable like treacle. His hand sank into the stone as Clarent's answering call, heard only by Camron, drowned out everything else.

And then, suddenly, he felt the cold hard hilt of a sword. He grasped it firmly and pulled back. In one smooth, fluid motion, he withdrew the Sword of Destiny from the Stone of Destiny where it had lain waiting, safe and secure, throughout the ages.

Camron stood transfixed, Clarent held before him, the ringing sound of steel against stone still echoing in his ears. The absolute perfection of the sword captivated him. The blade was as bright and sharp as the day it was forged untold centuries ago, engraved with magical runes like its twin. Both swords glowed with a radiant blue hue, almost as if they were overjoyed at their reunion after so long apart.

“I suggest you go outside for the next bit,” said Nimue. “I am not sure what magical forces will be involved in your attempt to control the sword, and being in a confined area might not be sensible.”

Camron nodded, still not taking his eyes from the sword and made his way outside, moving some distance beyond the visitor centre.

Nimue continued walking alongside him after the others had stopped. She placed her hand on his arm.

“Clarent can only be mastered by consent.” She said. “Only if you endure the *Trial of Truth* and suffer the same ordeal you would inflict on your enemies will Clarent deem you worthy and submit to your authority. Now, sheath Excalibur and grasp Clarent. Open your mind and your heart and surrender to the naked truth about yourself.”

Camron gripped the rune-covered hilt apprehensively. It grew cold in his hand, a wave of ice coursing from the sword into his palm. Startled, he took a step backwards and lowered the blade. His astonishment increased as, an instant later, a sharp tingling sensation spread up his arm, emanating from the sword. He winced reflexively in shock and a little pain. His fingers tightened around the ancient hilt. He felt Clarent touch his mind, tentatively at first, questioning and probing.

He tried to steady his nerves. His heart was racing, feeling trepidation at the ordeal to come. Fearful that he would follow in his father's footsteps and fail. That he, too, would be unable to wield the full power of Clarent and would be left holding nothing more useful than an ordinary sword. Taking a deep breath, he closed his eyes and opened his mind to the sword's probing. The tingling sensation rushed through him. He felt his mind connect with the sword, inexorably drawing him deep into himself. Images from his past assailed him as the magical blade sifted through them, flicking at lightning speed through his memories.

Camron's appearance was trance-like. His eyes were closed, breathing slow, and his face transformed into a white, death-like visage. The only visible sign of life was his fist, clenched tightly around the hilt of the ancient sword, which gleamed brightly in the morning sun.

Camron found himself carried inward, sucked into the essence of his being. Drawn into the maelstrom of emotion, the vortex of life at his very core that defined him. This was who he truly was.

Camron came face-to-face with himself!

A rush of jumbled images, confusing memories from all forty-two of his lives, engulfed him in a chaotic kaleidoscope. Pictures and impressions assaulted him mercilessly, each searing itself into his vision. Every one of his lives, from start to end, lay open before him. He was bereft of his own carefully cultivated illusions and open to the truth of his existence in all its starkness. No self-conceived blanket of illusion cloaked him. No glossy fantasies protected him from the harsh reality of these visions. He saw the Truth about himself with a cutting rawness he could not ignore.

Camron had no choice but to allow the images to flood through him, threatening to drown him. A seemingly endless procession of events, memories from his lives, revealing a part of himself he hadn't known or had simply refused to recognise. Like the precise entries in an accountant's ledger, each was listed. They detailed every hurt he had caused others, his lies and half-truths, those deep-seated prejudices, petty jealousies, and minor vindictive actions.

Not the crimes of an evil man, but the truth of the everyday wrongs of an average person. In his case, that brutal and open honesty was multiplied for each of his lives.

Most prominent were his self-doubts. An icy river of fear washed over him. He was drowning in it. His inner turmoil dragged him under. He couldn't do it. He simply wasn't up to it. The images paraded before him were relentless. He recoiled in horror at what he had to acknowledge about himself. It was too much. He couldn't accept it. He wasn't strong enough. Clarent had laid the naked, bitter truth before him, and he had been found wanting.

With a cry of pure anguish, he flung the sword from his icy cold hand. It flew end over end, glinting in the rays of the morning sun. Clarent landed, blade downward, in one of the giant stones the trolls had flung as missiles. The rune-engraved blade slid effortlessly through the stone, almost to the hilt, as if it were no more solid than sand. The Sword in the Stone came to rest, embedded, ironically, upright in stone. Held fast, awaiting the one who could withdraw it.

Camron collapsed to his knees, sweat pouring from him, emotionally and physically drained by the ordeal.

"I'm sorry," he croaked as the others rushed to his aid. "I couldn't..." He broke off with a sorrowful sob. "It was too much. I should have known I couldn't do it."

"It isn't your fault," said Geledhil kindly, but her eyes betrayed the anguish she felt at his failure. The battle was barely an hour old, and already their losses were horrific. The fighting had turned in favour of the Dökkálfar. It would only be a matter of time before they were completely overwhelmed.

"If I may, Your Majesty," said Findecámo. "I think my talents can be best used alongside the other mages."

Nimue nodded in assent, and Findecámo left the group, heading towards the Ljósálfar witches and wizards trading spells with the Dökkálfar battle-mages.

Hreidmar hoisted his heavy battle-axe in his rough, calloused hands.

“Well, I dunno about the rest of yer, but I ain’t giving up without a fight. If I’m going down, then I’m taking some of the beasties with me.” He looked at David. “Are yer coming, laddie?”

David hesitated a moment. Fear, his old enemy, rose within him. But he had grown in stature. The past year had changed him almost beyond recognition. He pushed down the fear, confining it deep within, locked away.

“Aye, I reckon I’ll take some of the beasties as well,” said David in a mock imitation of Hreidmar’s voice.

Smith unslung his own weapon from his shoulder and flicked the safety catch. “Mind if I tag along?”

Hreidmar nodded. “Just don’t slow me down, laddie,” he said.

“Geledhil?” David asked, looking at her enquiringly.

She looked from David to her grandmother. Nimue regarded her great-great-great-granddaughter for a long moment before nodding in consent. The two elves held each other’s gaze for a moment longer, both sets of eyes glistening with the threat of tears.

And then, Hreidmar, Smith, David, and Geledhil headed towards where the dwarves battled in bitter hand-to-hand fighting with goblins and orcs.

Camron glanced up from where he still knelt, looking towards his departing friends for what probably was the last time. Wretchedness and misery overwhelmed him. He had failed, as he secretly knew all along that he would.

Tears obscured his vision. The cries of the wounded and dying tore through him. Each one an accusation of his failing.

“I’m sorry, grandmother,” he said, the words wrenched from the depths of his being.

# Chapter 46

SATURDAY, 28TH AUGUST

As Rachel lay Gwenllian in her Moses basket, her eyes flicked towards the carriage clock on the mantelpiece. A slight furrow creased her forehead as she frowned. They were late. John was always punctual. He was part of the security detail watching over them since their arrival in London. Each morning when they changed shifts, one of them, usually John, came to the door with an empty thermos flask. Rachel had already made their coffee. It sat waiting for them in the kitchen.

She needed something to occupy her mind. To distract her from worrying about Camron. Would the battle have started yet? Would it even be today? Camron had thought so but couldn't be sure. Their parting yesterday had been painful. More painful, she admitted, than when he disappeared the previous year or when he had gone in search of the dwarves. This time she knew, deep down in a part of her that she kept locked away, that he truly might not come back.

She started at a sudden knock at the door.

"Xankira, would you answer the door, please?" Rachel called out as she went into the kitchen. She heard the front door open and then close again, but no voices in greeting.

Flint jumped from his basket and let out a low rumbling growl, his hackles raised, teeth bared.

"Flint!" Rachel admonished. "It's only John." The dog continued his warning growl. "Flint, onto your bed and be quiet." Rachel said, more sharply this time. Reluctantly the dog obeyed.

"Xankira?" Rachel called out.

She frowned in the silence that followed and stepped back into the lounge. A startled gasp escaped her lips as her hand flew to her mouth. Xankira stood in the middle of the room, tears streaming down her beautiful face.

"I'm sorry," she sobbed. "I didn't know who he was until it was too late." The object of her comment was standing beside her, holding her arm in a tight grip. Rachel stood horror-struck as she came face to face with a Dökkálfar once more.

"Flint!" she cried out. Flint, heedful of the urgency in his mistress's voice, bounded across the kitchen floor towards the doorway leading into the lounge. The Dökkálfar flicked his hand. The door slammed shut, trapping the now barking dog in the kitchen.

A second Dökkálfar, this one a female, stepped gracefully into the lounge from the hallway. Her gaze swept the room with a single glance. Her features were striking but not a warming beauty. There was no nuance of gentleness in her, no shading of care.

"This is the child's mother, Betshar," the male Dökkálfar said, indicating Rachel. He spoke in English, but his inflexion was harsh and guttural, contrasting with the lilting tones Rachel had gotten used to hearing from Xankira.

"I can see that, Raknarden." He cringed at the dismissive tone of her voice.

Betshar's eyes were glowing, a mixture of elation and pure delight suffusing her face. She had won. The power of House Dukker would be hers for the taking once she had killed the child, *the DoomBringer.*

Rachel tore her gaze from the malevolent triumph in Betshar's eyes and looked at Xankira. She appeared broken, and her voice cracked as she said, "I tried to fight it when I discovered who he was. But I wasn't strong enough. Rachel, I am so sorry. It's my fault."

"What do you want?" asked Rachel, returning her gaze to the Dökkálfar, summoning far more courage than she felt.

"To kill the child," Betshar announced coldly, "and you."

Reaching inside her robe, she withdrew an ornately carved dagger with an obsidian handle and black metal blade. Rachel started towards where Gwenllian lay in her Moses basket. She had barely taken a couple of paces when an unseen force, like an invisible hand, slammed into her chest, throwing her back against the wall and winding her.

"You can stay there and watch!"

Xankira had taken a pace towards Rachel but stopped under the withering look from Betshar.

"You stay still too," she said. Xankira obeyed as tears of abject hopelessness gathered in her eyes.

The two Dökkálfar stood, one on either side of the basket, looking down upon the peaceful form of Gwenllian. She was awake but didn't make a noise, merely gazed into the eyes of her antagonists.

Betshar, almost reverently, clasped the dagger in both hands, raising it above her head, revelling in the theatrics and savouring every moment of her triumph.

Rachel was numb with panic. For the second time in just a few months, her daughter's life was in peril. A thought flashed through her mind. Camron had arrived just in time to save her before. Would that happen this time? Would he know his daughter was in danger?

*The ring,* she thought suddenly.

She concentrated, trying to block out the image of the dagger poised above her daughter, focused on reaching out to Camron. Willing him to heed her call. And then she felt him and her mind reeled in shock. She would have fallen if she hadn't already been prone on the floor. Camron was suffering. His pain and anguish were intense. Rachel didn't know what was happening, couldn't comprehend his torment. *The ring,* she thought bitterly, was *the one thing that could have saved my daughter.* Suddenly, a second image flashed through her mind. The ring wasn't the only thing Camron had given her.

The dagger. She glanced at the bracelet on her wrist and then at Betshar, her back to Rachel. She tore the bracelet from her wrist, and it reverted to its proper form of a slim dagger. She pulled herself to her feet. Fear and adrenalin lent her strength as she rushed at Betshar, blade raised, ready to plunge it into the back of the Dökkálfar, threatening her child.

It might have been the sound of a footfall or an instinct for survival, but as Rachel's dagger plunged towards her back, Betshar sidestepped with the agility only an elf possesses. The blade missed its target. It grazed her arm, drawing a thin cut along her forearm, dark red blood slowly creeping out.

Caught off-balance, Rachel desperately tried to avoid Gwenllians' basket. She crashed into it, sending the baby tumbling out, before colliding with Raknarden. A tangle of human, Dökkálfar and cot crashed to the floor, with Rachel landing heavily on top of Raknarden. Their faces were centimetres apart. She lay there, breathing heavily. Her eyes reflected her shock and the realisation that she had failed to stop her daughter's assailant. She stared into the cold black oval eyes of the Dökkálfar and saw them widen in disbelief.

Rachel felt numb, her mind paralysed and unable to command her body to move. Her top felt damp and sticky against her chest. She glanced down and saw a rapidly growing red stain spreading across her white cotton blouse. She couldn't recall being injured, nor did she feel any pain. She gingerly lifted herself off him and looked down again. The hilt of her dagger was protruding from his chest. A tiny trickle of blood escaped the corner of his mouth as he took a laboured breath, and then his cold eyes went dark forever.

A baby's cry, almost drowned out by Flint's frantic barking, drew Rachel back to her surroundings.

*Gwenllian! Was she hurt?*

She looked around. Her daughter lay on the floor, crying. But the cries were more of indignation at her unceremonious ousting from the basket than pain. Another sound caught Rachel's attention. The remaining Dökkálfar was clambering to her feet, gingerly holding her forearm. It wasn't over yet.

Their eyes met. A look of hatred passed between them, almost cutting the air.

Rachel, at that moment, with her daughter's life still threatened, hated Betshar with an intensity she never imagined possible. But she had killed once and would do so again to save her daughter, regardless of what it cost her.

Betshar spat a curse in her own language.

"Same to you, you fucking bitch!" Rachel snarled with equal venom.

Betshar uttered a few words, and Rachel was thrown magically against the wall. She collapsed to the ground, momentarily stunned.

"You will die slowly and painfully," Betshar said.

Rachel noted the Dökkálfar had shown no concern for her comrade's death nor so much as glanced in his direction.

"No, she won't," interrupted Xankira, almost forgotten in the events of the last few seconds. She stood there, eyes blazing, one finger hooked under her necklace. Only now, it wasn't the beautiful oak leaf necklace. The illusion spell cast upon it had broken with Raknarden's death, and it was once again a twisted, ugly thing.

"I thought this my fault and that I was weak. But I wasn't, was I? Someone swapped my necklace for this one. It's cursed, isn't it? That's how you manipulated me. How you got me to help you."

Betshar's smile confirmed everything.

"Well, no more," Xankira said defiantly, grabbing the necklace and tugging at it. The necklace started to shrink, constricting around her neck, the chain cutting into her skin.

"Did you think it would let you go?" Betshar sneered. "Go on, try and take it off. I will enjoy watching you suffer."

Xankira grabbed the necklace with both hands and pulled with all her might. Rachel rushed over to help but never made it. She was once again flung against the wall by a spell.

Blood seeped from the wounds in Xankira's neck, her breath laboured as she gasped for air. But her eyes remained fixed on Betshar, meeting the cruelty and amusement with strength and determination of her own. Without looking away from Xankira, Betshar retrieved her fallen dagger and moved to where Gwenllian lay. She scooped her into her arm, wincing as the baby's weight aggravated her injured arm.

Xankira's struggled, matching the raw strength of her fortitude and will against the evil of the cursed artefact. Her breath came in ragged gasps as her aching lungs were starved of air. Her eyes bulged as her beautiful elven fingers tore at the chain around her neck, which, millimetre by millimetre, was slowly strangling her.

Rachel could only watch in horror from her prone position on the floor.

Xankira fought desperately to remain conscious. Just when she thought she had no strength left to resist, the necklace snapped, flying from her in shattered pieces. She gulped air into her aching lungs despite her exhaustion and pain.

"No matter," said Betshar, trying to maintain an icy indifference. She lay the dagger across the baby and pointed her fingers at Xankira, and uttered a spell with her free hand. Four magical darts erupted from her outstretched fingers, striking Xankira in the chest. Blood poured from the wounds.

"No!" screamed Rachel, horror-stricken.

Xankira looked down at the blood on her chest and then at Betshar. She withdrew her own dagger. Slowly, her breath still coming in shallow gasps, she hauled herself unsteadily to her feet.

"This ends now," she said, levelling the dagger at the Dökkálfar.

"Yes, it does," replied Betshar, raising her hand once more. Before Xankira had managed to stagger forwards, Betshar cast another *Magic Missile* spell. Four more glowing red darts struck Xankira. She cried out and collapsed, blood staining the carpet as Xankira gasped in pain.

Tears streamed down Rachel's face.

"Enough!" shouted Betshar, "I have wasted too much time already." She raised the dagger above her one last time.

“Tell Geledhil I’m sorry. Tell her she was always my sister.”

The words were soft, barely more than a whisper. Xankira raised her arm, pointing at Betshar, a look of grim determination on her blood-covered face. Sadness touched her eyes for a split second, and then astonishingly, they were ablaze with a bright white glow. The burning incandescence rapidly spread throughout her body, coalescing on her outstretched hand.

Xankira uttered a single word.

A glowing orb, white-hot in its intensity, sprang in a sizzling arc towards Betshar and Gwenllian. The ball of light touched them both, engulfing them. A scream of rage and frustration exploded from the Dökkálfar.

As the white light dissipated, it also dimmed from Xankira until only the intensity in her eyes remained. Her outstretched arm dropped listlessly. The light faded from her eyes, leaving them open but unseeing, the life in them having departed with the light.

Rachel felt warm tears run down her cheeks. She couldn’t believe what had happened.

Neither could Betshar. The elf uttered a howl of rage and frustration in her own language, a single word ringing around the room.

Betshars’ cry jolted Rachel and her gaze flashed to the Dökkálfar. Her eyes fixed on the dagger still held poised above the infant. She saw her knuckles whiten as Betshar grasped the hilt more firmly.

“No, please?” Rachel's plea escaped her lips in a whimper.

The dagger trembled in Betshars’ grip. Rachel watched as anger and disbelief flashed across the Dökkálfar’s face.

Slowly the Dökkálfar lowered the blade towards Gwenllian until the tip rested lightly against the infant's cheek. Rachel’s sobs muffled another plea.

Carefully, almost reverently, Betshar pricked Gwenllian’s cheek. A single drop of bright red blood appeared.

Through tear clouded eyes, Rachel watched as Betshar gasped, dropping the dagger as she raised her hand to her own cheek, dark eyes widened in shock.

Hatred quickly stifled her shock, and Betshar turned her malevolent gaze on Rachel. She carelessly placed Gwenllian on the floor and faced Rachel. She raised her arms and began an incantation. But Rachel realised something was wrong. The elf, through her rage, couldn't utter the words properly.

Rachel hauled herself to her feet.

The air between them almost crackled with their combined hatred.

With an incoherent scream of denial, Betshar twisted an ornate ring on her finger and pointed it towards the middle of the room. A glowing green circle appeared, hovering in mid-air. Betshar cast one last look around the room. A dead Dökkálfar, a dead Ljósálfar and a stunned and uncomprehending human.

Holding the baby tight in her arms, she stepped through the glowing circle and disappeared.

Her disappearance shocked Rachel into action. Betshar had taken her baby. Taken her away to be killed. The bright green glow in the middle of her lounge was dimming. She didn't stop to consider the danger. Throwing open the kitchen door, she called, "Flint. Come."

She turned and headed after Betshar but stopped as she passed the lifeless body of Raknarden. She hesitated just a fraction of a second before she bent and pulled the blade from his chest, fighting down the horror and trying to ignore the blood dripping from the blade. With Flint beside her, the pair raced towards the rapidly dimming magical portal and, together, ran through, disappearing just as the Dökkálfar had done, leaving behind the scene of devastation.

# Chapter 47

SATURDAY, 28TH AUGUST

Rachel and Flint appeared on a grassy knoll not far from a small copse. The unmistakable sounds of battle could be heard, coming from somewhere beyond the trees. Machine-gun fire, artillery and loud explosions assaulted her ears. Rachel looked around her, desperately seeking her daughter, but there was no sign of either Gwenllian or Betshar.

She knelt by the dog, pulling him close.

“Flint, where is she? Find my baby, please?”

Flint looked at his beloved mistress with his intelligent brown eyes and then pulled away, circling around and trying to pick up a scent. He ran back and forth for a minute, straining all of his scent receptors in his nose for a clue where his quarry had gone. Flint couldn’t detect a single trace of them, but he picked up something else. A scent he knew as well as any other. He looked at Rachel and barked once, then turned and bounded towards the trees, in the direction of the battle. Rachel hesitated for only a split second before she hurried after him.

After a few minutes, they came out the far side of the trees. Rachel pulled up short, horrified at the sight before her. A steady stream of injured troops poured into what had once been the Stonehenge visitor centre. The temporary medical triage unit set up in the car park had become overwhelmed by the volume of casualties. Rachel could see men laid out on stretchers alongside elves and dwarves. As she watched, a military helicopter carrying casualties took off from the coach park on the opposite side of the road. Her eyes followed as the helicopter rose into the air, and she saw another one approaching. Presumably coming to collect more wounded.

Flint stood panting a dozen metres away, awaiting his mistress. Rachel stared aghast at the turmoil before her for several long moments. The battle didn’t look to be going too well. Flint barked, and the urgency of her situation reasserted itself. She broke into a stumbling run, and Flint immediately turned, leading Rachel across a field towards the visitor centre.

Rachel stumbled and fell as they approached, grazing her palms on the gravel path. Flint was immediately by her side, joined a few moments later by a young woman in military fatigues and sporting a red cross on a white armband.

"Are you okay?" she asked, kneeling down beside Rachel.

Flint growled warningly.

"Oh, be quiet," the woman admonished sharply. "I'm only trying to help."

Flint looked at her, almost as if appraising her words. He sat down, quiet but still alert. The military nurse returned her attention to Rachel, who was trying to get up and gasped when she saw her blood-soaked blouse.

"You're injured," she said, putting her arms around Rachel to support her.

"No, it's not mine," Rachel said, shrugging the startled woman off.

"Who are you?" the military nurse asked.

Rachel ignored the question. Shrugging off the woman's arm, she started walking again.

"Wait," called the military nurse.

Flint stood and barked in a warning. Rachel ran further into the compound, followed by the woman still calling for her to stop. Flint ran alongside, barking. Rachel kept running, her grief at the loss of her daughter magnified by the dead and dying around her. She stopped suddenly, shock and confusion assailing her as she turned a full 360 degrees. The tears in her eyes misted her view of the mutilated bodies surrounding her.

"Halt, don't move," called a commanding voice. Two guards approached, SA-80 rifles pointing at her. Their eyes clearly showed suspicious as they viewed Rachel's blood-soaked civilian clothing.

Flint moved to stand protectively before Rachel. His eyes were wide, and his ears flat on his head. Long canine teeth and a vibrating growl deep within his chest gave clear warning.

"Who are you?" one of the guards asked, ignoring Flint.

"I need to find my baby," said Rachel.

The guards looked at each other and stepped closer.

The military nurse caught up, panting for breath and held her hands towards the guards in a placating manner.

"It's okay," she said to them, "I think she's suffering from trauma."

"Who is she?" one of the guards asked.

"Dunno, she just appeared from across the field. She looks like a civilian."

"She'd better come with us," the guard said, lowering his rifle and moving towards Rachel.

Flint started barking, a loud and menacing wolf-like snarl.

"Control your dog," bellowed the other guard, his rifle aiming directly at Flint.

Rachel dropped to her knees, arms wrapped protectively around Flint. Fear gripped her, and grief clouded her mind. She had to find her baby.

*Camron!* She cried out in her mind as she buried her face in Flint's fur and fresh tears streamed down her cheeks.

* * *

"Camron, come with me." Commanded Nimue.

"What?" Camron said confusedly, looking up at his grandmother from where he still knelt on the ground.

"Come with me," she repeated. "Rachel's here."

"What? Rachel? Here?"

"The *Family Rings.* Something is wrong, Camron. Did you not feel it from Rachel? Now come with me, and quickly."

Nimue and Camron hurried off in the direction of the Visitors' Centre.

Camron's pace quickened to a sprint as he approached and saw Rachel, covered in blood and clinging to Flint.

The two soldiers pointing their weapons at Rachel only increased his speed further.

"Leave her alone!" Camron bellowed as he approached at full pelt.

The guards looked up startled but lowered their weapons, clearly recognising Camron.

"Rachel?" Camron said gently, kneeling by her. Flint stopped barking but kept his eyes firmly fixed on the soldiers.

"Rachel?" he repeated.

"Camron?" Her tone was disbelieving that her husband could be there.

Rachel looked up at him through tear-streaked eyes, and the picture of abject misery drained everything else from Camron.

"What is it?" he asked thickly. Before Rachel had the chance to answer, another voice interrupted insistently.

"Where's Gwenllian and Xankira?" asked Nimue.

Rachel burst into floods of tears.

"Gone," she sobbed.

"Gone? What do you mean gone?" asked Camron urgently, his grip on her arms tightening subconsciously.

"Dead!" she cried, uttering the dreadful word that invoked such finality.

Camron gaped at her, unable to comprehend what she was saying.

"Dökkálfar. They've killed our daughter." The words came out one at a time, punctuated by sobs racking her body. Each one hit Camron like a physical force, stunning him. She must be mistaken. This couldn't be right. Their beautiful, precious little baby girl couldn't be dead. She couldn't be.

She raised her face to his, and as he stared into those midnight blue eyes, he saw the undeniable truth of her words. He saw her despair through the tears that glistened in the sunlight, and his eyes reflected her desolation.

"Xankira..." Rachel paused, stifling another sob, determined to denounce the traitor. "Xankira betrayed us. They came and took our baby away from us."

"Xankira?" Nimue uttered in disbelief.

Camron felt a rage rising within his chest like nothing he had ever felt before. His anger, fuelled by his grief, threatened to suffocate him.

*Gone! She had been with them for such a short time, and now she was gone?*

Camron couldn't believe this was happening. The image of his perfect, beautiful little girl in the hands of the Dökkálfar swam before his eyes. His anger, his misery and his disbelief at how cruel life could be coalesced around him, forming a new, powerful emotion.

Revenge!

They would pay. The Dökkálfar and their minions would pay for taking Gwenllian from him.

He looked into his wife's eyes once more. Saw the silent pleading for him to tell her it wasn't true, to make everything alright. But he couldn't. Taking his wife in his arms and telling her everything would be okay wouldn't bring his daughter back. His desire for vengeance grew, and his eyes hardened. He turned swiftly and strode away, drawing Excalibur as he went. Without conscious thought, he headed straight for the battle.

Camron heard a woman's voice behind, calling his name, but he ignored it. His determined stride carried him towards the battle that still raged. White-hot anger welled inside him like a volcanic explosion, searing him. He did not even break stride as he pulled Clarent from the stone it was embedded in.

As Camron grasped the hilt of Clarent, he felt the tentative probing of the sword as it brushed his consciousness for a second time. The icy cold of the ancient sword's hilt numbed his hand, and the now-familiar tingling sensation flowed up his arm, coursing painfully through his body. This time, he welcomed it, embracing it willingly. He almost craved the pain, the immersion the Truth would bring. The acknowledgement and acceptance of his shortcomings and failures were nothing compared to the heartrending grief consuming him.

Once more, Clarent drew him into himself, carrying him relentlessly in a whirlpool, ever deeper within the core of his being. He didn't fight it. He allowed the sword to take him where it willed. For the second time that day, Camron came face-to-face with himself, but this time, he didn't flinch from the harsh reality confronting him.

Again, images and memories of his past assaulted him. His mind felt like it would implode, and he reeled with shock. Despite all he had done over the centuries, he saw himself reduced to a momentary spark. This pitiful and insignificant life did not matter. His mistakes, wrongdoings and pettiness paraded before him. He acknowledged them, embracing his failings, for they were nothing against his failure to protect his daughter.

He accepted this side to himself that he had hitherto kept hidden. He could do no less. He couldn't deny it. He had to admit it unreservedly. For it was the Truth.

Camron drew strength from the cold hard pit within him where his hatred for those who had taken his daughter had formed an immutable iron core. And to this, he fed the pain, sorrow and anguish he felt at the Truth that Clarent revealed to him. He clenched the cold metal of the sword's hilt and felt the etched runes burn like ice into his palm, but he refused to let go.

And then, suddenly, he felt the force of the vortex slow down. His eyes snapped open. He saw Clarent held upright before him and his hand glowed with the same pure, brilliant white intensity as the sword. His eyes burned at the display of power. He shut them again, anticipating the return of the disturbing images that had laid his essence open to the Truth.

But they were gone.

Camron could still feel the sword's presence, the magical entity entwined with himself. But it was different now. The stark brutality had gone. He felt something else. Acceptance.

And Camron knew. His ordeal had ended. The *Trial of Truth* was over.

# Chapter 48

SATURDAY, 28TH AUGUST

Camron stumbled, unaware he had continued to walk while the *Trial of Truth* took place. He looked around at the battle before him, but none of the details registered. His mind remained connected to Clarent, although now it wasn't as adversaries, fighting for dominance. Now it was as partners, the sword willingly obedient to his will. In his other hand, Excalibur pulsed, humming almost joyously at being fully reunited with its twin. Camron knew how to control Clarent, the knowledge having been imparted to him by the sword, how to summon its' power and direct it against the enemy.

But the trial had not assuaged his pain or grief. His desire for vengeance was undiminished. If anything, it had increased, for the twin swords shared a magical bond with their wielder and fed off his thoughts and emotions. The magic of the swords magnified his yearning for retribution until it threatened to consume him entirely.

Camron didn't want to just force the enemy to undergo their own *Trial of Truth.* That wasn't sufficient. The retribution Camron would exact upon them had to be absolute. He strode towards the ranks of combatants engaged in savage and bitter fighting, much of it now at close quarters. Allies and enemies alike were oblivious to what had happened. They were equally unaware as to what was about to befall them.

Without conscious thought or design, Camron delved deep inside himself, driven by his emotions, searching instinctively for the core of pure elemental magic that elves and other magical creatures had as an intrinsic part of their being. The raw, wild magic that spells and incantations sought to tame and control. Very few of even the most powerful mages could access this power directly. It was dangerous and almost impossible to control. Camron reached deep within his own being, his need and determination driven by extreme emotions.

Suddenly, his eyes shone with a brilliant white light, burning with the intensity of a multitude of stars. His body began to glow. Softly at first but increasing in brightness until those nearby had to shield their eyes. The twin swords reacted to his call, aiding Camron of their own volition to channel and magnify his magic. He strode onwards towards the enemy.

Three orcs spotted him and charged, their pig-like faces split in evil grins as they bore down on the solitary human. Easy prey, they thought.

The first wielded a halberd, a vicious double-sided axe blade atop a long staff. The orc swung it in an arc with nonchalant ease, intending to severe Camron's head. Camron raised Excalibur, and as the weapons met, the blade sliced cleanly through the halberd. A look of dumb incomprehension crept across the orc's face as Camron swung Clarent towards its neck, accomplishing the feat the orc had intended for Camron. A spurt of dark green blood erupted from the orc's torso as the head, still bearing a quizzical look, toppled to the ground.

The two remaining orcs bellowed and charged together, one brandishing a huge sword, the other a battle-axe. Camron met their charge with a ferocity that exceeded their own. In three brief seconds, the fight was over. One orc lay dead, a wide gash across its midriff. The other was on its knees, clutching the remaining stump where its arm had recently been. A final swing from Excalibur and the orc head parted from its owner.

Camron continued into the fray, his body aglow with the magic coursing through him. Before him, a group of goblins were battling hand-to-hand with a contingent of human soldiers. Camron exploded into action, his twin swords whirling in perfect harmony, dancing a hypnotic dance that brought death to all they passed. Bloodied and dismembered goblin bodies flew to either side as he sliced his way through them. Those who remained turned and fled the terrible onslaught, battling each other to escape the blazing nightmare before them. But their cries of terror turned to shouts of triumph. Two enormous trolls lumbered towards Camron, knocking goblins out of their path with the tree trunks they used as clubs. The goblins halted their chaotic flight and gathered behind the trolls.

They stood jeering from a safe distance as they anticipated the death of the human.

Camron stood his ground. He watched as the trolls approached, their tiny black eyes squinting against the radiance he emanated. Camron let them get close before he raised Clarent and flicked the blade as a lion-tamer would a bullwhip. From the tip of the blade, a white ray of light erupted like a whip and with a resounding crack, the streak of light split the first troll in two, right down the middle. The second troll hadn't finished its bellow of pure rage when the whip-light cracked across its neck, silencing it forever. With truly impressive haste, the goblins turned tail and resumed their flight.

Camron drove deeper into the enemy ranks, his radiance increasing to a level of blinding intensity. Raw, untamed magic erupted from the tips of his swords in blazing white arcs that scythed through everything it encountered. Bodies were cut down, an abandoned tank was sliced in two, the metal glowing a bright orange where the magic had cut through.

* * *

Nimue watched as Ljósálfar and dwarves started to retreat, extricating themselves from the hand-to-hand combat with relative ease as their opponents stood confused.

She hurried over to General MacDougall.

"Pull your men back," she said to him.

"What!" he exclaimed, barely glancing at Nimue as he remained focused on the extraordinary sight of Camron, glowing with an iridescent intensity.

"Pull your men back, General. Now!" she repeated, the urgency in her voice wrenching his attention away from Camron.

"But why?" he argued. "Camron's got both swords. Look. See, he's doing magic stuff with them. Wasn't this what you planned? We should be attacking alongside him, not retreating."

"Yes, he has both swords and yes, using them against the enemy was the plan. But not like this. Something has gone horribly wrong." Nimue paused a moment, taking in the spectacle of her grandson. "General, I don't think Camron has any control over what is happening, and if anyone, friend or foe, gets caught up in his path, they will be killed. Obliterated entirely. Now, if you don't want half of your army slaughtered, then pull them out of his way!"

The general hastened to obey under the full force of Nimue's considerable authority.

Rachel stared in horror, her hands clasped to her mouth as the pure, blinding light consumed her husband. Camron waded through the massed ranks of the enemy like the grim reaper scything through a field of chaff. Nimue moved silently beside her and placed her arm around Rachel's shoulder, the distraught woman's head slumped against her.

"He's dying, isn't he?" Rachel murmured a statement more than a question. "He's being consumed by that magical light the way Xankira was." In her utter misery, she had forgotten her abhorrence of mentioning the traitor's name. She didn't notice Nimue's sudden sharp intake of breath.

"What do you mean, child?" Nimue asked, her voice soft, almost casual, "*The same as Xankira*?"

It took a couple of heaving sobs before Rachel could answer. "She died the same way. Her body glowed with the same bright light."

A moment or two passed, and then Nimue swung Rachel around to face her, strong hands gripping her shoulders. Her voice was firm and determined, but her eyes betrayed the faintest glimmer of hope.

"Tell me," she commanded. "Tell me exactly what happened."

Rachel's eyes stared over Nimue's shoulder. Camron was still shooting arcs of deadly magic at all in his path.

"Rachel!" Nimue shook Rachel's shoulders insistently.

The word snapped her mind back to the beautiful elven face right before her.

"This is important. Tell me what happened?"

Rachel paused, trying to muster her thoughts amid the raging torrent of emotions assailing her.

"She, Xankira that is, said something about her necklace not being hers and trying to wrestle it off...." The image surfaced in her memory. Her eyes grew wide, and her hand flew to her open mouth in shock.

"The necklace! It changed as if it came alive. It tried to strangle her." Rachel trailed off, her certainty as to Xankira's guilt challenged by that traumatic memory.

Another shake of the shoulders, gentler this time. "Go on, child, tell me everything," said Nimue.

"Well, after she got the necklace off, she grabbed a dagger and tried to attack the Dökkálfar, but she was hit in the chest by fiery red darts. She collapsed, and the Dökkálfar woman, Betshar I think she was called, raised her own dagger, saying she would finish it." Rachel sobbed again, unable to continue as the horror of the memory gripped her.

"But then," continued Rachel. "Xankira said she was sorry and to tell Geledhil she was always her sister, and then her body glowed as brightly as Camron's is now." She looked over Nimue's shoulder towards her husband once more, her eyes in the present, watching her husband die. Her mind in the past as she watched the same fate happening to her daughter.

"Rachel!" the retort was sharp, whipping her back to meet the elven queen's eyes.

"Sorry," she stammered under her penetrating gaze.

"That's alright," said Nimue, more gently. "But I must know exactly what happened?"

Rachel nodded. "When her body was glowing brightly, I could hardly look at her anymore. She pointed at where the Dökkálfar had her dagger poised to strike and called out to Gwen. And then she died as a burst of bright light engulfed all three of them."

Nimue stared into Rachel's misery-torn face, recreating the scene in her mind. "She called out to Gwenllian?"

"Yes. I think she might have been trying to say sorry."

“What did she say? What were her *exact* words? Think Rachel, this is important.”

Unwillingly, Rachel cast her mind once more to that awful scene. “Just her name, Gwen.”

“Are you sure it was Gwen and not Gwenllian?”

Rachel bit her lip as she forced herself to relive those terrible memories. “Yes, I’m sure,” she answered in a small, sad voice.

The faint glimmer of hope grew stronger in Nimue’s eyes as she took a deep breath, praying her guess was right.

“She would not have said ‘Gwen’. Elves never shorten names or use nicknames.” Nimue paused, watching Rachel absorb this, before asking. “Could Xankira have said the word *Gwedh*?”

Despite the turmoil in her mind, Rachel had caught the note of urgency in Nimue’s tone and thought carefully.

“Yes,” she said after a few moments, “it could have been *Gwedh*. What does it mean?”

Nimue ignored the question, asking one more of her own. “The burst of light as Xankira died. Was it like an explosion, or did it arc towards Gwenllian and the Dökkálfar?”

Again, Rachel faced the painful memories. “It was like a beam shooting from her arm towards Gwen.”

True hope lit Nimue’s face, making it even more beautiful than usual. The confusion on Rachel’s face contrasted with the hope radiating from Nimue’s, and she smiled as she uttered five words that Rachel had never thought to hear.

“Your daughter is not dead.”

Rachel collapsed but was caught before hitting the ground by the millennia-old elven queen, who still had remarkable strength and agility. Safe, comforting arms enveloped Rachel and held her close as shock, disbelief, joy, and grief clamoured through the human woman’s mind.

Nimue continued, kneeling as she held Rachel. "The word *Gwedh* is an ancient Elvish word meaning *Bind*. Xankira did not call out to your daughter to say sorry. She gave her life to do so. She invoked an ancient form of magic that uses the same raw elemental power that Camron is now wielding. She freely gave her own life to bind the life of the Dökkálfar to that of your daughter. That is why Betshar screamed in rage yet didn't plunge the dagger into your daughter. If Gwenllian dies, so does Betshar."

Nimue paused, allowing the words to sink in.

"Your daughter is safe, for the time being. I know of this Betshar. She is the First-Daughter of House Dukker, the First House of Svartalfheim. Her mother, Sallakray, is the most powerful Dökkálfar and Betshar is a formidable sorceress. She will keep Gwenllian safe while she tries to find a way to undo Xankira's magic."

"Can she?" asked Rachel, detaching herself from Nimue's clasp and looking at her. "Undo the magic, I mean?"

"No," Nimue answered. "This is ancient magic, and the binding of one life to another is permanent."

The brims of Rachel's eyes cupped shining tears of joy that slowly overflowed to trickle down her cheeks.

Nimue watched a tear wend its way down Rachel's face, hesitant to say anything to disturb her relief.

"You should know this, my child, the magic needed to bind one life to another has not been used for centuries. It requires the most precious gift and the greatest source of power. The spell caster's own life force. Xankira willingly gave her life to save your daughter."

Rachel looked stunned, her eyes wide as tears of sadness joined the joyful ones on her cheeks.

"Oh, Grandmother, it wasn't her fault at all, was it?"

"No, my child, it wasn't." And her own visage mirrored the sadness, hope and joy on Rachel's face. Sadness at the loss of Xankira, whom she had loved. Hope as a queen that all was not yet lost. And the joy that her great-granddaughter was still alive. The elven queen's lips curled into a smile, and her eyes sparkled with tears. And one more thing. Rachel had called her grandmother.

The sounds of the battle ebbed into Nimue's consciousness once more, bringing her mind sharply back into focus.

"Rachel," she said urgently. "Your daughter may be safe, but your husband isn't." They both stood, turning to look towards where Camron was decimating the enemy's ranks. Their own forces had now pulled so far back that Nimue and Rachel stood in advance of their troops.

Once more, Nimue turned to look at Rachel, but her look was soft and gentle, her eyes sorrowful.

"Do you remember when we first met at Avalon? I said that you would have to be Camron's strength?"

Rachel nodded, "Yes."

"Well, that has never been truer than now. Only you can be his strength."

Rachel's eyes widened, but she nodded again.

"He is lost, consumed within the swirling vortex of pure elemental magic. The raw eldritch power will destroy him unless we can bring him back to us."

"What must we do?"

"You, my child, must go to him. Make him recognise you and bring him back from the place where he is lost."

Rachel looked at the iridescent light that was her husband, its brightness painful to the eyes. In a broad circle around him, magic scorched the ground.

"Can I get close? Will he recognise me if I do?" her voice was small and carried a hint of fear.

"The love you have for each other is strong. I am sure he will recognise you when you call to him."

"How sure?"

As Rachel looked into Nimue's eyes, she saw, for the first time, all the barriers and guards the Queen of the Elves habitually had in place fall away. Her soul lay bare to her gaze. Rachel had a fleeting glimpse of the weight of responsibility this woman had carried through the millennia and her regret in placing this burden on Rachel.

“I do not know, my child,” Nimue answered with simple honesty. “In truth, he is far gone, lost in the raw power of his magic.” She paused, considering. “And I do not know what effect the twin swords will have. Camron’s magic is being channelled through them, they have a magical sentience of their own, and I do not know what they will do when you call to him.”

“But he is still Camron, deep inside? That’s still my husband out there?” Rachel asked, teetering between confidence and the need for reassurance.

“Yes, that is still Camron. His love for you hasn’t changed. You simply need to find a way to reach him.”

“And if he doesn’t recognise me?”

Nimue took a deep breath. She did not want to utter the words, but she would not lie to Rachel. “You have seen the effect his magic has on all it touches. If he doesn’t recognise you, then you will not survive.”

Rachel stared over the devastated battlefield, strewn with hundreds of their own dead and, further away, around Camron and beyond, thousands of dead orcs, goblins, trolls and Dökkálfar. Ten minutes ago, the thought of dying alongside her husband wasn’t so terrible but now, knowing Gwenllian was alive, could she make that decision?

She would have willingly risked her own life for Camron’s, but now her daughter also needed her.

“Rachel,” Nimue’s soft voice broke into her thoughts. “You should know that Betshar has most likely taken Gwenllian to Svartalfheim. Camron is our best hope of getting her back.”

Rachel took a deep breath. A sudden resolve arose within her, hardening in the pit of her stomach. This was her family, and she would not stand meekly by as they were taken from her. She turned to face Nimue, all trace of her earlier timidity gone.

“Grandmother, this is *my* family. I will have them back together, both of them. I will get my husband back, and then we will go after the bitch who stole my daughter.”

Nimue nodded, approving. “Go to him. Call his name loudly and focus on him through your family ring.”

The two women shared one final look before Rachel turned and determinedly strode towards her husband.

# Chapter 49

SATURDAY, 28TH AUGUST

Rachel concentrated on placing one foot in front of the other as she headed towards the iridescent brilliance that was her husband.

He was only about three hundred metres away, but it seemed much further. All around was carnage. The ground was churned up from both shells and spells. Bodies of the dead and dying lay discarded. Blood, both red and green, seeped into the soil.

She tried to avert her gaze but nearly fell as she stumbled over the corpse of a beheaded dwarf.

Rachel kept her thoughts fixedly on her family. Without her, they were both lost. She had never felt such an overwhelming responsibility, but she refused to give in. She began to appreciate the tremendous burden thrust upon Camron and how vital he was to winning the war. She couldn't comprehend what she could do to help win the war. That was for better, more important people than herself. But she would not give up the fight for her family.

Step after lonely step, she approached him, feeling the heat increase. She called out his name as loudly as possible while clenching her other hand around the family ring and conjuring up images of Camron and the happy times they had spent together. The family ring on her finger pulsed with a faint bluish glow. Its protective magic shielded her from much of the intense power Camron wielded, yet even at this distance, she could feel the heat emanating from him.

She willed herself to continue, ignoring the pain as the magic flickered and danced over her partially protected body. Determined to reach her husband. To get through to him and bring him back to her. She couldn't fail. She wouldn't fail. Their daughters' life depended on her.

Camron withered, lost deep in the maelstrom of wild, uncontrollable magic. This was raw elemental magic in its purest form, unfettered by spells or incantations. Very few had ever tapped into it, and fewer still had mastered it. Once released, it would not easily be restrained. Camron's pain and grief consumed him, mutating into vengeance by the raw power within him, magnified and channelled through the twin swords. Iridescent arcs of pure destruction shot forth from the blades, cutting broad swaths through the enemy lines. However, Camron was far beyond the point where he could differentiate friend from foe. Conscious thought had been replaced by instinctive elemental actions. Yet he was still there. The man who was Camron still existed. Buried deep within the vortex.

And it was this faint glimmer of being, the final vestige of the husband who loved his wife, that flickered briefly upon hearing a name, almost drowned out by the thunderstorm of power engulfing him.

There it was again. A name. His name. Camron.

Yes, that was his name. He was Camron. But he didn't want to be Camron. The pain and loss he felt as a father was too much. He could simply lose himself in the magic and not feel anymore.

The magic rose in intensity within him once again and threatened to consume him. He could let it. Let the magic consume him and all around him, including the voice. The pain would go away.

*'Camron'* echoed through his torment, and images accompanied it. He shut his eyes, trying to block everything out.

But the image was too strong. A slender, almost willowy figure with thick, luxuriant hair, the colour of deep burnished mahogany became sharper in his mind. Midnight-blue eyes pierced through the glow of magic.

*'Camron!'*

He couldn't ignore it. Slowly, painfully he clung to that name as a drowning man clings to a lifebelt. He concentrated on the voice. The woman's voice sounded like it was coming from the end of a long tunnel. He somehow knew he should recognise it. The voice felt familiar to him, but he couldn't quite place it. He followed her voice, and more images sprang into his mind.

Suddenly memories of his wife flooded back to him, and he remembered.

He was Camron.

He was her husband, and he loved her. He would never abandon her. It felt almost as if his body had been empty and was suddenly filling up with himself again, regaining his physical form.

He opened his eyes, turning towards the voice that called out his name in desperation.

The intensity of the raw magic slowly ebbed from him, its glow fading as he looked in wonder at the face, surrounded by dishevelled mahogany-coloured hair. His shoulders sagged with exhaustion, his breath ragged and his throat raw.

He wanted to run to her, but his legs felt leaden, and he almost fell when taking a staggering step.

Tearing his eyes from his wife, he looked around him. A scene of utter devastation greeted him. The battlefield now resembled a wasteland. The only features were the broken and mutilated bodies littering the ground in their thousands.

Camron cried aloud as realisation dawned on him. He had done this. In his grief-stricken madness, he had unleashed his fury on the enemy and slaughtered them mercilessly. Tears streaked down his bloodied face. He was not the monster who had done this. He would hate the Dökkálfar for killing his daughter. He would fight the enemy to his last breath, but this...

His eyes swept the scene once more. He let the swords fall from his grasp as tears fell on the scorched earth at his feet. But they weren't tears for the fallen. They were for himself.

"Camron?" a small, hesitant voice asked from beside him.

He turned slowly, fearing the look of horror and revulsion that his wife must surely feel for the monster he had become. Their eyes met. Dark green meeting midnight blue.

"Our baby..." she stammered, struggling to get the words out, her whole body still racked in pain from the effects of Camron's magic.

"Gwen, she isn't dead. She's alive."

# The End

The story will continue in *Daughter of Destiny*

Book Two of the Third War of the Realms

# About the Author

Martin J Lake was born in Southampton and now lives in Dorset, England, with his wife.

Beyond the Stones is his debut novel.

www.martinjlake.com